I0770819

DAWN OF CRIMSON

The Crimson Chronicles Book One

Ithildin
Northkeep
Ithildin Strait
The Stormspines
The Blackwoods
The Stormspines
Sea Of Storms
Vaentros
Glathwine Bay
Capital City
Stormkeep
Glathiri
Glaurost
Tears Of Rhys
Rhythiri Coast
Rhys Lake
Tears Of Rhys
South Lands
Eastern Hold
Rhyseria
Bardellian Coast
Sorrow's Bay
Baramore
Sunkissed Spires
Southpass
Rhyserion Empire

THE CRIMSON CHRONICLES

In reading order:

Dawn Of Crimson

Masquerade Of Blades

(Coming: 2026)

DAWN OF CRIMSON

The Crimson Chronicles Book One

KYLE SCARLETT

WICKED INK

PUBLISHING

Dawn Of Crimson (The Crimson Chronicles) : Book 1
Copyright © 2025 by Kyle Scarlett

Published by Wicked Ink Publishing Ltd.
www.wickedinkpublishing.com

Cover and book design © 2025 by Wicked Ink Publishing Ltd.
Editors: Raymond Griffiths & Adam Bamford

First Edition: September 2025
Printed in Canada

Library and Archives Canada Cataloguing in Publication

Title: Dawn of crimson / Kyle Scarlett.
Names: Scarlett, Kyle, author.
Description: Series statement: The crimson chronicles ; book 1
Identifiers: Canadiana (print) 20250225298
Canadiana (ebook) 20250225301
ISBN 9781998278237 (softcover)
ISBN 9781998278244 (EPUB)
Subjects: LCGFT: Fantasy fiction. | LCGFT: Novels.
Classification: LCC PS8637.C2654 D39 2025 | DDC C813/.6—dc23

DAWN OF CRIMSON

The Crimson Chronicles Book One

The Fate of an Empire Rests on the Shoulders of One.

PROLOGUE

THE RED DAWN

"These are to be the last words of the line of Eineriel, whose progeny saw both the rise of the Rhyserion empire, and the end of our world."

THE HEAVENS THEMSELVES SEEMED TO PART, FORCED ASUNDER BY THE smoke that poured from countless devastated buildings throughout the town. Death carried on the wind; the sickening stench that arose when the frenzy of battle subsided, and the tale of one's life, came to an abrupt conclusion.

When the sun set that evening, it was by the light of the candle that one navigated through the twisting labyrinth of the town's many alleyways. Yet now the warm glow of fires born from despair and devastation cast the city in an agonizing light. It was a sight that made one question if man had not yet equaled the strength of the Gods, and whether any that allowed such despair were even worthy of worship.

The hooded figure watched in silent amusement as slowly the screams were silenced, leaving in their wake the roar of a town on the verge of collapse. Through the eyes that bore witness to the waking world, he watched in perfect clarity as the souls he deemed forfeit tried desperately to bargain for their lives. It was a futile effort, and as one particularly shrill woman met the endless darkness gifted to her, he could do naught but smile. For those born from the Song, silence was all that awaited them.

From his vantage point, it was easy to make out the wondrous beauty of their sigil flying on standards erected throughout the town. Six bloodied eyes cast over a crimson backdrop served as both warning and prophecy for those that gazed upon it. The facile days of mortal comprehension were numbered, and every drop of crimson gifted to the insatiable earth was a step towards their grand finale.

He was pulled from his musings by the sound of footsteps approaching from behind, a familiar, if not tiresome familiarity. Even with the three eyes he bore when their crusade began, he could not foretell how draining his position would be, hardly able to spend a well-earned moment in consideration before being interrupted by any manner of concern.

"Speak, Diametrix." The hooded figure muttered, turning his head just enough so that he might look at the bloodied figure through his three eyes.

The man tensed immediately, feeling the weight of the many-eyed gaze fall upon him. There were few that could withstand the sight of him, let alone resist the fear that his unnatural eyes instilled in others.

"Lord Herald, the night is won." The man's voice, as were all that he considered his children, was low and raspy, sounding more like the scratching of claws through the woods than the mortal voice of man.

"Those that survive have amassed in the town square, cowering behind the Reeve who wishes to propose the terms of their unconditional surrender."

The hooded figure turned his gaze back to the town that stretched out before them, slowly lifting himself up from his perched position to stand upright. Long, flowing robes fell from his shoulders, fluttering out around him as the many eyes that adorned them seemed to dance about amidst the devastation.

Countless were the nights that he was graced with these sights, and yet with each one, the very definition of beauty seemed challenged in his mind. With the last of the rebellious screams silenced, he could drink in the town's serenity, engulfed by flames, marvelling at how it crackled and glowed beneath the might of their banner.

"We are close, Diametrix." He spoke, slowly clasping his hands before him as he opened the two eyes of clouded crimson.

"Soon the veil will obstruct me no longer, and when the sixth eye has awoken, I shall look upon the very face of our master."

The blood-soaked man did nothing but nod slowly, maintaining his silence until given the order to speak. He was bound by both blade and ear to serve, a fate he was ever reminded of by the terrible power which burned through his veins. For it was the gift from their master that ensured those that served would find their place far beyond the reckoning of the mortal mind, and in turn, all they needed to do was usher in his calamitous age. Break the very song itself and let a new one echo triumphantly.

"Butcher them like cattle, then begin the ritual." The hooded figure concluded, shooting the man a quick glance over his shoulder.

He was quick to nod, pressing a fist to his chest in a silent salute before turning and meandering back down the overlooking hillside.

Free from the company of his child, the hooded figure turned his three-eyed gaze back to the burning town. Even though two of the crimson eyes had awoken, all he saw were hazy outlines through their clouded gaze. A pitiful reminder of how close they were, and how much was left to do.

"So close." He muttered to himself, closing them as the clarity of the waking world came back into focus.

Even though he could make out naught through them, the colour splashed world seemed to him an overwhelming disgust. Only the crimson that poured from the alleyways of the town was befitting of the beauty of understanding, and he would drown the world in it by the time the final eye had awoken.

Once more was he pulled from his inner mind by the actions of his children, for in an instant a cacophony of sharp screams erupted from the streets below. His message was delivered. For one-by-one the screams were silenced, their agony cut short by the endless dark expanse that awaited them.

Pangs of irritation shot through him, for their cries seemed to him an insult. How could one be so reluctant to help usher in an age like none the world had ever seen? Was it not customary to accept a gift with eager hands and an excited smile?

They chose this small town, cast against the shadows of a forest that defined them as wholly unremarkable, for greatness. The men and women who lived unremarkable lives, earned for themselves a spot in the tomes of history. It was a gift that only those who could not understand it would look upon with disgust.

After what had felt like an irritating eternity, the last of the screams was silenced, leaving in its wake the blissful crackling of fire that continued to engulf the town. The six-eyed figure lowered his hood, drawing it back across the pale skin bereft of hair to reveal the ink-made markings lining his skin. There, in the flesh, he bore the prophecy that guided his every move.

The melody of a world was to come, imprinted upon the flesh of its harbinger. He took a step towards the precipice as the low chanted song hummed out from the town below him. With arms stretched outwards, the song grew louder, and he turned his gaze up towards the skies, bearing witness to their beauty.

"Do you hear the song of your Children?" He muttered, opening the two eyes of crimson in desperate hope of seeing the appreciative face of their benevolent master.

As the overwhelming metallic scent of crimson rose from the streets below, he closed his three-eyes, opting to gaze wishfully towards the heavens with the clouded crimson gaze.

The beauty of their ritual. The hum carried on crimson-scented winds to the heavens. All of it combined and enveloped him in a way that blissfully overwhelmed his senses. So distracted was he that he barely heard footsteps approach once more. Slowly, he closed the eyes of crimson, lowering his arms as he turned his gaze back upon the ever-ardent Diametrix. Only then did he realize the music ceased, and the silence of despair hung over the devastated town. How long had the ritual been completed?

It was impossible to gauge how long he spent trying desperately to peer through the clouded crimson eyes. Trying desperately to look upon the face he'd long to see for centuries.

"It is done, Lord Herald." The man growled, pausing as he glanced beyond the figure whose hood was drawn once more.

"None have survived, and by all accounts, the ritual seems to have worked. Though it still lacks completion, we draw closer to the perfection of the Song."

"Good." the hooded man muttered, feeling the weight of exhaustion wash over him.

How long was it since he closed his waking eyes to the world, allowing the splendour of respite to consume him? For though he was far beyond the mere mortals he was surrounded by, he was still bound by the chains of weariness. It mattered little, for she would reward the exhaustion plaguing him now when they roused her from slumber.

"Can you see her yet?" Diametrix asked, blurting out the question as the hooded man took a step closer to him. "Our master, that is."

Though others might have chastised the disobedience, the hooded man couldn't help but find something endearing about it. They were, after all, newly ordained in both power and servitude. They lacked the centuries of knowledge and understanding that flowed through his veins.

"No." He replied, slowly approaching the blood-stained man until he was close enough to put a hand on his shoulder.

"But with each ritual, the veil grows thinner. We are close, child. The sixth eye is on the cusp of awakening."

Diametrix nodded quietly, though excitement clearly lined his pallid expression. The words of the six-eyed man, the Herald, they called him, seemed to inspire a measure of confidence in the fledgling child, for as he let go of his shoulder and moved beyond him, the very air that surrounded them seemed alight with fervid excitement.

"Gather the men." The Herald continued, coming to a stop a few paces behind the servant that patiently awaited his order.

"Our gift has been accepted. We move onwards."

Once more, the bloodied man saluted the Herald before turning to descend the hill towards the still-burning town. Once the wretched morning sun awoke, it would bear witness to the destruction wrought the night before, and though the servants that enacted it would long since departed, the message of their banners would remain.

Taking in one final delightful breath of air they had tainted, the hooded figure slowly descended the hillside, watching as the countless shapes of his eager disciples came into clarity.

His robes, as dark as the crimson blood that was spilled that evening, dragged across the unlevelled earth beneath his feet. Leather boots, made for climate far removed from the island empire, crunched into the wet mud, staining the cloth as his slim form meandered down towards those who awaited.

Blood stained each of them from head-to-toe, and quick glimpses through tattered cloth revealed the mark of their power. Dark was the night that they created, but darker still were the powers gifted to them by a mother most benevolent.

"Let us march." The herald cried out, standing atop a small outcrop so that he towered over the figures who gathered.

"The blessed night wanes, and there is but one song left to sing."

A riotous cheer erupted as the figures all raised their fists to the air, and with all the eager excitement of one close to achieving that which they yearned, they turned and set off back into the welcoming darkness of the forest. When the light of the moon gazed upon them next, it would be as one final gasp before succumbing to the crimson glow of a new age ushered in.

The red dawn was rapidly approaching.

CHAPTER I

A COUNCIL DIVIDED

"Thus, it began during the celebration of the moon's blue light. The joyous festivities for Nalinyor were turned into a nightmare."

VANIMIRE, CROWN PRINCE TO THE RHYSERION EMPIRE AND SIXTEENTH IN the line of Einer of old, sat at the council table, contemplating whether he could survive a fall from the grand heights of the High Tower.

As he sat there, hoping for the ongoing debate to reach its conclusion, he thought about what he might do if given a series of wishes like the heroes in so many of the stories he had been told. When he was younger, he oft claimed his only dream was to rule brilliantly, as his father had.

Yet now, having experienced the soul-draining extent of daily bureaucracy, he was certain his wish would be to go back in time and smack his younger self.

The capital of the Rhyserion empire offered all the luxuries one might have hoped for in the island empire, at least, those who counted themselves amongst the denizens of the High City were afforded as such. Everyone who had the privilege of entering the High Tower witnessed the very height of the empire's exuberance.

Tapestries depicting the triumphs of the ages fell from beneath the domed glass roof that shone brilliantly overhead, allowing the day's light to dance upon the map of the empire that served as the council table. The white marbled stone was practically lost behind all that gathered in the hall. Paintings of fish seem to be born from myth and shields bearing the crests of the greatest noble families.

The offering of food and wine enhanced the majesty of the hall. Vintages from every corner of the empire were always kept in stock and quickly poured into magnificent silver goblets to sate the thirsts of the councillors, even when their meetings were held in the earliest hours.

Clearly, he took after his father in some sense, for as his gaze wandered to the crowned figure at the head of the table, it seemed he too shared in the exhaustion. *'The blood of Einor truly runs thick'*, he mused to himself.

Thankfully, the High King had the luxury of speaking, whereas the others who gathered were called upon only when necessary. Relief washed over the young prince as his father straightened in his chair, clearly tired of the conversation that had long since run stale.

"Over three-hundred meetings of the Lunar Council have taken place before Nalinyor's celebration and still we squabble over matters of inconsequence." Exhaustion clung to every word that passed through the lips of the High King.

Yet, when he spoke, a hush immediately fell over the council members that were, until a moment ago, bickering endlessly. Such was the greatest power of the High King, for when he spoke, his words carried with them the strength of the unbroken line of kings. Fourteen different crowns saw the blood of old Einor's progeny, and many believed that each subsequent ruler inherited the strength of his forebearers.

Despite only a few of those progeny steering the Empire in times of peace, the unbroken line of kings had provided for their successors the knowledge and strength of those that ruled before. Vanimire couldn't help but wonder if he too would command such a presence when the day came for him to be crowned the sixteenth of Eineriel.

"The extent of your concerns are well noted, Lord Alrick, though my position on the matter has not changed." With a sweeping hand the High King beckoned towards the table that they had gathered around.

There was naught a finer table in all the island, Vanimire

thought, for its carven face depicted a map of the Empire unlike any in the land. From the Southlands to the Blackwood forests of the North, and from the Stormlands of the west to the Rhyseria coast in the east, there was no greater tool for discussing the affairs of the Empire than over the table depicting it so brilliantly.

Small stone flags depicting areas of particular interest, or note, were placed across the table. With each meeting of the High Council, there seemed to be more-and-more flags placed through the expansive Blackwoods of the North.

Though it rapidly turned into an exhausting back-and-forth, Vanimire couldn't fault Lord Alrick for his concern. The Blackwoods were counted within his demesne, though crown authority was always weakest amongst the warring clans who thrived beneath the shadows of the ancient great trees.

"Under the blue light of last Nalinyor, we sent forth Daromir and his Red Cloaks to investigate whilst we tending to our celebrations. Until he returns, this council shall not take any rash action." The words of the High King, though wise, also carried the undertone of finality.

The debate raged long enough, and nothing further would come from it.

"Rash?!" the deep voice of Lord Alrick cried.

Disbelief etched in his expression as he stood upright and slammed a fist against the table.

"Not a cycle of the moon passes without my hearing word of more towns and settlements vanishing. Is it rash for one to care for the people he rules over?!"

Fire blazed in the amber eyes of the High King, who kept seated as he laced his fingers together. Broad-shouldered, even in his twilight years, the High King maintained a tall and imposing frame. With eyes burning with the fiery intensity which became his trademark in the days of his youth.

Sometimes it seemed impossible to notice the wrinkles that many-a-weary years and countless draining council meetings brought. Though time slowly sprinkled gray into his hair, he still maintained the power of his bloodline, and very few would wish to see his anger go unchecked.

Through the weight of his gaze did the distraught Lord Alrick quickly come to his senses, running a hand through his thick beard as he quietly lowered himself back down into his chair, desperate to shrink away as his anger cooled.

"You forget yourself, Lord Alrick." The High King muttered.

He had a penchant for maintaining a sense of regal order in his tone, even when his eyes betrayed the anger that swelled within him. Vanimire couldn't help but hope he, too, could command such respect with his eyes alone when it came time for the crown to weigh upon him.

Though he only saw twenty-five summers, ever was he reminded of how his father already made a name for himself on the battlefield by that same age. 'Maelstrom's malice', they had called him back then.

Even now, though the High King just witnessed his sixty-eighth summer, a title which ever seemed fitting. The crashing of time's waves served only to sharpen and hone the High King's ferocity.

"You of all my councillors should know of my desire to maintain order in the Blackwoods. It is worrying that so many moons have passed without a word from Daromir, but each of us is familiar with the power of him and those he leads. He *will* return to us, and only then will we witness the full might of the Empire, as it weighs upon whatever causes such chaos."

The words of the High King seemed to calm the angered Lord Alrick, or at the very least remind him of the prudence of muzzling himself during such deliberations.

The issues of the Blackwoods were long since a point of contention amongst the members of the High Council. Not a generation passed since the Blackwoods, once beyond the scope of the Empire, felt the crushing weight of the crown authority as the Capital tried to conquer the ruthless barbarity.

In the dense woods where shadows reigned, the empire seemed distant and uncaring, and thus the hardened bands of roaming forest-folk resisted supplanting themselves before the High King.

Even now, control seemed constantly in doubt, and though he was ever slow to applaud the uncouth councillor, Vanimire had to hand it to Lord Alrick. His family was just as instrumental in establishing any measure of control, and it was that precarious leadership that often justified his over-emotional reactions.

Vanimire glanced at the faces of the other councillors, trying to gauge what they thought of the proposition. Both lord Dayne

Vaentros and Lady Charlene seemed outwardly content, though each carried an air of dissatisfaction.

Lord Dayne's house ruled over much of the Stormlands, of whose northern borders came precariously close to the Blackwoods. The stress of such a dangerous position made itself manifest in the man's appearance. Hair as black as night fell disheveled over his shoulders, forming a hardened expression practically hidden behind a long and scraggly beard.

Those of the Stormlands stuck out in the upper societies of the Empire, though many found their more rugged appearance enticing. Vanimire understood he would want to resolve the matter quickly, as the Stormlands would have to accommodate the Blackwoods refugees in the aftermath of their renewed conquest.

Though such noble gestures were certainly accompanied by the knowledge of the resources that would be up for grabs, should the Blackwoods be tamed. The Stormlands saw their position in society shift dramatically, as if they were cunning enough to leap upon the opportunity.

Lady Charlene of Glaurost seemed to Vanimire a more curious disposition to ponder. Slender and refined, the picture of nobility, Glaurost sat as the head of the Southlands, though it was much closer to the Capital than any of the other settlements. To the hearts and minds of the Southlanders, the Blackwoods were a lifetime away.

Was she so empathetic that her heart broke for those she had never seen before? It seemed to Vanimire unlikely.

Lady Charlene was a strong and proud woman, and equally terrifying in anger. When her hair turned gray at a young age, it was said by many that it was the ire that burned within her that had consumed the colour. Her sharp, angled face held wrinkles born from scowling, though occasionally there were streaks of endearment in her eyes that swirled with a blue as bright as the ocean itself.

Were it not for the High King's presence, she alone would have maintained respect and serenity by the might of her gaze alone. No, empathy was not one of her stronger traits. It seemed more likely to Vanimire she wished only to see the strength of the Empire realized, since it was the Southlanders who primarily provided the arms and armour for their troops. Though war was often thought to be bad for the Empire, it was lucrative for the Southlands.

Just as he was observing the faces of the other councillors, so too had the High King. After silencing Lord Alrick, the remaining members each seemed content with the conclusion they had reached. Vanimire had little doubt both Lord Dayne and Lady Charlene would speak more on the subject in private council with the High King, and it would be only a matter of time before Lord Alrick brought the subject up again.

It was only the last member of the council who seemed perfectly content. Master Alros was, after all, Tomelord of the Capital. It was he who ordered the libraries of the Empire, and ensuring the historical tomes were both prolonged and not forgotten. Vanimire had long adored listening to the man, for when he spoke, which was rarely another reason for the crown prince's affection, he carried on his tongue the knowledge of countless centuries.

Each of the council members wet their throats with their respective goblets of wine, seeing as the High King had created an opportunity to do so. It was a trick the High King instilled in his son from their very first lessons: when you wish to change the subject, let each member drown their anger and opinions in their drink.

As a youth, Vanimire often thought this trick to be some form of magic, as it always seemed to work on the most agitated council members. Only when he came of age and could sit in on the meetings did the real trick reveal itself. Each of the council members were served from a specific wine of their choosing, and for Lord Alrick, the High King had ensured his was more potent than his peers.

"Now, let us turn our attention towards tonight's festivities." The High King sighed.

It was clear to Vanimire that he wished for nothing more than to conclude today's scheduled meeting, so that he might steal for himself a few hours of solitary rest before having to commit to a night of engagement.

For their part, each of the councillors seemed livelier for this topic. Even Lord Alros, who to Vanimire's knowledge had never been fond of either drink nor romantic company, seemed eager to discuss the festivities.

There was no grander holiday in the Empire than the celebration of the light of the blue moon. Nalinyor was its ancient name, and it was on this night that its light shone the brightest, adopting the blue hue that was seen in the evening sky but once a year.

Lords and Ladies from across the Empire would travel to the Capital to be in attendance for the greatest festival of the year and celebrate the passing of the year unto the next. For those that gathered, it would be a week or two of celebration and party. A time to reflect on the year's success and failures and partake in some of the bounty of the harvest.

For the High King it was an exhausting affair, but for Vanimire it was a night of both passion and excitement. For the celebration brought with it dazzling displays and captivating figures; anything that could entice one's senses.

"The last of the guests should be arriving as we speak." Lord Alros spoke, and Vanimire found comfort in hearing the deep smoothness of his voice.

In all his years of knowing the aged man, Vanimire couldn't recall ever hearing him show any measure of extreme emotion. *Mastery of emotion is mastery of oneself*; he had often told the over-excitable crown prince.

"Good, good." The High King mumbled, letting his gaze sweep across the carven table. "Any notable absences?"

Lord Alros opened his mouth to speak, but Lady Charlene abruptly interrupted him with her sharp voice.

"None, my lord. Some of the smaller houses could not attend, but theirs is a company not oft missed." The other councillors chuckled quietly at this, with only Lord Alros growing quiet.

He alone amongst them seemed to know the true extent and importance of even the minor houses. Vanimire couldn't help but wonder how many of the ancient histories were written in part because of the brilliance of small houses that were mocked so openly now.

Though each city in the empire was ruled by a high noble family - whose bloodlines were traced back to the allies of Einor of Old himself. Countless were the families that had come into prominence and riches in recent years.

Despite their wealth and prosperity, the relatively recent prominence of their bloodline ensured a cap to their vertical climb. An unfair system, constructed through a system that was already unfair unto itself. To live in the island Empire was to feel the weight of chains in every direction.

"Good." The High King concluded, pinching the bridge of his nose as a quiet sigh passed through opened lips.

"The Northern Lords are also not likely to be in attendance." Lord Alrick muttered, clearly trying to keep a hold of his emotions, lest he be responsible for another outburst.

"No houses of import." Lady Charlene said, looking at the irritable lord with a delightful grin as he squirmed in irritation.

Vanimire was thankful his father presided over these meetings, for he was certain that if left to their own devices, Lord Alrick and Lady Charlene would be at each other's throats in a matter of moments.

Lord Alrick's aged leather gloves cracked as he clenched his fists tightly, desperately trying to maintain control of the irritation that the Lady Charlene so easily inspired in him.

"Lady Charlene." The High King's voice carried on the tense air of the High Tower, instantly commanding the attention of all those in attendance.

"If you are so eager to antagonize Lord Alrick, then perhaps it best you accompany him to the Blackwoods, whereby you can be chiefly responsible for overseeing the situation."

Lady Charlene's face paled, not from fear of having to travel to the rugged lands, but that it would have to be done in the company of he who was most unagreeable to her. She bowed her head, lowering her gaze from the High King as she spoke.

"I apologize, my lord. I spoke out of turn."

The High King nodded, shooting lord Alrick a glance which was met with a quick nod of deference in reply.

"Good!" The High King roared, leaning back in his chair as he rested his chin against his curled fist. "There is but one more matter of discussion before we part."

Each of the councillors exchanged curious glances, with no shortage of them directed to the crown prince, hoping for some sort of answer. Though not necessitated by law, it was customary for the High King to prepare an itemized list of topics that were to be discussed during each meeting of the High Council.

Vanimire received the notice the night before, which prominently noted it would be a discussion on the state of the festival preparations concluding their assembly. For the High King to bring forth an unprepared topic wasn't unheard of, but it certainly was rare.

Finding the crown prince just as lost as they were, each of the councillors directed their gaze to the seated ruler, giving him a silent nod as if to affirm they refocused any wandering mind for this mysterious topic.

Much to Vanimire's surprise, the High King seemed hesitant to speak, as if dragged down by some unseen worry. He traced a solitary finger across the carven table, his eyes studying its intricacies as if it were the last time they would bear witness to it.

"During my speech at the end of the festival..." Never had Vanimire seen his father so uncertain in his words.

It was as if each of them was impossibly huge, struggling to have them pass through his dry lips.

"I intend to make it known this will be the last light of Nalinyor in which I am ruler."

Shock fell over the seated council members like a curtain flung from the highest tower. In all the known years of the Empire's history, not once had a High King stepped down from the position. To wear the lunar crown was to bear it until one's demise, regardless of how it occurred. For Vanimire, it was but another one of the many chains upon which their society rested.

The High King paused, letting his resolute gaze fall over each of the council members as he gauged their reactions. There was no doubt to Vanimire his father relished in this, for he had oft confided in his son that making the councillors squirm was a humorous activity he grew fond of in the days of his youth. Only when the curiosity of the councillors reached a point of desperation did he continue to speak.

"From the blue light of the festival, till the last blue light, my eyes bear witness too. I hope crown prince Vanimire serves as co-ruler." If shock fell over the councillors at the start of his speaking, silent amazement was quick to wash it away.

Vanimire, for his part, was stunned far more than the rest of them.

His father never mentioned this to him, despite their spending hours together every day. Vanimire was quick to look to the other councillors, hoping in their expressions he would find some measure of understanding. Much to his chagrin, they all seemed at a loss for words.

Uneasy were their faces, for though each had no doubt been considering it in the privacy of their chambers, that the king so directly mentioned his transition caught them entirely off-guard.

"It is a good decision." Lord Alros finally spoke.

His soothing voice piercing through the veil of uncertainty which fell over his fellow councillor members.

"Often the worst mistakes made by the kings of old were to not take succession seriously enough. The crown prince will certainly benefit from learning in a more direct approach."

The words of Lord Alros seemed to wipe away any vestiges of doubt lingering in the minds of those gathered around the council table. Vanimire watched as their expressions turned from shocked surprise to thoughtful acceptance. It *was* a brilliant idea.

His rational mind could agree with that, but why had no one thought to gauge his opinion on the matter? Each of the councillors looked to Vanimire, giving silent nods of confirmation on the notion.

By right of law the High King could enact almost anything he pleased, but the annals of history were littered with rulers who made a point of estranging their council, and how quick death was to find them afterwards.

"I agree," Lord Alrick added, running his hand through his thick beard as his gaze fell back down to the map of the empire sprawled out before them. "Though we will need to position it in such a way which clarifies the majority of power still rests in your hands."

"For once I find agree with our Northern advisor," Lady Charlene hummed, quick as ever to cut off Lord Alrick before his speaking gave way to rambling.

"So long as all see you as the central ruler, it should stave off the threat of rebellion amongst our... more energetic vassals." She flicked her gaze back towards Lord Alrick as she concluded, and though he did a magnificent job of containing his rebuttal, Vanimire could see how desperate he was to burst.

"What an age we live in!" The voice of Lord Dayne commanded the attention of all who gathered around the table.

Though he was one of the longest serving council members, his voice had become a rare gift during their meetings. He was slow to add his opinion on any matter unless it involved his house personally, or if he had strong opinions on the topic at hand. It was this sense of thoughtful self-control which many looked to as a voice of reason, and Vanimire always longed to hear the man speak on matters more often.

"We are blessed the High King has given to the Empire so many long years of both peace and prosperity. There is no doubt that some grew uneasy in knowing that his twilight years were upon him, yet to have not only named such a deserving successor, but to elevate him to ensure he performs his duty to the best of his ability. That my Lord, will be counted amongst your greatest achievements."

As Lord Dayne concluded, and the eyes of the councillors fell upon Vanimire once more, the crown prince couldn't help but smile softly. Never had he felt such a strong sense of resolve emanate from them. There was little doubt in his, or likely any of their minds he was unsuited for the role at the present. Each passing of the blue light of Nalinyor spent ruling alongside his father would serve to ensure its health and stability. Two facets of rule that ensured every councillor member would be able to line their pockets further.

"Good!" The High King roared, elation stretching across his once-weary expression as he clasped his hands before him.

"Then it is settled. I apologize for keeping each of you here longer than normal, especially on this most busy and joyous of days. That concludes this last meeting of the High Council. When next we meet, it will be in the new light of the moon. Enjoy the festivities, one and all. With all the planning we've put into it, I'm certain it will be a night to remember. You are all dismissed, though Vanimire, might I have a word?"

It never failed to impress Vanimire how quickly the council members cleared out of the chamber once the meeting concluded. The group could spend an entire morning gathered around the table of empire, discussing all its intricacies, and then, when given the word, fled the tower as if they were students dismissed by their instructor.

The sense of newfound strength seemed to depart the tower alongside them, for when the door had finally closed, leaving him with just his father, the feelings of uncertainty were quick to return.

"Well?" The High King asked, clearly sensing the questions that were so desperate to break free from the crown prince. "I suspect there is much you wish to ask."

"W…Why didn't you say anything beforehand?" Vanimire blurted out, unable to contain himself now that he could say what was eating at him.

"A warning. A heads up. *Anything* would have been nice!"

To his surprise, his father only chuckled, beckoning toward the nearby balcony as he slowly made his way towards it. With hands clasped behind his back, the High King paused at the railing, letting his gaze fall to the city that stretched out beneath them.

The magnificent white stone of the High Tower shone beneath the day's light, causing the balcony to appear bright and imposing. People claimed the castle, which extended from the mountainside, was built from the white stone to resemble a lighthouse for those who might gaze upon it.

A reminder that even in the darkest of nights, or the most wicked of autumnal storms, the blood of Einor was ever stalwart. From this height, one can clearly make out both the High City and the Low City, and remark on the differences between them.

If the High City were the embodiment of order, then the Low City was that of chaos. The wall defining the two seemed to carve right through the heart of the city, separating the wide, expansive roads of the High City with the twisting, meandering pathways of the Low City.

Where the High City bore estates and patches of green, the Low City appeared a mess of wooden buildings assembled with little care for order or cleanliness. The capital grew faster than its smiths and scribes could have managed, and thus, they seemed to work at odds with each other. Though stone, carved and painted in brilliant splashes of colour, was the signature of the High City, the Low City was home to weathered and stained wooden homes that had seen far too many sea-born storms.

"What is it you see?" The High King asked, glancing toward Vanimire as he rested his arms on the railing next to the man.

"What do you mean?" Vanimire replied, furrowing his brow as if the question itself was impossible to answer. "I see the Capital City."

The High King sighed, rolling his eyes before giving the boy a nudge.

"Vanimire, if I wanted such a simple answer, I would have asked Lord Alrick."

The pair chuckled, and Vanimire was once more thankful that when they were alone, he could engage with the High King as the father he was, rather than the title he held.

"Well…" Vanimire started, narrowing his eyes as his gaze swept across the city beneath them, searching for an answer.

"I see a city alight with excitement and life. From the houses and the people that own them, to the streets and those that walk them. Everyone is excited about the festivities."

"Exactly." The High King nodded, reaching over to place a hand on Vanimire's shoulder before giving it a gentle squeeze. "What you see is peace."

Vanimire turned to face his father, letting out a quiet sigh as his voice lowered.

"I'm just worried I can't protect it, father. My failure will destroy your life's work in an instant, and I will be known as little more than the weak and unready king."

The High King smiled, shaking his head as if to scoff at the very idea. "The blood of Einor of Old runs through you, Vanimire. To wear the lunar crown is to feel all those who wore it before you. When I am gone, I shall live on in the blood which runs through your veins. Just as all your ancestors do. You will be wonderful, my son."

Vanimire looked back down to the city below them, trying desperately to fight back the tears beginning to well. It was an uneasy thought, for though the inheritance of power always was alluring, it so often went forgotten that to wear the crown was to accept that he who wore it before you had left this mortal realm.

As a child, he often dreamed of what life would be like when the crown was his to wear. Yet now, as he shed the fleeting years of childish whimsy, he fully realized the truth of accepting his inheritance. When the crown was his, it meant his father departed this world, and with it, the closest living member of his family. When the masses look to him as their leader, would they see him as the worthy inheritor of the blood of Einor? Or would they see the terrified youth who wanted nothing more than to have someone, *anyone*, close?

"I will try, father," He muttered, sucking in sharply as if to steady himself. There would be enough time later for tears. For now, he needed to be strong.

"I know you will, my boy." The High King gave his shoulder one last squeeze before turning to face the city, leaning against the railing as he spoke.

"The peace I've spent a lifetime cultivating is threatened on all sides every day. Yet so long as the blue light of Nalinyor blessed our people, the empire shall remain strong."

Vanimire looked up towards the sky, trying to catch a glimpse of the appearing on the horizon. The sun was setting, and it was only a matter of time before fervour of excitement consumed the city.

Vanimire hardly made out the moon through the thick smoke pouring up from the bonfires scattered throughout the city. Its light was cast beyond the black veil of excitement, which seemed a perfect analogy for how the celebration of Nalinyor so often went.

"And they always will," Vanimire concluded, lifting himself up from the railing to face his father.

"We are blessed by the blue light, after all. Which, speaking of, I should go prepare for." The High King gave him a quiet nod, and Vanimire was quick to depart from the tower.

The hour grew later than he thought, and there would be precious little time before he was expected to attend the evening's festivities.

Left alone in the council chambers, High King Eineriel XV turned his gaze back towards the moon. Uneasiness washed over him as he barely made out its light, and once more, a chilled shock coursed through him.

He lurched forward, gripping the railing of the balcony as he clutched at his heart. The greatest medics and scholars across the Empire found nothing wrong, and yet every day seemed to heighten his sense of dread. *'Claim it. Use me.'*

The voice cried out in his head. With a shaking hand, he clutched his face, desperate for a moment of relief from the madness that seemed to entangle him. *'Claim that which is bound. Save your people.'*

The episode passed quickly this time, yet when the High King blinked back into realization, he found himself drenched in sweat. He knew not how much time had passed, for it seemed only a moment ago Vanimire departed him.

"T…The festival." He muttered, lifting himself up from the floor, which he fell onto before breathing in sharply.

Strength was, and always had been, his namesake, and he was

thankful the Gods seemed to have plagued him with these episodes only when he was alone. Turning, he slowly made his way towards the door of the council chambers.

With each step, strength seemed to course through him once more. By the time he departed, closing the door in his wake, it was as if none of this ever happened.

CHAPTER II

THE HEART OF THE SEA

"The capital of the Rhyserion empire was consumed in revelry like no other. If only we'd known it was the last celebration that we would experience."

ALE FLOWED MORE FIERCELY THAN A RIVER RAPID, FILLING THE TIGHTLY packed tavern with a sickly sweet scent which seemed only to heighten as the hours of the night grew long. The watered-down drinks, served in tandem with plenty of spiced fish, created an eerily comfortable atmosphere, though the denizens who frequented the tavern tried their best to contrast it. A fool might have expected a serene and orderly evening in the heart of the Low City, but many knew the Sunken Moon Travern's atmosphere was unique.

Walls, weathered with age and scarred by countless violent encounters, held a myriad of items that seemed to chronicle the history of the Low City itself. Strange and fascinating artistic depictions of fish hung between various tapestries, which people had donated over the years. Everything from fishing rods to countless shelves of various hooks and corks gave the tavern a sea-born life that served perfectly to cater to its preferred customers.

Indeed, if the moon itself sunk into the sea, one would easily rescue it after a brief visit to the tavern. Perhaps that was the point.

For her part, however, Eliira was content to sit in the tavern's corner where the light flickered low, and the dimness offered her some measure of privacy. Her brown hair, disheveled from yet another day of exploration through the twisting, senseless catacombs of the Low City, peaked out from the rain-stained hood she kept tightly drawn.

The shadow it cast over her tanned skin gave her a sense of invisibility, as if she existed beyond the eyes and cares of those who called the tavern home for the evening. Blue eyes shone behind the strands of hair that fell over her expression, keeping a wary eye on any who might have sought to wander too close. She was the perfect image of one wishing to be left alone.

She hoped that the aged, rain-kissed leather she wore made her appear like a passing vagabond and given a wide berth. So far it worked, though she certainly caught glances at the deep verdant cloth that flowed freely around her figure. She didn't care much for fashion, but she certainly wasn't going to appear as a fellow fisher. Hers were the seas of exploration and understanding, rather than the cerulean expanse so many in the Low City called home.

Not that she didn't have *some* affinity for the Sea of Storms. In fact, she had a connection to it that nobody else in the Capital could have understood. It was the sense of unknown she enjoyed the most. She was an outsider, and if that ever changed, then it would be the day where she knew once and for all that she had well-and-truly lost it. She enjoyed the city.

Of course, it would've been impossible not to, given that she spent the previous months stationed in it. Yet she wouldn't let herself forget why she was sent here to begin with. The Capital City, for all its allure of wealth and prosperity, possessed a shadow stretching far larger than the mountain peak looming overhead. No, her stay in the Capital was simply temporary, it had to be.

With a wave of her hand, one of the many servers came over to replenish her drink. The hulking figure seemed better fit to be leading a vessel through the worst of the winter storms, rather than serving drinks at a tavern, though it wasn't unlikely that he partook in both pastimes. He strode over without a word, snatching the half-finished mug before refilling it.

Eliira lifted her bundle of papers that were spread across the table as he did so, knowing full well after having been on the receiving end of countless battering fists and blades, the tables were ever prone to rock. Just as expected, Eliira noticed when he slammed the mug back down, the contents splashed over the edges, creating a foamy, half-water mess across the tabletop.

"Op…" the hulking figure muttered, his voice laced with the roughness of the salty ocean air. "M' apologies. Give m' just a momen' and I'll…"

"Don't worry about it," Eliira said, interjecting the man's blubbering with a wave of her leather-bound hand. "Happens all the time on board, doesn't it?"

"Ha!" the server roared, his laugh a booming noise that caused Eliira to wince at how sharply it cut through the near-overwhelming chatter echoing in the hall. "Tha' it does! Tha' it does! One can' help it when the boat is rockin', afte' all!"

"Indeed," Eliira muttered, already regretting her choice of engaging the man. "And when was the last time you found yourself a sea on such an expedition?"

"Ah! Wells, you see…" The man started off on some rumbling, broiling tale.

One need only have spent a single night within the Sunken Moon to have heard the selfsame story told over and over. One accumulated a handful of rather similar encounters when voyaging along the Sea of Storms, and yet, each made it *just* exciting enough to engage their fellow patrons.

For Eliira, however, she couldn't have cared less about the man's history. During her first few nights in the city, she noticed that many of the Low City's denizens often lifted their head when regaling of their time spent voyaging across the seas.

Perhaps it was their way of trying to spy some sight of it, even if they were within the halls of a tavern, or perhaps the memory brought them so much joy they couldn't help but straighten and bristle with excitement. Whatever the reason, it was *exactly* what Eliira needed.

She watched him with vested curiosity, waiting for when he inevitably straightened and looked toward the distant Sea of Storms.

As luck would have it, the man moved *much* faster than she expected. Almost immediately he straightened, and she had to fight the laughter that she felt bubble up deep within her. Their predictability was endearing, even if her ability to read them made her wonder how much longer she could stomach spending time amongst them. Hells, perhaps in a few months longer she too would act with such predictability, and *that* was a terrifying thought.

Regardless, the moment the man straightened, she got to work. Leaning back against the chair, she rested her left arm in her lap, concentrating as she felt that familiar warmth envelop her. Beneath the tightly bound criss-crossing leathers, the faintest flash of blue light emanated from within. Her eyes twinkled, swirling with a light which dazzled with excitement.

The blade, which lay sheathed and reclining at her side, buzzed with anticipation and delight, knowing full-well what was going to occur. Yet it was a spectacle saved for them alone, an act of unknown ability which dissipated as quickly as it had appeared. Eliira let out a soft sigh, resting her arms on the counter once more as she placed the papers back on the now dry tabletop.

The light vanished, and the buzzing of the blade slowly grew silent, offering only a final silent whistle that brought a smile to Eliira's expression. "I know," she muttered, gently bumping against the sheathed blade.

"'M sorry…" the man muttered. "Did y' say somethin'?" He focused his gaze back upon her, blinking as if realizing he was going on a long, albeit invited, tangent.

Eliira waved a hand, shaking her head as she forced her lips into a wide, gentle smile. "I was just saying how positively enrapturing your tale was!"

"En…I' was wha' now? Enrapping?"

"Ah…" Eliira let out a sigh. Her excitement got the better of her, and for a moment, she forgot where she was. "It was wonderful," she corrected, offering the towering figure another grin.

Her antics seemed to pay off, for he leaned back with another booming laugh, causing the chair beneath her to shake.

"It is!" He roared. "Bu' forge' me. Le' me help you with tha…" He pulled a dirtied rag from his apron, glancing back down to the tabletop.

"Oh." He blinked—once, twice, shaking his head as if clouded by some measure of confusion.

"'M' apologies. Though' I'd made a spill." He looked in amazement at the clean table, dry as one might have expected any tavern table to have been.

"You were so engaged in your tale you didn't notice you cleaned as you spoke!" Eliira clasped her hands together, still offering him a gentle grin.

"Thank you for both ale and tale. Though…" She paused, tilting her head to the side as another rugged figure slammed an empty mug on the counter across the tavern hall. "It seems you're needed."

The server, still puzzle about how he cleaned up the table and was left with a dry rag, seemed momentarily sated by Eliira's explanation. Regardless, he quickly put the cloth away, shaking his head one last time as he dismissed the incident from his mind.

"No' a problem a' all." He muttered, flashing a grin to Eliira before turning on a heel and meandering back towards the counter.

"Stop your bloody slammin'!" He roared, once more his voice echoing through the tavern at a near-terrifying degree.

Eliira let out another sigh as he departed, pushing aside the strands of dark hair that fell across her expression as she looked back down at the spread of papers. She sensed the familiar buzz at her side and stifled a small giggle.

"Come on, Kanah. It wasn't *that* rude. I helped! One might even think about commending me for such generosity." The blade responded with a silent buzz, earning a quiet laugh from the hooded woman as she ran her fingers along the various pages sprawled out before her.

The words never changed, and yet still she pored over them, hoping to find *something* she may have missed. Reports, annals, memos, and missives. They contained the same, simple truth: the blade was last known to have come to the Capital City.

Where exactly, it did not say, and though she thought it may have ended up in one of the countless catacombs sprawling out, twisting and turning beneath the city, so far, her search was wholly in vain. Hundreds of tombs, belonging to leader and peasant alike, and none of them contained even a passing reference to what she hoped to find. That which would be salvation, a relic like no other, vanished from their world.

How lucky she was to be chosen from all the members of their order to be the one tasked with such a headache inducing mission.

'As per the whereabouts of the Golden, we know only that it was brought to the island empire during the times of Eld. Thereafter, despite it belonging to one of the many ruling lineages, it passed

from record, as if it were consumed beneath the waves of the ocean itself.' Each report contained the same sentiment, despite conveying it in a great many words. 'The Golden was brought to the island, but what happened after that? Who knows where it ended up?'

The composers of such reports deigned to call themselves 'scholars', which brought no shortage of frustration to the beleaguered Eliira. They were clearly out of their depth and lost what they were entrusted with maintaining, even though they wished the truth was different. Now their failures passed to her, and given this was her first major assignment, she would stop at nothing to find *some* measure of success.

Her mind was pulled from its contemplation by yet another unwelcome distraction. The lumbering figure stumbled his way towards her with legs shaking so much one might have thought of him aboard his own personal vessel. Eliira paid him little attention, having grown used to the occasional curious eye wandering past her little corner of shadow.

This time, however, the man seemed intent on being a nuisance, for he buckled and bumped against her table with enough force to cause the recently topped up mug to fall over.

"Watch where you're going, sea brains!" Eliira hissed, lifting the parchments before the watered-down ale could stain them. "If you're looking for a table and conversation, look elsewhere."

The man, though Eliira thought such a description was hardly fitting of his oafish appearance, staggered to his feet, clutching his mug of ale as if his very life depended on it. Broad shouldered and molded by a lifetime spent in the rough streets of the Low City, the man's green eyes fixated on her.

"Ver' sorr' miss. I uh…" He stammered through his words, dropping syllables in typical seaborne fashion.

It took Eliira many weeks before she finally understood what the locals were trying to say, and even now, it was often difficult.

"Jus' wonderin' wha' you're readin' is all," He continued, reaching up to brush aside the thin strands of hair desperately in need of a wash. "Looks interestin'."

Eliira collected the papers, arranging them in a neat pile before stuffing them away in her satchel. Though she was certain the lumbering man would have struggled to parse any meaning from them, she could not afford him damaging what little clues she had to go off.

"Not to you," she snarled, lifting the now emptied mug and slamming it onto the table with a huff of frustration.

"Wha' you mean?" He mumbled, barely able to stand straight for longer than a passing moment. "They lik'…maps?"

"Something like that," Eliira grumbled, tightening the latch on her satchel as she looked at the man with eyes alight with irritation. "But not to *you*."

"Think I'd ver' much like to see them." There was a familiar edge to his words, a feigned niceness Eliira saw right through. The man wasn't *asking* to see the pages, he was demanding.

"It's getting late," she hissed, turning to excuse herself from the chair. As expected, the man slammed a hand on the table, positioning himself in a way that was clearly intentional.

"Let me see the maps," he repeated, his voice now soft and laced with aggressive frustration.

Having blocked her departure, Eliira had to concede the man was an excellent performer. Clearly his mind was as clear as her own, and yet he played the blubbering fool with dangerous efficiency. Still, this hardly was the first encounter of the sort, and she was certain that so long as she appeared, at least to the eyes of a sailor, distant and intriguing, it wouldn't be the last.

"I don't have time for this," she muttered.

Beneath the bound leather strips lining her left arm, a faint blue light emanated. Despite her efforts to conceal her arm, the glowing light still shone through softly. The would-be thief seemed to notice the emanating light, for he looked at the leather-bound arm with a curiously cocked brow.

"Wha' in the hells is tha…" He muttered, curiosity swirling in his expression.

Eliira could not help but smirk, feeling a familiar warmth surge in her. The light pulsed beneath its bindings, and her eyes swirled with a flash as she sensed the intimate press of the world around her.

The blade buzzed at her side, once more feeling the call. Rare it was for her to have to make use of such abilities outside the scope of her exploration. Having to call upon the power *twice* in one evening was certainly more excitement than she expected.

Eliira's eyes flashed, and faster than a rolling wave, she struck. The mug exploded in the man's hand, sending foam and slivers of wood outwards in all directions. He roared in both pain and confusion, stumbling backwards as he looked at the handle he still held. The sudden cracking of the mug, along with the man's scream, attracted many curious glances from those who gathered in the tavern. Yet before the man wiped the foamy ale from his eyes, Eliira grabbed her blade, slung it over her shoulder, and snuck past him, darting towards the door.

She hoped for a relaxing evening, one spent mulling over any possible missed leads with a disappointing, if not familiar, drink. Perhaps it was her lingering foolishness to suspect such an evening was possible. Still, it was best to depart before questions could be thrown her way.

With any luck, the man who hoped to accost her papers would believe their encounter to be exaggerated by the ale he was drinking, even if the lumbering drunkard was an act. Attention was something Eliira *didn't* want. If anything, it was antithetical to her purpose. Her two little 'acts', as she would call them, would have earned the ire of Kellear, but he wasn't here to chastise her.

The cool air rolling across the Low City was a welcome sensation. After sprinting a few strides away from the tavern, Eliira appreciated the night's gentle embrace. The soft chill carried on the rolling winds was the familiar sign that the celebration of Nalinyor was soon to be held. Aerturiel would then face another long and wretched winter.

She hoped to have returned long before the seasons gave way, and yet, she was no closer than was when she first arrived. At this rate, she would have to call the Low City home for several years, which was a *terrifying* thought.

Few figures were brave enough to meander the shadow-clad streets of the Low City this late. Though the main pathways were safe, one need not tempt fate by chancing an encounter with any miscreant who might skulk about once the sun set. The Protectorate's, whose sole purpose it was to maintain the safety of the Low City, couldn't be everywhere at once, after all. One only needed a moment or two to find a blade pressed between their ribs, and their belongings pilfered.

Breathing in the salt-laced breeze, Eliira turned her gaze back to the streets stretching out before her. A familiar hum reverberated against her back as she let out a gentle sigh, pausing only a moment before setting off towards home once more.

"You sense them too?" She muttered, stuffing her hands into her pockets to blend in. Her question was met with another buzz.

"Mm, I should've known he wasn't acting alone. Think it's *them*?" Another buzz. "One more show, and *then* we retire for the night. How's that sound, Kanah?"

Eliira continued to meander, moving along the winding streets of the Low City as if she were none the wiser. Order and planned expansion were traits inherent only to the High City looming above.

Here, the Capital grew faster than it could have accounted for, leaving the Low City a twisting, curling mess of alleys and throughways, with buildings leaning and held at awkward angles. Many saw it as a ship which took on water, listing to either side.

For them, this was the only home they ever knew, and it was in the chaotic nest of passageways they found both comfort and delight. For Eliira, however, the sprawling network of alleys ensured privacy, and most importantly, opportunity.

Turning off the cobbled street down one such alley, she picked up her pace, narrowing her gaze as if trying to focus on the sounds enveloping her. The afternoon's rainfall continued to drip from the hanging rooftops, masking the boot steps she sensed were still on her trail.

At best, she figured it was a handful of individuals. Any more would draw attention, even in the oft lawless underbelly of the Low City. If the gangs moved in such a number, it would inevitably draw the attention of the Protectorate, who would for reinforcements from the High City. Though such crackdowns occurred occasionally. The current crop of gangs knew better than to kick the lobster pot.

Eliira came to a sudden halt as the outline of a figure stepped out into the alleyway ahead of her.

"So this is where they wanted me," she muttered, still keeping her hands clenched in her pockets.

The light behind her shifted as she sensed the pursuing figures turn into the alley behind her. To them, it must have seemed as if they finally trapped their fleeing target. For Eliira, however, they fell into her trap with expected ease.

"Curious display you put on back there." The raspy voiced

called out behind her, causing Eliira to turn and face the group who continued to approach.

"Don't know many who can cause a mug to burst in one's hand." The man opted to forgo the usual seaborne dialect which told Eliira all she needed to know: this man didn't intend for her to be leaving the alley alive.

His mistake.

"Not sure what you're talking about, friend," Eliira called back, letting out another sigh. "Way I see it, he held the mug much too tight. You know how flimsy those mugs can…"

"Cut the fish shite!" The man roared. "Couldn't care less about the little display. You've got something curious on you, gutterfish, and I think we'll be taking it off your hands."

"Oh?" Eliira cracked a grin. "Let me guess, you and your little group here intend on making off with my satchel? Desperate for my little maps?"

"Don't know who you're dealing with." The man snarled, pulling out a serrated hook.

The man clearly used the makeshift weapon for fishing, though Eliira doubted he intended to use it for such a purpose now.

"No?" she muttered, sliding the sheathed blade off her shoulder and letting it rest against her leg. "You've been causing a great deal of mess lately, haven't you *Teethtaker*?"

The man paused, a toothy, misshaped grin stretching across his lips. "So, you *have* heard of me."

"Somewhat," she admitted, pulling back the weather-stained hood and shaking out her long, brown curled hair.

"I know the real Teethtaker operates far, far away from here. Though I suppose his legend is strong enough if it's caused such cheap imitations to masquerade as him."

Her words struck the nerve she anticipated, earning a snarl of anger from the leader of the group. Heeding his frustration, the other members of the group all brandished their weapons. Naught a real blade was among them, though Eliira expected that given the Low City's abundance of sharp tools necessary for fishing.

One need not spend the ludicrous sums for a proper blade when an afternoon with a hammer and anvil could fashion just about anything sharp and pointy into a suitable weapon for killing.

"Very well then," Eliira called, her own smile growing as she reached for the leather straps binding her left arm.

With a single tug, the crisscrossed leather pulled free, unwinding and falling to the ground at her feet. The sight caused the approaching individuals to pause, gazing in the moon's lowlight in both curiosity and terror.

One might have expected a matching tanned arm to be revealed beneath the tightly bound leather. However, much to the shock and confusion of her pursuers, a cracked, stone-like exterior consumed Eliira's arm up to the shoulder.

Beneath the cracks, a soft blue light seemed to pulse with excitement, matching the racing of Eliira's heartbeat. Her rocky fingers tensed, stretching into the cool autumnal air. "Hells, you don't know how nice it feels to have that binding off."

"W…What in the *hells* is that?!" the supposed Teethtaker impostor stammered.

"Oh, this?" She rolled her shoulder, stretching the gray arm as she wrapped her fingers around the handle of Kanah, pulling it from the sheathe.

"We call them the Akura. I'm the lucky one who inherited the Akura of Water, but to you?" She flourished the blade, swiping it through the air before levelling the tip towards the group. "To you, it's the last mistake you'll ever make."

Just as she hoped, her quip landed *exactly* how she wanted. There was little that annoyed the denizens of the Low City more than challenging them with such wanton bravado. Though she saw the uncertainty still tugging at the corners of their expression, by insisting they slipped up, she called into question all the traits and attributes making up their entire identity. For those who lived and breathed the briny air of the Low City, honour and strength were all that was worth safeguarding.

The thuggish men accompanying Teethtaker were the first to charge into action, brandishing their cruel and makeshift weaponry as they raced towards her. Despite its narrowness, the alleyway could easily fit two men standing side-by-side.

The crooked, hanging walls cast the pathway in shadow. Making it not only the perfect avenue for crime, but also for Eliira to flex what she so rarely got to make use of.

With a flick of Kanah to the side, Eliira stretched her legs, lowering herself into a battle stance as she awaited the perfect opportunity. Though certain that she was far, far stronger than any who called the Low City home, she so rarely got to flaunt the extent of her ability. Now, having managed the perfect opportunity to do so, she would not squander it.

The two men raced towards her, their boots splashing through the puddles that seemed ever present in the oft wet Low City. Though their charge started in unison, it didn't take long for them to become staggered, with the heavier set man falling behind his slimmer and lither companion.

'There', Eliira thought, her smile only stretching as she let them draw closer and closer. She sensed their eyes alight with irritation and scorn, bearing down upon her with a familiar glimmer of underestimation. People often looked at her with the same disdain, and she learned to use this to her advantage, allowing her to survive in a way few others could.

She couldn't help but feel a flash of irritation wash over her. After all she had been through, and after all she had shown to those who dared to overwhelm her in the alley, they still looked upon her not as the glimmering, terrifying warrior, but as a small, sheepish prey.

"Your loss," she muttered, biting back the frustration lest it threaten to overwhelm her and ruin her focus.

Power swirled around her, enveloping her in the warmth akin to being wrapped in a blanket. For Eliira, however, the sensation felt more like the embrace of a lover - at least, what she imagined that would feel like. The cracks in her arm shimmered with heightened intensity, emanating a roiling blue light that reflected against the crooked edges of the nearby walls.

Wave after wave of light shone from her arm, catching and swirling in her eyes as she levelled her gaze upon the slender thug racing towards her. The man's approach, though faltering, never stopped, despite the glow causing some measure of uncertainty as it illuminated his features.

It would be his undoing.

In an instant, the world around her drained of its colour. The sea-stained shadows coalescing under the jagged crooks and edges of the building, consumed in a flurry of pure, unbroken white.

As the colour drained, so too did the lines defining man from building, ground from sky. The blinding white void, brighter than the morning sun itself, engulfed her. To many, it would have been a confusing and terrifying prospect, yet for Eliira, it came as easy as one might draw breath.

She was trained for this. Weeks and months were spent practicing how to move through the unseen world, unguided by colour and definition. Though her mortal eyes could not see nor grasp the world around her, she could *feel* it. The man's charge seemed to still, his body hurtling towards her in slow motion as she flourished Kanah to the side.

Passing through the unseen world, blinking, as they called it, was an exhausting effort, even for those trained in its usage. She had precious seconds to act, and she intended to waste none of them.

Steeling herself for the often-nauseating act of moving through the unseen world, Eliira lurched forward, throwing herself towards the man, moving as slowly as an abandoned boat set adrift on a still lake. Her body passed through the outline of his, and with an arc of Kanah through the white-washed void, she spun on her heel. Moving the blade was as easy as dipping one's fingers into the river's current. It was natural. As the blade buzzed with excitement between her fingers, she knew her strike landed true.

As quick as the light had drained from the world, it came flooding back in. Like the crashing of a wave, the alley was flush with darkness and shadow once more. Eliira slid across the rain-slick alleyway, coming to a stop behind the slender man that staggered forward.

She quickly realized her surrounding again. Just as she flicked Kanah to the side, the familiar metallic scent of blood filled the surrounding air, crashing through the alley like a storm-born wave.

With an echoing clang, the slender thug dropped his weapon. Falling to his knees, clutching the elbow, which was severed as quickly as he could blink. Blood-curdling screams of agony echoed through the alleyway, a familiar chorus in the Low City's symphony of bloodshed.

Whether it be their companion's sudden agony, or the woman that somehow vanished and reappeared a few feet forward. Whatever it was, the remaining thug slowed his rapid approach, hesitation now battling irritation in his expression.

Yet Eliira was not content with just *one* display of power. Wasting no time, she spun to face the bewildered thug, swiping her stone-like arm through the air as the brilliant blue light shone once more.

Droplets of light, buzzing with excitement and rolling like beads of water, lingered in the air. Her eyes flashed, giving the silent signal before launching them forward like a surging tide. Whistling like a cannonball, they raced through the alley, smaller than a finger, yet far, far more terrifying.

The broad-shouldered thug, standing still with confusion and trepidation, was cut down as quickly as his companion. The shimmering droplets raced through the chilly air, piercing into his chest like a volley of arrows. Each one caused his body to twist and writhe, crunching through skin and bone as they tore through him with ease. The weapon in his hand fell to the puddle at his feet, the sound of its fall lost in the screams of the armless man that writhed behind Eliira. The heavier set man was not as lucky, for though his own lips parted to let forth his own agonizing screams, the droplets that ripped through his throat silenced them.

Immediately, the man dropped to the ground, clutching at the wounds in a vain attempt to still the blood surging between his fingers. He screamed, but the guttural sounds he gasped drowned out his cries, and the warm blood pooling around him obscured the rain-slicked stones at his feet.

The man twitched and writhed, clawing at the cracked stone of the alleyway to drag himself away from the woman who so clearly overpowered him. It was a vain effort, and Eliira only watched as that realization set in. The wounds were too deep, and the crimson that pooling beneath him was too much. The ferrymen of the Gods had called his song, and there was naught that could be done.

The blade that Teethtaker pressed through his back cut his terror short, bringing the man's frantic writhing to a sudden and merciful halt.

"Damn shame, that is," he muttered, wiping the blood on the now dead man's shirt. "Them two were among my best."

Eliira heard the clatter of metal on stone behind her, and the frantic patter of boots brought a smile to her lips once more. They were alone. The mighty and formidable crew sent scrambling after only a few moments of their clashing. She couldn't blame them, in truth.

When she first witnessed the Akura's might and prowess, she

was left dumbfounded, and even now, her power often amazed her. She saw the same confusion held in Teethtaker's expression, though it battled with the resolve born from his honour. He watched two of his best men cut down faster than one might have drawn breath, and still he was intent on clashing with her.

'Gods, men were idiots.'

"Leave now and I might just let you," Eliira called, flourishing Kanah through the air with a few swipes. It was a lie, of course, and she was certain he saw right through it.

"After what you've done?" Teethtaker shot back, snarling as he stepped over the body of the impaled man. "Not a chance."

His words gave way to a roar of frustration, the serrated blade held high in the air as he lurched towards her. He moved with far more deftness and agility than his underlings, alternating his approach with steps to either side as he drew closer. It was an excellent tactic, Eliira admitted, and had it been anyone else he clashed blades with, it might have even worked.

Kanah buzzed with excitement as it met the serrated makeshift blade. Despite the length of the blade, it felt impossibly light between Eliira's fingers. She moved it with familiar ease. Teethtaker continued to scream as he unleashed a flurry of blows, trying to slash across any bit of her he might have found.

Eliira parried these aside with ease, taking a step backwards with each deflected blow. Rare was it for her to get to hone and practice her skills, and though she was brimming with confidence, she would not let their clash end *too* quickly. In defeating the two thugs, she showcased her aptitude. Now it was time for her to have some fun.

Each blow deflected wayward only caused Teethtaker's frustration to grow. She knew in the way he continued his relentless flurry of attacks. They were increasingly sloppy. Kanah easily pushed aside desperate swipes of the serrated blade, meeting them as if it were a wooden sword held in a child's hand. For its part, the blade seemed just as delighted to prolong their clash. Each time Kanah met with the makeshift weapon, it buzzed with excitement, as if it were laughing at the lesser blade's efforts.

After only a few moments Teethtaker was huffing with exhaustion, stumbling towards Eliira with the desperation of one who knew their end was rapidly drawing near. Blue flashes emanated from her stone-like arm each time their blades met, and as he stumbled towards her in his relentless frenzy, he failed to notice the shimmering droplets that clung to the air of the surrounding alleyway.

The small shimmering droplets of light awaited their master's command, brimming with the selfsame excitement that Kanah exhibited with each deflected blow. In a way, it was almost too easy, and yet, Eliira was perfectly content with that being the case. It wouldn't do her any good having to work up a sweat, after all.

Blow after blow were easily deflected, the metallic clashes echoing through the meandering alley. Though occasional shadows passed alongside the main street that loomed ahead, no one stopped to cast a glance towards the cause of the commotion. The sound of combat was just another part of life in the Low City, a monotonous noise that was reduced to the familiar droning expected of life living in the shadows of the richer classes looming above.

Yet despite the joy that she had originally felt in getting to flex her powers, Eliira knew she couldn't keep flaunting her abilities for much longer. The night had grown late when she departed the tavern earlier, and she knew that another day of gruelling exploration awaited her when next the sun rose. Teethtaker was being kept alive so long as he proved entertaining, and that was slowly beginning to wane.

Frustration gave way to carelessness, as Teethtaker tried frantically to find any measure of contact with the easily maneuvering Eliira. One overextension was all she needed to bring their dance to an end, and she didn't have to wait long for the man to present her with such an opportunity.

With a scream of frustration that rattled the nearby rain-soaked walls, Teethtaker raised his serrated blade high over his head. Eliira could see his intent with ease, and though she could have just as easily ducked under his intended lunge, she thought it best their brief clash came to its natural - almost preordained - conclusion.

She needed not the limitless power of the unseen world to end their clash. As the man surged towards her, she tightened her hold on the blade, spinning it around as she turned on her heel, lurching forward with a swipe to the side. Eliira put her entire force behind the single blow, moving Kanah through the air as if it were a part of her arm.

Kanah struck true, and as Eliira ducked under the flailing arm of the now stumbling Teethtaker, she turned on a heel once more, spinning to face towards him as the roiling, shimmering blue light danced in her eyes once more. Kanah had cut cleanly across the man's chest, tearing through his leather jerkin with ease.

Blood poured through the torn leathers, dripping to the alleyway beneath them to join the ever-growing puddle of carnage that had formed. However, she still had more for him. Though the blow would certainly spell his demise in time, she had little intention of letting him get away, only to succumb to his wounds later.

The shimmering droplets continued to hang restlessly in the alleyway's air, heard their master's call, and shook with excitement. In an instant, they lurched towards their target, stretching and sharpening. Just as quickly as Kanah slashed the man's chest, the droplets skewered him in a dozen places. The man's serrated weapon dropped to his feet as he hung limply from the shimmering shards of light. Eliira heard the gasping attempts at screaming.

Pain hopelessly consumed the man, yet he was unable to give it voice. He would be dead in a matter of moments, for blood poured freely around the shards of light devastating him. Yet, as he showed mercy to his companion, so too did Eliira find some measure of it within her as well. He'd given her a decent enough workout, after all.

Both hands wrapped around the handle of Kanah, spinning it within her grip before slashing it through the air before her. Just as easily as it had connected with the chest of the man, so too did it sever his head from his shoulders. Blue light flashed from her eyes, and the droplets that had stretched unto spears shimmered and fell into pools of water that swirled with the warm blood that stained the alley. In an instant, the supposed 'Teethtaker' was brought to his untimely demise. That he proved himself such a threat in the Low City wasn't unsurprising, yet he met the same fate as all those who tried before him.

Eliira leaned down, dropping to a knee as she studied the body whose warmth of life was quickly fading. Kanah buzzed between her fingers, pulling her gaze as she let out an exhausted sigh.

"You're right. This *is* going to be a headache." The light faded from her eyes, and she felt the warmth of power dissipate as she wiped the bloodstained blade of Kanah along a strand of Teethtaker's cloth tunic.

Though the Protectorate would be relieved to know the gang was disrupted, they would certainly be keen on finding out just how such a feat was accomplished. The grisly scene certainly sung the song of their conflict, and if the Protectorate were to find her here amongst the bloodshed, they would have no shortage of questions.

Thinking on her feet, she rifled through the satchel clinging to her waist, pulling out a crumpled piece of paper and a spare piece of charcoal. She wrote frantically, scribbling upon the page before folding it and tucking the charcoal aside.

Sheathing Kanah, she threw the blade over her shoulder and pulled the leather strips around her stone-like left arm. Her effort at concealing it was shoddy, quickly done as she stepped over the bodies and made her way down the alley towards the flickering light of the main street.

She blinked a few times as she emerged into the scarcely lit street, giving her eyes time to adjust to the warm light before looking around. As expected, the main street was sparsely populated. Few were brave enough to dare challenge the nighttime life of the Low City.

Only those who had nowhere else to go or were adept at hiding dared to stand against the faceless beast. On any other evening, Eliira would have preferred long been tucked away in her place of residence. Yet, as the events of but a few moments earlier revealed, this evening was anything *but* normal.

Setting off down the street in a nonchalant stride, she stumbled across exactly what she was looking for. The small shadow scurried out of sight, ducking beneath the remnants of a market stall that clearly was re-purposed.

Peering over her shoulder, Eliira waited until the sole passersby meandered along the street before darting over towards the makeshift shack. Dropping to a knee at where she saw the shadow disappear, she knocked on the rain-stained wood.

"Hey, kiddo." She whispered, leaning in close. "Want to make a couple of coins?"

A dirty face appeared from within the stall. Blond hair, disheveled and muddied to the point of appearing brown, poked out from the hole. The boy, who couldn't have been older than nine or ten, blinked a couple times at the smiling Eliira, caution and curiosity alight in his green eyes.

"O…Oka," he mumbled, his words thick with the seabourne dialect.

It was a small wonder he could speak at all, at least, in a tongue Eliira could parse. In recent years, the orphans of the Low City, deprived of any semblance of upbringing or tutoring, developed their own system of communication. 'Mud-Speak' it was often called, and if one struggled with the seabourne accent, then Mud-Speak was wholly indecipherable.

"Take this paper, and when the sun rises, give it to the first member of the Protectorate you can. Okay?" A warm smile accompanied her words, and she saw the boy's wariness wane.

She put the piece of paper on the ground between them, pulling out a few coins from her satchel to rest atop it before sliding it towards him. The boy winced and ducked away when her hand drew close. *'Poor child. The life you have lived already, in so few years.'*

The boy's hand creeped out from the hole, grabbing both the paper and coins and pulling it inwards.

"O…Oka'," he repeated, scurrying back into the relative protection of his unseen abode.

"Thank you." Eliira whispered, giving the market stall a gentle few taps as she lifted herself to her feet and turned back towards the main street.

It would be only a few more hours until the sun rose, and life once more breathed in the salty air of the Low City. With any hope, Eliira would be long in bed by that point. Though she fully intended on rising from her slumber as early as possible and setting off on another day of exploration, the excitement of the evening warranted a few extra hours of sleep, or so she thought.

With hands stuffed into her pocket, she kept to the shadowy corners of the streets, moving with familiar ease as she made her way back home. Though the Low City was amongst the roughest and cruelest places she experienced, one had to admit it was easy to get just about anything taken care of. You just needed to flash a couple of coins and someone would gladly take any many of menial work off your hands.

Whether the blond-haired orphan delivered the missive to the Protectorates or not mattered little to her in the end. The paper detailed where they would find the so-called ruinous Teethtaker. Eventually, someone would discover the mess and another would rise to fill the void he left behind.

By then Eliira hoped she would find what she was looking for, and be far, far away from the Capital City. How fitting it felt. For a city straddling the coast of the Sea of Storms, one often felt like a fish set adrift in the turbulent, twisting alleyways of the city.

In a way, she was almost fond of it.

CHAPTER III

A MOONLIT DANCE

"The night was a myriad of colour, and yet, such resplendence served only to blind mortal eyes to the danger that lurked in the shadows."

FOR A CELEBRATION OF THE MOON'S BLUE LIGHT, THE EXTRAVAGANT banquet hall seemed intent on ensuring not a speck of it was cast in the darkness of night. The warm light of countless candles, each custom-made and imported solely for the momentous occasions, consumed the high arched ceilings. These candles, often called 'Redsticks', burned brighter and longer than the more common 'Whitesticks', thus lessening the need for the serving staff to replace them throughout the night.

Tapestries and banners, pulled from the heart of the castle's storage, hid the white marble walls of the banquet hall. Every noble family had their symbol dance with pride on the banners hanging from the walls behind the tables assigned to them. The history of the empire itself was on full display, held in the paintings and tapestries proudly showcasing the might of Einor of Old and his banner-guard.

For those invited from across the empire, the night was one of momentous pride. They alone were the inheritors of the legacy surrounding them. Though for many, the histories were best kept in their tomes, collecting dust.

Dancing was of the highest concern, and the dark wooden tables, crafted from ancient trees cut from the Blackwoods itself, were deliberately arranged to allow a spacious centre where the marble floors were meticulously cleaned until they shone. It was a spectacle like no other, and all of it stretched out before the raised dais housing the High King and his chosen companions.

It took weeks to prepare the hall adequately. The Capital burst with excitement as cart after cart rolled through the gates, bringing delicacies from every corner of the island empire. The finest fish from the shimmering seas of Glaurost were carried in boxes constructed specifically by their mysterious enchanters, allowing them to maintain their freshness despite the long journey.

Mushrooms from the heart of the Blackwoods, dangerously procured, were dashed in spices from the mainland of Aerturiel. No good was too expensive, nor fabric too luxurious for the occasion. For the single night, Aerturiel itself came together to celebrate indirectly, of course.

Rare was it for any mainlander to be welcome on the island, and after the great exodus enacted generations earlier, few non-Humans dared to make the voyage.

So rare was it for Vanimire to see the banquet hall in all its illuminated magnificence. He constantly looked around at all the painted illustrations, which seemed to have new life breathed into them by the excitement of the evening. Gone was the dust and malaise that hung over the depictions collected by his late mother.

Instead, the treasures now became a point of spectacle, with many nobles gathered around the various pieces of artwork to discuss and debate their meaning. For Vanimire, however, the fascination faltered when *she* finally made her grand appearance.

If Lady Charlene of Glaurost was the very embodiment of strength and terror, her granddaughter was the opposite. Emmaline was strong. Vanimire learned this quickly, but there were seldom few in all the empire who matched her warmth. He was so captivated by her that time seemed to slow down, the chatter and music growing dull as his senses drank greedily at the sight of her alone. No treasure that the island empire possessed came close to *her*.

They spent the early hours of the evening stealing glances at each other whenever they could. Just as he had social obligations to fulfill, so too did she, and it was with great pain the pair were kept at a distance from one another by their respective social tides. Life of two boats set adrift against the tide, they longed only to moor together, yet were dragged further, and further apart.

One after another, courses of food were brought into the hall, filling it with the aroma of spices from across the very world itself. Each dish was small, allowing for room to be saved for others, but were arranged with meticulous perfection.

Fish was grilled and set over herbs and vegetables to appear as if it were leaping from the heart of the forest itself. Soup carried the aroma of the distant north, hardy yet somehow inspiring more hunger. Fruits from the mainland, many Vanimire had never seen before, arranged in marvellous displays, highlighting their colour, and their strange prickly exterior. All of it was intoxicating, though the wines from across the empire, ales imported from the distant mainland Dwarven kingdoms, and a delicacy the northerners called 'mead' might have helped in that regard.

Even for one used to eating the heights of luxury, the meals were unlike any Vanimire ever experienced. Somehow it dwarfed the festivities from last year, though Vanimire suspected the extravagance was to prepare the nobility of the empire for the High King's speech that was to come. The thought made his heart race, though the games he played with the distant Emmaline served as a wonderful distraction.

After every course, their eyes met, and they silently commented on their opinions. A shrug of nonchalance after a dish which certainly blew them both away. A thumbs down after a dish resembling a squid strangling a sinking ship made entirely of potato, done in a way that the northerners referred to as 'mashed'. With each silent remark, their laughter grew, and Vanimire couldn't help but long for the evening to wane, and their expectations lessen.

Vanimire thought it was not possible for the social rounds to have been any more painful than they already were. Yet every time he looked over to see some noble upstart speaking with Emmaline, a twinge of jealousy shot through him like an arrow loosed. It was a foolish response, which only further led to irritation, as he knew how she felt about him, yet he couldn't help himself.

The dreadful social game continued for a few hours until, at last, the dinner concluded. The food itself was as extravagant as the hall they feasted in, yet Vanimire's mind focused only on what was to follow. With the last plates cleared and the attendees settled their engorged stomachs, the attention of all turned to dancing. He was quick to move, as he was certain there would be no shortage of nobles searching for her hand throughout the evening, but it was he alone who would steal her first.

How ridiculous the pair must have looked, taking to the dance floor before the music even began. Yet for them, it mattered not. She had raced to him with equal determination, clearly having much the same thought that he did.

As they moved in time with one another, the world beyond their closeness seemed to drift away. The eyes and ears of the Empire faded into blissful obscurity as he focused entirely on the amber haired woman who seemed intent on breaking his very heart with her smile. For if her beauty was enough to entice him from a distance, it was beyond comparison up close.

She inherited her grandmother's soft features, though, unlike her, they rested over a warm and inviting smile. The blue of her eyes seemed to Vanimire to hold the very light of Nalinyor within them. When strands of her long amber hair crossed over them, he sensed his very soul grow weak. With every twirl, the flowery scent that had ever been Emmaline's favourite consumed him. In truth, it was his as well, though he was certain she was responsible for that.

"How lucky am I?" Emmaline hummed, whispering softly so only he could hear. "To have the Crown Prince sprint across the banquet hall to curry my favour."

Her lips lifted into a soft smile, and her blue eyes seemed to catch the twinkling candlelight with playful enthusiasm. She was short, even by the standards of Glaurost, and though in childhood it was a point of playful jests, now it grew into something endearing. Slim from a sickly infancy, and lithe from a childhood spent darting around the castle together. In his eyes, she was the picturesque model of perfection. A beauty impossible to capture in any tapestry or painting.

"I had to steal you away first," Vanimire murmured, barely able to contain his growing smile as the two continued to move about each other.

"Steal me?" She shot back, a giggle escaping her as her expression grew playful. "If only my noble thief thought to act sooner. He might have spared me from the dull conversations that seemed never-ending."

Vanimire chuckled, sharing in her pain. The pair always shared a mutual disdain for the trappings of their respective positions. They yearned for the warm days of their youth, when they would spend hours together, playing carefree while the world's problems felt far away. The days when their greatest concern was whether to play pretend in the tower, or in the garden.

"The Lords and Ladies of Glaurost seem remarkably busy tonight," Vanimire continued, pulling his mind from its nostalgic musings as he cast a quick glance over to the table where Emmaline's relatives still engaged in their endless conversations.

"Yes, well, it's a momentous evening after all," Emmaline said with a sigh.

She didn't need to look back at her table to know of the endless courtiers and nobles desperately waited to grab her ear.

"Grandmother has been insistent. It's an excellent occasion for discussions and arrangements. Tonight's banquet is practically a who's-who of the Empire. What better time is there to forge deals or voice complaints?"

Vanimire blanched at the mention of complaints. His evening already was sprinkled with hearing those which the nobility deemed unnecessary to voice to his father, and as sure as the moon's light was blue, the trend would only continue as the dancing subsided.

"But what of my noble Crown Prince?" Emmaline hummed, her words dripping with the familiar teasing playfulness which so enraptured Vanimire. "I would be quite disappointed if his hand were given to another."

Vanimire's heart skipped a beat at her words. It took the pair much, much longer to admit to each other the feelings that were so dreadfully apparent to all who gazed upon them. Hells, he kept the letter she sent him confessing her shared affection, though he dared not to bring it up now.

"Oh? Does the thought of me being wed to some distant stunning noblewoman cause some measure of concern, Emma?" Vanimire's smile widened as he spoke, the teasing of his words dulling any edge they might have borne.

Emmaline's playfulness only increased. She spoke without missing a step.

"Mmm, yes. We of Glaurost were hoping to marry my grandmother off again soon enough. You know she's quite fond of you, Vani."

"You're the worst," Vanimire said with a chuckle, shaking his head as the pair continued their dance.

Emmaline giggled, lifting her foot between movements to gently step on his.

"I know," she said with a self-satisfied hum. "That's why you're insatiable for my attention."

Vanimire's lips parted to shoot back some sort of playful response, but nothing came. Once again, she verbally backed him into a corner, disarming him with such fervor and excitement he didn't notice how masterful her strokes were. If it were anyone else in the Empire, he may have been frustrated at being so masterfully outwitted. Yet for Emmaline, he found it only made his affection grow stronger.

The pair continued dancing, speaking in hushed whispers, catching the eye of those who looked upon them. And yet, the pair couldn't have cared less if they tried. Because of their roles, they were expected to spend most of the evening engaging with anyone who wanted their attention. But for this moment, this dance, the world beyond their embrace drifted into blissful obscurity.

The marbled walls of the banquet hall gave way to the gentle, warm air of the gardens they played in as children. He took his time pursuing her, but despite living so far away, she'd never felt closer.

They had much to discuss, and it seemed to Vanimire they would need no less than a week spent in each other's company to truly get through all that raced through his mind. His father and her grandmother would insist they speak about making their courting official, and all the political ramifications that would follow.

Yet Vanimire wanted to know more about *her*, how the flower garden she cultivated the previous summer was doing. If the nosey and rude serving woman was finally relieved of her post, and if her grandmother spoke any more about allowing more pets to fill the halls of Glaurost.

Since the moment they first met, the pair were nearly inseparable. Vanimire never knew of more happiness than the few months Lady Charlene stayed in the capital, bringing the young Emmaline with her. He longed for those moments. Longed for the chance to spend more than just a passing evening or day in her company. As they teetered on the edge of an official courting, Vanimire couldn't shake the nerves gripping him.

"You know…" Emmaline continued, and it was only then that Vanimire realized his mind had wandered. "If we speak to grandmother and the High King, we might convince them to let me stay in the capital for a few months. To begin our courting officially, that is."

"W…What?" Vanimire stuttered, his heart beating so strongly in his chest he was certain she heard it.

"Vani, how dense are you?" She said with an affectionate giggle. "The celebration of Nalinyor is a perfect time to make our intentions public. I also think it would be quite romantic."

Vanimire's smile grew as his heart continued to race. "I…I agree," He whispered.

"Perfect!" Emmaline said with a leap of joy. "Grandmother wishes to leave tomorrow afternoon. We'll steal ourselves a meeting with your father and my grandmother tomorrow morning, then?"

Vanimire was so dumbfounded, so overwhelmed with joy and affection, he could only nod, earning him a tight embrace from Emmaline before they fell back into the more socially acceptable distance and continued their dance. *Courting*, the word echoed in his mind. *'I'm going to be courting'*.

He did not know how long they danced for, only that when the music subsided, the pair were completely out of breath. It took every ounce of his strength not to steal a kiss from her. When the pair did their bows and departed, he sensed regret wash over him.

It always was his plan to discuss the idea of openly courting Lady Emmaline once the festival concluded, but it was in moments like these he wished he did it sooner. Both his father and Lady Charlene openly hinted at the idea, for it seemed the two lovers were not as discreet in their mutual pining as they once thought.

Vanimire stumbled off the dance floor, dropping himself into a chair next to the quiet and reserved Daelin Vaentros. The boy, though only a year younger than Vanimire himself, inherited much of his father's disposition.

They often joked that a banquet in Keep Vaentros was to be as quiet as a gathering of mice. Daelin's dark curly hair was pulled back into a ponytail, though it strained against its binding, hoping to free itself. His pink cheeks shone brightly over the pale features of his expression. Though he wore the finest silk vestments one would have expected, they seemed a bit too small for his broad-shouldered figure. They were likely inherited, but Daelin still made them appear *somewhat* presentable.

Vanimire reached for his half-finished goblet of wine, wrapping his arm around his quiet best friend as he pulled him in close.

"Come now, Daelin! You have the realm's finest food, wine, and company at your disposal, and you choose to watch it all from the shadows?" He drowned his love-struck grin with the remaining wine, calling for another goblet as he let go of the slightly irritated man.

"I shouldn't be here," Daelin muttered, gray eyes glued to the liquid that swirling in his goblet. "I should have left with the others."

Vanimire rolled his eyes, reaching for the fresh goblet of wine, which he was quick to wash down his throat. Unexpectedly to all, just after the meeting of the High Council concluded, word reached Lord Dayne that a supposedly terrible omen was observed back at Keep Vaentros. A branch of the white tree, believed to reflect the state of the world itself, withered.

As such, being the superstitious folk they were, all the representatives of their family departed at once, leaving only Daelin behind to act as their face and ears during the festivities. It happened before, though nothing ever came from the supposed omens. Descending from the banner-lord Vaentros, who was gifted with the foresight of prophecy, those of his bloodline thrived and flourished by heeding the supposed signals the white tree delivered.

Those they called 'White Whisperers' were strange folk, and Vanimire wasn't sure how they derived any information from the leaves and branches of the tree. Despite his proclivity for superstition, Daelin was a close friend.

When House Vaentros presented a seed from their white tree to Vanimire's father, it served as a testament to their loyalty not only to the High-King, but to the Rhyserion empire itself. The tree, and its progeny, were thought to be entrusted with the same sense of foretelling the bannerlord Vaentros was known for. Those bound by the bloodline attuned themselves not only to the tree, but to the very earth its roots pressed deep into.

House Vaentros had, because of the connection, proved to be an ever-stalwart companion and ally to the High-King. When Daelin came to the capital to study, it was seen by many as the mark of this friendship. Though whispers in the shadows thought it a more typical arrangement of ensuring one's ward was used to keep the noble house in line.

"If the missive was true…" He continued, though Vanimire was quick to interrupt him with a sigh before resting his goblet on the nearby table.

"It could mean anything, Daelin," he protested, turning in his chair to better face the man. "It could be as simple as bad soil."

Daelin scoffed, slamming his goblet on the table in irritation. "Countless centuries. The white tree has watched over my family, Vani. You know that! In all those years, not once has its leaves fallen, but now they do, and you think it's the *soil*?!"

Vanimire paused, breathing in quietly as he tried to collect himself. Many times in their friendship, the superstitious side of Daelin caused thorns in his side. He couldn't fault him for it. If anything, it was an honourable trait to have.

Though he was raised and educated in the capital, Daelin inherited all the traits of his family. Traveling home at a moment's notice if ever there was a need for additional hands.

Vanimire smiled as he watched his companion, who seemed more and more alike to his father, with each passing day. His dark hair was tied back, complimenting the sharper features of his face. By looks alone there was no mistaking Daelin as the son of Lord Dayne, though the former still hoped he could grow a beard as magnificent as his fathers.

In truth, Vanimire was thankful Daelin did not inherit the booming voice of his father, for he grew fond of the way his companion spoke softly. The pair seemed to complement each other well. Vanimire was wild and excited, and Daelin was reserved and collected. They kept each other out of trouble, which was likely why Vanimire's father was so intent on having the boys raised alongside one another.

"I'm sorry," Vanimire said, reaching over to grasp the man's shoulder. "That was insensitive of me, and though I would be quick to blame the wine, it does not excuse me being a neglectful friend."

Daelin seemed to relax beneath Vanimire's grip, reaching over to place his hand atop it. "No, no, Vani. I apologize. I'm just…tense, is all. It very well could be nothing but well…you know how we of the Vaentros are."

Vanimire chuckled, turning to pick up his goblet of wine before handing the man a fresh one.

"I wouldn't have it any other way, Daelin. The Gods only know what I would be without you keeping me in check."

This seemed to lighten the mood some. Daelin took his goblet in hand, clinking it against the other before bringing it to his lips.

After he downed its contents, Vanimire placed his goblet atop the table, standing up from the chair as he reached over to run his hand through Daelin's dark hair. "Alas, my friend, I should check in with my father. Why don't you try to take in some of the night air? Perhaps that will help?"

Daelin stood, sighing as he anxiously glanced across the banquet hall. Despite having been raised and taught in the capital, the boy never was one for large social gatherings. He tried to explain to Vanimire how it felt. A tightening of the chest, an inability to focus as his mind raced, but the crown prince did not understand.

Despite this, Vanimire was ever cognizant of his friend, keeping an eye out to make sure he was doing well. He noticed the fear swell in the man, and gave him a gentle shake, forcing his attention back upon him.

Daelin opened his lips but found no words passing through them. He simply nodded, smiling sheepishly to the crown prince before making his way to the far end of the hall, which opened outwards to the gardens laying quietly beneath the light of the moon.

Vanimire watched as the man departed, worried his anxious antics seemed more heightened than they usually were. With a sigh of his own, he forced his gaze to the table where the High King sat. His father was, as Vanimire expected, sipping from his goblet of watered-down wine, his gaze stalwartly glancing across the lords and ladies who occupied the dance floor.

Even at this distance, one could tell his father had long grown tired of the festival. Although he would have loved nothing more than to disappear from it all, he was bound by social etiquette to make an appearance until the very end.

***

It took Vanimire many banquets before he grew used to being seated before every pair of eyes in attendance. As he grew more comfortable with his role, so too did he grow confident in the position it afforded him during moments like these. Sure, the eyes of the realm were upon him, but from his vantage, he had an uninterrupted view of the lady Emmaline throughout the evening.

The pair continued to exchange glances even after their dance concluded. Vanimire found a strange measure of relief wash over him every time he looked to her and saw she refused another dance partner.

"Well?" the low voice of his father repeated, pulling the crown prince's wandering mind back to focus.

"Pardon, what was that?" Vanimire mumbled, shaking his head as he turned his attention back toward the seated man next to him.

The High King sighed, chuckling as he raised the goblet to his lips. Vanimire watched as his father seemed to chug through the remaining contents before resting the emptied glass on the banquet table.

"I asked when the pair of you intend to make your affections more formal. Lady Charlene has proposed countless arrangements should the pair of you wish to court." Blush immediately crept across Vanimire's face.

Though he was quick to hide the fact behind his goblet, it did not go unnoticed by the High King who chuckled softly once more.

"You two would make a good match," he added, his warm chuckle giving way to a sigh as he turned his attention back to the party at hand.

Vanimire downed the wine as if it were his first drink in many years, desperate to hide his embarrassment. It didn't come as any shock, for both he and the Lady Emmaline long since figured their respective families noticed their antics. He just did not think his father would bring it up so brazenly. Especially since he'd already planned to broach the topic *with* Emmaline present the next day.

"You must think on it, Vanimire. There isn't much time left." The High King continued, his voice lowering to barely a wisp.

The change in tone sent a shiver through the Crown Prince, for the words of his father seemed to carry with them a dreadful foretelling. Opening his lips, Vanimire found no words would form. It was only then he noticed his father's hands seemed to tremble against his lap, hidden from view except for his son seated next to him.

"I...Is it the dream?" Vanimire whispered, leaning in so that even the movements of his lips were concealed from the endless sea of onlookers stretched out before them.

The High King nodded, though as Vanimire drew close he already saw the answer to his question. The eyes of the High King, ever alert and focused, seemed to lose some of their edge in the previous weeks. It was as if the very fire that earned the man his reputation was being dragged down into the depths of the earth, lessening its intensive glow.

Despite having not gotten a proper rest in some time, the High King never faltered in his ability to put on appearances. Thus, it was only to his son that the true extent of his exhaustion was evident.

"Yes." The High King muttered, his lips quivering as his eyes seemed to grow unfocused. "I can still see it, Vanimire. The blue light of the moon giving way to a terrible crimson. T-The threads of the world's tapestry growing tangled and consumed in fire."

Vanimire listened with intense curiosity, for though he heard the recollection of the dreams before, it always sent a chill through him. The eyes of his father seemed to focus on that which could not be seen, their fire transfixed upon a world beyond the understanding and recollection of his son.

As the High King trailed off, Vanimire sighed, reaching for a fresh goblet of wine which he forced into the hands of his father. The sensation of the cup seemed to draw the High King's focus back to the banquet hall.

Vanimire watched as his gaze focused on him once more. The High King looked down to the goblet, which trembled between his palms, and slowly lifted it to his lips, hoping to drown the memory beneath the liquid contents.

"Last night..." Vanimire started, leaning back in his chair as he trailed his gaze to the banquet hall before them. "I had a dream of the most beautiful ladies of the realm were swarmed around me, fighting for my attention."

After the last of the goblet's contents were washed down, the High King lowered the empty cup back onto the table, looking to the Crown Prince with a raised brow as confusion etched into every line of his expression. Vanimire seemed unbothered, raising a hand through the air before him as if recalling every minor detail.

"Each of them wore naught but their necklaces and gems, as fresh and bare as the day they appeared in this life." Vanimire sighed, chuckling to himself as he turned his head to face his father once more. "Dreams don't always speak the truth, father."

The High King let out a weary sigh, sinking into his chair as he reached up and pinched the bridge of his nose.

"I should hope so," he replied, shaking his head as he laughed. "Or else the Lady Emmaline would have some choice words for you."

The pair's gaze met, and after a moment of silence, they both broke out into a riotous fit of chuckles, no doubt earning the confused gaze of many onlookers.

"I see much of your mother in you," the High King said with a sigh, settling back into his chair. "She would be delighted to see the man you've turned into, Vanimire."

He reached over, resting a hand on the Crown Prince's shoulder as he offered a weary yet loving smile. Vanimire's smile softened. He only saw five summers when the sickness descended on the capital. Even then, he knew those were dark days. Locked away out of fear it might spread, when at last the pestilence had lifted, it claimed countless individuals. His mother, sadly, was one of them. "In fact, I'm sure she'd…"

A wave of murmurs erupting through the banquet hall interrupted his words, attracting the attention of both Vanimire and the High King. Though neither could make out what was the cause for the confusion. All eyes were focused on whoever, or whatever, just came through the grand entryway. Surprised gasps erupted as the crowd shuffled, parting as the grumblings of discontent continued to build.

"By all the Gods. What is going on!?" The High King roared, lifting himself to his full height as he tried to see what was causing the commotion.

Vanimire looked uneasy, a twinge of concern shooting through him. Though they could not yet see what it was, that caused all the surprise. For the crowd to be alarmed was never a good sign. He found solace only in knowing the best guards in the empire were present, and so far, seemed unworried.

The irritation of the High King only continued to build as his demands went unanswered. Vanimire watched as the force parting the crowd grew nearer, waiting anxiously for their grand reveal. Silence befell the crowd, which contented themselves to watch the ongoing affairs.

When the last of the party-goers parted, their shock and surprise were both justified and shared with the seated royals. For the figures who parted the crowd stood in stark contrast to the other attendees. Their armour was as dark as the night sky and polished with all the regality fitting of their position. Red cloaks of intricate design covered their left arms, though none of the figures matched the beauty of he who marched at their head.

The High King's jaw dropped, and even Vanimire found himself in a rare moment of shocked silence.

"D...Daromir?" The High King uttered, squinting as if his very eyes deceived him.

The armoured figures continued to approach, their movements refined and graced with an almost otherworldly beauty. It surprised Vanimire despite wearing heavy plate armour from head-to-toe they could still carry themselves in such a regal manner. He supposed such excellence came from serving in a role that only accepted the most gifted swordsmen.

The Redcloaks came to a halt at the base of the raised dais leading to the table of the High King, flanking their leader on either side. The air of the banquet hall seemed to grow palpably tense, with every onlooker curious to see how the exchange would proceed.

It was known throughout the Empire that the Redcloaks were sent away, vanishing for months without sending word back to the High King who delivered their orders. Though Vanimire never questioned his loyalty, it was often a point of contention between Daromir and his brother, the High King. For though the Redcloaks swore to serve the crown, in truth, many of them looked to Daromir for their orders.

Vanimire looked at his father, curious to see how he was receiving the surprise guest. Only to find even though the tension was palpable throughout the banquet hall, nowhere was it more intensive than in his father's gaze. Beneath the façade of collected regality, Vanimire saw the High King was broiling with anger. The High King was never one for surprises, especially surprises in public settings. He always was a man of order and expectation, and in making this grand appearance, Daromir broke both tenets.

Worse yet, as Vanimire looked toward the collected Redcloaks, Daromir was relishing in the irritation of his brother. He stood before the High King after months without contact or word of their return, looking proud. No doubt words were to be exchanged once they were beyond the eyes and ears of the masses. However, in this moment, Daromir's playful teasing allowed him to pull one over on his younger brother.

Just as the tension was reaching its apex, and whispers spread that the Redcloaks were yet to kneel before their sworn lord, Daromir dropped to a knee, lowering his head in silent deference before the High King. The rest of the Redcloaks soon followed, and though unspoken, Vanimire sensed the tension in the crowd subside.

Only Daromir's Redcloaks could stand before the High King in such an ordinary fashion and evoke such a primal sense of surprise and confusion from the masses. Vanimire knew how much his uncle relished in that, having always enjoyed making a scene wherever he went.

The High King let out a long sigh, drawing Vanimire's attention. Whatever anger and irritation his father bore would be saved for discussion later. The banquet was exhausting enough as it is, without adding familial confrontations to the mix. Vanimire watched as a smile crept across his father's face, clearly relieved to see his older brother both alive and up to his usual antics.

"Rise, Daromir," he commanded.

His booming voice seemed to carry over the silent crowd with an intensity Vanimire had never expected. It was a rare thing to be in a banquet hall filled with all the Lords and Ladies of the realm and have not one of them talking about themselves.

"My Lord," Daromir replied, giving another quiet nod before lifting himself upright.

Daromir was always blessed with a soothing voice. Low in pitch, yet always laced with a playfulness that betrayed the gravitas of his position. Still, he was liked by both his men and the nobles, which was all one needed to accomplish to ensure a healthy and prosperous life.

The Redcloaks each rose, pressing their right fists to their chests in sign of respectful deference to the High King. None of them moved their left arms, which remained hidden beneath their intricate cloaks. It was said those who swore to the service of the Redcloaks would reveal their shield-bearing arm only to defend the Empire they swore to. Thus, the cloaks obscured their arms as a sign of peace.

"The blades of the Empire have returned, my lord." Daromir announced, a smile creeping across his expression as the crowd erupted with cheers and applause.

While they were known far and wide for the red cloaks they wore, everyone in attendance knew they served as weapons sent by the High King himself. If ever there were an issue of grave importance, it was the blades of the Redcloaks who were sent to deal with it.

Only when the crowd finally began to quiet did the High King raise his hand, ordering complete silence before he spoke. "We are truly blessed," he cried, voice echoing through the banquet hall.

"By the blue light of Nalinyor this evening. In truth, we are more blessed than we know, for the blades departed, have returned! Now come! Let us celebrate in a manner befitting Einor of Old!"

The crowd erupted into another round of cheers. As the High King lowered himself back down onto his seat, onlookers swarmed the returning Redcloaks, pushing goblets of wine into their free hands before probing them in conversation. Daromir resisted these offers, instead of ascending the dais towards the table of the High King. He stopped at the edge of the table, lowering his head in silent respect once more.

"By the Gods, Daromir," the High King groaned, waving a hand dismissively towards him. "Lift your damned head before you hurt your neck."

Daromir looked upwards, a playful smile clinging to his lips. He flashed Vanimire a quick glance, winking as he tried to contain himself. Their time apart did nothing to change their relationship, for Daromir seemed content to be the teasing older brother.

"Grab a chair, would you?" The High King muttered, beckoning to the chair beside Vanimire. "I'm sure we have much to discuss."

CHAPTER IV

BLOOD-KISSED PETALS

"Life itself seemed so easy before that night. If only I appreciated the ease that my position had afforded me."

"THERE WE WERE, BESET ON ALL SIDES BY THE MOST VICIOUS NORTHERN bandits I've ever laid my eyes upon. Syraxis and Ealric were keen to attack. They were never the most tactically brilliant after all, but I held them back, for a plan formed in my head."

Daromir had a way of telling stories, which delighted Vanimire for as long as he remembered. Though the older man would always claim the blade was his only skill, in all his years of searching, Vanimire hadn't yet encountered another who matched his uncle's wondrous manner of storytelling.

When the man spoke, it was as if his very words breathed life into the tale he spun. Though Vanimire sat on the edge of his seat at the table of the High King, his mind was carried the vast distance to the north. It was as if he were truly there.

"Oh? And what was this ingenious plan?" The High King asked, trying to maintain his feigned mask of indifference in the story being recited.

"Wouldn't you care to know?" Daromir shot back, smiling with such playfulness the High King couldn't help but let out a weary sigh.

"You've returned to us for all of a single evening, Daromir, and already I long for the evenings of sensible silence." The High King turned his gaze from them, casting it back towards the ever-moving hall of banquet attendees.

Vanimire saw through the feigned veil his father created and knew beneath all the indifference he was overwhelmed with relief at seeing his older brother return.

Daromir scoffed, giving his younger brother a soft nudge before turning to better face his inquisitive nephew. "You've become an old man, Verrick. An old man who has robbed himself of a brilliant story. But it matters not. I'll just tell it to dear Vanimire then."

Vanimire noticed a momentary flash of irritation in the eyes of his father. Seldom few referred to the High King by his given name. In all his years of life, Vanimire recalled only once when he used the name out of anger, and the consequences which followed. No, he was afforded the luxury of referring to him simply as father.

For everyone else in the island's empire, he was High King Eineriel XV. For Daromir, however, he was the younger brother who, in their youth, often butt heads. The lovable, if not stoic, Verrick.

The irritation was gone in a moment, and the High King turned to speak with some nobles who approached the table. It afforded Daromir and Vanimire the perfect opportunity to lean in, lowering their voices to a conspiratorial whisper as Vanimire listened with an intensive childlike curiosity.

"Here's what I did, little nephew," Daromir continued, pausing for a moment as he shot a glance at those who approached. When it was clear they had no wish to speak with him, he resumed his tale.

"I realized the ferocious Northerners were itching for a fight, and perhaps so too were we. I knew we could take them, for a single Redcloak is worth twenty useless Northerners. However, the storm was rapidly approaching, and if we weren't able to make it back to town soon, we would face the most dangerous foe in this world: the forces of nature."

Once more, Vanimire was entranced, and in his mind's eye, he visualized the scene exactly as it was described. He always yearned to travel beyond the suffocating walls of the capital. It was always a rare event, leaving the capital. In all the years of his upbringing, he could count on two hands the number of times he was afforded the luxury.

He hoped, perhaps naively, when he came of age, he would spend some years acting as an envoy for his father. The role seemed perfect, in that it afforded him the opportunities to see the stretches of the empire and take in all the distant faces of its denizens.

But life is, as Vanimire was so often reminded, never as sweet as it appears in the mind of a child. He could likely spend a summer in Glaurost once his courting of the lady Emmaline became official, but his dreams of travelling throughout the Empire grew more and more distant with the passing of the moon.

"So, what was it?" Vanimire asked, barely able to contain his curious excitement as his uncle stalled dramatically.

"What was what?" Daromir replied, reaching for his goblet of wine, which he was quick to bring to his lips.

"Come now, Uncle, don't play those games," Vanimire groaned, leaning over to punch the man's armoured shoulder softly.

"Fine, fine." Daromir cleared his throat after placing his goblet back onto the table, taking a quick moment to push aside the plate of food he hadn't taken a single bite of.

"I reached for the horn at my waist and held it high into the air. I noticed the Northerners were uneasily studying it, so I figured it must mean something terrifying for them. Then, with the horn pressed to my lips, I let forth such a fantastic blow the very earth seemed to shake around us. The Northerners must have thought I was calling for aid, for they all turned and bolted back into the shadows of the night."

With the story concluded, Daromir leaned back in his chair, smiling wickedly at the stunned Vanimire. Not that the conclusion of the story disappointed the Crown Prince, but that it was entirely not what he expected.

"You blew into a horn, and they fled?" Vanimire asked, raising a curious brow as he looked to his uncle for answers. "Surely you don't expect me to believe that?"

"What!" Daromir cried, his jaw dropping as if pained by the accusation. "I speak only the truth, dear nephew. Have you ever known your uncle to be a liar?"

"Don't answer him," the High King muttered, leaning back over to join their conversation at the perfect moment. "I've known him longer than you have my son, and if there is one thing I know for certain, it's that he can lie just as well as the rest of us."

Daromir leaned back in his chair, raising his uncovered hand into the air as if to plea his innocence.

"I leave the Capital for such a short time and come back to find my younger brother colder than the lands I traveled!" He cried, holding his head in hand as he fought back against the imaginary tears. "Is this the gift I get for such valiant service?"

Both the High King and Vanimire rolled their eyes at his exaggeration, which evoked a riotous fit of laughter from the older man. "You two are more alike than you know!" He roared, reaching for the goblet of wine once more before washing away his laughter with its contents.

"So, what was it then, Uncle?" Vanimire asked after washing the contents of his own goblet down his throat.

"What was what, Vanimire? How many times must I tell you? You must annunciate what it is you're inquiring about."

"What was it in the Blackwoods that caused all those villages to go missing?" Vanimire added, giving his uncle a swift nudge with his elbow in response to his playful teasing.

"Ah…that." Daromir seemed to deflate, letting out a long sigh as he ran his hand through his hair. "Nasty business."

"And perhaps one best saved for a council meeting," the High King interrupted, flashing Vanimire a quick look before turning his attention back to the armoured Daromir. "I will not have the mood of the evening ruined by the horrible realities which faced you. This *is* a night of celebration."

Daromir nodded, giving Vanimire a quick apologetic glance before offering a weak smile to the High King. "Of course. All the details are recorded in missives and tomes and delivered to Lord Alros, after all. I will say this, dear nephew, to sate your interest."

Vanimire leaned in closer, eager to hear of his uncle's expedition. His father, for his part, seemed far less keen about hearing such talk on what was supposed to be a night of festivities. As if sent by the Gods above, a group of nobles approached, bowing low at the edge of the dais before approaching the table with grins on their faces.

The High King scoffed at Daromir's antics and rose from his chair, greeting those who approached with outstretched hands as his attention was pulled elsewhere.

"One village, hoping to take advantage of forgotten treasures, established itself atop an ancient ruin. In their avarice, they stumbled upon a terrible ancient evil that had lain dormant. A curse, left by those whose bones littered the forgotten sanctuary. The evil manifested as a dragon of old, wreathed in a terrible shadow as dark as the night itself. When the sun dipped beyond the horizon, one could only see its terrible eyes glow a furious crimson."

The description of the beast sent shivers through Vanimire. Were it not for the sincerity of his uncle's tone, he might not have believed him. Gone was the nonchalant aloofness of his earlier story, replaced by a faint measure of genuine fear making Vanimire uneasy.

He realized even the mere mental recollection of this terrible beast brought back all the terror his uncle must have experienced facing it. Though he was curious about how such a beast was dealt with, he didn't want to make his uncle remember those memories again.

"Well, I'm glad the Empire is safer, and you've returned to us," Vanimire muttered. "But how was it that…"

The High King cut Vanimire off, slamming his fist into the table, making the others jump in surprise. Immediately, Vanimire looked at his father, and realized they had dwelt on the topic for far too long. A fire of irritation blazed within his eyes, causing Vanimire to bow his head in a silent apology.

"That is enough for one night," the High King hissed, letting out a long sigh before he continued. "Vanimire, return to your socializing. There are countless individuals who I'm certain wish to speak with you."

Vanimire exchanged a glance with his uncle, who only shrugged in response. Though the pair of them wished to continue, neither would go against the direct orders of the High King.

Vanimire reached for a fresh goblet of wine, lifting it with a hand, as he departed from behind the table. He turned, as was customary, to face the High King after he excused himself, bowing before him in a show of respect before giving a nod to his uncle. Daromir smiled playfully back, before mouthing the words 'we'll talk later'.

THERE WAS NO EXHAUSTION COMPARED TO WHAT CAME AFTER HAVING to spend any amount of time listening to haughty nobles speak of themselves. After spending the opening hours of the banquet with Emmaline at his side, Vanimire wondered why his father regarded the events with such disdain. The truth was painfully quick to remind him.

He hoped forcing himself to be more talkative at these events would slowly grow a measure of familiarity with the role assigned to him. Though he could not act as a stand-in for his father, many nobles saw the Crown Prince as a way their complaints might travel to the High King's ear.

It took a few minutes after departing from the table of the High King before Vanimire found himself lost amidst the never-ending torrent of the Empire's nobility. Though each of their concerns was valid, Vanimire couldn't help but wonder if they could have waited till after the festivities ended.

As Vanimire heard endless recounts on the lack of harvests, or the need for additional garrisoned forces, it was the occasional glimpse of the Lady Emmaline that gave him the strength to carry on. She, too, was bound in her position to speak with various members of the houses that aligned with her family. Even across the distance separating them, he saw how little she enjoyed the duties.

Though it seemed a never-ending source of exhaustion, he would try his best to shoulder the burdens of expectation levied upon him. If not for his own future, then for the one he hoped to provide for her.

Eventually, the last of the nobles demanding his attention were content, and Vanimire found himself with the rare opportunity for freedom. It was not a chance that he would squander, and after grabbing a fresh goblet of wine, one he most certainly deserved after having gone through all that he had, he was quick to meander through the crowd towards the large arches leading to the outdoor gardens.

It was a couple hours since he last spoke with Daelin. To the best of his knowledge, his friend hadn't returned to the banquet floor. He hardly blamed him, as it took speaking to one demanding nobleman before he, too, had wished to sneak away.

The chill of the night air seemed like a wave of delightful relief to Vanimire. The sound of his boots clicking against the carven stone brought back endless memories of times spent running through the gardens, much to the delight and chagrin of his father. Only when graced by the silent serenity of the evening did Vanimire realize how loud the banquet hall was. Though he meandered through the expansive hedge lined walkways, he still made out the indistinct sound of chatter from behind him. A constant reminder of what awaited him before too long.

The change of pace was nice, and it made him thankful that he found these moments of tranquility, even on a night filled to the brim with excitement. The chatter in the banquet hall was almost overwhelming, but it quickly faded beneath the serene sound of flowing water.

Before the festivities, they completely redid the garden's immaculate and intricate series of ponds. Waterfalls provided a quiet ambiance, beneath the soft sounds of frogs imported from the north, and fish brought in from all over played in perfect harmony.

Vanimire cast his gaze across the garden, hoping to find the figure of his friend through the blue canopy of the moon's light. Such was the intensity of the moon. Although torches were hardly needed, some still burned brightly in the areas where the shadows were deepest. Vanimire knew firsthand how quickly any area away from prying eyes was sought after.

A few individuals inhabited the gardens, for whom the cool evening air was made tolerable by either drink or company. He exchanged glances with some figures as he meandered about, not keen to invade anyone's private business. There were a handful of reasons two individuals might steal away from the excitement of the banquet, and none of those were something Vanimire wished to interrupt.

Vanimire followed the hedge-lined pathway through the garden, knowing where Daelin was likely to be found. The gardens stretched out farther than one imagined. Filled with flowers gathered from across the empire, and benches arranged for couples to bask beneath the beauty of the stars overhead as the flowery scents danced around them. Just as was to be expected, he saw the figure of Daelin with a hand pressed against the aged trunk of the white tree.

For as long as they were friends, the younger boy always found the shade of the white tree to be a place of unmatched serenity. In a city full of excitement and an uncountable number of faces, it was here the boy found a connection to the home he left behind. Many generations ago, the seeds were gifted to the line of Eineriel by the house of Vaentros.

"There you are," Vanimire called out as he approached the tree.

The clouds covering the light of Nalinyor shifted, allowing for the garden to be cast once more in its blue illumination. It was supposed to be an evening of unparalleled beauty, yet when the figure of Daelin came into clarity, it sent a wave of shock coursing through the Crown Prince. He dropped his goblet as he sprinted toward the trunk of the tree. The sound of the crashing metal attracted some confused glances, though most were likely to assume it to be the clumsiness of intoxication rather than anything else.

Vanimire drew closer to the unresponsive figure, which seemed to intensify the shock that consuming him. For though he expected his friend to be resting against the symbol of his home, he found Daelin's outstretched hand digging into the very trunk itself. Daelin was unresponsive as Vanimire shook him, his lips moving at a rapid pace as he chanted in some language unknown to the Crown Prince.

"*Fale gal mat. Fale gal rak. Fale gal elorie, rath!*" His fingers pressed into the wood of the tree with such an intensity blood welled at their tips, dripping down and staining the grass sprawling out beneath them.

He trembled as he continued to chant, his eyes closed as his expression maintained an eerie calmness.

"Daelin!" Vanimire screamed, grabbing hold of his friend with both hands as he violently tried to shake some measure of sense into the boy.

Nothing seemed to work. The boy's chanting continued at its intense pace. Vanimire looked around desperately for anyone to help. The self-absorbed individuals lining the gardens ignored his cries of panic, clearly thinking it to be some jest born from the alcohol they consumed.

A sickening crunch brought Vanimire's attention back to the boy, whose hand seemed to have broken with the pressure exerted upon it. Still, Vanimire tried to rouse his friend from the madness taking hold of him. Nothing seemed to work until, in an instant, the chanting stopped. Daelin's hand fell from against the trunk of the tree, his eyes rolled back in his head before blinking back at the subconscious manic gripping him. He turned to face Vanimire, his expression lined with confusion.

"V-Vanimire?" He asked wearily, looking around him as if he had no recollection of the events that had just concluded. "W-Where am I?"

Terror had yet to leave the Crown Prince, who continued to hold the shoulders of his confused companion. His mouth parted to form words but found nothing would come. Both terror and confusion gripped him, and though he knew not what the entranced man muttered, there was something about the words which gave him a shiver of genuine terror.

Daelin continued to look around, and slowly Vanimire saw some semblance of consciousness flood his gaze once more. "A…Ah, the gardens. Yes, I…I came out here for a breath of fresh air."

"W…What was that?!" Vanimire asked, looking at the disfigured and bloodied hand as it lay at the man's side.

"What was…what?" Daelin replied, looking back at the confused man with a similar look of confusion.

"D…Daelin, when I found you, you were chanting some nonsense, and your hand!" Vanimire reached for the wounded hand, lifting it upwards to the shock of his companion.

This too confused Vanimire, for Daelin regarded his wounded hand as if it were the first time he ever saw such an injury.

Daelin's face twisted in shocked surprise, turning the hand over beneath the blue light of the moon. His lips quivered, as if the pain of such an injury only just became apparent. Despite being roused from whatever came over him, Vanimire realized the clarity had not yet returned to Daelin's eyes. The younger man seemed lethargic, as if every motion required every ounce of his strength to perform.

Though confusion still wracked him, Daelin lowered his hand, turning his gaze wearily to study the surrounding garden. His gaze rested on the goblet, reflecting the light of the moon upon the ground where it was dropped.

"A…Ah, that was it," he muttered, lifting a shaking hand to point toward the fallen goblet.

Vanimire's eyes followed the man's outstretched hand. "My goblet? I dropped it when I saw you chanting."

Daelin shook his head, turning his gaze wearily to the Crown Prince.

"I've had far too much to drink tonight, Vani. Perhaps I should get some sleep." Those who stopped at the sight of the commotion, but didn't dare draw nearer to it, seemed to accept this answer.

With a soft spattering of chuckles, the couples continued their way. One hardly blamed anyone for having the excitement of the festivities go to their head. Although no one wanted to cause trouble, a party without any drunken shenanigans would have been considered quite a dull affair.

Vanimire's jaw hung slack for a few moments, suddenly aware of how chilly the evening became. Though he still held the weary man in his arms, he wasn't sure if he believed the excuse given. In all his years of attending banquets, Vanimire had yet to see an individual who drank so much to where they were breaking their hand against the bark of a tree. Then again, if ever there was someone who would drink so much to the point of chanting and communing with trees, it would be someone from house Vaentros.

Vanimire sighed, shifting the man within his arms so he had a better hold of him. Daelin always was a confusing sort, and though there was a part of him still shivering in horror at the mental image of the man's hand breaking against the tree, he figured guiding the man to his chambers and fetching for the healing staff might be the best course of action.

"Come on, then," he said, grunting from exertion as he lifted the weight of the man upwards. "We'll get you back to your chambers, and I'll call for the healers to have a look at that your hand."

"T…Thank you," Daelin groaned, struggling to walk even with the help of the stronger Vanimire.

"Just promise me you'll lay off the drinks next time, hm?" Vanimire groaned as they walked away from the shadow of the tree.

He found for the first time in his life he was thankful to see the shape of it slowly get lost in the shadows behind them.

"I…I promise. You're a good friend, Vani. I hope you know that." Daelin's footing seemed to elude him, for his gait was more of a stumble rather than the refined manner of walking the nobles were used to.

"Yeah, yeah. Tell me that when the sun rises, and the pain of your hand clears that mind of yours."

Daelin smiled wearily. As the chatter of the banquet hall grew louder, he whispered beneath his breath. "If it does."

IT TOOK LONGER TO GET THE INJURED MAN SETTLED THAN VANIMIRE realized. Despite the constant protests, he refused to leave the man's side until the healers took care of him. The wound appeared worse than it was. His nails were shattered, and there were a couple of cracked bones, but none of the damage seemed so devastating that it wouldn't heal in time.

When his hand was set and wrapped, the healers gifted him the relief of their concoction, which was quick to bring the groaning man sleep at last. Only then did Vanimire thank the healers and see them off.

Quietly, he closed the door to the house of Vaentros' chambers, exiting into the quiet halls of the capital complex. What was usually alight with life and excitement was now draped in quiet solemnity. All the members of staff were tending to the banquet raging on overhead. It was still far too early in the evening for most of the partygoers to be anywhere other than the centre of entertainment.

Vanimire opted to enjoy the moment of quiet serenity, strolling through the expansive hallways. Even though art and decorations adorned the walls, Vanimire ignored them. Those who looked upon it often enough remarked on the extravagance of the palace. But for one who spent every day of his life trapped within its walls, it was the city beyond that seemed far more captivating.

Pressed into the side of the mountain itself, the palace loomed over the heads of those that called both the high and Low City below their home. Its marbled exterior, white as ocean foam, seemed to twinkle beneath the radiance of the summer sun, acting almost as a lighthouse to those who looked upon it in awe. Its multiple levels shrunk as it stretched upward, appearing almost like a tall and imposing tower at its heights.

Vanimire's boots clicked against the marble floors, bringing him thoughtlessly back toward the banquet hall. He knew every inch of the palace by heart, for in the days of his youth he had to evade the guardians that, to him, were his captors.

Only in his recent years, he came to feel apologetic for how hectic he made the lives of those who existed, only to keep him safe. For them, it was a matter of life and death. The young and energetic prince rarely considered the dangers that might have presented themselves in the city below, especially once the sun went down. The tough realities didn't occupy his mind, only the desire to steal a few precious moments of delight in a world altogether foreign to him.

"How simple things had been then," Vanimire whispered, quietly smiling as he remembered how terrible he used to be.

As he turned the corner, Vanimire noticed something which made him freeze on the spot. At the end of the long hallway, moving through the shadows lining the walls, was a figure wrapped in a long white cloak. It moved slowly, but deliberately, sticking only to where the shadows were strongest.

At first, Vanimire thought it might have been a partygoer, for it wouldn't have been the first time a new face to the capital got lost amidst the twisting and turning labyrinth-like hallways sprawling out through the complex.

Yet, as Vanimire took a step towards the figure, he sensed a shiver of fear once more tear through him. It was as if he still stood next to the injured Daelin, his blood pooling beneath the white tree. Something about the shadow-clad figure seemed to create a strange mix of curiosity and terror in the Crown Prince, who continued to tip-toe towards it.

As he moved, so too did the figure. It seemed to exist only at the edge of his vision, for as Vanimire picked up the pace, he could not make up any ground separating them. Before he knew it, he was sprinting down the endless hallways, desperate to figure out what eluded him.

He must have looked a madman, tearing through the marbled hallways as fast as his feet took him. The shadowy figure looked as if it were going nowhere, for as it was heading toward the banquet, it would turn and draw farther away from the main hall. Everything about the figure confused and intrigued Vanimire, who found his insatiable curiosity swell and grow with every passing moment.

After it felt like a lifetime, he cornered the shadow-clad figure. Though it evaded him, it made a crucial mistake, turning down a hallway leading toward a section of the capital labyrinth not yet completed. Vanimire turned the last corner, and as he expected, the cloaked figure clung to the shadows at the very end of the hall. The chase was exhilarating, but it had at long last reached its conclusion.

Vanimire paused, catching his breath. The Crown Prince would revel in questioning the robed figure that started their endless game of chase. With nowhere left to go, they were at his mercy.

As Vanimire walked toward the figure, he felt a heavy gauntleted hand grab his shoulder, making him yelp in surprise. The hand turned him away from the cloaked figure, and much to Vanimire's surprise, it was Daromir.

"Is everything alright lad?" Daromir asked, confusion apparent in his expression as he studied his panting nephew.

Vanimire was at a loss for words. How long was his uncle following him? His lips parted, though no words would come. All he could do was point toward the end of the hallway behind him.

"What?" Daromir asked, moving his gaze from beyond his nephew, curiously studying the hallway. "By the Gods." He gasped, letting go of Vanimire.

Vanimire turned, looking down the hallway to where the shadow-clad figure stood, only to find that it now empty. Once more shock washed over him.

"It was right there!" He protested, walking toward the end of the hallway. "I chased it through all the halls, and now it's gone!?"

Daromir looked at Vanimire once more, his confusion clear. "Slow down, boy. What did you see?"

"I...I don't know!" Vanimire cried, walking toward where the hallway ended.

He pressed his hands against the uncut stone wall. Languished that the cloaked figure was indeed nowhere to be found.

"It was a cloaked figure."

Daromir raised a brow, joining his nephew in curiously feeling the cool stone wall.

"A cloaked figure?" His confusion and disbelief were clear in his tone. Vanimire found a twinge of irritation course through him.

"I swear it was right here!" Vanimire said, exasperated. "G... Gods, what is going on tonight?"

Daromir chuckled, turning, and taking a few steps away from where the 'figure' vanished.

"You've had too much to drink, nephew. A shame, since I was hoping to share a rare vintage, I brought back with me from my travels."

Vanimire paused, thinking over his uncle's words. He was drinking since the council meeting earlier in the day. Did it explain the strange occurrences plaguing him all evening? With a sigh, he turned, walking over to where his uncle awaited him.

"Perhaps you're right. Though it will not stop me from trying out that vintage. Especially if we share it by hearing another of your stories?"

Daromir let out a loud laugh, which bellowed through the empty hall, draping his arm around the curious Vanimire.

"I suppose there are a few things I can tell you about!" The low light caught his uncle's expression, casting long and curious shadows.

With the heart of the party still beating strong in the banquet hall, there was a calmness surrounding them. Even here, the radiance of the capital was on full display, with flower pots hanging along the walls containing all manners of greenery that the botanists of the city grew and cultivated.

Vanimire smiled, eager to return to the banquet hall. What a strange evening it had been, for it seemed every moment since he left the party he faced some strange occurrences. Perhaps it was the Gods way of letting him know he should enjoy the luxuries of the party for once.

Who knows when next he would get to experience such extravagance?

CHAPTER V

AN UNEXPECTED GUEST

"For the most terrible sin was committed. I refused to believe my senses. I saw the outline of a monster, and I ignored it."

Once more, Vanimire found himself beneath the cool and refreshing blue light of Nalinyor, though this time under much more enjoyable circumstances. The vintage Daromir kept safe through all the long months of his expedition was worth the effort, for Vanimire never quite tasted anything like it. Cool and fruity at first, yet it left a faint burning of the mouth after it settled. As if the dark-red liquid hoped to leave a powerful reminder to any who consumed it.

Though the chatter from the banquet hall carried on the quiet winds of the garden, it too subsided some, as most of the attendees became content after all the wine consumed. The party dwindled to its embers, and Vanimire was more than content to see out the evening in the company of his uncle, who had an endless supply of interesting stories too regal.

"So…" Daromir hummed, placing the near-empty bottle on the stone railing the pair leaned against. "Lady Emmaline, hm?"

Vanimire choked on the wine he was sipping, earning a riotous laugh from the older man. After sputtering for a few moments, he caught his breath, collecting his thoughts before he dared answer the inevitable barrage of questions that would follow.

"Y…Yes. We have been…well, I suppose interested in one

73

another for some time, though it remains to be anything serious." Only with the gifted courage of a day spent drinking did he speak so frankly about the situation.

His willingness even surprised himself, though perhaps he hoped to earn his uncle's favour.

"I see," Daromir muttered, hiding his growing smile behind the rim of his goblet.

Vanimire couldn't read his uncle as well as he could his father, and so the inner workings of his mind remained a curious enigma.

"Well, she is a suitable match, at the very least. A wonderful family, a terrifying grandmother, and well, she's stunning." He added, leaning over and giving the younger man a playful nudge.

Vanimire had no response to this and so tried to hide his growing blush by chugging the rest of his goblet. He knew his uncle meant well, and it warmed his heart to know his selection of potential partner earned his approval.

"I'll stop teasing you, boy..." Daromir said with a chuckle. "How goes your training? I hope you haven't been neglecting that."

Vanimire sighed, reaching over to fill his goblet up one last time.

"It's been a slow process," he admitted, taking a gulp from the goblet before continuing. "It's difficult to find the time, in truth. I spend my days with the tutors or attending meetings of the High Council. After those have concluded, it's responding to missives or attending to any other manner of issues demanding my attention."

"I take it you still cling to the dream of yours, little nephew?" Daromir asked, downing the last of his goblet before resting it between them.

"Of course I do!" Vanimire shouted, earning the curious glances from the few individuals lingering in the serene garden.

He felt embarrassed, though he was thankful his father was kept busy in the banquet hall. If he was there to hear his son's outburst, it would have almost certainly led to an endless reminder of the need for self-control in the role which was expected of him.

"It's always been my dream to see more beyond the walls of the capital, Uncle. That much has never changed. Though, I'm not sure what father would say if I told him I dreamed of being a Redcloak like you."

"I see," Daromir muttered, turning his gaze from the younger man to stare down at the twinkling lights of the city below.

People built countless fires for the celebrations, and while most were extinguished, the city still overflowed with more light and energy than usual.

"I know you see the walls of the city as little more than the walls of your cage, dear nephew, but there is safety in living within them."

Vanimire's gaze followed, looking down at the city stretching out beneath them. How many days did he spend in his youth in this very spot, yearning to grow wings and fly beyond the horizon? Not once had he gotten close, even when he eluded his guardians and spend a few precious hours roaming the twisting streets of the city. It was no straightforward thing, leaving the city to which he had such an important role to fulfill.

It was easy for him to sit at its highest peak and dream of seeing the world beyond, but every time he drew nearer to those walls, he found his fear building. In this way, his uncle was right. The walls were a visible reminder of the safety afforded to him. More chains.

"I know," Vanimire sighed, turning his gaze back towards his uncle. "But when I hear tales of your adventures, I can't help but yearn to create stories of my own. How will the history books remember me, uncle Daromir? As the High King who was born and lived within the safety of his walls, too afraid to see the world beyond them?"

Vanimire swirled the contents of his goblet, holding it between either hand as his vision grew unfocused.

"You and father already made names for yourselves in your battles against the mainland invaders by the time you were my age. Leading the cavalry charge with your men-at-arms as you pushed them back to the seas. Hells, even then, you two couldn't get enough! Leaping into the boats left behind and…"

"And we gave chase, boarded the vessel, and cut them down." Daromir was quick to interject, finishing the tale he had both lived, and heard recanted far, far too many times. "Those were little more than rogue pirates, Vani. Disgruntled tradesmen from the Republics who sought to find a better life for themselves in distant lands."

Vanimire sighed, shaking his head as he took another long gulp from his goblet.

"Still. People *remembered*. Even now I'm sure there are those who re-enact the scene on many a wobbling tavern tables. Somehow, I can't imagine many leaping at the opportunity to play the tavern role of *Vanimire*."

Daromir looked to the boy, his expression growing soft as he reached over to rest a gauntleted hand on his shoulder.

"I am certain you will be remembered as the greatest High Kive we ever knew. The line of Eineirel will not end with you, nephew. Yearning to see the world beyond the walls is only natural, but you must never forget the stories of my adventures are built upon the backs of countless friends who have been buried."

At first, Vanimire was confused because his uncle's words made little sense. *'The line of Eineriel will not end with you'?* Of course, it wouldn't. Not that Vanimire hoped to find a glorious death beyond the walls, only to see the world eluding him. Yet whatever confusion plaguing him was soon forgotten as his uncle's expression grew solemn.

"I'm...I'm sorry," Vanimire added, feeling embarrassed.

Though the council meeting would discuss the exact details of their year-long expedition, rumours already spread that far more men were lost on it than ever recorded in the history of the Redcloaks. It was rare for even a single Redcloak to die, so any expedition that saw the death of multiple members would undoubtedly face criticism.

"If only there was more time to see it all," Daromir whispered.

Although lost in thought, Vanimire's uncle's solemn tone refocused him. His attention turned to him, his brow narrowing as confusion lined his expression.

"What was that?" Vanimire asked, leaning forward to garner some measure of an explanation from his uncle's gaze.

To Vanimire's surprise, it grew distant, weary, sorrowful. Not once in all the years of his life was his uncle like this, and the very sight made his heart race.

"Life is far too short for us to truly enjoy it, nephew." Daromir added, lifting his eyes upwards to gaze at the moon as he spoke. Though directed at him, his uncle's words felt distant, as if he were speaking to someone else entirely.

"Now you're the one who's gone and drank too much," Vanimire said, looking down at the empty bottle of wine with a low chuckle.

The quip pulled his uncle from whatever came over him, for he too looked down and snickered.

"So, it would seem!" He muttered, shaking his head as the pair broke into a shared fit of laughter.

It felt good for laughter to once more return to the gardens of the capital. The recent months saw a heavy veil of malaise draped over the capital as rumours carried regarding the complete destruction of the Redcloak expedition.

Before the High King even ordered Daromir to investigate, that entire towns were vanishing in the Blackwoods sent constant waves of panic through the citizens. When the updates ceased, it became a point of near total panic as some whispered the threat of the north turned its gaze southwards.

For their part, both Vanimire and his father never once lost hope. The struggle was trying to maintain order amongst the council members, who were constantly at odds. Now that Daromir returned, his seat would no longer be empty during the meetings, and Vanimire hoped his presence alone would bring peace to the embattled council.

His uncle's return marked a turning point, and one Vanimire hoped would lead to better, calmer days spent within the walls of his captivity. Hells, perhaps he would pester him into resuming their training, now that the Redcloaks were certain to enter a period of rest and recuperations.

"I'm glad you've returned, Uncle," Vanimire said with a sigh, reaching over to rest his hand against the man's gauntleted arm.

"As am I, boy. As am I. There were many moments where I thought for certain I wouldn't live to see the spires of the capital." The older man replied, collecting himself after the fit of laughter subsided.

Vanimire's elation faded as his lips drew to a line. There was much he wished to ask, and yet, he worried that to get the answers he was so desperate for, it would require bringing up memories best left behind. He always struggled to read the emotions of his uncle, but even he saw the toll that the year long expedition exacted on him. He was different, though Vanimire couldn't quite put his finger on what changed. Had the aged lines of his face grown deeper with all the stress he endured?

"You've never been good at hiding when your mind is turning,"

Daromir muttered. The corners of his lips lifted in a gentle smile as his words pulled the younger man from his musings.

"W…What?" Vanimire asked, turning his gaze back to focus on the man.

"Your face scrunches up when you're thinking. It's always been this way, and I'm sure, knowing you, it always will be. So, out with it. You wish to know of the expedition, I take it?"

Vanimire paused, blinking in pure shock as his eyes widened. Was he truly so easy to read? It was remarkable how cognizant his uncle had always been.

In the days of his youth, he often lambasted against those who claimed Daromir's only talent was with the blade, for he knew just how talented his uncle was in almost all walks of life. Only recently, his uncle revealed this was by his own intention, for it was easier to read those who believed he was nothing more than a simple swordsman.

"The dragon," Vanimire whispered, as if scared his voice would break the tranquil serenity of the gardens. "What was it like?"

Daromir chuckled, turning his gaze from the boy to once more cast out over the city sprawling out below them.

"It was beautiful," he sighed, much to the surprise of Vanimire. Of all the responses that might have been given, this was easily the one Vanimire least expected.

"Beautiful?" Vanimire asked, unable to contain his surprised confusion at the response.

"Aye. It was terrifying, and terrible, and yet, it wielded a power the likes of which the world has not seen in countless ages. Covered from head to tail in scales housing the light of the very stars itself. It moved with such slender and grace, one might think it impossible given how it loomed so tall overhead. They say there was an age where dragons were more common than man, and when I looked upon it, Vani, I almost wished I lived in that forgotten age." Vanimire watched as his uncle's gaze grew distant as he spoke, as if he were transported back to the very confrontation.

He expected terror to coat his uncle's expression at recalling such a memory, but once more, to his surprise, a sorrowful smile tugged at the older man's lips.

"I almost regret killing it," he whispered, once more sending a surprised shock through Vanimire.

Rare was it for anyone to see a living dragon, let alone wield one's weapon against it. Even with his privileged lot in life, Vanimire only ever saw depictions of the curious beasts in ancient tomes of lore. The age of dragons met its end when the age of man came into dominance.

"It had to be killed, of course…" Daromir continued, his vision still cast far beyond their surroundings. "But it spoke with such a beautiful tongue. A shame it was, dear nephew, to assign to oblivion a mind containing centuries of wisdom. All it might have known is now lost to us, for by my blade, I denied us the gift of knowing."

Silence fell over them as his uncle's words trailed off. Vanimire could hardly contain his surprise at how his uncle answered. He expected to hear a tale filled to the brim with heroic details, flourished by the unparalleled storytelling ability his uncle possessed. Instead, his uncle appeared sorrowful, as if the memory remained eternally mournful.

"But it was evil, right?" Vanimire asked, his gaze wandering from his uncle's expression.

He noticed as the story carried on, his uncle's clenched fist trembled, and Vanimire sensed his uncle was uneasy with the topic at hand.

"What?" Daromir replied, his gaze focusing once more on the city below. He turned his head towards Vanimire, lifting a curious brow as if complete confusion gripped him.

"The dragon," Vanimire continued. "It was evil, wasn't it?"

"Ah. Yes. Of course, it was." Daromir paused, seeming to deflate some as understanding washed over him.

Vanimire sensed his mind was somewhere else entirely, and his question brought him back to the present. Had it been any other day, it might have unnerved him, but given all his uncle went through, it seemed natural exhaustion was setting in.

"Is everything alright, Uncle?" Vanimire asked, tilting his head to the side slightly as he narrowed his gaze.

"W…What?" Daromir blurted, blinking as he shook his head.

"You're acting…strange. Has all the wine and talk of glory gone to your head?"

"Ah…" Daromir muttered, looking down at the goblet as he let out a quiet sigh.

"We should have never freed it from its prison. How foolish we were to not realize it was a trap." Daromir added, his voice lowering to little more than a whisper.

"Freed it?" Vanimire asked, raising his brow in confusion. "How does one even imprison a dragon? Especially one that appears as you've described it."

Daromir glanced at the younger man for a few moments, confusion once more etched along his expression. Slowly, he removed his hand from Vanimire's shoulder, turning to lean against the railing as his gaze once more wandered beyond the garden.

"Of course. It was a dragon. It couldn't have been imprisoned." He muttered, shaking his head.

"Uncle?" Vanimire turned to face the man, fear brewing in him once more. Was his entire night to be cursed with all these strange experiences? "Are you sure you haven't had too much to drink?"

"Enough, nephew!" Daromir hissed, digging his fingers into the stone railing. His uncle's tone came as a surprise, causing Vanimire to stumble backwards in shock.

"U…Uncle, what's wrong?" Vanimire asked hesitantly, his heart racing as his uneasiness continued to grow.

"Nothing!" Daromir spat back, bringing a clenched fist down against the stone railing.

The gauntleted fist made a terrible cracking noise, causing Vanimire to once more jump in surprise. "The mortal drinks affect me no longer, nephew, so quit with your ceaseless worrying!"

Vanimire's jaw hung slack, unable to form any manner of words. In all the years he knew his uncle, not once had he raised his voice as he did now. He was certain the man experienced anger, for he was still as much a human as the rest of them, but he always had a soft spot for his younger nephew. It was a rare enough sight to see his uncle upset, let alone so quickly given to fits of anger, and never had such darkness seem to fall over him.

"I…I'm sorry, uncle," Vanimire said, stuttering as he stepped away. "Perhaps it's best I return to my socializing…"

Daromir turned, moving like a crack of lighting as he reached out and grabbed hold of Vanimire's shoulder once more. His grip was tight. Waves of pain coursed through him as Vanimire gasped in both surprise and shock. Before he realized what happened, Daromir pulled him in close, lowering himself so their gazes were level. Vanimire could see that his uncle's eyes were trembling and strained, as if fighting against an indescribable pain.

"V…Vanimire!" He gasped, voice weary and drained. "You must leave the capital. T…Take your father and g…go. I…I'm so sorry. It's all my fault. I…I failed. I tried to stop them but…"

Vanimire stood in silence, unable to move even after his uncle released him. "D…Daromir?" He asked, watching in terror as his uncle lurched from side-to-side, twisting and tensing against the stone railing.

Daromir made no noise through this fit of madness gripping him, and Vanimire wondered if he suffered from whatever seemed to have come over Daelin earlier in the night. Unlike his younger companion, Daromir straightened as the fit subsided, leaving him panting and weary as he turned his gaze back to face him. Despite himself, Vanimire couldn't help but shrink beneath his uncle's gaze.

"I…I'm sorry, nephew," Daromir muttered, bracing himself against the stone railing as he collected himself.

"The dragon's talons dug deep, and it has left my mind prone to moments of…I'm sorry." His gaze faltered, and Vanimire noticed tears welling in his eyes. At once, Vanimire felt sorrow wash over him.

"N…No." Vanimire said, taking a step closer and resting a hand on his uncle's armoured shoulder. "You are fine, uncle. Exhaustion and wine are never pleasant companions. I can see your expedition has left you…altered, and weary. Come, let us return to father."

Daromir seemed uncertain, confused. Vanimire couldn't put his finger on it, but there was something off about the way his uncle carried himself. Had the year away from the capital been so draining it left him little more than a shadow of his former self?

Only time would tell, though Vanimire hoped with an almost childish naivety his uncle would return to his former self in no time.

As he was about to snake an arm around his uncle to bring him from the gardens, the quiet serenity was once more disrupted. Both Vanimire and his uncle's gaze shot towards the arched doorways leading to the banquet hall. Gasps and quiet, shocked murmurs carried on the wind. Vanimire found his heart sink into the depths of terror once more.

The soft music filling the banquet hall, and carrying gently on the winds through the garden, paused. In its place, distant, wordless chatter heightened. Vanimire gazed upon the outlines of figures through the grand windows and watched as they darted nervously back-and-forth.

Gone was the memory of his uncle's outburst, replaced with the uneasy curiosity of what might have provoked the widespread chattering this time. Vanimire exchanged a glance with his uncle, who, unlike him, was alert and ready to spring into action. Vanimire tried to turn, but felt the gauntleted hand of his uncle pull him back. The man's strength had clearly returned, though *that* made Vanimire uneasy for another reason.

"Stay behind me, nephew!" He roared, releasing his hold on the younger man.

Vanimire nodded quietly before they set off, breaking at full speed through the hedged lined pathways of the garden. His excitement and terror grew as each step brought them closer to the banquet hall. For Vanimire, the night air itself became cooler as they sprinted through it.

His heart raced in his chest, both from the sudden exertion and the growing adrenaline. There was something different about how the crowd's confusion emanated. When Daromir made his grand appearance, it felt as if the crowd were abuzz with curious excitement. Yet this time, despite being unable to make out a single word being said, Vanimire sensed the collective nervousness of the crowd build.

One voice seemed to rise over the collective uneasy chattering as Vanimire and his uncle sprinted back into the warmth of the banquet hall. Much to his shock, Vanimire saw everyone in the hall turned toward whoever had entered. As they drew nearer, he heard the booming voice of his father cry out, demanding to know who it was who dared to interrupt their festivities. Something wasn't right, that much was certain. Vanimire sensed the terrified uneasiness of the crowd roaring so fiercely it was almost palpable.

"Stay here!" Daromir commanded, pushing Vanimire against a pillar lining the marble-floored hall. "I know not what danger has appeared, but I would not have you put in harm's way as well."

"B…But uncle…" Vanimire protested.

"Now is not the time, Vanimire!" Daromir screamed, giving him another push before forcing his gaze to find his own.

"Y...You must run!" He added, voice trembling as he gave his nephew's shoulder a gentle squeeze.

Confusion washed over him. It was as if his uncle spoke as two separate individuals. Vanimire did nothing but nod quietly, which earned him an appreciative smile from the older man before he turned and bolted towards the High King.

His growing fear made it impossible to still himself completely, though the wine coursing through his body helped to stifle the more outlandish thoughts clawing at his mind. Were he with anyone else, he would have certainly lost himself in his panic. Yet with his father and uncle nearby, Vanimire hoped all would be taken care of.

Despite his orders, Vanimire was insatiably curious to discover who earned both the gaze and ire of all those in attendance. Free of his uncle's presence, he slowly made his way through the crowd, desperate to catch a glance at this mysterious figure.

"Redcloaks to me!" Daromir screamed, causing a wave of silence to fall over the crowd as the armoured figures pushed their way through.

Though it earned him no shortage of irritated glances, Vanimire pushed his way to the front of the crowd. Unnoticed by both his father and uncle, who were soon flanked by armoured companions.

Vanimire's eyes followed the crowd, directing towards the cloaked figure standing in the centre of the banquet hall. Dark robes tattered and ripped along the bottom, dragged behind as it moved through the hall with terrifying confidence.

Whoever it was, they were unbothered by the stunned looks they received. As they moved, the cloak continued to stretch behind it, further revealing countless eyes inscribed in a sickening crimson. All the gazes that beheld it in the banquet hall were dwarfed by those that it wore on itself. As if the strange individual was gazing back to every one of them tenfold over.

His heart lurched up into his throat as he looked upon the same cloaked figure that had eluded him in the halls of the capital earlier in the evening. That time it was just he who borne witness to the mysterious figure that was clad in white. Though the cloak they bore was unlike any Vanimire ever seen, he was certain the same individual hid beneath it. All the eyes of the empire looked upon it in horror and confusion.

Daromir, flanked on both sides by the Redcloaks who entered

earlier, descended from the raised dais, drawing nearer to the figure whose cloak concealed their identity from the world. The High King roared in anger, hurling no endless barrage of questions and accusations against the figure whose very presence disrupted the warm atmosphere built over an entire evening of festivities.

Despite his uneasiness continuing to build, Vanimire experienced a wave of relief wash over him as the Redcloaks awaited their orders. There was nowhere safer in the entire empire than in the presence of the strongest swordsmen the world ever knew. He doubted one cloaked figure would hold his own against the might of the entire Rhyserion empire.

The murmurs, which were silenced somewhat by Daromir's roaring orders, continued to build as the cloaked figure lifted their trembling hands towards the hood. Time seemed to slow to a standstill as Vanimire watched in uneasy anticipation, desperate to know who, or what, caused him so many issues.

The hood of the cloak fell back, revealing a pallid head free of any hair, yet adorned in a brilliant mosaic of crimson tattoos. The eyes on the cloak shimmered as they drew back, creating the illusion of blinking for a moment. Others thought the same, for when the pale head was revealed, the banquet hall erupted into gasps and silent cries.

Everything about the figure hidden beneath the cloak was unnatural. Skin as pale as the dead. A face angled and sharp, with high cheekbones causing its skin to pull inward. Yet for all the terror of its visage, it paled compared to the sight emerging as it straightened and opened its eyes. Though its cloak held hundreds of them, the skin on its face twisted unnaturally as each pair of eyes slowly opened, blazing with a red intensity as they levelled upon the High King standing before it.

Six eyes lined the figure's face, and immediately Vanimire felt a shiver of horror course through him. It was unlike anything he ever saw, for each eye blazed with an intense fire. Each of which was directed towards the High King who looked on in complete shock. His father grew pale as the figure revealed itself. Vanimire noticed, and even from this distance, he realized he trembled in terror.

The uneasy murmurs of the crowd continued to build as more-and-more of them caught a glance at the mysterious six-eyed figure. The noise grew so loud Vanimire could barely hear the thoughts in his head. He wished everyone would control themselves so he might hear what the figure had to say. For though it opened its mouth, it quickly closed it when the screams of the crowd drowned out any words passing through their lips.

Vanimire noticed the figure was growing irritated, for though faint, its silver eyebrows twitched. It raised its hand, swooping it through the air, which brought about an immediate cessation of the screams. The sudden silence made Vanimire leap in surprised terror, as he noticed countless individuals in the crowd, who were amid their panic, drop to the ground.

Their hands clutched at their throats as they rolled and writhed in muted agony. Though their lips remained parted as if to scream, no noise carried through the banquet hall. Many of those who peered on in surprise only watched in terror as their friends and loved ones writhed and choked on whatever invisible force the figure unleashed. Their own screams drowned in their throats, unable to give voice to the sounds that might have earned their own demise.

"Progeny of Eineriel. High King of the Rhyserion empire, heir to Einor's legacy. Lord of the song unworthy." The figure spoke, its voice raspy yet determined.

Vanimire could not draw his attention away from the individual as they stepped towards the edge of the raised dais. The Redcloaks still separated them, though they too appeared uneasy.

"I am the Six-Eyed Herald, the harbinger of our new age. Let me be the first to congratulate you on hosting such a fantastic feast. There is no better way to bring about the age of crimson than gathered in this most ancient and remarkable hall."

The High King could not form a reply, though the mysterious figure who called itself the Herald, waited with outstretched arms. Vanimire noticed his father tremble, his lips quivering as if trying to form words that would not come. Slowly, the figures writhing on the floor fell into a terrifying stillness. The light in their anguished faces extinguishing as their life drifted from broken, silenced lips.

The Herald took another step towards the raised dais, to which the Redcloaks took a step forward. The High King, stumbling back against his chair in genuine terror, could do naught but raise his arm, casting his hand towards the six-eyed figure as he cried out. "D…Daromir! K…Kill him!"

With his gaze still intently focused on the six-eyed Herald, Daromir nodded, clearing his throat before his voice once more carried through the banquet hall.

"Redcloaks! Forward!" Relief washed over Vanimire as the Redcloaks surrounded the Herald.

For their part, the six-eyed figure appeared at ease as the greatest swordsmen in the realm encircled them. Vanimire wished desperately to see them struck down, if only to bring an end to the strange circumstances plaguing him this cursed evening.

Daromir exchanged glances with his fellow Redcloaks, who stood shoulder-to-shoulder encircling the pallid figure. Though some of them seemed uneasy, Vanimire saw most of their expressions were alight with a fire unlike anything he had ever seen. It was as if they stood upon the very precipice of battle, and with a desperate urge to be unleashed, they chafed against the chains binding them.

"W…Wait…" Vanimire whispered.

A sickening truth formed in Vanimire's mind as he studied their gazes. *They were chained, but not by…*

"Redcloaks!" Daromir screamed, raising his gauntleted arm up towards the cloak hanging from his left shoulder.

"N…No!" Vanimire screamed, trying to lurch forward but finding his body was far too heavy to move in response to his orders.

"Defend the *Song!*" Daromir screamed, tearing the Redcloak which hung from his shoulder.

All his companions followed suit, and Vanimire watched in horror as they bared their left arms to the world. Gone was the arm of the Redcloaks, which were to remain covered unless in moments of protecting the Empire. Their armour, torn at the shoulder, revealed arms as dark as the night sky. Cracked and battered like a maelstrom collided with the earth. Lines of glowing, *pulsing* red shone through.

Terror and confusion gripped the crowd, whose eyes were all drawn to the unnatural and ominous arms hidden thus far. Such was the terror gripping Vanimire that as he struggled to move, even as he saw the Redcloaks take a step towards the Herald before turning to face the crowd that surrounded them.

"N…No…" Vanimire muttered, tears flowed freely down his

cheeks as the blackened arms of the Redcloaks raised towards the crowd.

The Herald's mouth twisted as its lips parted, revealing long, serrated teeth lifting into a wretched grin. At that moment, the figure appeared more monster than a man. Its arms lifted, his hands set beneath long, twisted fingernails stretching out like the jagged teeth lining its jaw. Every aspect of the Herald was twisted and stretched, as if the unnatural, terrifying figures of one's deepest nightmare were given life.

The Herald's chest rose and fell from long, ragged hiss-like breaths as its excitement heightened. A laugh bubbled up from the depths and echoed over the terrified murmuring of the crowd that filled the banquet hall. Set on all sides by the Redcloaks, continuing their slow, unwavering march towards those who gathered. With every step, their armour clanked, and the marble beneath their feet seemed to shake and quiver beneath the terror of their frenzied resolve.

Vanimire watched as panic spread through the crowd, who, having control of themselves, returned once more, tried to push themselves away from the Redcloaks, whose attention turned on them. Time seemed to slow to a standstill.

Vanimire could do nothing but watch in complete horror as the blackened arms of the Redcloaks glowed a terrible crimson. The crowd, pushing against itself in a desperate attempt to flee in the face of danger, could not move any further back, and Vanimire watched in horror as the cracks that lined the Redcloaks' arms flashed, and terrible bolts unleashed.

The bolts shot out from the cracks, sizzling through the air as they tore through the gathered nobility. Screams were silenced as bodies crunched and writhed, and the night of festivity, gave way to that of carnage.

CHAPTER VI

A BANQUET OF BLOOD

"In the weeks that followed, I kept wondering what might have happened if I remained strong. If I dared to look the monster in the eye and hold my own."

Neither fairy tale nor the most wicked of nightmare could recreate the horror that so quickly consumed the banquet hall. The blackened arms of the Redcloaks were a weapon the likes of which Vanimire had never witnessed.

Whether by divine providence or simple luck, he avoided the initial onslaught, throwing himself to the ground as the Redcloaks unleashed terrible crimson spikes through the crowd. Few were as lucky, for countless bodies hit the ground in a battered, broken mess. Their lives were snuffed out in a single, terrifying instant.

Screams of the guests were deafening, their terror near enough to cause Vanimire to lose himself to the panic clawing at him. With every barrage of spikes unleashed by the Redcloaks, more screams were silenced.

When the first drops of blood spilled, all sense of reason and nobility vanished. Nobles from across the empire clamoured over one another in desperate, but vain, attempts at saving themselves. Fathers pushed aside brothers, and mothers stepped over daughters.

Like rats fleeing a sinking ship, they sought only their own salvation. The Redcloaks, however, were relentless in their barbarous devastation.

Vanimire lost all sense of his surroundings as the screams consumed even the roaring orders of his father. Never had the High King failed to pierce through the commotion with his booming voice. However, despite his efforts, the terror gripping the banquet hall drowned out the High King's orders and pleas for the carnage to cease.

Vanimire watched as the High King summoned his courage once more and stood tall and defiant atop the raised dais. The Redcloaks attacked his people. Though Vanimire's vision swirled and darkened at the edges, his father projected the image of the empire's defender.

Vanimire did nothing as the terror consumed him. He needed to flee, to adhere to the words of his uncle and escape from the carnage. Despite his every effort, he could not force his body to move.

Another onslaught of spikes caught more of the partygoers, one of which fell on top of the terrified Crown Prince. The noble's weight, ballooned from an evening of lavish consumption, pinned him in place. Warm, slick blood poured freely from the wounds that he'd sustained, pooling beneath the pinned Crown Prince. Vanimire watched as the Redcloaks continued their slaughter.

They easily killed the few remaining guards, overwhelming them in a frenzy that seemed to consume them wholly. The blackened arms of the Redcloaks twisted and jut out at awkward angles, forming terrible crooked blades that sliced through armour and flesh with ease.

The screams were deafening. As the seconds passed by in a flurry of slaughter and carnage, they slowly subsided. Their symphony of despair giving way to the eternity of darkness that consumed them. The Redcloaks acted as if they prepared for this very moment, cutting through the nobles with ease.

Some of them had more courage in the face of death than Vanimire and tried to run to the massive doors at the end of the banquet hall. They were quick to find out that the doors were locked, causing another outburst of despair. Another barrage of crimson spikes impaled them to the doors like a missive nailed into a noticeboard. Any hope for salvation fleeting as their bodies grew limp.

Through it all, Vanimire tried desperately to find where his uncle and father had gone, as he lost them both in the carnage. His mind also wandered to the Lady Emmaline, though he hoped with a childish naivety she was not present in the hall when the bloodshed began.

He couldn't bear the thought of her becoming just another one of the lifeless bodies piling around him. Their blood pooled and spread so thickly that the exquisite floor of the hall was no longer visible through the crimson veil created.

Vanimire tried to move, desperate to find his father. With each passing moment, more partygoers continued to be massacred. Vanimire's chances of escape were dwindling. If he could find his father, they might steal themselves away while the eyes of the Redcloaks were distracted. He understood his father was in the most central and recognizable spot in the banquet hall when the massacre began, making the hope of escape foolish and naïve. But it was the only thought that would keep him alive.

With a strained effort, Vanimire shifted beneath the bloodied body of the nobleman, crawling out from underneath him as he shuffled through the pool of blood that formed. He needed to sneak away from the centre of the banquet hall, relying on the shadows along the wall to mask his escape. It was no easy expedition, for just as Vanimire crawled away from the bodies, another torrent of spikes ripped through the crowd. How he managed to not meet the fate of so many was beyond his knowing. He survived another barrage, though a searing wave of pain consumed him as one spike ripped across him.

Vanimire screamed in agony, clutching his side where the spike grazed him. He sensed the warmth of blood seep between his fingertips. The shock of the pain coursed through him, followed by throbbing agony that threatened to make him fall once more to the ground. The terrible shock to his senses immediately freed his mind from the crippling thoughts and terror engrossing him.

Summoning as much of his strength as he could muster, Vanimire broke into a sprint, though he stumbled and tripped over the broken and battered bodies. He slid under a table at the far end of the banquet hall, throwing himself into the shadows, desperate to be unseen.

The thin veil created by the silken tablecloth would not protect him if the Redcloaks unleashed more crimson spikes, but it was here, enveloped in the shadows, where he sensed the faintest measure of safety. Tucked away from the eyes of the world, and the gaze of the maddened Redcloaks, Vanimire felt the weight of all the evening's affairs finally fall upon him.

He leaned his back against the chair of the table, pulling his legs up against his chest as he buried his head between his knees. Pain shot through him as he moved, the wound still bleeding, though he hardly paid it any mind. The screams beyond the veil of the tablecloth continued, and Vanimire, unable to do anything save listen to their agony, finally broke down.

Rocking back and forth as warm tears stung his eyes, hoping all of this was nothing more than a terrible dream. However, the pain was still pulsing from his side and spoke a truth he wished desperately to ignore. He could do nothing to save his people. He couldn't even summon the courage to see if his father had survived. His failures became so pervasive, he felt perhaps it was best to accept the same fate that had befallen others.

The world would not remember him, for there would be no one left to write the histories of his lineage. Perhaps it was better this way, for what would the historians of the future even care to write about him? *Vanimire, the last of the line of Eineriel, whose bloodline traced its birth to Einor of Old, died under a table, crying, and forgettable?* Perhaps being forgotten was the last blessing gifted to him by the benevolent gods above.

The last of the screaming voices fell silent. Never had Vanimire felt so alone. If they were lucky, Daelin and Emmaline would have escaped, though even if they had, he knew he would not live long enough to meet them. No one who was trapped in the banquet hall survived the massacre wrought by the Redcloaks. Not even his father. He didn't even see where his father fell, though his booming voice had long since been silenced. Vanimire paused, lifting his head from against his knees as he heard the muffled voice of the Herald speak.

Vanimire sensed a surge of hope course through him, for if the Herald was speaking, perhaps it meant someone survived. Despite his body screaming in agony, he shuffled beneath the table, pulling aside the cloth just enough so that he could peer past it.

In his frantic attempt at escape, he found the furthest table away from the center of the banquet hall. Many of the torches lining the walls were destroyed in the onslaught, allowing shadows to stretch and envelop him once more. Feeling a measure of safety in them, he ducked out from beneath the table, pressing himself against the wall as he moved along it.

Hidden from the eyes of the Redcloaks, Vanimire continued to shuffle through the shadows until at last he saw all that happened. Not a soul was left in the banquet hall, except for the Herald and the Redcloaks who were serving him now. Partygoers littered the floor, their blood pooling in such a horrifying amount Vanimire couldn't make out the tiles of the floor beneath them.

The Herald stood where he was when the carnage erupted, flanked by Daromir and the Redcloaks. Vanimire was desperate to make out his uncle's expression, hoping it would hold some sort of answer. Much to his irritation, the distance that provided him a measure of safety also made it impossible to make out the fine details of the Redcloaks. Yet, as he stood there quietly studying them, he realized they were all facing the raised dais.

Vanimire followed their gaze. His heart skipped a beat as he saw the figure of his father standing proud and defiant in front of the dining table. Gone were the tremors and uncertainty, and in that moment, it seemed to Vanimire he looked upon his father as he so often was depicted in the songs and stories of his youth. He was elegant, refined, and powerful in his posture, and despite the circumstances screaming otherwise, Vanimire experienced a measure of hope build.

His father appeared certain of something, and even with all the distance between them, Vanimire felt the flames of courage emanating from him. In the chaos and blind panic, he lost sight of his father, yet it seemed the old man was unshakable in his resolve.

"So…this is it, then?" The High King muttered.

Glancing at the senseless carnage sprawled out before him.

"This is how the Rhyserion empire falls?" Vanimire's heart sunk as the realization overcame him.

His father wasn't standing strong and courageous with confidence, but with the knowing all was lost, and his life reached its end. As brave as he was in his youth, the High King seemed intent on standing face-to-face with death itself.

"Falls?" The Herald's scratchy voice called out. "This is the advent of a new age! The birth of the Song itself! Rejoice, oh last of the line of Einor, for you bear witness to the era foretold. The blood pooling beneath us will usher in an age of peace and prosperity."

The High King's laughed roared, echoing through the now-emptied hall.

"Peace!? You speak of peace after what you have wrought? Only fools and madmen speak of peace earned through sword and bloodshed. What you have brought is not peace, no, it is chaos. You speak of a new age, a new Song, yet you're no better than we were!"

Anger gripped the Herald's expression as he scowled.

"You are a fool, last of Einor!" He hissed. "You stand before the Gods themselves and refuse to acknowledge them. It is no wonder you are unfit to rule. I see far more with one eye than you can ever hope. I see the face of *Her!* See what she was robbed of!"

The High King laughed once more, shaking his head as he scanned the room once more. Vanimire spotted the pain hiding behind his father's expression, and despite it, he mustered the strength to peer at his foe and laugh. Yet something concerned the High King as his gaze wandered. Vanimire watched as his brows furrowed and realized his father was staring at him.

There was so much Vanimire wished to say, wished to do, in that one fleeting moment. Uncertainty gripped him as his thoughts raced and fought one another. Vanimire, the son, wished nothing more than to sprint towards his father, clasping him in his arms, even if it meant experiencing their last moments together.

Yet, Vanimire, the Crown Prince, knew such an action was folly. It was paramount he survives the evening to tell others what happened. Faced with this internal battle of wills, he could do nothing but grip the wall. Terrified of whatever action he'd choose would be the wrong one. How did his father do it? Summon the strength and courage to be decisive when his words would see either the survival or fall of countless individuals?

Vanimire's mind continued to race as panic gripped him again. His vision faltered, the edges of the hall growing dark and blurry as his breathing quickened. He noticed only his father, who appeared to gaze at him with the faintest hint of a smile as time beyond them grew still.

Vanimire's eyes focused on the smile, finding in it a warmth he so desperately needed. Even with the distance separating them, his father's smile was remarkable. When his lips parted, Vanimire felt his heart sink. For his father muttered only a single, unmistakable word. The last command to his Crown Prince, his only son. *'Run'*.

It was to be the last gift to the son he cared for more than life itself. The High King clearly experienced the terror and confusion gripping him, stealing from him the burden of choice. He often said he would have denied his father nothing, for doing so would be to go against the Crown itself. This rule was so often forgotten, but in this very moment, when the weight of the world and the empire itself hung in the balance, Vanimire would honour his father's last request.

Tears stung his eyes as he shuffled along the shadows of the wall. He sensed the night's crisp air flowing through the doors leading to the gardens. It appeared so close now, and yet still a lifetime away. The Herald and his father's voice continued to echo through the banquet hall, but Vanimire couldn't understand what they were saying. He focused all his senses on achieving what his father had entrusted to him. He knew the shadows wouldn't hide him forever, and he had to escape before the Herald and the Redcloaks noticed him.

Despite knowing he was condemning his father to death by fleeing, he felt helpless to intervene. He painfully realized the best thing he could do for his father was to ensure his memory lived on, and the betrayal of the Redcloaks would not be forgotten.

A scream echoing through the banquet hall pulled Vanimire from his concentration, forcing his gaze to turn back towards the raised dais. He recognized the voice, and in an instant, it made his blood run cold. His father, once standing tall and defiant, hung in the air with his arms stretched out to either side.

Vanimire watched as he writhed in agony, twisting and turning in the air as the Herald approached with an outstretched hand. He was so close to escaping, so close to the freedom his father yearned for him to seize, and yet, he found himself once more powerless as the Herald's voice screamed out.

"The blood of Einor is the last of the ancient bloodlines to fall, oh mighty High King!" The Herald's laugh seemed to boom as the High King writhed in unseen agony, twisting, and turning as if his whole body were engulfed in flames.

"P…Please. S…Stop!" The High King screamed.

His voice battered and broken, carrying with it the desperation of one who knew their demise was near at hand. Vanimire fell to his knees, tears streaming down his cheeks, as he watched in muted horror. His hands covered his mouth, not wanting to draw attention to himself but unable to silence himself completely.

"Long have you stood in our way, wretched High King, but now yours shall be the blood which concludes the incantation, and with it, the new age will dawn." The Herald waved his free hand, and Vanimire watched as the Redcloaks approached his writhing father, stretching out their blackened hands as they held them towards him.

"Y…You can't!" The High King screamed, clawing at his arms. "Y…You will bring about the end of our world!"

The Herald's voice grew impatient, as if having grown bored with their exchange. "The wretched Song stained by mortals shall end, and with it, birth a new world created solely for the dominance of Veristeriax."

The High King's lips parted to respond, but no sound escaped. Vanimire screamed out in terror as the blackened arms of the Redcloaks glowed with newfound intensity. In an instant, large spikes burst out from the High King's body, making a sickening crunch bringing his twisted torment to an immediate end. Vanimire gazed as his father's blood fell freely from his lifeless body.

The Herald's laugh echoed in the hall, but Vanimire could barely hear it. A loud ringing grew in his ears as he observed his father's body fall onto the raised dais with another crunch.

Were it not for the low chanting the Redcloaks performed, they might have heard his muffled scream. He lost complete control of himself, giving way to the terror and uncertainty which gripped him. Vanimire did nothing but rock back and forth along the ground, clasping a hand over his mouth as tears continued to sting his eyes.

Bearing witness to an event that was both untimely and cruel broke something in him. His father always was a constant in his life, there to remind him and guide him when his path appeared uncertain. Now, he lay in a crumpled and twisted mess on the floor of the banquet hall, his elegant clothes stained with the blood of all those who have fallen. Long he yearned to travel beyond the walls of the capital, and yet now he wished only to throw himself from their parapets.

He turned, unable to watch the carnage any longer, as he crawled out into the gardens. The sickeningly sweet night air suggested the night's carnage was yet to be finished. There were no more souls left in the gardens, for the Redcloaks onslaught had extinguished them all. Vanimire struggled to lift himself to his feet, stumbling through the hedge-lined pathways as he sought desperately to bring himself to the railing. What a fool he was, running into the gardens. There was no method of escape from here, for every door led back to the banquet hall. Jutting out from the side of the capital tower, a fall from the gardens would send one hurtling down countless levels before crashing into the lower reaches of the complex. Had his feet always known this was his destiny? To run not to salvation and escape, but to the one way he knew would reunite him with all those lost that evening?

It didn't take long for Vanimire to stumble to the edge of the gardens once more. The stone was chilly beneath his fingertips, which emerged in stark contrast to his body, that was alight with warmth. The pain that ached from his side where the ripped through him paled compared to the claw ripping through his heart. He was alone. He knew not if Emmaline or Daelin had, but the thought of them brought little hope to him now. What good would it make in the end? He hoped for his father's salvation, but his death, so brutal, had cast aside any hope for the rest of them.

Now, he had only the cool stone railing to dig the tips of his fingers into. The city sprawled out before him. Its lights blurred by the tears flowing down his cheeks. If he closed his eyes, he could almost faintly make out the sound of laughter and excitement down below. Was it only the palace that was attacked?

There was no evidence the Herald fought his way through the city, as the only fires burning were the massive bonfires of celebration constructed in the more popular centers.

Vanimire almost pitied them, engulfed in the heights of excitement and carelessness. In a way, it reminded him of how simple life had seemed but a few hours earlier. Not a care in the world beyond consuming more wine, enjoying food, and finding warmth in the company of others. The thought struck him of how quickly the luxuries of life could be taken away.

Whether one danced in the High City, or in the alleyways of the Low City, everyone would wind up facing the same fate in time. There would be no more warmth or enjoyment for him anymore. All he needed to do was summon one last burst of courage. Just as his father had, before he…

Slowly, he lifted his gaze upwards from the city that was his birthright. If he were to draw his final breaths, it was to be one final blessing he would do so under the blue light of Nalinyor. Yet, as his vision became focused, he saw yet another horror painted across the night sky.

The blue light of Nalinyor was fading, giving way to the white light of the regular evening. The incantations carrying through the gardens from the banquet hall appeared to increase in their fervour. Vanimire watched as the white light of Nalinyor drained as well. Like an arrow loosed into the night, Nalinyor itself seemed to flee from the world it hung over.

Even though they were a lifetime away, Vanimire heard the collective cries of surprise and terror as the evening sky darkened, draping the world in a veil of darkness. When the last light of Nalinyor vanished, the very earth roared beneath Vanimire's feet.

The screams of the city below grew louder as the buildings shook. Vanimire tightened his grip on the stone railing, terrified that the rumbling earth would consume the palace. Vanimire was lucky because the palace was built into the mountain itself, but some people in the city below were not so fortunate. The ground beneath shook with a terrible intensity, causing several buildings to fall. So loud was the chaos Vanimire covered his ears, unable to bear the noise any longer.

With his hands clutching his ears, the darkness draped over the city seemed to heighten, and as the melodic chanting of the Redcloaks increased in volume, the shaking of the earth ceased. A terrible crimson glow from Nalinyor shattered the unnatural darkness enveloping the city, blazing in the evening sky as if it were the sun itself.

An eerie red light bathed the world around him, making Vanimire long for the few moments of darkness. The citizens of the city below shared his sentiment, whose screams carried on the icy night air, sending a shiver of terror coursing through him. Everything about them was strange, yet none of it compared to the supernatural circumstances of Nalinyor's light. Was this what his father predicted?

A terrible inhuman scream ripped through the skies above, interrupting his musings. Others, which cried out in their terrible cacophony, answered its call, earning yet another wave of tortured screams from the city below. With his ears still clenched, Vanimire lifted his gaze upwards, desperate to witness what made such a terrifying noise. The black evening skies hid whatever it was from his view. Only when they soared across the crimson moon were their horrifying shapes apparent.

What flew through the sky was no beast Vanimire had ever witnessed before. They ranged in size, some appearing as big as houses, and others as small as little specks. Yet all of them were twisted and flew on unnatural wings, sending pinpricks of terror down his spine.

It was as though the world was coming to its end, for the winged beasts were quick to descend upon the city below. Pulling their wings in tightly against misshapen bodies, they fell from the heavens, falling at such an intense speed that the surrounding winds whistled. Crashing through the buildings and unleashing carnage making the events of the banquet hall seem a dull affair.

Vanimire couldn't bear the sight any longer, for as he lifted himself to his full height, turning his gaze towards the city consumed in complete chaos. Fires quickly spread through the city, unleashed by the winged beasts as they tore through everything. Screams carried on the winds, and in an instant, Vanimire experienced the same feeling as he did when the Redcloaks began their onslaught.

He was helpless, terrified, and uncertain of what should be done. From this sea of tormented thoughts, only one idea bubbled to the surface. Not wanting to see what further carnage would follow, he found the strength needed to climb up onto the railing.

'Let the world see how the last of Einor's progeny takes his fate in hand. Let them see how even the mightiest may be brought low.'

The world, which represented beauty and strength, stood in stark contrast to that of only an hour earlier. Gone were the vestiges of peace and tranquility, of hope and celebration, replaced instead with terror, carnage, and bloodshed. Many thought the capital of the Rhyserion empire to be the single greatest city in the entire world, at least, those who knew only the shores of the island empire. Here, beasts resembling the most terrible nightmares imaginable tore it apart.

This city was his birthright, its denizens his to protect, yet here he stood, bearing witness to the very sight of his failure. He failed to save his father, and he failed to save his people. The line of Eineriel failed, and if any survived to write his story, they would say he witnessed the fall of his house and his people.

Vanimire lifted a foot from the railing, moving it over the abyss, calling for him. There was nothing more to think about, nothing more to ponder. He knew it was only a matter of time before the Redcloaks discovered him, or one of the winged beasts would descend to tear him apart.

"Goodbye," he whispered, feeling the tears roll down his cheeks.

As he was prepared to throw himself beyond the precipice, a gauntleted hand grabbed his shoulder.

"Trying to escape, are you?" The voice roared, yanking him from the ledge and hoisting him in the air.

Vanimire tried to struggle, blinking back the surprise as he tried to face whoever ruined his plan. The man threw Vanimire to the ground before he glimpsed at him. The impact knocked the air out of his lungs and made the world spin. Waves of pain coursed through Vanimire as the man swiftly rammed an armoured boot into his stomach.

Vanimire coughed and sputtered as he tried desperately to recover. On uneasy hands, he tried to lift himself off the stone. Instincts taking over as his mind was a foggy pain-addled mess. He tried to put distance between them, but the armoured figure was quick to lean down and grab hold of him, yanking him into the air.

To his horror, Vanimire saw the face of his uncle Daromir. His expression was more terrifying beneath the red light of the moon.

"H...How could you?!" Vanimire screamed, desperately slamming a fist against his uncle's armoured arm.

Pain shot through him as he struggled to free himself from his uncle's grip, each blow barely leaving a dent in the reinforced armour.

"I...I had no choice," Daromir muttered, turning and throwing Vanimire onto the freezing ground.

"H...He was your brother!" Vanimire coughed, bracing himself on an unsteady arm as he turned his gaze toward Daromir.

There was little point in trying to run from the man, for the Redcloaks were stronger, faster, and better trained than Vanimire ever hoped to be. Daromir silenced Vanimire's cries by bringing his armoured boot down onto his nephew's stomach again.

Vanimire retched as the wind escaped him. His vision swirled, straining to maintain focus on the man who betrayed everything he ever knew. Vanimire glanced at him as he had his entire life. The man towered over him and surpassed Vanimire in every way imaginable. There was nothing he could do that his uncle couldn't have done better. His uncle kicked him in the chest, forcing him into silence as tears prickled his eyes, and warm blood poured from cracked lips.

The world was a blur as his head spun, not able to catch his breath between his uncle's blows. Daromir heaved him into the air again, and Vanimire went limp in his grip. Resisting was futile and would only earn his uncle's ire.

"I...I'm sorry," Daromir whispered, tightening his hold on the shirt he held Vanimire in the air by.

He was slow to approach the edge of the railing, giving Vanimire an agonizing amount of time to come to realize his fate. Tears rolled down his uncle's cheeks as he held him over the edge, and the air of the city below came up to greet him.

How quick his fate seemed to change again, for though it was only a few minutes since last he stood upon this very precipice, he faced it now with terror and fear. There was to be no noble sacrifice.

His hands came up to grab hold of the obsidian arm, holding him aloft, desperate to maintain a grip on it. He was foolish to think if his uncle were to let go of him, he could save himself by holding on. Yet it was all he thought of in that moment. Gone was the gifted decision making of the line of Eineriel. He squirmed against his uncle's grip, acting on base, primal instinct alone.

The crimson lines adorning the arm of obsidian glowed brightly. Vanimire sensed an unnatural warmth course through it before the spikes shot outwards, piercing through his wrists, and sending a burning agony through him. His scream echoed across the empty garden as he writhed in his uncle's grip.

The pain was unlike any he ever experienced. Though he had been cut before, the spikes retracting back into the obsidian arm made Vanimire feel as if his blood were on fire. With a crunch that made his stomach churn, the spikes pulled back through the 'skin' of the obsidian arm, disappearing back into the crimson light.

In an instant, this terrible agony consumed his entire body, and though he screamed and cried, it would not subside. His vision blurred from the pain, and as he glanced at his hands, he thought for a moment they appeared as black as the arm that held him. Like paper thrown into the hearth.

"Vanimire!" His uncle screamed, shaking him in his grip. "Y-You must listen to me before it is too late!"

Vanimire could barely focus. Such was the intensity of the pain wracking him. It felt as if his blood was boiling within him, and in an instant, the autumnal world was consumed in hellfire. He did not feel the icy sting of the air any longer, for it felt his body faced the very heat of the midday sun itself.

"Vanimire!" His uncle repeated, forcing his agonizing nephew to open his eyes.

The world, still a colourful blur, and his uncle little more than a shining splatter of red paint against a canvas of agony. Though it took every ounce of his effort, he strained to focus on the man screaming at him. There was something different in the way he spoke, in the way his voice cracked against the tears. It reminded him of days long forgotten, and of an uncle he thought was deceased.

"I cannot take back what I have done, but you alone can save us!" Daromir screamed, his voice barely audible over the rising sound of chaos and devastation that was unleashed upon the city below them. "Remember, my words: *A Goste I-Telerachdi Veste!*"

He spoke in a tongue unlike any Vanimire ever heard, for it was both elegant and powerful in its cadence. His uncle dug his teeth into his lip, drawing blood which flowed as freely as the tears. Vanimire strained to open his lips, desperate to ask what it was he meant, but before he could, Daromir let go of him.

The night moved around him faster than he could process. It appeared to be a lifetime ago now when he was dancing with the

Lady Emmaline, revelling in what he didn't know would be the last moments of a life worth enjoying. Time was never fair, for it so often took from those who deserved it and gave to those that hadn't earned it. Yet none of it seemed to matter now.

The figure of Daromir disappeared against the backdrop of the crimson moon as the walls of the castle raced past him. He knew he was falling, yet the agony burning in his very blood made him unable to scream. He did all he could, and still he would meet the fate he feared.

There would be no redemption, no salvation, and no tomes of history that told of his exploits. His mind raced over his thoughts until the ground below came to meet him, and thus, in its bloody and terrible puddle, would spell the end of the line of Eineriel.

In the joyful days of his youth, he often wondered how he would die. It was impossible not to consider it when one's days were spent reading of the exploits and lives of the prominent figures preceding him.

It always was a humbling and bewildering experience, for in those heroes of old, Vanimire did not see himself. He knew from the start he wasn't destined to die in battle after winning glory and victory for his people. No, he was fated to live the life of an administrator, where death so often came in the nonchalant days of one's twilight years. A life spent enjoying the arts and gorging oneself on festivities. The life spent arm-in-arm with your life partner, surrounded by children that bore his likeness.

Yet, in his most wild fantasies, he would not have predicted how his journey would conclude. In the end, even a memorable death was denied to him, for no tales would speak of Vanimire's fall.

His eyes opened slowly, barely able to see as the wind of the night air rushed past him. He made out the distant edge of the gardens and knew the stone of the lower courtyards would soon come to claim him. Perhaps this was a blessing, for he smelt the blood and devastation of the city carry on the winds that enveloped him.

All his senses appeared to burn at their limit, for though he perceived the terrible wound Daromir inflicted upon him, he had no energy left to react. Blood still poured freely from his wrists, creating trails of red that danced beneath the shining crimson canopy of night. He couldn't bear the sight of his blood any longer, so he contented himself to close his eyes and enjoy the last moments of his life.

It came quickly. There was a terrible noise of stone being ripped and torn from the castle walls alongside him. He only hoped he would not live long enough to be subjected to whatever terrible beast that crashed into the castle. His body jerked to the side, sending a terrible wave of shock through him, and then the chill of the stone ground raced to meet him. Darkness enveloped him.

As he breathed his final breaths, the terrible noise of the Low City silenced against his broken ears. Tears welled in his eyes, and as his chest lowered one last time. He swore he saw his father gazing down upon him, his mother held in his embrace.

The pair looked at their dying son and extended a hand towards him. He thought dying would have been more painful, though perhaps this was the last gift of the Gods. Reunited with family once more.

Perhaps it wasn't such a terrible way to go.

CHAPTER VII

THE NIGHT OF CRIMSON

"I was unworthy of my position. Surrounded by those whose prestige was etched into the annals of history already. Theirs was a shadow I feared I'd never escape."

Names were a mark of the privileged, but no one ever gave him that luxury. People called him *'Skitters'* for most of his life, though one voice made him think it was more an insult than a name. He wasn't even sure what it meant, in truth, yet he grew fond of it. He was Skitters, and Skitters did what he did best.

The screams roused him from his sleep. A familiar sound, though this time the cries sounded more like a nightmare than anything he ever heard before. The terrifying cries were so loud the very ground beneath his feet shuddered, as if the stone itself was petrified by what roared overhead. He tried to silence the cries echoing in his head, pressing his dirty hands to his ears, but the sound still descended upon the Low City in a terrifying frenzy.

His home had thin walls, the broken-down market stall having been built for storage instead of living. Walls of stone were another mark of privilege. Yet Skitters hoped the inconspicuous nature of his hideout would ensure whatever was behind the screams and roared overhead would leave him alone.

Then the fires came.

Warmth enveloped him like a blanket, forcing him to skitter out of the stall through the front hole making up his doorway. What he witnessed was far more terrifying than the screams he heard. Smoke and flame consumed the meandering street of the Low City, casting it in a flickering light illuminating the night unnaturally.

Scrambling to his feet, Skitters looked around as panic struck. Flames danced along the rooftops, casting smoke high into the sky above. A sickly red hue, which seemed to dance between the flames consuming the Low City with an insatiable ferocity, illuminated the night.

Even the rowdiest of parties paled compared to the noise that now consumed the recently slumbering Low City. The same screams which roused him from his sleep roared overhead, racing through the clouds of smoke in shadows which moved faster than anything Skitters ever seen. The ground beneath his feet shivered with every pass, though the terrors seemed distant compared to those that stretched out before him.

Everywhere he looked, Skitters saw chaos and confusion, carnage and devastation. The wooden walls of the nearest home splintered and buckled beneath the flames, consuming it, succumbing to its frenzy with a sickening shriek as wood burst, and screams that echoed a moment earlier were silenced.

He stumbled away from his hideaway, which was now wholly consumed by flames, as he tried to find some measure of understanding amidst the waves of chaos. His foot caught on a lumping shadow, and he fell to the ground with a crash that was muffled by the puddle which caught him.

To his horror, he saw that the familiar rainwater, which often collected and danced through the misshapen stone streets, wasn't lining the streets of the Low City. Blood as thick as water, and darker than the crimson stained skies above, filled the streets.

So overwhelmed were his senses he didn't notice the sickly metallic scent wafting between the smoke bellowing from the shattered wooden walls surrounding him. The flickering light caught on the shadows that lining the streets, revealed the faces and bodies who were frozen at sickening angles.

"W...Wha' happen'," he stuttered, pushing himself up from the pool of blood as he searched for any source of explanation.

The streets were full of people, darting about with the selfsame confusion. No one seemed to have any answer, as they ran in all directions to flee from some unseen terror. He tried to join them, moving on instinct born from the years spent clinging to survival in the city that was already a danger unto itself. Yet his greatest asset now condemned him.

He always skittered along the streets unseen, meandering beneath the eyes that found no value in his recognition. Now, however, it proved little more than a nuisance. Skitters picked the first individual who came close to him and opted to follow the tall, imposing figure. The confusion and terror which suddenly became commonplace gripped the man, hardened by years spent on the open sea. *That* was a source of fear unto itself. For if those who braved many countless terrors were now blinded by panic, what was it that caused it?

Skitters had little time to ponder the question, for the man, desperate to flee from whatever shadow was looming ever closer down the street behind them, ran full speed into the boy. The man stumbled, though regained his footing without so much as a second glance at what was the cause. Skitters, however, was not as lucky.

The boy fell to the ground *hard*. His head hit the misshapen stone, causing his vision to swirl and the colours of the world to blend as he rolled along the street. When he stopped moving, he was dazed and more confused than before. The ground was shaking beneath him.

A roar grew louder with each passing moment, joining the terrified quivers from the overhead screams. He experienced the sensation before. Something was approaching, something far, far bigger than any brute of a man he encountered. Far taller than the belly of a ship lifted in the shipyard.

His innate senses of survival kicked in, flaring as he rolled onto his stomach and tried desperately to push himself up from the stone path he fell onto. As he heaved, a sharp sting of pain raced through him, causing him to crash back down as he screamed out in agony. He broke *something* in his fall. His arm seemed the most likely, given how he could barely feel his right fingers. A shame, since those were always his favourite ones.

Whatever was the source of the growing shadow drew nearer, and certainly wouldn't care about the broken and battered boy. He needed to get up, needed to run away from the shadow looming through the bellowing smoke. He rolled onto his back, cradling his broken arm across his chest as he pushed himself up with his other arm.

It was too late.

The figure continued to grow, its terrifying shadow loomed through the fire illuminated smoke. With a roar, Skitters to fell backwards, clutching his ears with either hand to silence the scream which shook the ground beneath him. Pain, as searing and hot as bonfires they constructed for the celebration, rocked him as he moved his broken arm.

The monster clawing through the smoke was bigger than anything Skitters had ever seen. Its head was level with the rooftops of the buildings, and its form was crooked and angled to a sickening degree. Too much bone jutted out from the beast, barely covered by its skin, like spears that scraped along the wooden walls. Row after row of serrated, spike-like teeth filled the mouth, all lined beneath lips stretching from one side of its face to the other.

The sight of the monster was so terrifying Skitters could summon the air to his lungs to scream. All he did was gaze resembling something born from the depths of one's worst nightmare. Its eyes–or what appeared to serve the function–levelled upon the boy.

Dark circles, devoid of colour and deep as the night sky, noticed the scrambling boy in an instant. Its mouth opened and Skitters could hear bones break in its jaw as it unhinged itself. Flames flickered in the back of its throat, and light shone through the holes torn in its skin. He did not know what the monster was doing, but he was certain he was its chosen target.

So petrified with fear, he froze in place, watching as the crimson flames pooled in the back of the monster's throat.

"P…Plea…" He stammered, reaching towards the beast with his broken arm, desperately trying to reason with the monster that seemed devoid of any sympathy.

"I don…wan' die…" Air rushed past him, the smoke itself feeding into the beast's maw, as the crimson light grew with terrifying intensity.

With a scream, it leaned its head back, and Skitters hunched over, closing his eyes and hoping the process of passing into the next realm was less painful than living in the current one.

"Not today!" The familiar voice screamed. Her words carried

above the deafening sounds of the chaos consuming the Low City. A blue blur ripped through the street, throwing the battered boy to the side with terrifying speed.

<hr>

KANAH ROARED WITH EXCITEMENT, RELISHING IN THE SENSATION AS ITS icy edge ripped through the dark red skin with ease. It cut through the monster as if it were made of little more than softened butter.

Eliira raced forward, carried on the winds she summoned at her side as the blade arced around her. She moved with inhuman prowess, spinning through the street with Kanah held out to her side.

The blade sliced through the beast's side, causing it to stumble and crash into the street as the squad of Protectorates came rushing in behind her. Their spears were raised overhead with a defiant scream before plunging them into the beast's back, pinning it to the stone as she flipped through the air. She landed on her feet against the side of a building, crouching, and pushed off with another leap.

She wasted little time racing to the pinned beast when she landed on the ground, raising Kanah over her head and bringing it down to sever the monster at the neck. With a final terrifying scream, it grew still, and its skin immediately began to bubble and steam.

"Retreat!" she roared, and the Protectorates were quick to dislodge their spears and stumble away from the body consuming itself.

Blue swirled in her eyes as she looked around, taking in the sights of the street she meandered down so many times before. Box-Rest Lane, they called it. A common dumping ground for unused crates and disheveled orphans. It was hardly recognizable. The buildings lining it were a broken mess of flames and devastation.

How many individuals were consumed by the chaos already?

The legends contained a great deal about the crimson night, but even their descriptions paled against the heart-wrenching, terrible reality.

"He's okay!" One of the Protectorates called, forcing Eliira's illuminated gaze to find the boy who was being helped to his feet.

"Ah…" she muttered, taking a few strides over to where the boy was shaking with fear. "I remember that face."

Her lips lifted into a smile as she dropped to a knee, letting her gaze draw level with his. He took a step back out of instinctive fear, though summoned the courage to hold her gaze, as strange as it was.

"The market stall." Was all she said, earning a slow nod from the boy stained with both dirt and blood. "It's okay. We're going to bring you somewhere safe."

"Ma'am…" The gruff voice huffed out behind her.

"Eliira," she corrected, standing upright and turning to face the hardened face of the Protectorate Commander.

"Though I'll forgive you on account of the…well." She waved a hand to the crimson skies above.

"Ah…y…yes. Anyway, we can't keep pressing into the Low City. We're already dangerously far from the chapel. If we keep going, we might not…"

"There are still people out there!" She hissed, cutting off the commander with a tone which caused him to take a step back. "If we stop now, then they'll…"

An explosion at her side cut off her words, sending her flying across the street as smoke and debris consumed the air. She skid along the ground, rolling from the impact until she collided with the wall of the nearby house. Kanah scraped and ground across the stone, ripped free from her grip by the sudden burst that tore through the street.

Stumbling to her feet, she swiped a hand through the smoke. "Kanah to me!"

She sensed the blade arc through the street, heeding the call of its master as she wrapped her fingers around its grip when it drew near.

"Ma'am!" the voice called through the smoke. "We lost two in the blast, but the boy is okay!"

"Dammit!" Eliira hissed, clutching the blade even tighter. "Fine! Head back to the chapel! I'll meet you there!"

"Got it!" The voice called back. "Grab the boy and let's go!"

"Now, where are you?" Eliira muttered, lifting the blade and thrusting it forward. This was not the first blast which was unleashed upon her. Though it caught her off-guard, she was familiar with what was behind it.

The smoke lessened, clawing upward to the crimson skies above. As it waned, it revealed what she was searching for. Eyes, black as the night had been before, all the carnage shone through the flames.

"Got you." She hissed.

Eliira thrust Kanah to the side as she lurched her left arm forward. Free from its bindings, blue light shone and swirled between the cracks of the stone-like exterior. Small droplets of glimmering light leapt into the air, swirling and dancing before she swiped through them with her fingers, sending them hurtling towards the flames.

The racing streaks of azure power found their target, ripping through the alley faster than one might have been able to draw breath. Flames danced and parted as the droplets tore through them, letting out a sharp whistle as they passed through the intense heat.

Just as quickly as their release, they found the red flesh of their target and erupted in a dazzling display. Blue as radiant as the tranquil sea burst forth from the droplets, vanquishing the flames that were born from the crimson night's devastation. Smoke erupted as water met flame, though the resulting burst sent it scattered across the meandering street.

The winged beasts screamed in agonizing horror as the explosion consumed them, the final melody in their wretched symphony. They posed a minor threat to Eliira, especially with Kanah at her side. Theirs was a power born from rapidly overwhelming their target, hurtling themselves down towards it at terrifying speed.

If she weren't careful, then they might have found some measure of success in their opening onslaught. Yet the moment that failed, they were little more than a distraction.

Kanah buzzed with excitement between her fingers, forcing her attention to level on the remaining set of eyes glowing through the withering smoke. "Seems we have some lucky ones, Kanah." The blade responded with silent, yet familiar excitement, buzzing between her fingers in response. "I agree."

With the blade held at her side, Eliira crouched down, drawing forth that familiar enveloping warmth as her eyes swirled with power. The street drained of its colour, the brown and black buildings consumed with flickering orange flames slowly giving way to that overwhelming, all-encompassing white. *The World Unseen*. Against the untouched canvas, the remaining winged beasts stood out like wretched, vile splotches of paint. They were an abomination; a stain upon the dual-worlds.

Kanah roared between her fingers, and Eliira was ever eager to give the blade that which it craved. Pushing up from her crouch, she lurched forward, moving with sickening speed through the street that seemed to move at little more than a stand-still. The winged beasts were barely moving, hung in flight amidst the carnage and devastation that she unleashed upon them but a moment earlier.

Silently, she pushed through the overwhelming brightness, bounding between her leaps as she raced along the street. The winds stilled, but she flew in their embrace, hurtling in the blink of an eye towards the remaining foes.

Kanah moved with familiar ease, arcing overhead before swiping downwards as she ripped through the bellowing smoke. The silence was eerie but offered a momentary reprieve as she blinked past the winged beasts, landing on the jagged stonework behind them. Color poured back into vision, dragged inwards from the corner of her gaze as she passed back into the familiar world of colour and carnage.

The onslaught of sensations overwhelmed her, instantly making her feel as though she had to catch up on everything she missed. Eliira couldn't help but wince as she blinked back into the world of colour, dropping to a knee as the winged beasts burst into flames behind her. Their bodies, split cleanly from Kanah's strike, fell to the ground, sizzling and bubbling as they consumed themselves in their defeat.

"Have to...stop using that." She muttered, clutching at her head with the stone-like hand.

Kanah buzzed between her fingers, and she used the tip of the blade to ease herself back up to her feet.

"I know, I know. I just..." She paused, glancing around at the street that grew momentarily still. "I have to do something. *Anything*."

Fire continued to dance along the wooden buildings, revelling in their wicked consumption. The thick scent of blood and death carrying up to join in their jubilation of despair. Distant screams carried on the winds as shadows continued to race overhead.

Between the gaps of smoke, the crimson moon hung eerily overhead, watching in silent, delighted contentment. Long would the night be, and the devastation amplifying with each slow, agonizing passing hour.

"Kanah…" Eliira muttered, clutching the handle of the blade tighter. "Has it awoken? Is there *any* sense of it?"

The blade grew uncomfortably still, silent between her fingers for a few moments before buzzing weakly.

"Damn it all. One God's damned mission and *still* I've let them all down."

Theirs was an order divinely ordained, and despite their efforts and prowess, it still seemed hopeless against the foe that had entwined the very moon itself. *The conjoining*. Their order had known about it for a long time. Now they were the unlucky successors that inherited dealing with it.

Would they even be able to manage it?

Without the strength of the Golden, it seemed hardly likely. Hells, it was *centuries* since last they were united and fully empowered. In the long years since then, they had done little more than lay in wait, desperately clinging to the shadows as they chased after their lost power. What right did they have to think of themselves as guardians? Especially now, when Aerturiel itself was being torn asunder.

Kanah buzzed intensely in her grip, pulling Eliira's wandering mind back to focus on what was chiefly important.

"You're right. You're right." She muttered, shaking her head and letting the long, disheveled strands of brown hair fall over her shoulders. "Survive. Then we can figure out what to do next." She huffed out a sigh.

"Though that seems much easier said than done." Her eyes trailed across the devastated street, swiping away some of the smoke that bellowed from broken windows. "The chapel. That's where we start."

The blade hummed in agreement, and Eliira swiped the blade through the air, falling into familiar, practiced movements. Even before she awoke, swordcraft had ever been a source of comfort, a way for her mind to focus and silence the world that was often overwhelming. Kanah moved with ease, as if the hefty blade were a part of her arm, and weighed less than silvered cutlery. It was still as fascinating as it was when she first inherited the blade.

"Alright, Kanah. Let's get to it." Blue swirled in her eyes, the familiar powerful warmth dancing around her form as she lurched forward.

With the blade at her side, Eliira raced through the meandering streets, flying on the winds themselves over the lifeless, battered bodies of man and beast alike. She sensed the world around her, *felt* its presence as she drew upon that which gave her strength.

Even in the depths of night, as the world itself was torn asunder, she felt the familiar hum coming only from water's unspoken call. Hers was a realm that surrounded her every waking moment. *This* was what she inherited.

This was the power of the Song.

Eliira moved so fast she passed through the flames, extinguishing them for a moment through the fury of her winds alone. She rushed through the Low City like a wave, bouncing between the devastated walls of broken homes and street alike with catlike prowess. With reckless abandon, she threw her body, tugging on the hums she felt all around her to ensure she didn't meet her demise in such an embarrassing fashion. It took only a matter of minutes before the familiar sight of the chapel came into view.

The peaked rooftop of the chapel towered over the nearby buildings, serving as a marker for many who called the twisting, meandering streets their home. Eliira slowed her approach, dropping from the winds back down to the jagged stone streets that twisted beneath her.

The efforts of the Protectorates were all around her. Sizzling, broken bodies of the red-skinned monsters cut down in their rushed return to what they had hoped would be a haven. Despite her frequent complaints about their methods–she often thought them a bit cruel towards the downcast–Eliira conceded that the members of the Protectorate were remarkably well-trained. It seemed necessary, after all, given the often unruly domain of the Low City.

She came to a halt at one of the bigger bodies, crouching down to inspect the recently felled beast. Its body consumed itself, burning away as life itself drained from its hulking, monstrous form. Bones that appeared deliberately broken jut out awkwardly, causing the skin to stretch upon it like a spear. It was as if the bones and skin were crafted by two different creators, both of which were constantly at odds. She never, in all the long years of her training, seen anything like it. These were beings most unnatural, handcrafted by some wicked and cruel master.

That she saw no Protectorate bodies was a relief, though it was equally likely that someone dragged any injured members back to the chapel. With any luck, the twisting, spiralling crypts that stretched out beneath the Low City would offer some measure of safety, or, in the worst case, serve as a fitting tomb.

"Alright Kanah, let's see how…" She froze as she rose to her feet. Her eyes narrowed as she felt *something* press against her. The sensation was strange, and unlike anything she experienced. It felt neither wind nor flame. Nor was it the hum of the *Song* emanating from water. Malice clawed at her heart, its talons dragging and ripping against her very mortal coil. Something was wrong, very, *very* wrong.

Holding Kanah ahead of her, Eliira slowly made her way around the edge of the building, crossing down the alley that led to the entrance of the chapel. Her heart raced with uncertainty, and the wretched, vile talons continued to claw at her. *Something* was trying its very best to undo her, to ruin the would-be saviour before she even lay her eyes on it.

Though she had no notion of what might cause the sensation, she felt confident in knowing it wasn't one of the red-skinned misshapen beasts. Those were a terror, but *this* was something different. The beasts were mindless; weapons unleashed by a distant master to cause as much devastation as possible. They acted on instinct alone, driven by an insatiable hunger for carnage. Whatever was causing the terror that clawed not against skin nor armour, but her very soul itself, was doing so *deliberately*.

She pressed herself to the wall of the narrow alley, clinging against it, hoping to find some measure of safety from the shadows it draped over her. The chapel was one of the few spots in the Low City that was afforded some measure of a square stretching out before it. What was once the spot of local gatherings and conversation was now the final, terrifying stretch before salvation.

There, free from the shadows of the twisting alleyways, one was at the mercy of the beasts that raced overhead. There was no cover or safety to be found. Only in making it across that last stretch did one have any hope of the Gods-inspired sanctuary that the chapel might have offered.

Of course, that is where the source of the terror was waiting.

Eliira caught a glimpse before it noticed her, and the sight caused her heart to sink. There, standing before the chapel, was a member of the Redcloaks. It was an unmistakable image. The paragon of strength and virtue, defenders of the High King, and beloved knights of the Empire. Its red cloak bellowed over its left arm, and as Eliira studied it with bated breath, she was certain that the sense of dread and terror was emanating from it.

A slender, robed figure accompanied the Redcloak. The pair seemed to be amid some manner of discussion, for Eliira watched as they took occasional glances at the chapel they stood before.

Terror and uncertainty clawed against her very soul, latching onto the sparks of doubt that bubbled up from the depths of her conscious. Her breathing quickened as the waves of terrifying power washed over her. There could be no escaping to the chapel while the Redcloak stood before it.

As she crouched pressed against the wall of the alleyway, Eliira was certain that she would have to clash with whatever this monster was. Though it masqueraded as a man, she knew with all the certainty in the world that all semblance of good had disappeared. She saw the Redcloaks before, though only at a distance. Even then, she was certain the man standing before her was stripped of anything noble and earthly.

The ground beneath her feet shook violently as the sickening, monstrous screams echoed through the alleyway behind her. Eliira's attention was pulled from the figure, who seemed hardly bothered by the beasts that continued to ravage the city.

Blue swirled in her eyes like the crashing of a wave as she looked away from the chapel square, staring down the alleyway that was quickly consumed by an ever-growing shadow. The ground cried out in terror as a handful of crimson-skinned beasts came to a halt at the end of the alley. Eliira's breath hitched as she pressed tighter against the wall. For a moment she hoped that the hoard of beasts would continue meandering down the street, their attention drawn by some other manner of pursuit.

Alas, when was it ever that simple?

The misshapen beasts turned their gaze down the alley. Blackened eyes as dark as the ocean's depths locked onto their prey, and the group let out a collective scream of delight as they turned and began racing down the alleyway towards her. The beasts, pursuing so recklessly, squeezed themselves against the tight walls of the alleyway, scraping along wood and stone. Their bodies, twisted and unnatural, cracked and ground along the walls.

Eliira watched in confused horror as the beasts crushed each other against the walls, killing many of their own members long before they even drew close to her.

Even with the monsters that were battered and broken against the walls, far too many were squeezing into the alleyway after her.

"Damn it!" She hissed, sparing one last glance over her should towards the chapel square.

The robed figure accompanying the 'Redcloak' departed, leaving the armoured figure alone to gaze upon the chapel. She had no other choice. Tasked with either being overwhelmed in the tight alley by the rapidly approaching sea of crimson monsters or having to cross paths with the sickeningly terrifying 'Redcloak'.

"Kanah!" she roared, pushing off the wooden wall before lurching into the chapel square.

The blade roared between her fingers, answering its master's command. Warmth and power enveloped her as she stumbled into the square, turning on a heel and thrusting the stone-like arm towards the alley. Blue surged and swirled from beneath the cracks in her arm, once more causing droplets of shimmering cerulean to pour into the air like petals caught in the breeze. The droplets shook with excitement, clearly knowing they needed not to wait long before being called upon. They enjoyed being useful to the lord of their domain just as much as she enjoyed calling upon.

After all, no matter where one was in the world, water was *all around you.*

With a swipe of her hand, she threw the droplets down the alley. Shining brighter with each passing moment, they were quick to find their target. The blue flash ripped through the misshapen bodies of the beast, leading the charge, cutting them down in an instant. They fell to the ground, crunching and sizzling beneath the ceaseless footsteps of those that raced behind them. The monsters gave little concern for their fellows, though they too would soon accompany them unto whatever void it was they were born from.

The droplets of power, lodging into the chests of the monsters that were leading the charge, glowed, and in the blink of an eye, stretched and grew in a rapid burst. The ground shook as the droplets exploded, bringing much of the walls of the alleyway down upon the beasts' desperately racing between them. Smoke and debris erupted from the alley, forcing Eliira to throw herself to the side to avoid the ensuing carnage.

Weakened by the flames that had consumed them, the buildings on either side of the alleyway were quick to collapse in the wake of the blue explosion. The wooden homes creaked and groaned as they gave way, falling into each other and crashing down upon the beasts that had been surging between them. That which protected and housed the downcast denizens of the Low City was turned into a weapon of their revenge.

With any luck, those who called the building's home would have been among the first to find shelter in the chapel, but such fanciful hopes were hardly to be had in the cruel and unfair reality. There would be time enough later to ponder such morality.

Eliira pushed herself up from the ground as she coughed and tried to steady herself. The dust settled, and if the 'Redcloak' hadn't known of her presence before, then they would have certainly been alerted now.

Eliira felt the handle of Kanah in her grip once more, the blade giving the silent warmth that its presence always seemed to provide. Though uncertainty and terror still clawed at her with the blade in hand, it was difficult to fully lose hope. After all, Kanah knew and served countless masters, and the Azure Akura was also something born from legends as old as the world itself.

It was through them that the *Song* was possible, and with such power at her disposal, Eliira felt no small measure of confidence. The 'Redcloak' or whatever the masquerading monster truly was, there was no one better suited to deal with it in the empire than her.

"Quite the entrance." The deep, feminine voice called, causing Eliira to bristle and straighten as the smoke from the collapsing buildings slowly continued to wane. "In a night of so many spectacles, it seems another is quick to join the stage."

Eliira couldn't help but scowl at the woman's voice. Disinterest laced her every word; she spoke as if she were attending some banquet or gala, rather than standing amidst a city on the verge of annihilation.

"Quite a long way from the High King." Eliira called, her eyes narrowing on the outline of the figure as it slowly came into view once more. "Curious place for a *Redcloak* to be."

"Strange indeed. Yet it is hardly the role of the performer to question the orders of the director."

"A troubadour masquerading as a Redcloak?" Eliira shot back. The words were hissed out through a clenched jaw. She couldn't hide her disdain for the woman that still emanated unseen terror.

"Something like that."

As the last of the dust settled, the armoured figure once more came into unobstructed view. As expected, she wore the familiar armour of the High King's elite guard, with the famous red cloak billowing from over her shoulder.

One could have thought she was pulled from the pages of a child's fantasy. The darkened armour, etched and lined with streaks of crimson, shone as bright as the skies above. Flame kissed the thick plate, and it barely held any stains from the blood of men or monster. In comparison, the blood-soaked, disheveled Eliira must have been quite the sight.

The pale woman glanced at Eliira with a glimmer of intrigue. Blond hair, cleanly shaved on one side of her head. A hairstyle that was popular in the Northern Realms of Aerturiel, though rarely seen in the island empire was neatly kept, a curious fact given the chaotic carnage that consumed the Low City. For one who spoke of being little more than a performer on the stage, she seemed to have hardly moved.

"Well, then..." Eliira muttered, slowly raising the tip of Kanah towards the armoured woman. "I take it you'll not let me get to the chapel with ease, will you?"

The Redcloak's lips twisted into a terrible smile, excitement dancing in her expression.

"Never." She reached up to the cloak that hung elegantly from her shoulder.

Armoured fingers crunched as it grabbed hold of the cloth, ripping it free to reveal a sight that caused Eliira's heart to sink.

Eliira could have lived a thousand lifetimes, and still she would have never guessed what was revealed as the cloak was torn and cast aside. Scorch marks scarred the jagged and twisted edges of the Redcloaks' battered and broken armour at the shoulder. Extending from the armour was a solid, stone-like arm, dark as the night sky above. Beneath the cracked ridges, a deep, sickening crimson light swirled.

Though it bore the familiar appearance of her own Akura, there was something unnatural about it. The sight of the arm, which the Redcloak flexed with pride, filled Eliira with revulsion. It felt as if she were looking into a mirror that distorted and corrupted one's appearance. Clearly crafted with every intent to mimic the Akura that the members of her order bore with pride. That which the Redcloak flexed was little more than a sickening, terrifying deception.

"W…What in the hells is that!?" Eliira spat. Her grip tightened on Kanah to still the shaking that she hadn't even noticed had started.

"It is but one of the many instruments of despair. A gift from the harbinger of Aerturiel's new master." The Redcloak's smile widened, revealing the serrated, unnatural teeth that lined her smile. "It is terror made manifest."

"It's a cheap imitation!" Eliira hissed, lowering Kanah as she held out her own stone-like arm. "An attempt at grasping that which you know far too little about."

The azure light of her arm swirled and danced, calling forth more droplets of power that she hurled towards the Redcloak with a swipe of her hand. She was certain the figure would love nothing more than this verbal back-and-forth, but Eliira had little time or stomach for it.

The blue droplets raced forward, whistling with the winds that carried them across the chapel square. Red flashed beneath the cracked, darkened arm of the Redcloak, blood laced with power poured freely, pooling in the air and merging into spikes that were sent racing forward. Crimson met the cerulean in a terrible burst, sending light and power arcing in all directions as they met and exploded. The Redcloak met Eliira's tried-and-true method with ease, matching and nullifying the attack with a similar display.

As the dust settled, the armoured woman's laugh echoed through the square, causing Eliira to grimace and scowl.

"A weapon empowered by the might of the crimson moon!" The 'Redcloak' roared, extending her arms to either side as she lifted her gaze upward.

In an instant, winged beasts raced through the skies, coming to a halt overhead as they gathered into a huge, terrifying shadow. The flapping, beating orb of beasts grew larger as more raced to follow their master's command.

"See now how outmatched you are! A relic of an age forgotten!" The Redcloak's gaze levelled back on Eliira, and her arms thrust forward in some unspoken command.

The ground shook violently from the collective scream of the beasts that raced forward. They surged towards her, thrust carelessly down upon the bearer of the blue Akura.

Eliira could think of no other option. The swarm of beasts was too large to stop with another barrage of droplets. Before she could throw them forward, the hoard would be upon her, raining down with neither care nor concern as they heed their master's command.

"Kanah!" she cried.

Power enveloped her as the colour drained from the world around her. Time itself slowed as she blinked into the World Unseen. If she didn't use the power as much as she did, then she might have used it for a fatal strike against her foe. Yet she was well-and-truly exhausted and could think of nothing more than simply avoiding the barrage that was unleashed upon her.

She turned on a heel, clutching the blade tightly as she bounded away from the ever-growing shadow. One step, two, three. When her foot pressed against the stone on that irrevocable step, she lurched forward, throwing herself on the winds as colour seeped into the world once more, and she passed back into the Seen World.

As the winged beasts crashed into the stone ground of the clearing, the explosion launched her body into the air. The bust of carnage and devastated sent Eliira hurtling away, carried by the winds.

As colour bled back into the world around her, Eliira felt that all-too familiar twinge of pain course through her. With all the long years of training, passing into the World Unseen, even for a moment, was incredibly taxing. Never had she relied so heavily on that power, and it was certainly taking an effect on her body. Were that she inherited the full might of the Akura. If only she was one of the…

Eliira forced herself to stand upright, holding Kanah towards her opponent as the dust and debris settled once more. She couldn't show any measure of weakness, not against a foe that came much closer to matching her than any had before. If she was a moment too slow, or careless for even a fleeting second, it would certainly spell her demise.

"Better than expected." The Redcloak called, her voice still laced with that tangible measure of disdain. "Though you remain far, far outmatched."

"Who are you?!" Eliira hissed. "*What* are you?"

"Rhamun, was what they called me in the life before. In those days before salvation."

The name meant little to Eliira. The Redcloaks, though each a legend, were, to her, little more than faces and names. Theirs was the realm of heroics her order sought to protect; champions that wielded the glory that would inspire the masses.

Meanwhile, Eliira and the others would content themselves with operating from the shadows. The fanfare could ring for the Redcloaks, and it mattered little to them of the order. For they alone were entrusted with ensuring that the *Song* maintained its harmony.

"Why?" Eliira asked, lowering the tip of Kanah ever so slightly. "Why did you betray those you were ordered to protect?"

Rhamun paused for a moment, as if her mind was trying to come up with some measure of an answer. The true aim of the Redcloaks stood contrary to that which they now seemed to unleash. Redcloaks, who swore to protect the Empire, became the instrument of its destruction. The quills dipped in the ink of ruination.

"Our goal has never faltered." Rhamun finally responded. "We defend those worthy of being cared for. The citizens of the Empire were naught but imitations, much like that arm of yours. A relic of the past; chains that hold us back."

Eliira clenched her jaw, causing the panted breaths that passed through it to turn into wispy snarls. "You're a monster."

"To them?" Rhamun beckoned a hand to the chapel behind her. "Perhaps, but their opinions are as short-lived as the flesh from which they were born."

Eliira could bear the insults no longer. She screamed as she lurched forward, blue swirling in her eyes as the surging warmth of power emanated from between the cracks in her arm. Once more did the shimmering droplets pour forth, arcing and spiralling around her as she raced towards the Redcloak. Kanah was held so firmly between her fingers that the blade trembled beneath her fury.

Blue light continued to pour from her arm, the droplets catching and merging as she raced towards the Redcloak. It seemed as if she raced on the might of a wave itself; a boat set adrift amidst a turbulent storm.

With each step she took towards her foe, she could feel her resentment growing. The Redcloak that stood before her was antithetical to the purpose of her order, a foe to life itself. She might have failed in her pursuit of the Golden, but she would *not* fail in vanquishing the demon that dared to masquerade as a hero.

As Eliira surged forward, Rhamun lifted her sickening arm. Crimson light poured freely from the cracks of the obsidian stone, and Eliira watched as those familiar spikes of blood shot outwards before hanging in the surrounding air. She braced herself for the blast that she had expected, a repeat of the clash of blue and crimson from a few moments earlier.

To her surprise, the crimson droplets coalesced around the Redcloaks hand, joining and forming into a long, extended shape. The shimmering red light teemed with power as it raced together, taking the shape of a blade *much* faster than Eliira expected. The smile Rhamun wore sent a shiver down her spine. *'What is it you're anticipating?'*

With a flash of blue, the droplets raced forwards like a rolling wave, stretching into spikes as they lurched towards their foe. Eliira was not far behind them, screaming with frustration as she held Kanah pointed forwards. The winds seemed to carry her, moving her at a speed that seemed impossible for any human to reach.

The arcing, twisting blue lights found their target just as Rhamun wrapped her fingers around the blade that had manifested. With sickening crunches, they pierced the Redcloak, causing the metal armour to buckle beneath their frenzy. Each one caused Rhamun to stagger and scream. Her voice was a mix of irritation and agony. For any other foe, the spears ripping through the

Redcloak would have been their demise. Yet, Eliira would leave nothing for the wills of the fate to decide.

Their blades met a moment later, Eliira lurching forwards on the winds with all the strength that she could muster. Kanah hummed with excitement as it met the blood-formed blade. Metal scraped on metal, and the momentum that Eliira carried herself on caused the pair to stagger backwards. Winds raced past them, causing the smoke to shiver around their mortal dance.

Eliira had hoped that the might of Kanah would have cut through the Redcloak's blade with relative ease. That it was no mere mortal weapon was clear enough, and yet, the sickening, serrated blade managed to not only catch the Kanah's strike, but guard against it with ease. Eliira panted as her momentum slowed, and as the single slash proved ineffective, she pulled Kanah back towards her, desperate to unleash another frenzied strike.

To her terror, however, Rhamun let out a sickening laugh. Before Eliira could even call the sound into question, the answer presented itself. The blade that Rhamun formed a moment earlier began to shimmer and give way, dropping back into droplets that raced towards the staggering Eliira.

"Kanah, please!" She cried, desperately swiping the blade upwards to ward off the barrage of crimson racing towards her. Kanah buzzed in silent terror, humming between her fingers an unspoken plea.

Colour once more drained from the world around them, a final, desperate attempt at staving off the death that was almost certain to follow. As the world around her became consumed in that overpowering white, she wasted no time turning on a heel and throwing herself to the side.

The first droplets, aimed at her, already struck, ripping across her side as she scrambled to safety. Each blow caused a flash of pain, followed by a wave of subsequent terror. It was agonizing, but every droplet that slashed against her leather tunic was a reminder of how close she had come to meeting her end.

I'm still not good enough.

The force of the returning colour sent Eliira hurtling to the side. Though she dodged the bulk of the barrage, the blast that followed when the blood struck the stone floor sent her spiralling. Kanah scraped and roared against the stone as it was ripped from her fingers, and her tumbling finally came to a stop with a crunch as she was thrown into the pile of debris.

Her senses swirled, and her vision waned as she struggled to focus on the Redcloak that laughed with great satisfaction.

"See now the might of the crimson children!" Rhamun screamed. Her arms reached up to the skies above as her head fell backwards. "Bear witness to all that the Six-Eyed wields! *This* is the Song reborn!"

Eliira struggled to draw breath. The blast ripped all the air from her lungs. She held a shaky hand forward, still barely maintaining her vision as she felt the sickening familiar shadow grow around her. Overhead, she could barely make out the endless flapping of the winged beasts, their cries little more than an added note to the symphony of devastation that enveloped the Low City around her.

Though Kanah was quick to return to her grip, she still struggled to brace herself upright. The last blink through the World Unseen sapped her strength, and she knew it would take time before the power had returned to her veins once more. Meanwhile, the shadow overhead continued to grow, and for the first time since the chaos was unleashed upon the Low City, Eliira was scared she was going to die.

Yet the shadows departed, and as quickly as Eliira's terror fleeted, it gave way to another. For though the shadow no longer hung overhead, it hadn't vanished completely. Her vision strained, still unable to focus entirely from the injury she sustained. Her legs refused to heed her call, feeling little more than stones beneath her as she watched the shadow drag across the square.

"No!" Eliira screamed.

Kanah slipped from her fingers, clattering to the ground at her side as the shadow narrowed, and raced with increasing speed. It took her a moment, but the realization of Rhamun's intention slowly became clear. *She was never the target for the gathering swarm of winged beasts.*

"Rhamun! Please! Anything but..." Her pleas were silenced by the ensuing blast.

Screams so loud the very ground trembled beneath their fury shook Eliira to her core, causing her hands to press tightly against her ears. The swarm struck like a crack of lightning, throwing themselves into the chapel with terrifying and reckless abandon.

The damage they wrought was amplified by how little they cared for their own wellbeing. As the swarm burst and battered against the wood and stone of the chapel, crunching against it as wave-after-wave of beasts descended.

The blast sent dust and debris racing through the square, forcing Eliira to release the grip on her ears. She threw herself to the ground, pressing her face against the carved stone of the square as the winged beasts continued to rip through the chapel. The roar of the collapsing chapel quickly drowned out the sickening crunch of the broken bodies of the winged beasts. The chapel, desperately trying to stand tall and proud amidst the chaos, became the greatest victim of the carnage. In an instant the building collapsed, caving in on itself as its structure helplessly was cut through.

As the devastation of the beasts was consumed by the collapsing building, so too were Eliira's screams. She shut her eyes tight, wishing—hoping the evening was naught but a wretched nightmare. It was a foolish hope, yet, as the chapel collapsed, and with it, consigned all who were trapped within to oblivion, it was the only thing she could do. She continued to cry out, screaming desperately into the chaotic void.

Seconds passed in sickening terror; screams silenced in the chaotic frenzy of the chapel's collapse. Stone and wood were sent in all directions, and Eliira was certain that some of it sliced across her. Any wounds she had were small, thankfully, though that couldn't have been said for those who were trapped in the chapel when it fell —those who she *directed* to the chapel.

If there was any hope to be had, it was the wish that many of them, having continued to hear the ongoing destruction, would have fled into the twisting, meandering catacombs that stretched out beneath it.

"All that, and you still failed to protect them." Rhamun's voice cut through the square like a blade, inflicting a wound far deeper in Eliira than any she received.

As the dust settled, Eliira could once more make out the armoured figure that had unleashed such devastation with delight. She stood tall and imposing, with her arms stretched out to either side as if she were giving a sermon. No trace of the crimson droplets remained, save the light that still emanated from the abomination of her left arm.

"A shame." Rhamun continued. "That I can't stick around and be your undoing. I was so *close*, after all."

"S...Shut *up*!" Eliira hissed, lifting herself up with shaking arms. "I am *sick* and tired of hearing you speak!" She felt the familiar warmth of Kanah between her fingers and pressed the tip of the blade into the stone to ease herself up to her feet.

"Good." Rhamun muttered. There was a difference to her cadence, and Eliira could only look at the Redcloak with marked confusion. "Use that against us."

Eliira's lips parted to speak, but she was interrupted as the physical form of the Redcloak shimmered. Red flashed through the cracks of her abomination of an arm, and soon the figure dropped to the stone in a pool of blood. The liquid seeped between the cracks, twisting and pooling, eventually sinking into the very ground itself, and disappearing from sight.

"W...What...?" Eliira muttered, blinking in confusion as she tried to make sense of what occurred.

If the Redcloak passed through the World Unseen, then Eliira would have felt it. She sensed when the others in her order managed it; a way for them to both train and hone their own ability.

Yet when someone passed beyond the colours, they always appeared in the blink of an eye, thus it was often referred to as 'blinking' through the World Unseen. Yet the Redcloak hadn't managed that. Somehow, against all odds, she *shifted* her physical form. Revert it back to that which it likely derived, and with that, vanished.

She pushed the thought from her mind. The exact abilities of the Redcloaks would be a concern for later. For now...she turned, facing the pile of burning rubble making up all that remained of the chapel.

"I failed." She muttered, dropping to her knees as she continued to take in the very monument of her shortcomings. "I failed *them*. I failed the order. I failed them all."

Despair crept in, uninfluenced by the Redcloak. *That* had been a despair made manifest by the will of another. This, however, was the sinking, terrifying feeling that came when one knew in their heart that they were chiefly responsible.

"It's...over. I..." Her words were silenced by the frantic, excited buzzing of Kanah between her fingers.

"K…Kanah?" She blinked, gazing down at the blade as it physically vibrated in her grip. This wasn't the calm, reassuring voice of her companion trying to rouse her from her despair. This was different. This was… "Y…You sensed it!?"

Immediately, she bolted upright, peering at the blade in her hand as if it had a face to gaze upon. Never had she felt it hum with as much excitement as it did now. Were her grip any less on it, then it would have slipped from between her fingers.

"You *felt* it." She added. "Then it's been awakened!"

Her breathing quickened as all the pain she felt a moment earlier seemed to dissipate. The chapel might have marked her greatest failure, but there still was a chance for her to make things right. To *earn* her redemption.

Were she any less exhausted, she might have jumped for joy, yet it hardly seemed appropriate. Calming herself, she turned to face the burning rubble of the chapel. "I failed you…*all* of you…but I can make it right. I *will* make it right."

Her grip on the blade tightened, and she turned on a heel to face the meandering streets of the Low City once more. "I *will* find the Golden Akura."

Power, warm, familiar, and empowered, swarmed around her, and as she lurched forward, she raced on the winds towards the redemption she desperately sought.

CHAPTER VIII

AN UNEXPECTED AWAKENING

"Yet on the night I died, I was born anew."

WHEN HIS EYES REOPENED, VANIMIRE HAD THOUGHT THAT ALL THE wonders of the afterlife would have appeared before him. As clarity returned to him, he saw only the wretched crimson moon beset in the night sky above. Confusion was quick to follow as he realized that despite all odds, he somehow looked death in the face and deny it.

He could barely make out where the railing of the gardens had been, for its height stretched far into the night sky above him. It was almost unrecognizable with the devastation that was wrought to its stone-laid fortifications. Massive tears ripped through the stone itself, clawing haphazardly, as if the beasts were flaunting the power of their talons.

Was that the source of the terrible crashing noise he heard just before colliding with the ground? Whatever it was, it clearly grew bored with destroying the outer walls. As Vanimire lifted his head, wincing as a wave of agony shot through him, he saw no sight of the beast.

To his horror, he realized he was laying in a pool of his own blood, and despite having fallen from an insurmountable height, only the pain in his head bothered him. He sat upright; the motion sending another wave of pain rippling through him as he lifted his arms before his eyes. He saw where his uncle impaled him, for the skin on the wrists seemed soft and new, and there was no visible sign of any wound. He was certain he didn't dream up the entire encounter, for no dream was ever as agonizing and terrible. Yet, he could not deny that as he slowly lifted himself up on his feet, he had, against all reasoning, survived.

Were it not for the winged beasts still flying overhead, or the terrible cries of devastation in the city below, he might have let out a scream of joy. He *survived*. Even thinking about the realization seemed unbelievable. How he had managed it, he still did not know if this was to be the one gift from the gods he would ever receive, he would not take it in vain.

A high-pitched scream forced his attention back to the world that surrounded him. At first, it sounded like someone called his name. The voice seemed vaguely familiar, yet he refused to believe that it belonged to the Lady Emmaline as he hoped at first. There was little doubt in his mind that she had been claimed by the same fate that he narrowly avoided, and his heart fluttered, hoping perhaps she was more cunning and smart than he had. Perhaps she called out to him, or perhaps his head was still ringing from the fall.

Before he could fully come to his senses, a terrible boom echoed through the sky above him. His gaze immediately lifted to see the unmistakable smoking aftermath of the palace's cannons having fired. Hope swelled in him as he realized he was not alone. Some had not only lived but began their preparations to defend the palace against the foes claiming the very skies as their domain.

A shadow crossed over the crimson moon shining overhead, and Vanimire threw himself to the side to avoid the desecrated body of a winged beast crashing into the courtyard alongside him. It clawed at the shattered stone pathway with long, twisted knife-like talons. Its bones, which jutted out at terrifying, unnatural angles, ripped the very skin stretching across it.

Vanimire saw the massive holes that were torn through the flesh of its wings, and its loud, agonizing screams softly gave way to gargled, sizzling cries as its flesh poured in on itself. He scrambled to his feet as it let out one final terrible scream, twisting and writhing along the battered stone before it grew still.

The aim of the palace's cannoneers always amazed Vanimire, and though he was thankful for their service, he was never more relieved to have them than at this very moment. Their blast cut through the beast at the waist, severing its legs from the rest of its body and guaranteeing its fate long before it crashed into the courtyard.

The beast was unlike anything Vanimire could have ever imagined, let alone seen in either life or tome. Its skin seemed to be stretched across misshapen bones, which jutted out in twisting and horrifying fashion. Vanimire wasn't sure how it even flew, for its webbed wings were torn through with stretching induced holes.

Even as its crimson body lay still, it still provoked an uneasy feeling in him, for the talons stretching from its two hands were still wet with blood that was clearly not its own. How greedily had the beast feasted in the city below before it grew too bold in its attack, Vanimire wondered. Its head was nearly as big as he was and filled with crooked fangs that drew to a narrow tip and were slick with the same dripping crimson that lined its talons.

His curiosity was piqued like never before, and it took every ounce of his self-control to stop himself from approaching the felled beast and reaching out to touch it, if only to ensure that it was real.

It seemed to him an image pulled from the most terrible of nightmares, inconceivable in mortal minds to be a living, breathing creature. Yet, blood as black as the night sky above pooled beneath his boots, and Vanimire sensed the fleeting warmth of its life slowly dissipate.

Once more was Vanimire pulled from his musings as the wall at the far end of the courtyard buckled beneath some terrible blow. Before he raised his hands to cover his ears from the terrible noise, the door was torn apart, bringing with it much of the stone wall it rested in. When the smoke finally cleared, Vanimire saw a two-legged figure slowly crawling through the gap it made.

It rose to its full height once it ducked through the destroyed wall, standing almost as high as two floors of the palace structure it so easily destroyed. Even with all the distance between them, Vanimire noticed how muscular the misshapen figure was, and how the blackened horns stuck out from its crimson fleshed head.

The beast's glowing red eyes focused on him, and its terrible scream shook the ground as it leaned back, vanquishing any hope he had of avoiding it. His jaw was larger than any human Vanimire ever seen, despite the beast appearing mostly humanoid in appearance, and was filled with the same crooked fangs that had adorned the mouth of the winged beast.

A low growl reverberated through the terrifying monster as it took a step towards him, and Vanimire watched as the very stone beneath it cracked and buckled. The beast must have weighed more than it appeared, and yet it moved with a measure of finesse that seemed impossible. Vanimire was certain his earlier miraculous survival would soon end once the monster reached him.

If he only chosen to wear a sword, then he might have defended himself, yet he always thought that the practice was gaudy and so forewent one. How foolish he was before the very world itself unraveled.

Vanimire felt the cold stone of the railing behind him once more and knew he could run no farther. He created all the distance between them he could, and if the beast continued its approach, then he would have no hope left but to finish what Daromir started. His fingers dug into the stone, desperate to stop the trembling consuming him. He peered death in the eye so many times this evening, and with each passing moment, he still felt the same fear gripping him.

For its part, the beast seemed content to simply play with the cornered Crown Prince, knowing he had nowhere left to run. Its lips parted, tearing flesh and breaking bone to reveal the lines of fangs. It seemed to Vanimire as if the beast were smiling at him. Yet its approach halted as glass shattered in the window behind it.

Vanimire closed his eyes, waiting for the fate that seemed inevitable. Yet hearing that crash, he immediately looked to see what had caused the commotion. Even the beast seemed surprised, for it slowly turned its head towards the noise that had pierced through the chaos of the night.

Vanimire heard only the scream of whoever broke through the window. Not the scream of a man meeting his final moments, but the enraged, adrenaline-induced scream of a man meeting his foe head on. Someone launched themselves through a window one floor above where the beast broke through. He hurtled through the air, descending upon the beast as he thrust his blade forward, digging it into the back of the monster's skull.

The beast ripped its claws through the air, twisting and writhing in agony as its scream shook the very foundation of the surrounding palace. Despite its protests, its efforts were in vain. The man never wavered in his resolve, holding the blade deep in the back of its skull until its screams silenced, and it crashed to the stone of the courtyard.

Vanimire raised an arm to shield himself from the dust that ripped past him, waving a hand as he coughed. Every one of the monsters seemed terrible. That the man threw himself upon it with such reckless abandon Vanimire's curiosity inflamed.

When the last of the dust settled, Vanimire saw the unmistakable golden armour of the Kingsguard shine beneath the crimson moon blazing overhead. Suddenly, much of it made sense. The Kingsguard were certainly second only to the Redcloaks among the realm's greatest swordsmen.

The bearded man pulled his blade from the monsters' skull, flourishing it in the air overhead before bringing it back down in another, decisive slash. Vanimire winced as the beast's bones were broken, crunching inwards as the blade cut through them with ease. Despite his disgust, he was thankful that the man ensured the beast wasn't clinging to life.

With the monster defeated, the man removed his blade once more, leaping down from the skull of the beast and sauntering toward the confused Vanimire.

"Crown Prince!" The man's deep voice boomed. "By the Gods, we had thought you dead!"

Vanimire blinked in surprise, feeling the tears well in his eyes once more as relief washed over him. Ser Ralick was the Kingsguard for whom he grew the most acquainted. When Daromir was sent beyond the walls of the city, it was Ser Ralick that had taught him how to use the sword. The tall, tanned man dropped to one knee, reaching out and placing a hand on Vanimire's shoulder.

It had been some time since Vanimire last seen the man, yet he still kept his head clean shaven, and his dark beard straight. It always seemed a strange combination to Vanimire, yet he quickly grew fond of it. '*It was always best to stand out in a crowd*', Ser Ralick often told him when questioned. '*For it means the women are certain to see you!*'.

Time slowly caught up to the man, who always seemed the model of brawn and bravado. Gray was sprinkled through his hair. The man's face held more lines born from weary exhaustion than

Vanimire remembered. Then again, the life of the Kingsguard was never an easy one.

Though the Redcloaks were the force that was sent throughout the Empire, the Kingsguard was entrusted with ensuring the peace and safety of the High King himself. Vanimire had little doubt many of the wrinkles the old man bore came from ensuring each and every recruit was trained and inspected by him alone.

Ser Ralick dropped his sword to the ground, running his hands carefully along the torn fabric of Vanimire's sleeves. The weapon clattered to the stone beneath them, its blade engraved with the single word 'Devotion'.

The evening's ominous crimson light danced along the blade, which maintained its regality despite the blood dripping from it. Above all else, it was a blade worthy of the Kingsguard. Concern coated Ser Ralick's expression, and Vanimire watched as he turned his arm over, inspecting the spots where the flesh was discoloured.

"Are you… injured?" He asked, looking at Vanimire with a raised brow.

"Y-Yes." Vanimire muttered, uncertain of how exactly he could summarize all that he went through in the last hour. Hells, even if he told Ser Ralick every detail, he was certain the man wouldn't believe him. Having experienced it himself, Vanimire still could hardly believe all the details.

Ser Ralick glanced from the wounded arm up to the wall of the castle that was torn through. His breath hitched in his throat, and he quickly glanced back at Vanimire with even more confusion.

"How in all the hells did you get here, lad?"

"You wouldn't believe me if I told you," Vanimire replied.

It was the first moment of genuine human interaction that he had felt since the massacre in the banquet hall.

"W-What's happening, Ser Ralick? Where were the Kingsguard? W-Why didn't they protect father?" Tears welled in Vanimire's eyes once more as he clutched the man's arm tightly.

Ser Ralick's lips opened, but no words came. Vanimire saw that behind his stoic features, there was a pain consuming him. Ser Ralick lowered his head, and Vanimire could feel his hands trembling as they held gripped his shoulder.

"I am sorry, lad." He whispered, clenching his jaw tightly as if to stop the torrent of emotions pour out. "We were as surprised as everyone when Daromir and his Redcloaks returned. He told us that he had it on good authority that some of the city folk might try to storm the gates. He sent us away, told us to reinforce the entrances and he would oversee the Palace security. I…I should have known better."

It brought Vanimire some measure of relief to know that word of Daromir's betrayal spread throughout the palace. There were many who would struggle to believe the words.

After all, Daromir was a legend, and adored by all those who beheld him. That he'd played a pivotal role in such a massacre… Vanimire could still hardly believe it.

"T…The banquet hall…" Vanimire started, shaking the man to force his gaze back on him. "Y…You saw?"

Ser Ralick nodded slowly, his eyes darting side-to-side as if trying to make sense of all that he had seen.

"Aye. We heard the commotion and came running. By the time we broke through the door, it was already too late. We saw the body of the High King and tried to get to him. T…The Redcloaks were quick to cut us down. I only narrowly escaped. Torvin… tried to rescue the Kingbanner. He…"

Vanimire's heart sunk. If the Redcloaks turned against them, and the Kingsguard was destroyed, what hope was left for trying to fight against the hell that was unleashed upon them?

Vanimire lifted his head, looking toward the railing of the garden that loomed so far overhead. The sight of the crimson moon, which was now outlined by a glowing dark ring, continued to loom ominously overhead. The shadows of the terrible winged beasts still crossed over it, further making Vanimire's heart drift towards despair.

"S…Ser Ralick…" Vanimire muttered, forcing his gaze away from the moon that sent despair through him. "H-How long ago did the massacre happen?"

Once more Ser Ralick seemed confused, his eyes narrowing as if trying to recall from memory. Exhaustion dug its claws into the man, and Vanimire was certain that he didn't have a moment of rest since the beasts first appeared.

"At least a few hours." He muttered, flicking his gaze back to the man. "Perhaps four or five?"

Vanimire's eyes widened as he looked back at the sky above

them. If the massacre took place relatively quickly, then it would have been almost six hours since the light of Nalinyor was corrupted. Despite it, the moon still hung clearly at its apex, towering over the night sky and unleashing the full extent of its terrifying presence.

"T…The moon." Vanimire muttered, causing Ser Ralick to gaze upward in confusion. "It's barely moved. You'd think only an hour of night has passed."

Ser Ralick sighed, giving a quiet nod.

"Aye. Seems like we are forced to live beneath it, at least for a few days." He muttered. "Damned thing has barely moved. Though its presence has clearly summoned these wicked beasts that plague us now."

Warm tears stung Vanimire's cheeks as he turned his gaze back towards the man. Despite all he went through, all that he survived, every step forward still seemed as hopeless as the one that followed it.

What point was there in resisting his fate? Whether he died valiantly in an hour or curled up sobbing in a minute. His end would always be the same.

His hold on the armoured man tightened as he dug his fingers into his arm.

"S…Ser Ralick, what…what do I do?" He whispered, voice cracking as despair quickly overwhelmed him. "W…We're going to die!"

Ser Ralick was quiet for a few moments, and Vanimire could see a flash of doubt behind his otherwise stoic features. He breathed in sharply, narrowing his gaze on Vanimire as a warm smile stretched across his lips.

"Aye, lad. We might. However, we are born into this world knowing that one day we will leave it. We have been blessed to make it this far, and so long as I live, I swear to you that you will continue to see the next. My sword is yours, Vanimire, just as it was your father's."

Vanimire stood in silent awe, unable to form any words in response. Ser Ralick always inspired others through his words alone. There was something about his low, smooth voice that carried an impressive weight behind everything he said. His quick speech, delivered beneath the canopy of death and despair that loomed overhead, made Vanimire *want* to believe his words.

He felt a warmth of courage course through him. The path forward was terrifying, and yet, already he gazed death in the eyes and done the unthinkable by denying it. Whether the Gods gifted him, or simply lucky beyond his measure, none of it mattered. He *survived*. Better yet, he believed that so long as he was in the company of Ser Ralick, *they* would survive.

"A…Alright," Vanimire muttered, releasing his hold on the man as his hands curled into fists. "What shall we do then? I fear that every moment spent in this palace will bring us closer to our demise. We must escape it, surely."

Ser Ralick gave the man one final clap on the shoulders before lifting himself to his full height. He stuck the toe of his boot beneath the sword that he had tossed aside, flicking it into the air before grabbing it by the blade. He turned to face Vanimire, proffering the sword to him with a head bowed low.

"I could not have said it better myself." He smiled as Vanimire reached for the blade.

Ser Ralick turned, pushing his cape aside and pulling out another equally impressive blade. He flourished it through the air, getting accustomed to its weight and design as he studied the broken courtyard that stretched out before them.

"The armoury." He stated, casting a glance to Vanimire over his shoulder. "That blade of mine will do you well for now, but if we are to have any hope of surviving, we should rescue that which your father cherished above all else. That which he would want you to have as High King."

Vanimire, despite feeling foolish about how rusty he was, swung the sword through the air, trying to imitate the movements of Ser Ralick. At his suggestion, Vanimire paused, raising a curious brow as he tried to figure out what exactly Ser Ralick was alluding to. It took a few moments but eventually it clicked, and his jaw lowered.

"The ancient blade of Einor." He whispered.

"Very good, little Prince!" Ser Ralick said, laughing as he continued to flourish the blade through the air. "I am glad to see that the affairs of the evening have not dulled your senses! If we can get to the armoury, we increase our chances. Hells, we might stumble upon more valiant defenders!"

It seemed so obvious to him now, and he couldn't help but feel stupid for not having considered it beforehand. Only a few knew the ancient blade of his bloodline, although its legend extended far into the past. In the days of old, when the Rhyserion Empire was little more than an idea, it was said that Einor himself took up the blade and cut through darkness itself.

His father said that all who possess the blood of Eineriel could wield it. Though Vanimire never witnessed his father wield the blade. It was a secret most paramount. A relic that precious few could know of. It was kept locked away and hidden in the armoury, supposedly a sign that the Empire was at peace.

"Alright." Vanimire nodded, taking a few steps towards Ser Ralick. "I'm sure the road ahead won't be easy. But we'll get out of here, together."

Ser Ralick nodded, lowering the blade to his side as he reached over to clasp Vanimire's shoulder once more. "You remember all that I taught you, aye? Just imagine that the Lady Emmaline is watching. That way, I am sure you will manage just fine."

Vanimire gave a quiet nod, sorrow washing over him once more at the thought of Emmaline. He could have sworn that it was her voice that roused him from his anguish earlier, though perhaps that was just hopeful thinking.

Ser Ralick turned, breaking into a stride as Vanimire followed closely behind him. The man always had a flair for the dramatics, and even the end of the world wouldn't conquer that. For though the wall of the castle was largely destroyed by the two-legged beast from earlier, Ser Ralick opted to leap through a window, leaning into it with his shoulder as it shattered and gave way.

Vanimire couldn't help but smile as he followed suit, and in that moment, he believed.

Believed that perhaps they would make it out of this castle. Together.

CHAPTER IX

THROUGH THE LABYRINTH

"The blade was more beautiful than anything conceived in mortal minds. When my fingers brushed against it, I felt the strength of countless generations in the line of Eineriel. I felt Einor of Old."

HE SPENT YEARS NAVIGATING THE HALLWAYS OF THE CITADEL, YET WITH the chaos and carnage that consumed them, they were hardly recognizable. Every step of their journey through the palace was a struggle, as if at every turn they needed to prove to the very Gods they deserved to live. Vanimire was thankful that so far none of the terrifying, colossal monstrosities appeared.

Though Ser Ralick said the tightness of the hallways made their movement through them impossible. That which protected them from the colossal monstrosities encouraged the smaller ones to flourish. They poured through cracks in the walls of the citadel, rushing through from the High City in a terrifying number.

The beasts were equally terrible as their larger counterparts. Ser Ralick called them *'Bloodsmiles'* on account of the dark, serrated spikes lining their unnaturally enormous jaw. When their lifeless gaze fell upon a foe, the skin around their lips would crack and tear, causing dark blood to pool between the lines of teeth. It was a decent name, if not inventive.

Ser Ralick enjoyed it due to how quickly he could bellow out the word, alerting Vanimire in an instant when more of their ranks descended upon them.

Similar to the colossal monstrosities, and the winged foes, thin skin stretched over the Bloodsmiles' form, breaking and cutting along the bones that jut out like spears from its human-sized body. They clamoured through the halls like a man that had too much to drink that evening. Though something was sickeningly off-putting about them. They moved with an unnatural gait, clamouring uneasily, yet never faltering in their approach. It seemed as if they imitated the corrupted form of a human itself. They were single-minded in their intention, desiring only to destroy and consume any life that crossed their path. This marked them differently from the colossal ones ravaging the city.

As they descended through the labyrinths of the palace, they stumbled upon no shortage of desecrated nobility. Their chest cavities torn open, and flesh gorged upon, as if *they* were part of the festival's offerings. Vanimire's stomach emptied itself the first time they stumbled upon such a sight.

Vanimire sensed the terror clawing at his soul. Long, twisted talons sought to undo his resolve with every step through the castle's endless labyrinths. His hands still trembled with uneasiness, born from uncertainty. Every step felt as if it would be his last, for as they made their way deeper into the heart of the castle, the signs of devastation and despair only intensified. The banquet hall was the first note played in the Six-Eyed Herald's bloody symphony, but it was certainly not the only one.

Ser Ralick, however, stood in stark contrast. Though stained by the blood of the lumbering crimson beasts, his armour still maintained the air of its prestige. As the pair meandered through the countless hallways, Ser Ralick moved with the determination of one born and hardened on the field of battle.

So tight was his grip on his blade, Vanimire almost thought the man was trembling from his strength alone. Every beast was cut through with ease, and when their numbers appeared once more, Ser Ralick was the first to let out a roar of fury as he charged the group like a man possessed.

Under the guidance of Ser Ralick, the pair was quick to figure out an effective way of dispatching the Bloodsmiles. The pair turned another corner in the endless labyrinth of the palace and saw a pair of lumbering Bloodsmiles at the far end of it.

Ser Ralick's voice *boomed through* the hall as he let forth a frenzied roar. The pair of Bloodsmiles turned to face the cause of the commotion, and upon seeing a potential feast before them, let out an equally terrifying scream. Where Ser Ralick carried the warmth and strength of a man hardened by battle, theirs seemed little more than cries of blades dragged across the stone. Lifeless. Purposeless. *Wretched.*

Vanimire moved quickly, knowing every moment was precious and important. Theirs was a mortal dance, where even one misstep would spell their demise. This wasn't the training grounds or the tournament fields. There would be no second match, no chance of rising through the ranks of the losers.

The roar that Ser Ralick unleashed attracted the beasts. Vanimire was thankful, for it allowed him to duck to the side, pressing his shoulder against the warm stone of the hallway as they sprinted towards the Bloodsmiles. When only a spear's length separated them from their foe, they came to a sudden halt, and Ser Ralick let out another cry signalling to Vanimire for their moment to attack.

As Ser Ralick ducked to the side, passing under the swipe of a hand filled with clawed talons, Vanimire lurched forward. The blade he was given slashed with familiar ease, severing the outstretched arm of the first Bloodsmile. Its mouth parted in the terrible, blood-soaked grin that had earned its moniker, skin cracking and breaking as it screamed and writhed from the pain.

Ser Ralick silenced the beast's cries as he moved in tandem, plunging his blade through its gaping maw. With a sickening crunch, the blade pressed out through the back of its neck, and the beast went limp before Ser Ralick kicked it free.

The fleshy arm dropped to the floor beneath them, rolling across the stone, staining it with blood as dark as the night sky as it began to sizzle and consume itself. Its writhing stilled as the body it belonged to was cut down. The first of the Bloodsmiles fell forward, and Vanimire had to duck under the broken bones jutting out of its back like spears. Ser Ralick, clearly not as bothered, simply let them scrape against his armour as he stepped over the felled beast, his fiery gaze now turned upon the remaining one.

The hallway was narrow, and Vanimire needed to be careful not to get too close to Ser Ralick, otherwise he might disrupt the other's movement. The spikes jutting out from the back of the beasts scraped and ground against the stone wall that enveloped them, leaving long, serrated black marks wherever it found purchase.

Where once the hall was filled with the quiet trinkets of life that knew peace, now the many paintings, carpets, and potted plants were destroyed amidst the carnage. Wherever Vanimire looked, the beasts born from the crimson moon upended the life he knew. Only the cruel reminder of his world's end remained.

Even destroying the monsters felt inhuman, for though their muscled body would resist the movement of the blade at first, as soon as it cut through, it found no resistance. Vanimire rolled to the side, dodging out of the way of the reflexive swipes that were launched at him.

Ser Ralick stole the opportunity to leap upwards, kicking himself off the wall to redirect his blade through the neck of the other beast, bringing it down with one simple motion.

The beast twisted and writhed against the blade, piercing it. Serrated talons swiped through the air as it called upon every drop of resolve to resist the fate that Ser Ralick hoped to impart upon it.

As Ser Ralick struggled to pull his blade from the beast, one of the wooden doors lining the hallway behind the pair flew off its hinges. Wood shattered as it met the wall, sending splinters in all directions as a lone Bloodsmile staggered through the opening.

Lifeless eyes were turned towards Vanimire, the beast no doubt having heard the screams of its companions as they were felled. Its scream caused Vanimire to stiffen, tightening the hold on his blade as it clamoured towards him.

Vanimire's heart pounded in his chest as he watched the Bloodsmile lurch towards him. Spear-like bones scraped against the stone wall of the hallway, leaving serrated marks against its face as stepped through the body of its fallen companion. As carelessly as one skipped through a puddle, the beast continued its slow, unrelenting approach.

With each step forward, blood raced in Vanimire's ears. His heart could hardly stand the anticipation, and, feeling the blade tight in his grip, carelessness got the better of him. Perhaps it came from the never-faltering wish to impress the hardened Ser Ralick. Or perhaps Vanimire simply wished to show the older man that *he* could be helpful as well. Ser Ralick had, after all, led the charge through the labyrinth of the palace hallways. Vanimire cut down a fair share of beasts, but it paled compared to Ser Ralick's prowess.

As the Bloodsmile drew near, Vanimire lurched towards it, letting out a scream that he hoped imitated Ser Ralick's battle cry. The beast swiped through the air, and Vanimire ducked under the talons with ease. If nothing else, the beasts had *some* measure of predictability. His fingers tightened around the grip of his blade, feeling a sense of power swell in him as he lunged forward, aiming the tip of the blade at the beast's chest.

The blade found little resistance, pressing through the chest of the Bloodsmile with a sickening crunch. Vanimire put his weight behind the blow, throwing himself upon the Bloodsmile, hoping his blade would sink deeper. The beast screamed as Vanimire's blade pierced it, and though his hopes had been successful, his inexperience in the fight was made manifest only a moment later.

Vanimire failed to deliver the killing blow. Instead, his blade had skewered where one might have expected the lung to have been. Though the beast screamed in agony, its taloned hand came slashing through the air a moment later. Vanimire tried to duck under it as he always done, but his feet got tangled up beneath him. The heel of his boot pressed into a slick pool of blood, and as he threw himself away from the beast that sought to undo him, he went stumbling to the stone ground with a cry.

He yelped in shock, falling to the bloodstained floor as his blade escaped his hand. Vanimire's breath hitched, terror immediately swelling in him as he worried he once again finally met his end. The beast, still writhing and screaming in agony, threw itself towards Vanimire, its serrated maw ripping open as it descended upon him.

Just before it could sink the endless rows of jagged teeth into him, Vanimire heard a sickening crunch as the tip of Ser Ralick's blade jut through its open mouth. The beast went limp in an instant and Ser Ralick, with all the flair and confidence he exuded, rolled the beast to the side before pulling his blade from inside it. Vanimire let out a soft sigh as he reached for his own blade, gripping it before reaching for the hand that Ser Ralick had offered him.

"I would chastise you, little prince, but I am sure the sight of that wicked mouth was enough of a warning." Ser Ralick chuckled, helping Vanimire to his feet before wiping the blood from his blade on his stained cloak.

"You could say that again." Vanimire sighed.

"You ready to continue, then?" Ser Ralick asked, putting a hand on Vanimire's shoulder as he tried to force his gaze away from the carnage. Dwelling on the terror that faced them would only slow them down.

"Y…Yes." Vanimire muttered, blinking as he turned to look at the older man.

The pair were practically unrecognizable after their hour spent navigating the palace's internal labyrinth. Blood from man and beast soaked them from head to toe. Vanimire marvelled at how, even while soaked in blood, Ser Ralick seemed to look both heroic and imposing. It was as if the carnage only served to further heighten his grandeur.

"Good! Let us carry on then, lad. We should be drawing near to the armoury now. With any luck, the Redcloaks were busy with that abomination they worship and have not yet had time to pilfer it." Ser Ralick let out a deep laugh, which echoed through the surrounding hall.

His ability to remain cheerful even when looking death in the eyes brought a measure of comfort to Vanimire. With each step they took, it felt as if their goal was almost a guarantee, for he could think of no man or beast that would bring down the last of the Kingsguard.

In truth, Vanimire had no notion of how close they were to the armoury. Even in the days of his training, he seldom walked through it. It had always been a place of busied excitement, with Kingsguard, Redcloaks, and other members of staff spending time preparing and discussing beneath its vaulted ceilings.

Only once, Vanimire travelled there with his father. In the middle of the night, the two quietly made their way to stand before the enclosed sword of Einor, which even then shined with an aged brilliance. A relic entrusted to his progeny, the line of Eineriel. The sword stood as a reminder of their ancient inheritance; of oaths that were long forgotten, sworn to the nameless masters who entrusted the weapons to Einor and his Bannermen.

His father highlighted the importance, and as he rambled on about the history of the blade, Vanimire had, much to his sorrow now, dozed off. The weapon was a symbol of their family and possessed within it something that his father had hoped would never be needed. That was all he remembered, and now that fact broke his heart.

It was on that night, when Vanimire asked about how one would even uncoil the bindings that held it for a century, that his father imparted upon him the secret. Within the ring he wore, a gift from his father on his thirteenth name-day, was the key to unlocking it. Though the ring was now blood-soaked from all the carnage, Vanimire could still make out the twisting lines of gold dancing along the silver band. He was certain that even if Daromir stole every blade in the armoury, he could not touch the ancient blade of Einor.

After what felt like an eternity of running, the pair turned a corner and found a sight that made Vanimire's heart sink. More Bloodlines than Vanimire could count filled the hallway. The scent of death carried so heavily on the air that it took all Vanimire's resolve not to fall to his knees and empty his stomach. The horde descended upon a pile of bloody carnage. A host of nobility that had, in a vain effort, tried to conceal themselves in one of the many hallways of the palace.

Ser Ralick raised a hand, immediately drawing to a stop as they studied the terror that sprawled out before them. Luckily, it seemed they weren't spotted yet, though it was clear they would have to press beyond the beasts to get to the armoury.

Only one set of doors lined the hall between them and the collected group of monsters, and to get through it, they would have to come dangerously close to the horde gorging themselves on their fallen prey.

Vanimire swallowed nervously, pressing himself close to the armoured Ser Ralick. Though in his mind he knew it was a terrible idea, he scanned the faces of those being consumed, hoping desperately he wouldn't recognize them. He was thankful most of the faces were unknown to him or were so terribly disfigured as to be simply unrecognizable.

There were a couple of faces belonging to members of the palace staff, though none that he was close with. Still, it was a fate that he wouldn't have wished upon even his worst enemy. To be eaten through after your demise was one thing, but Vanimire learned quickly how the beasts had revelled in the terror they wrought. It wasn't enough for them to simply kill their prey; they wanted to gorge themselves on the terrified screams of those they played with.

Ser Ralick lowered himself, squatting closer to the ground in a motion Vanimire was quick to mimic. He gently lowered his blade, resting it on the stone floor beneath them as he fiddled with the straps of his arm brace.

Vanimire watched in silent confusion, trying to figure out what crazy idea the man had formed. Before he pieced it together, Ser Ralick leaned back, ripping his arm brace free.

"When I say run, we run. Got it, little prince?" Vanimire's brow furrowed with confusion at the whispered command.

Ser Ralick sighed, turning to look down the hall that stretched out before them.

"Just follow me." He muttered.

Ser Ralick slowly moved into the hallway, lifting himself up to his full height as he clutched the arm brace tightly in his hand. Vanimire watched in silent awe as he hurled the metal brace down the hall in one quick motion, turning to look at Vanimire before giving a quick nod.

The metal arm brace soared over the heads of the occupied beasts, vanishing into the darkness of the hallway before it clattered and crashed on the stone floor. In an instant, all the beasts let out a terrible screech, lifting their blood-soaked heads from their feasts as they turned towards the source of the commotion.

In the chaos, Ser Ralick screamed, "Now!"

The pair sprinted towards the beasts, all of which seemed viciously focused on whatever had caused the crashing noise behind them. They screamed in a terrible cacophony, which echoed through the hall and sent chills of terror rippling through Vanimire as they moved.

It was a terribly risky plan, and yet, it somehow worked. With every passing moment, Vanimire was growing more certain that one of the Gods must have woken up that day and thought it fun to watch him specifically, for there was no other explanation for the luck he seemed to have.

The pair bolted through the hallway, racing towards the horde of beasts before throwing themselves through the door that lay before them. As the door slammed shut, Ser Ralick moved quickly to push the nearby bookshelf in front of it. Its wooden frame scraped against the stone, and it took their combined effort to push it into place.

They knew it would barely save them if the beasts were intent on breaking through, but it represented a moment of relief. Vanimire fell to the ground, stumbling away from the now-barricaded doorway as he heard the beasts move beyond it. He was quick to cover his mouth with the palm of his hand, worried the sound of his terrified breathing would be enough to earn their attention.

It seemed, however, the beasts grew tired of their feast, and sought fresher haunts deeper within the palace labyrinth. Only when the stone floor beneath them stopped shaking did the pair let out an exhausted sigh, turning to find each other's gaze as they chuckled wearily.

Both knew just how unexpected the success of their plan was, and yet, finding a fleeting moment of serenity, they were quick to take it.

The pair found themselves tucked away in a small storage room that clearly saw little use in recent years. Builders carved much of the palace labyrinth into the mountainside, and with each expansion, an exhaustive list of rooms needing repair or completely forgotten grew.

Legend often spoke of a particular head scholar that would determine who to take as students based solely on if they could estimate how many rooms the palace had at its disposal. Even Vanimire had no notion, and he was certain his father cared little for such trivial matters. Still, the labyrinth of the palace was often a nightmare to navigate. He was thankful for it now more than ever. The same twisting hallways that proved exhausting to navigate now provided them a chance at survival.

Death carried thickly in the air of the storage room. Vanimire tried his best not to investigate every room laying beyond broken, and battered doorways. The blood pooling thick between the stones was enough for him to know what happened. Fires no doubt raged elsewhere in the castle, for the ceiling of the hall became lost beneath the hazy, ever-constant reminder of his world's undoing.

The metallic scent of blood mixed with the deep smell of smoke, enveloping Vanimire in a cloud of terror and dismay. When he closed his eyes, he was back in that banquet hall, the scent of blood pooling around him—his father's blood. *His* blood.

Ser Ralick rested his sword against a nearby crate before sauntering over to a nearby torch that flickered in its sconce. That it still burned must have meant someone tried to hide there earlier in the evening, and Vanimire couldn't help but wonder what might have happened to them. If they were lucky, they would have managed an escape, but he knew it was far more likely that they now lay resting in the hallway just beyond them.

"How long do we have?" Vanimire asked, pushing back his sweat slick hair with a hand that was far more disgusting.

"Not long." Ser Ralick sighed, fiddling with the torch in a vain attempt to steal more light from it. "Just enough time to catch our breath, then we should head out. The armoury can't be much farther."

Vanimire nodded, pulling his legs up against his chest before wrapping his arms around them. He rested his forehead against his knees, letting his eyes slowly close as he tried to find a moment of respite.

It was impossible, of course, to find any measure of relaxation, given all that surrounded them. Though the screams of terror slowly faded, Vanimire knew that the cause, for it was because of the devastation of those who were caught in the palace, rather than their escape. He wasn't sure if he could ever relax fully again after all he went through.

When his eyes closed, he could see the broken and battered body of his father as it had lain limply in the banquet hall. He heard the screams of terror erupting when the Redcloaks began their slaughter, and he saw their faces twisted and writhing as they were so terribly devastated. No, there would be no relaxation for him. Not now, and perhaps never again. He could only catch his breath in the silence that fell, and even that felt like a monumental task.

It was crucial they reached the armoury and escaped the palace before the adrenaline of the evening had subsided. Vanimire was certain that when that occurred, he would almost certainly pass out from the exhaustion. Though they were drawing so tantalizingly close to their destination, it still felt like a lifetime away. Their every step would be challenged, every hallway a fight.

By the time they reached the armoury, it will have likely come after another exhausting push through the palace labyrinth.

Vanimire couldn't help but sigh as his thoughts swarmed, overwhelming him, and his hands trembled.

"Hey, Crown Prince." Ser Ralick said, shaking the trembling Vanimire from his thoughts.

Vanimire lifted his head up from against his knees, blinking back the surprise as he turned his gaze to find that of Ser Ralick's. "It is time to move."

Vanimire nodded, though his mind was still in a daze as he uncurled himself. He reached for his blade, finding an eerie familiarity with it, before he lifted himself upright. He wasn't sure how much time passed, or whether sleep unexpectedly grabbed him, yet as he lifted himself up, his muscles screamed in tense agony. Wincing, he fought back the growing soreness as he stumbled over to help Ser Ralick move the bookshelf.

If it was a struggle to move it the first time, then it seemed to Vanimire that moving it now was an exhausting nightmare.

With the combined force of the two of them, it slowly scrapped along the stone floor, eventually resting against the far wall, before Ser Ralick quickly ducked his head through the door. Vanimire's mind was still slowly rousing from its respite as Ser Ralick gave him a quick nod, and the pair departed back into the hallway they recently escaped from.

The beasts were nowhere in sight, though they left in their wake a visual testament of the carnage they wrought. Vanimire tried not to look at the bodies that were ripped and torn beneath them as they moved, though the scent of them alone was nauseating.

It felt to him as if it had taken a lifetime to navigate this single hallway, such was his desperation to be free of it. When they finally turned a corner, leaving the bloodied carnage behind them, Vanimire felt a wave of relief wash over him. There was something about having to navigate through the pool of chaos that had threatened to overwhelm him with every step. It was as if his very soul was being tried and tested, and he wasn't sure if he had the strength to carry forward.

All he could think about was how likely it was he would end up as one of them, a body to be stepped over after having been ripped apart and devoured.

It felt like a lifetime before. At last, the curled arches of the armoury came into view. In the time between departing from their moment of respite and finally finding their destination, there were countless foes that stood between them. Through their combined efforts, these enemies were easily conquered, and yet, with every passing moment, Vanimire sensed dread continue to claw at his heart.

The more he watched Ser Ralick, the more he was certain he was unfit for the role given to him. In every category Ser Ralick excelled, he seemed lackluster. With every movement, the man exuded both flair and confidence, and Vanimire felt he was left to keep up; that with every swing of his blade, he just narrowly avoided the inevitable doom awaiting him.

The sight of the armoury was a relief, if only in knowing that at last there was something only he alone could accomplish. Despite his protector's wondrous aptitude, only his inherited gift allowed him to retrieve the blade that would save them. Though Vanimire was initially reluctant to believe a simple weapon might possess the power that legend alone provided it, with every passing moment, he hoped more and more that it would be true.

Ser Ralick ducked beneath the swing of a enormous beast, laughing wildly as he brought his blade upward to pierce through its terrible jaw. Vanimire winced as he heard the visceral crunching of its skull. The beast could barely let out a wicked scream of pain before it fell limply upon the weapon that had brought about its demise.

Yet, as if simply conquering that which seemed to Vanimire a nightmare wasn't enough, he spun about the beast, bringing his blade outwards, and severed its head at its terrible crimson neck.

Vanimire sighed, shaking his head as if Ser Ralick acted to prove the very doubts wracking him. A large part of him knew his worries were simply the folly of his childish naivety, and even with the realization, the pain still burned within him.

He often felt the crown of the High King was better suited for another, but whether through a cruel joke, or divine providence, the Gods ordained him to be the one to wield it. All his life he was surrounded by those who swore the inheritance was his alone to burden, and not a single one offered him the reassurance that he possessed the aptitude necessary to make good on it.

His father believed in him, that he had known, yet it still didn't quash the endless feeling of ineptitude wracking him from his earliest days.

Vanimire dodged beneath the claws of one of the crimson beasts, letting out a loud scream of frustration as he severed its arm at its shoulder. It seemed useless to dwell on his feelings of inadequacy, especially when every step demanded his complete and undivided attention.

No, it seemed much better to unleash that frustration upon his foes; to mete out unto them a measure of the terrible pain that they so happily inflicted upon others.

Vanimire rolled out of the way of the claws that followed as the beast writhed in agony, and though he reviled in hearing its screams, he was quick to push his blade through its throat; bringing a choked silence to the monster as it fell to the ground.

Whether by necessity or coincidence, much of his training returned to him in the time it took them to navigate through the labyrinth of the palace. He thought naught else was a better teacher than looking death itself in the eyes; and when faced with such, he had learned quickly.

His body seemed to move as if acting on its own accord, instinctively processing the terrible necessity of self-preservation through his movements.

With the last beast choking and writhing on the floor beneath them, there were no more foes separating the pair from their destination.

Though relief flooded Vanimire, he wouldn't let himself relish in it until they reached their destination. The armoury was little more than a stopping point, for the actual destination lay beyond the walls of the city itself.

CHAPTER X

THE BIRTHRIGHT FROM LEGEND

"In that moment, I felt all those that come before me. In wrapping my fingers around the blade, I felt the blood of Einor in my veins. I felt every Eineriel upon my shoulder."

Vanimire turned, falling into line behind Ser Ralick as the pair broke into a sprint towards the large doors of the armoury. They moved quickly as the pair leaned into them, ancient hinges creaking as the doors slowly opened. They squeezed through as soon as they were able, a feat much easier for Vanimire, as Ser Ralick wore the full plate of the Kingsguard.

His armour scraped against the doors as they turned on a heel, looping a hand through either of the massive iron rings that rested on the back of the doors. Vanimire threw every ounce of strength into closing the doors behind him, growing red in the face from his exertion.

When at last they slammed shut, Vanimire stumbled backwards. Silent amazement formed along his expression as Ser Ralick thrust his hand towards the wooden door. His eyes closed as he muttered something in a language unlike any Vanimire heard. Light shone beneath his fingers, twisting and turning as if carving into the face of the door a set of strange runes which lie around a large and intricate circular symbol. Vanimire had heard of the ancient oaths recited by the Kingsguard, but not once had he seen them performed.

The surrounding air warmed with excitement, as if it were dancing with delight. Vanimire continued to study the sigil in silent amazement, marvelling at how the light seemed to emit an ethereal hum.

It pulsed and swayed like light dancing upon a gently flowing river. The oaths of the Kingsguard were a strange art, one that saw little use in their modern age. Hells, he only saw Ser Ralick call upon the ability to mend a chipped blade in the days of their training.

When the light softened, Ser Ralick turned towards him, giving a quiet nod as beads of sweat trailed across his dirty, bloodstained expression.

"The seal will buy us but a few moments, Princeling. I hate to think of what that wandering hoard might do if they return. You must retrieve the blade!"

Vanimire nodded, scrambling to his feet as a massive blast rammed against the doors. The hinges screamed in agony, though the door did not shatter. A testament to the ancient power of the Kingsguard's oaths.

It bought them a few moments, and for that Vanimire was determined not to have Ser Ralick's effort end in vain. He bolted towards the back of the armoury, passing row after row of emptied shelves. In the immediate aftermath of the attack, much of the Kingsguard and Cityguard had attempted to arm themselves. That's what he hoped, at least.

For if they were to have any chance against the beasts of the crimson night, they would need all the arms and armour they could find. If the armoury was pillaged by the Herald, or hells, even worse, the Redcloaks? Vanimire tried to push such thoughts aside.

Vanimire's sprint came to a halt before the statue of Einor of Old that loomed over the now emptied armoury. Tall and depicted in a set of armour that exuded both power and prestige, the founder of the empire stood at the height of nearly three men combined.

With one hand gripping the handle of a sword larger than Vanimire, its tip pressed against the stone dais it stood upon, and the other reaching forward with palm facing upwards, as if inviting any who gazed upon it to approach. Its stone expression seemed imposing and disappointed. Its lifeless eyes, carved of stone, seemed cognizant of how the empire he formed was unraveling.

It was the custom for each departing member of both the Kingsguard and Cityguard to salute the statue before they departed, offering silent praise to him who formed the empire by blood and conquest. A shame it was that they didn't have the time for such customs.

Vanimire clawed at his hand, wiping away blood and dirt as he pried free the ring he was gifted. His mind raced as he tried to recall what exactly his father told him all those years past. The ring was the key to retrieving the weapon he inherited.

All he needed to do was…"Dammit!" Vanimire hissed, sucking in sharply as he pressed a hand to his head. "What was it? What *was* it!"

He studied the statue, hoping to find in its lifeless appearance *some* measure of an answer. It offered little help. Einor of Old stood as imposing and condemning as ever, holding a hand forward as if inviting Vanimire to join him in the realm beyond. Reaching for him as if…

The hand.

Vanimire stepped forward, raising his hand up towards the statue of Einor of Old. He rested the ring of his birthright, stained with blood, his *own* blood, upon its open palm. His breath hitched as he took a step back, hoping to see some sort of sign his intuition was correct. To his dismay, Einor of Old remained lifeless and still. *'Dammit.'* Vanimire cursed, curling his hands into a fist. *'What was I thinking? It's just a Gods damned statue after…'*

Light slowly pooled in the palm of Einor of Old. Pulsing light, a beating heart, it poured from his hand like a mist, vanishing into the air as the statue rumbled. Like a knife carving through stone, sigils etched themselves along the statue's blade.

Vanimire knew they meant *something*, but they were in a script that seemed otherworldly to him. One by one they etched into the blade, twisting and carving through the stone like Ser Ralick's oath bound the door of the armoury behind them. They began at the grip of the stone blade, slowly etching downwards towards the tip as the armoury doors continued to boom from repeated blasts.

When the last of the sigils appeared, they all pulsed in unison, and Vanimire's heart raced. The light intensified, beating as fast as a drum until the stone itself cracked. It started slowly at first. Slight breaks along the edge of the sigils, as if the intensity of the light was too much to bear. Yet each successive crack came faster than the previous.

Vanimire raised his arm, shielding his eyes from the light, continuing to intensify as the stone sword itself *burst*. Vanimire staggered backwards, hearing the sizzle of stone fragments race past his ears. To his relief, the burst avoided him completely, and as he lowered his arm, he saw that which they sought desperately to claim.

It was unlike any weapon Vanimire had ever seen. Its hilt was made of solid gold that contained within it the very light of the sun itself. The blade shined silver, like the light of Nalinyor at its zenith. Vanimire could see his dirty, blood-stained reflection in the blade, which caused him to wince at the disheveled sight. It seemed to glow as if it were a star cast amongst the canopy of night. He only realized he'd been holding his breath as he took a slow, reverent step towards the blade that hung in the air, waiting for him.

Einor of Old stood proudly behind the blade, its stone hand now wrapped around the grip of the blade that exploded. The weapon of his birthright was *entombed* within the statue. Countless members of the Kingsguard and Cityguard were so close to the weapon of legend, and yet they were wholly unaware.

Vanimire had little time to appreciate the weapon before the door of the armoury was shattered, sending shards of wood ripping through the room as dust poured from the blast.

"Ser Ralick!" Vanimire cried, turning to look at where the blast occurred.

He coughed as the dust enveloped him, but found relief as he heard the older man coughing at the far end of the armoury.

"I am okay, Crown Prince! But we need to leave now!" Ser Ralick roared, his voice echoing through the armoury as the dust settled.

Vanimire turned back to the statue. The blade of Einor of Old glowed through the dust filling the armoury, pulsing with a warmth that almost seemed inviting.

Wretched screams echoed from the hallway, and Vanimire knew it was only a matter of time before the beasts were upon them once more. He leaned forward, gently wrapping his fingers around the grip of the blade as he pulled it from its ancient tomb. The warmth that called for him now seemed like a hug, wrapping around him with an excitement as he felt the blade pulse between his fingers.

He felt undeserving, in truth. Like the blade passed to the most unworthy of heirs. Yet Vanimire was certain of one thing. Vanimire, the forgotten Crown Prince, died when Daromir threw him from the gardens. *That* Vanimire remained a broken and crumpled mess. As he took the sword of legend, feeling its warmth surge through him. Vanimire the High King was born.

Vanimire heard the terrible screams of the crimson beasts as they poured into the armoury, yet something was off about them. Their hungry, terrifying cries echoed through the pilfered armoury, but they seemed restrained.

Like dogs whimpering in the chains of their kennels. As Vanimire turned to face the cries, Ser Ralick came bolting over, readying his weapon alongside the Crown Prince. A shadow appeared through the dust, which quickly came into focus as it passed beyond the battered doors and into the armoury proper. The red cloak, though in tatters, that bellowed over its shoulder was indistinguishable, and though he felt a surge of strength course through him, the sight of the Redcloak terrified him.

Vanimire recognized the Redcloak sauntering into the armoury, flanked on either side by Bloodsmiles that seemed perfectly tamed. It wasn't an individual he had gotten along with.

Even before donning the Redcloak, Syraxis was a proud and condescending individual. His chiseled face gave way to sharp angles, causing his lips to always twist into a disgusted grimace. Black hair long began to fray and thin, fell haphazard across his pale, and imposing expression.

He was born on the outskirts of the Empire, and through his proficiency in fighting, he changed his fate, eventually bringing him to one of the highest positions in the realm. He was a brilliant fighter, and he knew it all too well. Vanimire tried to train with him once, but found the man was far more interested in proving his prowess than imparting some of it to another.

The sight of him made Vanimire's heart sink. To go up against any Redcloak would have been a monumental task, especially with the strange power of their obsidian arms, but against Syraxis, it seemed an impossible feat.

The man stepped over the rubble that littered the armoury,

coming to a halt as his eyes slowly scanned the room. Vanimire watched as he lifted his armoured gauntlet, pushing long, slick black hair from across his face. He bore a terrible smile that, were it not for the beasts chaffing under their master's command, would have been the most terrifying thing in the armoury.

"You've brought me a gift!" Syraxis hissed, waving his armoured hand toward Vanimire. "I wondered where that old fool of a High King hid such a weapon. A shame the Herald killed him before we could have made him speak."

Vanimire inched closer to Ser Ralick, who tensed as the former Redcloak spoke. Ser Ralick kept his blade held close, holding it upright and across his body in anticipation of the attack he was certain would come. Vanimire hoped he might have some time to grow accustomed to the new weapon.

Though its warmth continued to pulse through him, bringing with it a measure of familiarity, he would have preferred to test its strength on some of the Bloodsmiles, rather than the greatest swordsmen of the Redcloaks.

"I had not thought the Redcloaks were privy to such legends!" Ser Ralick called back, dropping into a defensive posture. "You should know who it belongs to in such a case."

Syraxis shrugged, shaking his head as if disappointed by the Kingsguard's response.

"I care little for children's stories, Ser Ralick. I've been commanded to fetch the blade, and in doing so, I will not fail. Even if I must bring it back to my master with Vanimire's arm still clutching it."

"How could you serve that monster!?" Vanimire screamed, clutching the blade tighter as he moved from behind Ser Ralick. "You've broken every oath you swore, Syraxis! That monster killed the man you made them to!"

Vanimire saw as a flicker of anger ignite in Syraxis' expression, though it was quickly buried. Clearly, what he said got through to the man, though Vanimire knew it would do little in dissuading him from his intentions.

"My master sees far more with one eye than you could with two, little princeling. Imagine what he can see with all six! I've seen it Vanimire. I've seen beyond the veil clouding our world. When my master gifted me the power, I caught but a glimpse, and it was more beautiful than anything you could ever imagine. The Song was… was perfect!"

"You traded your humanity to become a monster!" Ser Ralick cried, flourishing his blade through the air before him.

At the sight of it, the Bloodsmiles let out a terrible scream, clearly desperate to sink their fangs into the men looming so close to them. Vanimire caught sight of the Bloodsmiles trailing behind Syraxis and shuddered. Had it just been the hoard, they might have managed. However, to face the Bloodsmiles *and* Syraxis would be no easy feat.

"Enough!" Syraxis screamed.

His roar shook the floor of the armoury, causing dust and stone to fall from the ceiling overhead. Vanimire sensed their deliberations were reaching a conclusion.

"I'm tired of your wretched squabbling. There is much left to do, and I will not waste time debating with those who are unfit to hear the Song that we will create! One High King has fallen tonight already. I see no reason for anyone else to live."

Syraxis slashed his obsidian arm through the air, and Vanimire saw as its skin cracked and ripped, forming into massive spikes that were shot through the air toward them. By reflex alone, Vanimire ducked out of the way.

The statue of Einor of Old, which stood for centuries, erupted as the spikes ripped through it. Dust and debris shot out in all directions, and only the faint coughing that echoed told Vanimire that Ser Ralick avoided the barrage as well.

They only allowed the pair a moment to collect their thoughts before attacking them again. Syraxis screamed out a command in some foreign tongue, and immediately the Bloodsmiles raced towards them.

In the chaos that followed, Vanimire lost sight of Ser Ralick. The blast separated the pair, and just as the dust settled, the Bloodsmiles were upon them.

Syraxis unleashed waved after wave of crimson spikes, forcing Vanimire to be on the move constantly. He threw himself to the side as another barrage ripped through the air, and, moving on instinct alone, thrust his blade forward, severing the jaw of a Bloodsmile lurching towards him.

Syraxis unleashed another barrage, and Vanimire rolled out of the way as the talons of a Bloodsmile accompanied it. His body seemed to move as if acting on its own accord.

Whether this was the adrenaline of once again fighting for his very survival or being inspired by the warmth of the blade that already felt natural in his hands, he could not tell. Yet as he spun around the side of another beast, ducking under the blow that followed and bringing the blade upward to sever through the arm itself, Vanimire felt *powerful*.

The monster screamed in terrible agony, though Vanimire was forced to duck away from another barrage of spikes. This wave ripped through the roaring Bloodsmile, silencing its cries as it fell to the ground in a crumpled mess. Syraxis focused solely on killing Ser Ralick and the last High King. The capture of his own monsters clearly didn't concern him.

Vanimire was thankful, for Syraxis saved him from having to bring about the beast's demise himself. He ducked under another swipe of claws through the air, watching as Syraxis turned his attention towards where Ser Ralick must have ended up. Vanimire heard the occasional roar of the Kingsguard, a welcome reminder that the older man still lived.

After leaping out of the way of another claw swipe, he broke into a sprint, trying to put some distance between himself and the monsters that endlessly assaulted him. He slid across the stone floor, dodging underneath another torrent of spikes before leaping upwards to plunge his blade through the head of a Bloodsmile, bringing it to the ground as if it put up no resistance.

There was something about the ancient blade that changed him. It seemed as if time itself were altered when he picked up the blade. He ducked under the arm of a beast approaching him from behind, allowing his body to act on the impulses that seemed to carry it.

For Vanimire, it felt as if he were simply watching as his body acted with a smooth finesse he never knew he had. He rolled out of the way of another blast of spikes, turning on a heel to sever the head of the Bloodsmile that lumbered towards him.

An idea formed in Vanimire's mind as he leapt out of the way of another flurry of claws. He turned on a heel, spinning towards where the spikes came from, and once more broke into a sprint.

He heard another scream rip through the armoury, shaking the very stone of the floor beneath him as he moved towards Syraxis. It was clear the Redcloak was unleashing the blasts in either direction, aiding his near-endless waves of Bloodsmiles in their assault on the pair. Clearly, Syraxis hoped to kill them both without having to fight them properly.

The ultimate display of how his power dwarfed theirs. It was a sound enough strategy, but like the cadence of a melody, Vanimire recognized the pattern. A barrage of spikes had been unleashed upon him, which meant he had a few precious moments before the Redcloaks attention would be turned upon him once more.

He burst through the cloud of dust, and for the first time since the fight started, he glimpsed Ser Ralick. The Kingsguard clearly made quick work of the Bloodsmiles, no doubt making use of the crimson spikes to kill some of them. He positioned himself in a way that put many of the beasts between him and the Redcloak. Turning the monster's own weapon as an advantage for himself.

To Vanimire's surprise, Ser Ralick reached Syraxis, cutting through the final Bloodsmile separating them. With a scream, Ser Ralick slashed his blade towards the man, though Syraxis easily ducked out of the way. Lurching forward, Syraxis curled his obsidian hand into a fist, punching the chest of the Kingsguard, who was sent stumbling backwards from the weight of the blow.

Vanimire let out a wicked scream as he burst towards the Redcloak, who turned to him with a look of surprise. Vanimire clutched his blade tighter, hearing the beasts that still chased him growing closer as he sprinted towards the Syraxis. That same terrible smile crawled across the man's lips, and for a moment Vanimire couldn't help but wonder if he impressed the former Redcloak.

Syraxis raised his arm, turning his frenzy upon Vanimire once more. The cracks in the stone-like exterior pulsed with a sickening light, and Vanimire had to throw himself to the side to avoid the spikes that were thrown his way. He hit the ground hard, but was quick to scramble back to his feet, resuming his charge with unwavering determination. The barrage ripped through the Bloodsmiles that clamoured after him, giving Vanimire an opportunity to throw himself against the prowess of the corrupted Redcloak.

Syraxis' eyes widened as Vanimire continued his charge, screaming once more as if to summon all the courage he could muster. He still bore that terrible smile, and as time itself seemed to slow down, Vanimire quickly realized something must be wrong.

This was not the smile of a man caught off-guard, or of a warrior impressed. No, this was the smile of one who was confident in his own victory. The smile of a general that watched his troops' demise yet knew that a cavalry charge was moments away. The realization hit Vanimire harder than a blow to the head. Syraxis planned this.

Vanimire, carried on the winds of his own momentum, lurched forward, bringing the blade of Einor of Old in a downward arc from above his head. Syraxis' smile grew as he raised the obsidian arm to meet it.

Much to the surprise of the former Redcloak, the blade met with obsidian flesh and immediately ripped through it. Syraxis screamed in agony and shock as Vanimire brought the blade down until it caught at the elbow. Syraxis lurched towards Vanimire, blood as dark as the evening sky pooling beneath the pair.

Vanimire watched as the lines of the obsidian arm brightened, and he realized immediately the mistake he made. It surprised Syraxis that the blade cut through the arm so easily, but in the end, he still achieved what he originally wanted. The elbow snag held Vanimire close, preventing him from pulling free the blade. As the light intensified, new stone sinews formed, reaching around the blade to connect the two halves of the arm together once more.

The terrible red light reflected in Vanimire's eyes. Instantly, he found his mind transported back to the banquet hall, to the start of the slaughter. Vanimire recalled how the arms glowed with the same terrible light before the crimson spikes formed from their very flesh. Though he surprised Syraxis knowing that the blade of Einor of Old could trough the arm that seemed to be made of stone, in his haste Vanimire made the one mistake that would spell his ruin.

Ser Ralick's roar forced Vanimire to refocus, blinking back the memories of earlier in the evening. Time itself seemed to slow as the crimson light grew brighter. Syraxis' smile widened as Vanimire tried desperately to escape his grip.

The pair were too close together for him to pull the blade from the arm that reformed around it, and Syraxis' grip on Vanimire's shoulder dug so roughly he could barely move. He watched as the flesh of the obsidian arm cracked and twisted, forming the tips of the crimson spikes that would surely rip through him in a matter of moments.

Ser Ralick's scream roared in Vanimire's ear as he closed his eyes, accepting that his demise was near at hand. It seemed to Vanimire the noise was getting increasingly louder, though in his dejected acceptance he didn't pay it much mind. It was then that Ser Ralick crashed into him, leaning a shoulder into his back.

In an instant, Vanimire was sent stumbling to the ground. The blade ripped from his hand as it lay embedded in the obsidian arm that had reformed around it. The armoury swirled around him as he hit the stone floor *hard*. Ser Ralick put every drop of his strength into the blow, knocking Vanimire free even as it sent him rolling along the bloodstained stone.

Vanimire lifted his head in immediate terror, a new realization washing over him.

"Ser Ralick, no!" He screamed, raising a hand toward the man just as the torrent of crimson spikes ripped through him. The sound of the man's armour crunching beneath the onslaught made Vanimire's heart sink immediately.

Ser Ralick did that which Vanimire never seemed able to do. He had fought till the very end. When Vanimire was frozen in an acceptance of his fate, Ser Ralick fought bitterly to change it. Many of the crimson spikes ripped completely through the man, shattering into the stone wall behind him.

Blood immediately poured from the impaled man, pooling on the ground beneath him as he somehow stood upright. Vanimire watched as Ser Ralick curled his armoured hand into a fist, bringing it up to strike the laughing Syraxis right in the jaw. The former Redcloak stumbled backwards, his obsidian arm lowering to the side.

Surprise once more washed over the Redcloak as Vanimire's blade crashed onto the stone floor, echoing through the hall. Even being as broken and devastated as he was, Ser Ralick used one last burst of strength to put distance between Vanimire and the Redcloak, and in doing so, pulled free the blade that started this run of mistakes.

Ser Ralick trembled as he tried to take a step forward before crashing to the ground, his legs unable to bear the weight of him any longer. Vanimire felt the warm sting of tears fall once more as he glanced at the broken body of Ser Ralick. Blood poured from countless wounds, mixing with all those they overcame to pool beneath him. Syraxis' shrill laughter filled Vanimire's ears once more as he felt an adrenaline like no other surged within him.

The weapon of Einor of Old seemed to share his anger, for its blade glowed with a light that rivalled Nalinyor herself. Vanimire scrambled to his feet, screaming as he ran towards the glowing blade.

Ever since the Redcloaks first made their appearance, strange events tormented Vanimire. It was supposed to have been a night of festivities, of great food and drink, and of time spent in the company of the Lady Emmaline.

Instead, in an act of cruelty, the Gods deigned to steal everything from Vanimire and would not yet give him the satisfaction of death. He watched as everyone he ever knew, everyone he ever loved, was taken from him, and yet he alone was left alive. He alone was *forced* to survive. Against all the odds.

How many more friends and loved ones would he have to watch die before the Gods would allow him to join them? He was powerless to save his father, and powerless to save even a single soul in the banquet hall, and yet the Gods denied him the silent serenity of death when Daromir hurled him from the gardens.

He spent hours navigating the twisting labyrinth of the palace interior, bringing death to countless beasts, and stepping over those that weren't so lucky, and somehow, he survived. Even now, Ser Ralick, who was everything Vanimire wished he could be, was allowed to die, and yet he was forced to carry on.

To die was easy, for one did not have to shoulder the painful memories of existence any longer. No, these were given to Vanimire, who seemed, despite his every intention, unable to die.

Syraxis raised the obsidian arm upwards once more, and Vanimire watched as the lines glowed. He lowered himself mid-stride, grasping the blade as he continued his charge. He was certain the next blast of spikes would spell his end, for there was no conceivable way the Gods could deny it yet again, but it mattered not. Bringing Syraxis with him would make his death a happy one. There were few in the world who could kill a Redcloak one on one. Most of their kin fell when facing overwhelming numbers. For Vanimire, this would be his greatest achievement.

Vanimire's scream grew louder as the distance between the pair lessened. Syraxis seemed to hesitate for a moment as confusion etched into his expression.

Vanimire clutched the glowing blade tighter, caring not for what might have bought the Redcloak at this moment of hesitation. His eyes burned as the colours of the world seemed to fade. The deep hues of the armoury fled to the edge of his vision and vanished beneath the overwhelming whiteness that consumed it. Vanimire only saw the Redcloak standing ahead of him.

Though he struggled to see the outline of Syraxis, he *knew* where the monster was. A splotch of deep, sickening red paint against the white canvas. Heat seemed to burn deep within his chest as he drew closer to Syraxis, who still stood in complete shock. The blade between his fingers seemed to *sing* with excitement, buzzing in his grip as Vanimire threw himself upon the man that represented everything he loathed in the world.

The Redcloak realized his error far too late. He raised his obsidian arm towards Vanimire once again, clearly intent on catching the blade as he had before. The blade of Einor of Old met the obsidian arm with a burst of light, and as Vanimire felt it slice through the stone-like exterior, he screamed out in determination.

For all those he lost that evening. For all those he could not save; Daelin, his father, Lady Emmaline, and Ser Ralick. For the people he let down, and the empire he inherited. He moved like a man possessed, the overwhelming whiteness of the world consuming his vision completely. He no longer saw Syraxis, but it didn't matter. He could *feel* him.

The blade ripped through the arm with ease. As soon as Vanimire felt it reach where the elbow *should* be, he pulled to the side, twisting his grip and bringing the blade to the side. He threw his weight to the side, rolling under the armoured gauntlet that swiped at him.

Carrying himself on the momentum, Vanimire spun on a heel, bringing the blade of Einor of Old into the air, only to plunge it downward upon Syraxis' shoulder. Though it felt as if Vanimire's eyes were closed, he *knew* his slash hit true.

The blackened obsidian arm fell to the ground, and Syraxis was sent stumbling as bloodcurdling screams of agony escaped him.

Blood as dark as the evening sky poured from the Redcloak's shoulder, sizzling as it met the stone ground beneath it.

Syraxis gazed at the arm in surprise and agony. Blood continued pouring freely from the wound, though the pain burned so intensely that Syraxis could not feel it. Shocked silence fell over them as Vanimire stood panting with the blade of Einor of Old still gripped tightly in hand.

The adrenaline continued to course through him, though the exertion of the evening was making itself known. The thought of Ser Ralick, crumpled and broken behind him, seemed to provide an endless font of strength from which to draw from.

Syraxis glanced between the fallen arm and the blade Vanimire held tightly. Though weariness set in, Vanimire would not let himself fall victim to another surprise. The Redcloak's lips parted, but no words seemed to form, which made Vanimire's lips lift into a delighted, albeit exhausted, smile.

Even if he failed to kill the Redcloak, he silenced him, which was a feat accomplished by few in the world.

Vanimire breathed in sharply, clenching his hands around the grip of the blade as he strode forward once more. Color flooded his vision once more, and he saw the devastated Redcloak in all his wretched hues. The shock had still not left Syraxis, and Vanimire was intent on using the moment to accomplish that which he thought was impossible.

There would be time enough to contemplate why the blade suddenly glowed, and why in the heat of his approach, the world itself seemed to drain of colour. For now, he focused entirely upon finding the revenge that Ser Ralick deserved. It seemed to Vanimire a quick death would be far too kind a fate for one as wicked as Syraxis. Still, the end point would be deserved. Vanimire was intent on making every moment until then agony.

His approach was halted when the obsidian arm that was freed from its body began to crackle and burst. Vanimire followed Syraxis' gaze and watched in silent confusion as it writhed along the stone floor. Smoke poured through the cracks that formed in its stone-like exterior, and Vanimire watched as it melted in on itself, much like the beasts the Redcloak had ordered around. The blackened shape pooled out along the floor before burning away, as though a page torn from its tome.

Nothing about the evening made sense so far, and Vanimire hardly found the almost liquidus breakdown of the arm to be surprising. All that mattered was that Syraxis was stripped of its power, and as Vanimire turned his gaze back toward the still shocked Redcloak, he was relieved to see that it hadn't immediately reformed. Vanimire tightened his grip on his blade, resuming his slow approach as Syraxis watched in confusion.

"Y…Your eyes…!" Syraxis hissed, pointing with his remaining hand toward the man that approached him. "What in the hells…" His words were cut short as Vanimire raised the blade overhead before bringing it down against the arm that was stretched out towards him. The blade of legend, which still glowed with the intense light of Nalinyor, cut through the obsidian arm with no resistance. Human flesh and bone were like warmed butter.

Syraxis fell to his knees as another agonizing scream filled the hall. The blade of Einor of Old cut through the armoured hand with ease, casting it to the ground with a sickening crunch as Vanimire rested the tip of the blade against the floor. Countless questions about the weapon bounced in his mind, each vying to be answered, but so long as it aided his escape, they could wait.

Vanimire loomed over the devastated Redcloak. With no more hands to raise in an attempted plea, the Syraxis contented himself to rest on his knees, consigned to the fate that Vanimire would deliver unto him.

"Speak." Vanimire hissed, tightening his fingers around the handle of the blade as he looked down upon the defeated man.

"And what, you monster, should I speak of?" Syraxis replied, leaning his head to the side as he spat aside the blackened blood that poured from between his lips.

"After all that you've done, you would dare call *me* a monster?!" Vanimire roared, lifting the blade overhead before bringing it down with a terrible crash.

It took every ounce of his self-control to not silence the wretched beast, instead slamming the blade into the stone of the armoury floor. To kill him now would be an injustice, for there was much he could hope to learn.

"Why do you follow that six-eyed nightmare?! *Who* is the Herald!?"

Syraxis laughed wearily, shaking his head as blood continued to pour from between his lips.

"We have no choice." He muttered, and Vanimire saw him slump down as he spoke.

Gone was the cockiness and condescension that he had in life. Syraxis seemed to deflate as he faced the oblivion that awaited him.

"We serve because we must, the same reason you fight against us. The light of Nalinyor was wretched and cursed. Only Veristeriax has the power to remake it."

Vanimire's brow furrowed at the mention of this Veristeriax. It was not the first time this evening the name was uttered, and yet Vanimire, despite all his years of tutoring, had never heard it before.

"Who is this Veristeriax? What does he want?! And why did Father have to die for it!?" Vanimire asked, his voice lowering as the anger slowly receded.

"V…Vani…" Ser Ralick groaned, resting a weary hand on the man's shoulder.

Vanimire turned to see the near colourless Ser Ralick, barely able to hold himself upright without the assistance that he earned from bracing himself against Vanimire.

"He is gone lad." He muttered, nodding his head toward the kneeling Redcloak.

Vanimire turned his gaze back toward the conquered foe and found, much to his disappointment, he succumbed to his wounds. Syraxis' eyes were unfocused, gazing toward the blade that still shone with the light of the moon. Vanimire saw the corner of his lips lifted in a faint smile, and he wondered if the blade brought back some semblance of serenity in the man's last moments.

Vanimire sighed, turning to wrap an arm around the wounded Ser Ralick. His wounds were countless, but Vanimire noticed the faintest hint of golden light dancing around them. Perhaps another of the ancient oaths of the Kingsguard.

The spikes which pierced him gave way to blackened blood, which now stained his armour. Ser Ralick desperately needed a healer, but the armour of the Kingsguard proved its worth.

"Take it easy, Ser Ralick. We'll get you fixed up once we get out of here. We're almost there." Vanimire hoped his words feigned more confidence than he felt.

Were it anyone else, the wounds Ser Ralick received would have been fatal. The man was as resilient as the stone itself, yet he was still, much to his chagrin, a man.

"Aye. I…I am sure that I will be fine." Ser Ralick muttered, his voice hoarse and raspy, as he tried to chuckle. "T…Though with that blade, I am more certain *you* will be fine."

Vanimire tried to inch his way towards the broken entrance of the armoury. Now that they navigated the complex labyrinth of the palace, it would be only a few moments before they could escape the palace compound entirely.

In the days of his youth, Vanimire learned of a secret passage that snaked through the walls, bringing one into the depths of the High City below. In a matter of weeks, Vanimire used the secret passageway to escape his protectors, enjoying a night of excitement and entertainment in the city.

"Come now, Ser Ralick. We're almost to one of the secret passageways. We'll get you settled there, then we'll see to your wounds. I'll be needing your help in growing more familiar with this new blade." Vanimire tried to remain optimistic, fighting back the tears welling in his eyes.

He was thankful he had not lost Ser Ralick as quickly as he once feared, though he knew Ser Ralick's departure was inevitable. At the very least, he would get to take his final breaths away from the chaos of the palace, and that seemed to Vanimire a blessing, given the world that was ending all around them.

"A…Aye." Ser Ralick muttered, still relying on Vanimire's strength to move.

The pair made their way from the armoury, ducking back into the long hallways of the palace interior. Were they both capable of moving, then it would have only been a few moments before they came to the section of the wall that swung inwards when pressed in a certain way, yet with the gravely injured Ser Ralick, it was an unbearably slow process. Vanimire was thankful the beasts roaming the palace seemed intent on unleashing their carnage elsewhere, for it meant their journey was safe; albeit slow.

Only when the stone wall was closed behind them did Vanimire let out a long sigh of relief. Although the pair faced danger, the secret passageway almost guaranteed their uninterrupted journey until they reached the High City.

Vanimire lowered the injured Ser Ralick, doing his best to

remove the broken pieces of armour and laying them aside as he set to work beneath the flickering torchlight he started. Only the faint light at the entrance broke the total darkness of the passageway. It was there that Vanimire did his best to ensure his friend would be at peace, and when the last of his wounds were attended to, they figured it was best to steal for themselves a well-earned rest.

Though chaos undoubtedly awaited them in the city below, they survived the chaos of the palace, and that was worth a well-earned moment of respite.

CHAPTER XI

INTERLUDE

THE CITY DANCED AMIDST ITS DEVASTATION. MUSIC, UNLIKE ANY BEHELD by mortal ear, lifted unto the very stars above. The symphony of despair seemed lost to those who were blessed to behold it, for though their screams added to its splendour, they refused to stop and bask in its delight.

They moved like rats, darting through the meandering streets of the Capital City, searching for respite and safety in a world which offered none. Fires licked the many rooftops, dancing in jubilation as they engorged themselves in endless revelry. They were the insatiable children who would inherit the city; the revellers proclaiming new and better age. A new *Song*.

From the heights of the palace gardens, it stretched out as far as the eye could see. Amber flames danced beneath the smoke, crawling ever slowly towards where the Sea of Storms consumed it. Boats set off from the harbour, subjecting themselves to the terror of the crimson moon's winged children. Perhaps it was a better fate, but for the Six-Eyed Herald, it perfectly highlighted the hubris of the undeserving world.

The chorus of despair echoing through the ballroom slowly gave way to the satisfying silence of the efficacy of their hunt. With the blood of Eineriel finding its way back into the earth it was born from, the Herald took a moment to behold the extent of the crimson moon's wonder. Though he sat atop many familiar scenes, all those paled to the one that he now beheld. Each of them was little more than notes in the song of his efforts, a slowly building melody unto that which he spent many, many years.

"How does it look?" He whispered, eyes lifting from the waves of fire that rolled beneath him. "Oh, how it must seem from there up high. Imprisoned as you are, does the burning sight of the World that was Lost fill you with the same excitement as it does I? Does it not sound like the music of *that* night oh so many lifetimes past?"

The questions, as always, went unanswered. Such tantalizing music lifted only so high before the notes fell on dead, distant ears. Yet soon it would change. Every note, every melody, all of it formed a song that was creeping ever closer to the finality he long sought.

The ears of Veristeriax would remain closed for now, but with each passing moment, each delightful dance of the flames, they were closer to opening once more.

The Capital City was but the advent of the crimson moon. There was still much left to do. The symphony, though intoxicating, was hardly complete. Only when the world's cries created harmony would the symphony achieve its intended effect, fully opening the six eyes. Yet all could wait, for now. After all, the evening was one of celebration, was it not? Though they were late to the festivities, the Herald was intent on partaking in them now.

"Worry not, oh Veristeriax, for the night has only just begun. Soon you will bear witness unto a world re-imagined…a world sung from your very heart." His lips twisted into a grin as he continued to cast his gaze up to the crimson-born moon.

Rare was it for him to show such delight, yet he couldn't deny the excitement consuming him in seeing their long-awaited plan finally bear fruit.

How typical, in the World that was Lost, for something to dash that excitement so quickly.

Someone's boots clicked along the stone garden path, approaching him with great trepidation that belied the wearer's identity before the Herald turned. He lowered his arms, the jubilation of their achievement interrupted by the reminder of those he had to deal with.

"Speak!" The Herald hissed. Disdain and disgust replacing the reverence of his tone.

"M...My Lord." The pair of attendants lowered to their knees, robes muffling the sound of their uncertain movements. One redeeming quality of the vermin he ruled over was their knowledge of an acceptance of their subservient lot in life. That, and they were *remarkably* expendable.

"Did I not make myself clear?" He snarled, turning to face them with a weary sigh. One pair of eyes would have been enough to see how wretched they were, let alone three. "*Speak!*"

"We bring word from the castle." The first one stammered. "Word of its ongoings..."

"And of your child." The other interrupted.

The Herald glanced to him, six eyes narrowing on the uncertain cadence in the attendant's voice. He grew used to their fearful subservience. It was one trait that first led to their use, yet this was laced with something... more. "*Speak.*"

"S...Syraxis, your lord. He was leading the search of the castle, trying to find the..."

"I *know* what I entrusted him to do!" The Herald roared. The two attendants fell forward, pressing their faces to the stone as they knelt before him. "What *news* do you bring of my child!?"

Silence fell over the attendants, quivering in terror as they kept their heads press firmly to the stone, with arms stretched out towards him. He was rapidly losing patience. That which made them useful, also made them incredibly taxing.

"H...He was k...killed." One finally managed, her voice shaking with such intensity it seemed to break on every syllable she spoke.

"W...What?" The Herald blinked, unable to hide his surprise at the revelation. "B...But how, and...why!?"

He expected many of his children would be bested through the evening, but killed? No, that seemed impossible. A handful of well-armed men could have overwhelmed any of his children, temporarily forcing them to retreat and gather their strength before returning in all their glory, but...killed?

"Tell me what you saw!" he hissed.

His ferocity was so intense the stone beneath them seemed to tremble amidst his fury.

"In the armoury, my lord…" the attendant continued, her voice breaking with tears as she spoke. "He was kneeling, with a… with a…"

"With a *what?!*"

"A smile, m…my lord. H…He was…" Her words cut off sharply as she writhed, consumed by a warmth burning all manner of thought.

The screams were quick to follow, pouring from her lips as she fell to the side and rolled upon the ground as if consumed by some unseen flame. She writhed and flailed, clawing at her robes as her blood boiled and her bones cracked. The Herald's eyes shone intensely as he watched her, inflicting the unseen devastation as her body cracked and split, blood pouring from the wounds as she continued to writhe.

The other attendant trembled in place, hoping to be spared the carnage inflicted on his companion. Though each of them knew the danger that came with presenting the Herald ill-tidings, they were beholden to the expectation of their role. His companion had spoken up where he couldn't, and she had paid the price for delivering the news expected of her.

With a final, sickening crack, her screams were silenced, her body slumping to the blood-soaked ground. The Herald let out a long, weary sigh as he turned his gaze back towards the remaining attendant.

"And what of the castle?" He hissed.

"They are gathered, my lord." The attendant managed, trying his best to make good on the opportunity that his companion provided. "A…As requested, in the banquet hall."

"Good. On your feet, then."

The attendant lifted his head just enough to see the Herald's beckoning fingers, and with trembling limbs, he forced himself up to his feet. As the Herald lifted another hand to the crimson skies, a swarm of small, crimson-winged monstrosities descended, as if heeding some silent, unspoken command.

A shriek of terror escaped the attendant at the thought of being attacked, but as he watched them descend upon his now silenced companion, relief and terror washed over the trembling man.

"Never forget what it is we do," continued the Herald, forcing the attendants' gaze back towards him with another curl of his finger. "All that we do is in service of the world re-imagined."

"Y…Yes my lord." The attendant's head drooped, falling into the familiar bow.

"Now, tell me of those who gathered."

"O…Of course, m…my lord. As instructed, the castle was scoured for all those who assembled." His voice still trembled, but it seemed the robed figure found some measure of strength from reciting the orders that were imparted unto him, likely from Syraxis himself before he…

"And who did they find?" The Herald asked.

"L…Lords and ladies, m…my lord. F…From across the empire."

"Why were they not cut down like the others?"

"T…They wished to swear fealty. S…Syraxis thought it best to gather them before you, rather than simply…"

"So, this was his doing?" His last wish, but the Herald would not give voice to such words. Though his children acted on his behalf, they still contained some measure of self-thinking.

"I…I…Yes, my lord. T…Told us to gather those who wished to swear fealty before you. L…Let you decide on their fate."

In life, Syraxis was a great many things. Though, as a father, he loved all his children equally, some were far more capable than others. That he had favourites wasn't a cruelty, but a truth that was found ever present in the World that was Lost.

The Capital City, and the castle which ruled over it, were the playground for such fanciful notions. The looming shadows of expectation filled with the bodies of those deemed unsuitable or unworthy. In comparison, the devastation wrought in the ballroom had seemed a grand vengeance.

"Very well." The Herald sighed. "We shall see who…if any…are worthy of beholding the symphony we are creating. You shall assist me, *vermin*."

"Y…Yes my lord." Fear laced his words, and yet, he knew the orders of the Herald were paramount. Even if he wanted to run to the shadows, he could not do so.

"Let us see what the Empire's best have to offer." The Herald folded his arms over his chest, setting off along the stone path of the garden back towards the banquet hall, stained with the earlier devastation.

THE AIR WAS THICK WITH DEATH. THE FLOORS OF THE BANQUET HALL were stained from the crimson they drank so greedily. Uncleaned and quite content, the Redcloaks and their attendants left a tangible reminder of the crimson moon's dawning. The final High King's body, battered and broken, lay in a crumpled heap where he fell. Pausing, the Herald glanced down at the lifeless form, his face still showing the pain and torment that killed him.

"How low we all fall." The Herald said with great amusement, giving the richly robed man a kick with his boot before stepping over him.

The banquet hall was full of similar sights, nobility clad in the finest clothing and jewels the empire offered, and yet, none of it earned them a measure of salvation. In the World that was Lost station mattered little for the last moments of one's song. Rich or poor, high or low, all of them left the world screaming and terrified. The unworthy world was anything but fair, and yet, only in those moments of the advent and demise of life was it close.

The banquet hall was frozen in the carnage that consumed it earlier. In their search for hiding or fleeing nobles, the Redcloaks overturned and destroyed the long, illustrious wooden tables. Silk garments, worn in the haughty fashion of their station, lost their vibrant colours, becoming the same crimson that now stained the floor beneath them. Those in high society now lay in a similar crumpled mess. The unworthy world lifted them up, but they were undeserving of hearing the music that was to come.

The blood of Eineriel remained unbroken through the centuries, yet now it pooled beneath his heel. Frozen in the state of chaos that was unleashed within it, the banquet hall held the uncertain discomfort plaguing it earlier in the evening. As per Syraxis' last request, the noble families who bought themselves time by insisting they swore fealty gathered before him. Acolytes, to whom they were entrusted, shuffled them into the hall.

The gathered nobility was a wretched and undeserving sight. Their expressions revealed their fear and trepidation; their disheveled, ripped, and torn silk attire poorly represented their former high station. Now it served as a physical recounting of the evening's despair. From their highest towers, they ruled the World that was Lost, but a single blow reduced them to the level of those they exploited in their greed.

There were more than the Herald expected; families gathered from across the Rhyserion Empire to celebrate the most jubilant of evenings. Though their revelry was dashed, something far, far more wondrous and deserving supplanted it. With great terror, they stumbled their way into the banquet hall, stepping over the battered, crumpled bodies of their companions as they gathered before the raised dais.

The Herald kicked the body of the High King to the side, stepping over the arm that stretched out at an unnatural angle as he gazed upon those who Syraxis sought to gather. The door to the banquet hall boomed as it closed behind them, the robed acolytes standing with serrated, twisting blades drawn as they awaited their lord's command.

"Fortune..." The Herald began, his voice echoed through the hall and forced the gaze of all those who assembled. "Has smiled upon you already, for you alone have been gifted this fleeting moment."

The nobles shied away from his gaze as he glanced across at them, quivering in terror as they pressed close to one another. He scowled, unable to hide the extent of his disgust at the sight that was arranged before him.

These were supposedly the greatest minds and bodies in the Empire? *These* were the individuals who had strangled out power for themselves, ruling over the far-reaching borders of the island Empire? It made him sick and were there even the fragment of a crack in his resolve, then the sight would have certainly wiped it clean.

"The last wish of my child was for you all to be brought before me. That, I'm afraid to inform you, was *not* something that I had arranged. He acted of his own volition, for I have little need for those who are unworthy of beholding the melody that is to come." The sharpness of his words caused many in the gathered group to fall to their knees, screaming in terror as the finality of their position was made clear.

"Enough!" The Herald roared, demanding silence from those that trembled before him.

Though some were quick to heed his order, there were still those who were lost to the depths of their terror. The banquet hall echoed with screams, as if the noise would somehow undo everything that happened that evening. With a nod of his head, a pair of acolytes approached the group of nobles, causing them to wince and step back. They feared the *acolytes* of all people, showed how unworthy they were. After all, did the moon wince at the sight of a rat?

As the acolytes plunged their serrated blades into the backs of those overcome by fear, their fervent screams ceased. With sickening crunches, their cries gave way to the uneasy silence hanging over the crowd once more.

A swift kick to the side caused the offending nobles to sprawl out on the floor, their fear forever silenced as the acolytes dealt with any subsequent outcries. Only after the acolytes silenced the protesting nobles and cast a few into the endless darkness of their demise did the Herald continue.

"Fortunately, I am bound to heed his last wish. For that which binds a parent to their child is stronger than the disgust that I bear for you all." His eyes narrowed on the remaining nobility, and with a sigh that further belied the revulsion, he raised a hand towards them.

"You balance upon the edge between worlds. You hear the fleeting melody of what was unworthy, what will soon be lost to the sands of time. Explain why you deserve to hear that which we create. Tell me why you should be allowed to heed it. Tell me why you are *worthy* of it."

The command went unanswered, the group of nobles consumed by their terror. Whoever the six-fold gaze fell upon was quick to shy away from it, terrified of the unnatural visage the Herald presented. It was among his strongest weapons, and yet, it brought with it some small measure of headache.

Were that he could look upon them as their fellow, though the thought made him sick, then perhaps he might have been able to inspire them to an answer. Their fear of choosing incorrectly and sharing their companions' fate prevented anyone from answering. Like rats fearing the paw of the cat hunting them.

"No one?" The Herald asked, scanning across the crowd as his scowl grew. "Syraxis' last wish and *none* of you would deign to appreciate it? Even by the standards of the unworthy world, you are all..."

"I will try," a voice echoed, interrupting the Herald's remark.

It alone would have earned even his acolytes their undoing, and yet, as the slender figure moved through the crowd, the Herald couldn't help but feel a measure of surprise. Despite his sparkling azure silk, similar to that of many of his companions, the man was unimposing. Thick curls of black hair set over a tan complexion, which seemed–at least to the Herald–far more defiant than those who parted around him to allow his slow approach.

He moved with the lithe grace of one who was used to being unseen, and as the Herald set his unwavering gaze upon him, the boy of some two decades steeled his nerves.

"And who are you?" The Herald asked, tilting his head to the side ever-so-slightly.

"Saylen." The boy answered, dropping to a knee in deference. "Ward of the House of Glaurost." His cadence was unlike his companions, though the Herald cared little to parse which dialects came from which region.

To the Herald, the title was little more than some conjecture of little meaning. Though Glaurost and its ruling family were paragons of the island's northern reaches, the city was of little concern for the armies of the crimson moon. The Capital City was where the bloodline of Eineriel was, and it was their initial target of concern.

"Saylen." The Herald repeated, feeling out the word between his lips. It was wretched and ugly, though the same was true, when they first met, for those who became his now cherished children.

"What is it that makes you worthy?"

Saylen paused for a few moments, lowering his gaze to study the blood pooling around him. The Herald watched as the boy tried to find some sort of answer, as if his mind were sifting through the twisting, meandering currents of a sea of thought that was near overwhelming.

"Give me a blade, and I'll prove it."

The Herald paused for a few moments, narrowing his eyes on the kneeling boy who still could not meet his gaze. The Herald's interest piqued. Though uncertain whether the boy would live up to his expectation, the Herald was never one to pass up the opportunity for entertainment. The boy would be a fool to take the weapon and try to charge the dais.

The prowess of the six-eyes would have him writhing in agony before he could even take his second stride. So it was that he nodded to the acolytes, who seemed nervous with the response but heeded his order. The nearest faceless, robed figure took a few steps towards the kneeling boy, offering over his serrated, wretched blade.

Saylen rose from the ground, taking the blade in hand. As the acolyte stepped back, he weighed the weapon in his grip, easing it up and down as if to get a feel for how it felt. Clearly the boy had some measure of training, though that alone would have hardly proven him worthy of a life in the world that was to be remade.

"Well?" The Herald asked, the question laced with rapidly fleeting patience. "How do you intend to make yourself..."

Once more, Saylen interrupted his words by tightening his grip on the weapon's handle. Spinning on his heel, the boy lurched forward, plunging the weapon through the chest of the azure-clad nobleman who stood behind him. Gasps and screams poured from the group as the boy continued forward, pressing the blade deeper into the man's chest until, with a sickening crunch, it broke through his back.

So surprised was the nobleman that he had no time to even utter screams of terror and pain as the blade pressed into him. Stumbling backwards as blood poured from between his cracked lips, he blinked in pure, unfiltered shock as Saylen pulled the blade back as he slumped to the ground.

"Curious." The Herald muttered, watching as the screaming nobility clamoured to get away from the boy who stood proud over the dying nobleman.

Saylen plunged the blade downwards, silencing the writhing man's blubbering protests and ending his squirming as his brilliant blue silk robes stained purple, then a deep, dark red.

"One of the many lords of Glaurost," Saylen spat, wiping the bloodstained blade on the man's silk robes. "Whatever he might have said, he was unworthy."

The boy turned on his heel to face the Herald once more, dropping to his knee as the blade was held overhead as if in offering.

"Though I am too, I would ask only for the opportunity to right some wrongs that have been inflicted upon me." A pause. "Allow me to partake in the fight against Glaurost…against the city that was my gaol."

The Herald pondered the request for a great many moments. With hands raised up, the terrified screams of the gathered nobility were once more silenced by the threat of the approaching acolytes, helping to ensure their compliance. Saylen never wavered, kneeling in the pool of blood with the blade held overhead.

Though he was a wretched sight, he was *slightly* less wretched than those who gathered alongside. Time would determine his worthiness to witness the Song that was to come. For now, however, the boy presented a unique and interesting opportunity. Though the Herald alone acted as the harbinger of the crimson moon, there were others with which he had the occasional council. Were they to learn that he passed up such an opportunity because of his disgust alone, then they would have been mighty displeased.

"To what lengths are you willing to serve?" The Herald asked, lowering his arms back to the side.

"Any of them, my lord. *All* of them."

"I see." The Herald shifted his gaze away from the kneeling boy to the group of nobles who were creeping their way towards the locked doors of the banquet hall.

Saylen's eagerness for betrayal clearly caught them off-guard. They were scurrying akin to rats desperately trying to find safety amidst a sinking ship. It was a vain effort, if not an entertaining one.

"When I prove myself worthy…" Saylen continued, flourishing the blade in his hand as if he inherited it long, long ago. "I ask only for one trifling object."

The Herald's scowl deepened. Betraying one's fellow was not nearly enough to make one worthy of beholding the world that was to come. The boy's eagerness proved intriguing, but that too was hardly enough.

"Go on." The Herald hissed, barely able to hide his growing disdain.

"Glaurost." Saylen responded, his words once more infused with a strength and confidence not known to the other nobles that were gathered. "I will deliver the city to your hands. In return, I wish to become its new lord."

The Herald contemplated his offer in silence. Though it was the mark of the hubris born from the world unworthy to make such a bargain, that which he asked for *was* little more than a useless token. Glaurost, the grand coast city to the north.

For a time, the Herald considered the possibility of unleashing the crimson moon there, though that plan fell to the wayside when the bloodline of Eineriel was fully scouted. Now it remained little more than a radiant reminder of that which was to be undone. If using the boy and his readiness to betray those, he knew for a lifetime would accelerate their plans by even a day or two, then so be it.

"Very well," he said, eyes trailing across all those who wore the brilliant blue of the distant coastal city. "Prove your worth and we'll see to handing the sceptre of Glaurost to more deserving hands."

Saylen dropped to a knee, pressing the tip of the blade to the ground as he bowed his head in deference to the six-eyed figure towering above him. "Thank you, lord Herald. Your orders shall be my command."

A scream burst out from the back of the room as a noblewoman clearly realized the futility of their attempted escape. With the doors locked, and acolytes still laying in wait, the cry of terror was silenced with the slash of a blade. For those who were so eager to swear their fealty to him, the nobles proved anything but cooperative.

Did the world truly forget the tranquility of silence when standing before one's superior?

The trembling trepidation of the nobles had only continued to grow as he spoke with Saylen. In their foolishness, they hoped to sneak their way out of the banquet hall whilst the two were engaged. A ludicrous hope, given that the ever vigilant acolytes continued to wait in the shadows for their master's command. Even the disposable vermin had their uses.

The Herald lifted his arms to the side as he spoke once more. "Pain alone is the pathway to paradise, Saylen. Even those that are unworthy of beholding the Song that is to come can find some measure of comfort in the oblivion which awaits them."

Saylen, for his part, maintained his deferential knee, his forehead pressed to the pommel of his blade as he let the wisdom of the six-eyed Herald wash over him.

"When the first of the crimson nights concludes, we shall gather once more. Until then…" He paused, narrowing his gaze upon the nobles that continued to claw against the locked banquet hall doors. "Deliver the unworthy unto oblivion."

Saylen rose with a nod, tightening his grip on the blade before turning to face the quivering group of nobles. He understood such a command and was eager to fulfill it. Another point in his favour as far as the Herald was concerned. Though the boy impressed him thus far, the path towards worthiness was a long and difficult one.

As Saylen walked through the ever-growing pool of blood, the gathered nobles burst into screams. With their fates sealed, they could do naught but watch as the executioner approached them. He moved with a deliberate slowness which belied the revelry he was having with following the command. Saylen wouldn't just cut down the nobility, he would *toy* with them.

Perhaps there would be a use for him after all.

As their screams heightened, the Herald turned his back towards those who gathered. Waving a hand to the nearest acolyte, he descended the dais, the long trails of his robe dragging through the pooling blood of Eineriel as he made his departure.

"Keep your eye on the boy." The Herald said with a snarl when the acolyte approached him. "Have him carry out Syraxis' last wish…" He paused, leaning in closer to the trembling acolyte. "If he steps out of line, silence him."

The acolyte nodded, taking a couple steps back and bowing low before the Herald before moving past him to join the carnage that was being wrought once more. Though they were little more than pests beneath his boot, they had their uses, and so the Herald was more than content letting them carry out his will as he passed into the cool air of the gardens once more.

Screams echoed from the banquet hall, slowly being silenced one-by-one, and joined the tantalizing chorus of despair consuming the Capital City in its entirety. As he returned to the ledge where he was marvelling at the sight earlier, that which stretch out before him seemed even more beautiful than before.

"Can you hear it?" He muttered, casting his six-fold gaze up to the moon overhead. "Hear how they cry out for your mercy?"

Like flames cast amidst the tides, the Capital City danced beneath the warm glow that consumed it. Shadows of his children flew overhead and poked through the bellowing smoke below. It was a playground of terror, a circus of despair. The first of the endless nights, and it was *perfect*.

"Oh, how it pales compared to the Song that you sang, fair Veristeriax." He sighed, lifting his arms up to the sky once more in quiet jubilation as the moon seemed to shimmer in his gaze.

"But not for much longer."

CHAPTER XII

BENEATH BOTH TREE AND MOON

"The palace became a garden of despair; the flowers of all I knew wilted and drowned in pools of crimson."

SER RALICK DID NOT LIVE TO SEE THE SIGHT OF THE HIGH CITY OF THE Capital. When Vanimire finally awoke, he found the deceased man's arms wrapped around him. It was both beautiful and heartbreaking. Vanimire spent several hours afterwards, unable to move from the spot. He watched his father die and saw Daromir's betrayal; all those he knew and loved were dead or deranged. With the death of Ser Ralick, Vanimire felt well and truly alone.

When he could sit still no longer, he set himself to carrying the broken body of his friend through the passageway. It took hours, but when at last he emerged into the light of the crimson moon, he felt the tears flow once more. There was nothing more he could do for his fallen friend than to bury him beneath the nearby tree, hoping his spirit might find comfort in getting to gaze out upon the sight of the city sprawling out beneath them. If it would even survive that long.

The monsters tore through it, and Vanimire watched in agony as fire and terror continued to consume much of the city. It was not a sight Ser Ralick would have enjoyed, but Vanimire hoped in time he could bring beauty back to the capital, and then he would return to this spot and tell Ser Ralick all that he accomplished.

The crimson moon still loomed ominously overhead, casting the city in a terrible low red light. An umbral ring formed around the edge of the moon, which served to further heighten its terrifying image.

Vanimire tried desperately to keep his gaze from wandering towards it. Hopelessness settled in once more as Vanimire sat on the edge of the railing, peering at the city stretching out beneath him.

Were it not for the low light emanating off the ancient blade, he would have sat in the crimson darkness. With Ser Ralick buried, the blade alone remained to give him hope and inspiration. He sensed a warmth surge through him when his fingers graced the handle. It was enough that even now, sitting upon stone cooled by the night air and soaked from head-to-toe in blood, the cool sting of the evening air was beyond his feeling.

Fires continued to engulf the city, sprawling out as far as he could see. Their terrible orange flames dancing in Vanimire's weary gaze. The hulking, disfigured shapes loomed over many of the buildings, and the mere sight of them made his skin crawl. With his father so brutally deposed, the mantle of High King now fell to him, and yet he felt powerless to do anything.

Screams poured out from the city streets, mixing with the terror and ineptitude surging in him like a tumultuous storm. There he sat, running his fingers over the blade that rested upon his lap as if it would provide him the answers he needed. Yet, down below, the terror and chaos Vanimire had only recently escaped still engulfed his citizens.

His eyes drifted across the shapes that danced beneath the light of the flames consuming the city. The Fourth's Wall, it seemed, still defined the boundary between the High City and Low City. Supposedly its ancient, twisting figure defined where the city limits were in the time of Vanimire's ancestor, the fourth High King.

In the centuries that followed, the Capital City exploded in growth, with the Low City nearly tripling in size compared to the city that lay behind the Fourth's Wall. Fires spread easily through the wooden buildings which largely consumed the Low City, with all its twisting, labyrinth-like streets.

The High City, with its larger stone estates, were largely spared from the twisting infernos, but the shadow-clad crimson beasts roaming about consumed the gardens and vistas that were central to the serene life of the city.

It appeared to Vanimire now that class and status meant little in the end. The same carnage, and onslaught that tore through the Low City, still consumed the richer vistas of the High City. Hells, the biggest beasts Vanimire saw, could easily been able to scale the ancient wall dividing them.

From the mountainous peak of the palace complex to the docks that lay in the furthest reaches of the Low City, the hellish carnage that was unleashed upon them consumed all the capital. Vanimire read several tomes that depicted what the end of the world might have looked like, and yet none of them came close to the gruesome terror of reality.

It was then, as he continued to run his fingertips over the edge of the ancient blade, that an idea formed in his mind. From his vantage point, he could easily make out the unmistakable shape that marked the ancient Watchtower resting at the edge of the city's docks. The crimson light of the moon danced upon its dome glass roof, as if it were reaching out to Vanimire and calling for him.

Centuries ago, the Watchtower was built to stop any threat to the entire Empire. Despite repeated explanations to Vanimire, he didn't grasp its workings. However, each major city in the Empire had a similar tower. If one of them signalled a terrible threat, it would pass the message along to each of the others, immediately alerting all corners of the island Empire.

Vanimire wrapped his finger around the grip of the blade, standing upright as his breath hitched. Realization immediately washed over him, and he felt like an idiot for having not considered it earlier. His gaze was far too narrow.

When his father died, he inherited the title of High King, and though he spent a lifetime within the walls that felt like a cage, the empire that stretched beyond them was just as much under his command and purview.

Although the Capital City, often considered the gem of the Rhyserion Empire, was almost certainly lost, the Empire didn't need to fall with it. Perhaps it was naïve to hope the same chaos that was unleashed in the capital didn't also consume the rest of the Aerturiel. Yet it was the first plan Vanimire formed on his own accord, and it immediately felt right. Despite the loss of his life and the capital, Vanimire clung to the hope of warning the rest of the Empire.

Vanimire's gaze traced through the city, trying to figure out a sensible path that might bring him to the Watchtower. Traversing the High City might prove easy, given all the carnage and chaos was focused near the larger estates lining its esteemed pathways. If he were smart about how he carried himself, then it might be possible to get to the Fourth's Wall within the hour. However, it was the Low City that terrified him.

Even in the days of tranquility, the Low City was a nightmare for the inexperienced princeling to navigate. Although the High City had meticulous planning and organization, the capital's exploding population made planning the Low City impossible. Its narrow pathways twisted and turned without rhyme or reason, giving life to the chaos that so often consumed the denizens of the Low City.

For the princeling that was used to life in the castle, it was practically impossible to make sense of the streets that spiralled through the Low City without rhyme or reason. One never knew what awaited around every turn. Where it seemed likely to bump into an attendant or aide in the castle, one was just as likely to find a thief or assassin in the salty aired Low City.

To get to the Watchtower, Vanimire would have to navigate the terrible chaos gripping the Low City, fighting against both the inconceivable layout of the district, and the beasts that continued to roam freely through it. If only he wasn't so foolish when facing Syraxis, then perhaps Ser Ralick might have lived. The older man would have certainly known the best route to take.

Yet, Vanimire tried not to dwell on the thought. Focusing on his failures would have kept him sitting exactly where he was, awaiting the death that seemed inevitable.

Vanimire lifted his gaze upward, trying to determine any sort of marker in the sky that he could use to orient himself when surrounded by the chaos of the Low City. Only the crimson moon, looming overhead, broke the total darkness consuming the night sky. With no other notable sight to make use of, he contented himself to keep the crimson moon over his left shoulder. Hoping it would point him in the general direction of the docks.

If that failed, then he would have to stumble through the narrow alleyways until he heard the water lapping at the coast. It was a terrible plan, and Vanimire sensed his confidence waver, but it was all that he had to go off. He would have to hope the Gods would give him one final blessing.

With the weapon held tightly in hand once more, Vanimire felt the power of purpose surge through him once more. It was as if he figured out what his purpose in life was, for there was little doubt in his mind that even if he activated the Watchtower, he wouldn't live long enough to see the far reaches of the Empire.

He was thankful that in his lifetime; the Watchtower had always been little more than a reminder of their past, and as such, he did not know how it worked. However, it made sense to him that if it could alert every other major city in the Empire, then it would certainly attract the attention of the beasts ripping through the Low City.

As Vanimire gazed at the Watchtower, it appeared more and more certain he was looking at his death. In the past, this might have terrified him. Hells, there were a handful of moments that evening alone which he felt the same terror.

Something was different now. There would be no better way to die than hoping to save the Empire that was entrusted to him. Perhaps then the historians who lived could write of Vanimire's brief reign in a good light, though even that seemed so minor to him now.

Vanimire tightened his grip on the blade, feeling the familiar warmth course through him from its handle. He turned his gaze back to the disturbed mound of dirt resting beneath the nearby tree.

"Looks like I'm not able to rest yet, Ser Ralick." He muttered, hopping down from the stone ledge before taking a few quiet steps towards where Ser Ralick rested. "I bet you're laughing at me right now, aren't you? Going on about how you get to relax in the company of all the finest women in the heavens while I must continue onwards, hm?"

Vanimire laughed quietly, the sting of tears beginning to well once more.

"Well. Save some for me, will you? I can't imagine I'll be long."

Vanimire reached down, placing his hand against the disturbed earth as he breathed in sharply. He knew every second that passed was a matter of grave import, and yet, he couldn't bring himself to rush away from the side of his departed friend. He lowered the sword, resting it against the quiet mound as he reached for the dirtied cloak he put aside.

It would have been customary, given Ser Ralick's position in life, for the cloak to be draped over his final spot of resting. Vanimire hoped wherever Ser Ralick was watching from, he would excuse his breaking of protocol. Only when his last job was completed, would he return to drape the cloak over his friend.

For now, Vanimire lifted himself to his full height, unfurling the cloak and shaking off the dirt clinging to it. In a single motion, he waved it over his shoulder, letting it hang over his left arm as he tied it around his neck. Though the cloak would have normally been white and gold, the blood that soaked it made it seem more akin to that which the Redcloaks wore. The irony brought a muted smile to Vanimire's face as he lifted the blade.

"How do I look?" He asked, spinning around as if to let the silent friend gauge the full sight of him.

"I thought so," he added, lowering his head for one last moment of respect before he turned on his heel, facing the road that led downwards to the High City.

"I'll be back soon, Ser Ralick. Until then...well. Hang tight." Vanimire set off, the cracked stone path of the road crunching beneath his boots as he made his way towards the destiny awaiting him.

CHAPTER XIII

THROUGH THE DUAL CITIES

"I flew on wings of despair. Though my burdens weighed heavy on my soul, freedom came from knowing I had nothing left to lose."

Just as he expected, Vanimire passed through the High City with little problem. He encountered a few of the two-legged Bloodsmiles, but the blade's power, and his imitation of Ser Ralick's brilliance, enabled him to swiftly overcome them.

The winged beasts were a constant threat, though Vanimire learned quick that if he stuck to the shadows and took care not to move when they were swooping overhead, then they seemed to be unaware, or uncaring. To them, he was a meal that resisted fiercely. Hardly worth the effort.

Waves of flame from the dense buildings obscured the salty air blowing in from the nearby Sea of Storms. Cracked beams fell inward, sending dense bursts of bellowing smoke that nearly concealed the light of the crimson moon. The blood and fire were overwhelming the senses in the Low City, a place known for its dense, seaborne air that one could have thought himself thrust into the depths of hell.

The massive hulking beasts appeared to contend themselves with gorging on the extravagance that flowed freely from the massive estates of the High City. It was eerily quiet as Vanimire traversed through it, though he hoped, perhaps naively so, that most of the citizens escaped.

The retinues that guarded their estates undoubtedly surrounded any noble that wasn't caught in the palace's frenzy. Though they were trained to dissuade thieves and pickpockets, rather than the nightmarish creatures.

Even in the best protected part of the city–save the palace itself– the beasts easily tore through their defences. Bodies lined the street, twisted and broken, just as they did in the palace.

Vanimire saw some signs of resistance, for there were occasionally the skewered and sliced body of a Bloodsmile. He thought for all the centuries of their progress, and all the years of their experience in the arts of war, the resistance of mankind was a folly when put up against these nightmarish beasts.

The sight of the Fourth's Wall was a relief for Vanimire, in only that it allowed him another opportunity to gauge his course of action. Large sections of the ancient wall were torn apart, the years of history putting up little resistance against the claws and fangs of the crimson beasts. He quickly scaled the broken segment, using the height of the wall to determine how best he might navigate the Low City.

If the Low City seemed alight with the flames of chaos and carnage from the overlook, then it was a scene from a nightmare up close. The scent of blood and death tainted the very air itself, making Vanimire's stomach spin in revolt.

The cobble streets, twisting and turning through the Low City, were barely visible beneath the blood and carnage littering them. Every step through the city would be a reminder of what they lost, and yet Vanimire tried to push the thought to the back of his mind.

Standing atop the broken Fourth's Wall, Vanimire saw only the dome roof of the Watchtower looming in the distance. He already traveled far more in a single day than he ever recalled. Yet it seemed a lifetime separated him from his goal.

The dome-roofed tower stood defiant of the devastation surrounding it. Settled upon a small mound overlooking the nearby harbour, it now watched in silent agony as ships were cast out to sea in a vain effort at salvation. The water of the harbour appeared as red as the blood that lined the streets. Only the gently rolling waves distinguished the Sea of Storms from the harbours carnage.

It was clear he would have to stick to the twisting and chaotic alleyways that cut through the Low City, lest he brave the open streets that would subject him to the winged beasts above. Were it not for the broken arches that offered some protection, then even the Fourth's Wall prove unsafe.

If there was any relief to be found, then it was only in that no hulking colossal beast lingered in this section of the town. He could see their hulking shadows in the distant eastern section of the Low City, towering over broken and battered buildings as they gorged on whatever they could find.

No, the Gods seemed content to pit him against only the winged beasts and the smaller two-legged monsters.

Vanimire was quick to scurry back down the broken segment of the wall, landing on the blood-soaked path with a gentle splash. With every careful step Vanimire took, the stench of death grew stronger in the narrow street. The stones, worn down by the boots of many, became slick with the freely flowing blood of numerous bodies left hanging in different states of desecration.

Luckier individuals found themselves ensnared in their houses, their bodies consumed by the flames that danced through shattered windows and doorways. The unlucky tried to run, and in doing so, came face to face with the terrors unleashed upon them.

Vanimire could not bear the stench any longer. Death carried thick on the air that bellowed out from the fires consuming much of the Low City. With every step, he sensed the thick, metallic, rotting scent desperately try to encase him in a hug of despair. He broke into a careful sprint, desperate to get through the grisly scene before turning a corner.

Immediately, he lurched to the side, bracing himself against the nearby wall as his stomach gave in, and emptied its remaining contents. Never had he seen such a terrible sight. The faces of countless citizens held the agony of their demise on their broken expression. The dead could not speak of their torment, but their depictions spoke far more than Vanimire ever imagined.

When his stomach settled, he pushed himself off from the wall, stumbling down the alleyway as he tried to keep his head from spinning. The stench was overbearing, and the endless images of tormented agony only served to further unsettle him.

He suddenly believed those caught in the palace inadvertently escaped a worse fate. Despite being terrorized by unimaginable beasts, many still enjoyed the luxury of space. Gifted with the opportunity to die in solitude, rather than piled upon each other like refuse.

Vanimire gagged, turning his gaze away from the terrible scene as he tried to maintain his focus on what must be done. All it would take is his sense of direction to grow wayward and he would no doubt meet the same fate that was inflicted upon so many.

Even with this knowledge, it still proved difficult to maintain control over his senses. Every new grisly sight that greeted him sent his head spinning, and his stomach threatened to release itself with each dismal display.

Only when a terrible scream ripped through the alleyways could he regain his focus. The beasts, as Vanimire quickly learned, were often the first to be heard, rather than seen, and just as he expected, a pair of lumbering Bloodsmiles appeared at the end of the alleyway he moved through.

Their screams carried on the winds, shaking the ground beneath his feet as if the very earth itself was crying out in terror. Sharper than the loudest birdcall, yet booming like the firing of a cannon. Their screams appeared to come from the depths of nightmares, just as their bodies twisted into a distorted imitation of mankind.

The monsters turned, setting their lifeless faces towards him as their twisted fangs emerged from behind cracked lips. They noticed him, and it meant they needed to be dealt with before he continued onward.

Vanimire held the sword with both hands, levelling the tip towards the monsters slowly clamouring down the alleyway towards him. It was not the most ideal location to be fighting in. The alleyway could barely hold two individuals standing shoulder-to-shoulder, a fact the beasts quickly learned as one fell in line behind the other.

Even as they marched towards him, their shoulders scraped along the stone walls that lined the alley, and their various spikes and horns occasionally got stuck on the mismatched bricks jutting out unevenly.

Vanimire breathed in, trying to maintain control of his senses as the monsters approached. If the narrowness of the alley proved to be an unavoidable reality, then he would simply have to turn it into an advantage. His mind raced. The world beyond the Bloodsmiles drifted away into obscurity as he focused intensely upon them.

Power and confidence flowed through him like never before. It appeared to him as the monsters made their slow approach, they were marching to their demise.

Whether it was from the warming power flowing from the blade or simply being in the close presence of Ser Ralick for the hours that they spent together, Vanimire had felt different. He felt *powerful*.

Vanimire watched in quiet anticipation as the beasts drew closer. He did not move backwards, for the narrowness of the alleyway was vital to the attack he had planned in his mind. All he needed was the singular moment of opportunity. When it would appear he had every intent to act upon it, stealing for himself the moment of victory, and relishing in the continued existence that would follow it.

Was this how Ser Ralick felt with every engagement? Was this the confidence born from victory? Or was it masculine folly to think of oneself better than everything that appeared before him?

The moment came as he expected it. As the beast's spikes caught in the jagged bricks jutting out from the misshapen walls, Vanimire leapt forward. The blade felt a natural extension of his arm as he screamed, surging towards the two beasts caught between the buildings lining the alleyway. Like hares caught in a trap, Vanimire descended upon them in a frenzy.

Vanimire lurched towards the first beast, ducking under claws that came instinctively towards him before leaping upwards. The blade of Einor of old seemed to move as if acting on its own accord, piercing easily through the crimson flesh of the monster's throat before lifting upwards. Vanimire winced as he heard the sickening crunch of the beast's skull breaking beneath the onslaught of his blade.

There was something about hearing its brutal demise that continued to unnerve him. The beast let out one final, gasping scream, the noise fleeting and waning with the strength that was once its terrifying trademark. As the last throes of its life vanished, its skin began to sizzle and burn, tearing away at itself as the body collapsed into a sickening, bubbling mess.

The hopeful part of him wished the sensation would forever be unnatural, for it meant that such necessities were forever foreign, though he knew it was unlikely to remain that way.

With the first beast dispatched, Vanimire moved to bring death to the other. The crimson beast fell so quickly it proved somewhat inconvenient, for now he needed to clamour over its sizzling, broken body to dispatch the other monster lumbering behind it.

Vanimire leapt upwards, pressing a foot against the felled monster's shoulder as he soared upward through the air. The sudden appearance of the one who quickly disposed of his companion caught the second beast off-guard. Yet, before the beast bored his jagged teeth into a terrible scream, Vanimire brought his blade down through the air in a vicious lunge.

Once more, the sickening crunch of a shattered skull echo through the alleyway. As the beast slumped down, letting out a long sigh, its eyes of black rolled back into its head as death claimed it. With every monster Vanimire bested, he felt his confidence grow.

There was little doubt in his mind that it would have taken him years to match the prowess Ser Ralick or Daromir exhibited, and yet, so long as he remained on his feet, and continue fighting, it mattered little to him in the end. He accepted long ago that his was the path of the scholar and diplomat, for the sword would forever be secondary to the prowess of his mind.

Vanimire pulled his blade from the felled monster's head, leaping off from its sulking body to land in the blood-soaked stone of the alleyway once more.

He knew this would not be the end of the encounters before he would reach the Watchtower. The tendrils of exhaustion already worked their way into his limbs. Vanimire couldn't recall a single day which brought with it as much exhaustion as the evening had, and still it seemed far from over.

With the crimson moon forever hanging overhead, it was impossible to sense the passage of time. His body, however, seemed to expect the sun to have long since risen.

Vanimire continued through the alleyway, quick to resume his usual stride that would bring him ever nearer to his destination. Though a lifetime still separated them, with every step forward, he knew he was one closer to finding its ancient glass edifice. His mind didn't consider what might occur after that moment. It still appeared unlikely that he would even accomplish such a feat. Even with his growing confidence.

There would undoubtedly be far more beasts than just the two that assaulted him, and each encounter would pit his expertise and luck against the monsters that were crafted from the very nightmares that plagued mortal minds.

Vanimire often believed life guaranteed nothing, yet facing the world's end, that tenant seemed more certain than ever.

The stench of death never seemed to lessen through every alleyway that Vanimire traversed. Every few minutes a new atrocity would present itself to him, and in those moments, he felt the selfsame worry and trepidation that first plagued him.

If his reign lacked other memorable achievements, people would know him as the High King of the dead. The chaos and carnage that ripped through the capital earlier that evening continued to consume his citizens. Despite this, Vanimire continued onward, pausing only momentarily to grasp his left arm through Ser Ralick's bloodied cape.

Ever since he began his descent through the city proper, he sensed a growing burning pain that ripped through him, unlike anything he ever felt. The pain of the crimson spikes and the burning sensation of Daromir's twisted flesh piercing through him seemed little more than a scratch compared to the blazing sensation that occasionally rocked him.

It felt to Vanimire as if his very blood was alight with the fire ripping through the surrounding city. His mind swirled as he leaned against the cool stone of the nearby building, digging his fingers into his arm as he waited for the flash of pain to subside.

The tremors as he lacked any other word to describe the sensations he felt were growing in their duration. The first came not long after he set off to the High City. It was little more than a shock, as if his arm were bashed against a pinprick. After some time, the episodes grew longer, and before he knew it, they became debilitating.

Vanimire screamed in agony as he writhed against the wall, waiting for the particularly bad tremor to pass. He was as knowledgeable in the ways of healing as he was in the ways of war, and yet he had no notion of what gripped him.

Did the terror of all that he saw finally break him down completely? Was his fear and uncertainty manifesting in the physical pain that seemed to boil his blood?

Vanimire slammed himself against the wall, sending a fresh wave of shock rippling through him that made the pain in his arm subside. He steadied himself, lifting off from the wall as he wiped the beads of sweat that formed along his forehead. His breathing stilled, though his chest still rose and fell from exertion.

There was still so much to accomplish, he couldn't even bear the thought of letting the pain of his arm distract him from the task at hand. No, it was so monumental that he would rather sever it now than see it disrupt what he had to achieve.

Vanimire continued down the alleyway, turning at the end as he tried to orient himself. As the pain of the tremors grew, so too did they engulf his senses, casting his mind adrift through the pain-addled waves. Vanimire came to an intersection and began searching overhead, desperate to find the crimson moon that was his only guiding beacon.

After a few tense moments, he found it through the canopy of smoke. A quiet sigh of relief escaped him as he reoriented it over his shoulder. So long as it loomed overhead it meant the world itself was ending, which wasn't ideal, but also it directed him towards the docks of the Low City.

Vanimire positioning himself with the crimson moon over his left shoulder before taking off down the alleyway that stretched out before him. There, amidst the twisting labyrinth of alleyways, it was impossible to gauge how much time passed since the world itself ended.

His natural body clock wanted to believe it had been at least a dozen hours. How strange, he thought, in half a day, the world he once knew could be so completely torn asunder. The monsters thriving beneath the crimson moon reduced the centuries-old walls and buildings of the capital to dust in moments.

The Low City was a never-ending series of twisting alleyways, especially as Vanimire continued to avoid the main throughway. He was thankful he avoided the winged beasts casting shadows overhead, especially after seeing some unfortunate survivors be whisked away into the night by their talons.

Still, he traded the safety from the beasts overhead for the obscurity of the pathway unknown to him. Every alley was just as the same to the one before it, and Vanimire could only tell he made progress in finding fresh sights of grisly devastation the crimson beasts unleashed upon the terrified city folk.

The deep roaring of the palace cannons pulled his mind from its ruminations, and he turned back to catch a glimpse of the smoke blasting out from the palace's upper reaches.

It amazed him despite the threats of both the Redcloaks and the crimson beasts, there were still members of the guard who maintained their post. His heart sunk in hearing so few of the cannons rip through the crimson sky, and he could only wonder how long it would take before the palace itself would grow disturbingly quiet.

Vanimire returned his mind to the world surrounding him, for the Low City would undoubtedly consume him if he lost his focus. With little notion of how much time passed, he wasn't certain how much further there was before the Watchtower would appear. His eyes were ever watchful for a collapsed building that he could scale, but so far there was nothing that would not have brought with it a terrible risk.

Flames consumed the devastation, or it would have made him precariously vulnerable to the winged beasts. For now, Vanimire gauged his general direction by the moon that sat at its apex. Turning to place it over his left shoulder once more, he took off through the twisting alleyways.

Occasionally he heard quiet sounds of struggle, the adrenaline filled screams of men, and the clashes of blades against claws. Though hearing that resistance still offered him some hope, his heart sunk, knowing he could not help them.

How many men would die in the coming hours because he could not assist them? How many would spend their last moments in twisted, writhing agony as he raced past, secretly, and ashamedly, glad the beasts didn't direct their focus towards him?

The questions racing through his mind were endless, though he knew if he dipped a toe into those endless pits of despair, he would be pulled asunder.

Vanimire ducked under a partially collapsed archway, spinning on his heel as he moved to lift the blade upwards. As he expected, he heard the gut-wrenching sound of flesh being cut through, and once more did the terrible screams of the beasts rip through the darkness of night.

As the beast fell from its vantage point, Vanimire wasted no time in bringing the length of the blade downwards, severing its head at the neck as the blackened blood pooled in the street beneath him. The Bloodsmiles were hardly capable of tactical thought.

Occasional beasts found themselves in advantageous positions when their gorging on fallen bodies had coincidentally provided them with such a vantage point. The red blood dripping between broken stones told Vanimire that this was another such case.

Or so he thought.

The blood dripped from the battered body of someone that was crushed by the falling stone. Where Vanimire expected to see signs of consumption, the body was left relatively alone. Some of them *were* capable of a measure of intelligence, for this beast clearly was lying in wait.

It was much smaller than the others Vanimire saw, and the spikes jutting outwards from the flesh of its head appeared much less defined. What it lacked in the disproportionate back spikes, it made up for with its claws. Long, talon-like serrated edges protruded from webbed fingers, scraping along the ground beneath it as if each were the length of a sword itself. Were the beasts like anything in the reckoning of man, then Vanimire might have thought this one to be akin to a child, or somehow half-formed.

Despite this newfound revelation, he saw remarkably little that suggested they were similar to the beasts of the mortal world.

Vanimire turned his gaze away from the beast as the spasms of death appeared. With every passing moment, new questions and curiosities formed in his mind, and yet, it was painful knowing it was unlikely he would ever receive the answers that would sate him.

He was long curious about the relationship between the Redcloaks and the crimson monsters. For though Syraxis seemed able to maintain a measure of control over them, most of them appeared little more than rabid and terrifying beasts. They acted in packs, that much Ser Ralick, and he learned quickly, but each of them acted solely for their own survival. A crimson beast wouldn't care about its captured companion. Instead, it would double its efforts to devour its prey. They were single-minded, and viciously efficient.

Vanimire paused as the alleyway reached its end, pouring out into a slightly wider crossway. He pressed himself against the stone wall nearest to him, grateful for its touch was still cool. Though many of the initial city fires subsided, their effects remained visible, palpable, and odorous wherever Vanimire went. He learned early in life one could experience the pain of heat that long since vanished from the naked eye.

There appeared to be no monsters in immediate sight, though the there were fewer shadows than he would have hoped. However unlikely it seemed for a winged beast to descend and grab hold of him, it was not a fate he wished to leave to chance.

It took only a moment for Vanimire to decide, seeing that one alleyway across the small crossway would offer a much more significant level of protection from the beasts soaring overhead.

After giving one last glance to the avenues of immediate danger, Vanimire burst across the small crossway, breathing in sharply as he threw himself into the relative protection of the shadow-laced alley. His body fell with a crash as he rolled to a stop, and though he was quick to lift his gaze upward, the world around him swirled from the exertion.

Vanimire desperately needed a moment of respite, and yet, it became apparent to him the world itself would afford none to the denizens that experienced their extinction.

Once he felt the air return to his lungs, and his senses stop their dizzying swirling, Vanimire stumbled to his feet, bracing himself against the nearby wall as he held the glowing blade before him. The faint light it gave off was useful in moments like these, where so much obstructed the night sky above that it was almost completely pitch black.

Vanimire had no notion whether the beasts could see in complete darkness, though he could only hope that they would be just as blind as he was. The faint glowing of the blade might have made him a target, but it was crucial to helping him find his footing.

Even here bodies lay in twisted and deformed agony. There clearly were some who thought the darkness of the tight alleyway would have been their sanctuary, and now their blood echoed softly as Vanimire quietly moved through it.

What hope was there for safety when the world itself was ending?

To hide might buy you an extra hour or two, spent in terrified exhaustion as you awaited the fate that was clearly coming. Yet, to fight was to earn a similar fate. With every step that brought Vanimire closer to the Watchtower, he wondered if he, in his efforts to resist the fate that was assigned to him, was more foolish than those who tried desperately to avoid theirs. He thought the twisted bodies he stepped over acted more rashly according to their nature than he did.

Only a fool would stare upwards against insurmountable odds and claim they could overcome them. Who was he to think himself worthy of such a legend?

The darkness of the alleyway seemed to stretch onwards for an eternity, and with every step, Vanimire's terror continued to build. Though he appeared relatively safe from the threat of the crimson monsters, the weight of that which he traversed was difficult to push aside. Faced with only the darkness of the path before him, his mind wandered and conjured up the terrible images that were seared into his mind.

It was a great relief when the darkness of the alley gave way to the low crimson glow emanating from overhead. At the end of the alley, Vanimire found a rope ladder that was thrown from one of the opened windows overhead. He didn't know if someone used it to escape or for frivolous excitement before the world ended, but he was thankful. With the blade held in one hand, Vanimire climbed, hoping to see the outline of the Watchtower looming beyond.

Seeing the domed roof of the Watchtower at last, Vanimire was overcome with relief and almost wept. The Watchtower was still a distance away, but it was significantly closer than it was when he first set off, and that alone was worth the excitement.

Perhaps in an hour or two at most, he could finally push through its ancient doors, and in doing so, would have succeeded in the most foolish endeavour he ever undertook. The path ahead would not be easy, for he was all too aware of what stood between him and the Watchtower, but the end was in sight.

Vanimire was quick to lower himself back down to the ground, splashing into the shallow pool of blood that covered much of the roads of the city. Relief washed over him once more as he emerged from the darkness of the alley, giving a quick glance across the roadway before darting through a narrow alley on the other side of it.

Overhead lights allowed him to see the world beyond, a sight he enjoyed, though another terrible scream, which shook the earth beneath him, was quick to dash that excitement.

Pain ripped through Vanimire's left arm, causing him to drop to his knees and let go of the ancient sword. He clenched his teeth to stifle the scream that threatened to escape him, knowing there were certainly monsters nearby. His eyes watered from the intensity of the pain, as he threw himself against the stone wall to distract his mind from the arm that felt engulfed in flames.

The skin of his arm paled, growing almost as white as Nalinyor itself. Though the first episode of such searing intensity happened whilst in the High City, in truth, the arm felt off since Daromir threw him from the parapets of the gardens.

Vanimire writhed and twisted, breathing in sharp and exhausted gasps as the pain subsided. That episode was the worst by far, and even after it passed, he still shook from the memory of what he went through. Somehow, he survived, though he wasn't confident he would repeat such a feat.

He was certain that the next time the pain in his arm would consume him, bringing him to the finality he knew awaited him. He knew with all the certainty he had that the pain of the next episode would be his undoing. If the Gods were kind, it would come only after he activated the ancient Watchtower, though he wasn't ready to bet on such odds.

With trembling fingers, Vanimire reached for the blade, finding relief to wash over him as he sensed the warmth course through him once more. In only a few hours, he grew attached to the weapon in a way he thought impossible. It became an extension of him, and the thought of being separated from it made him shiver in fear. He used the blade to lift himself upright, steadying himself as he wiped away the sweat that formed along his exhausted features.

Another terrible scream ripped through the air, causing Vanimire to press himself tightly against the wall as he watched in anxious anticipation for the monster to appear. There was some distance between him and the end of the alleyway, and Vanimire watched the flickering crimson light as a shadow slowly appeared. It was impossible to gauge what sort of monster was creeping closer, but Vanimire knew a fight would soon be upon him.

If Ser Ralick were alive, he might have opted to race towards the beast, stealing for themselves the moment of surprise to kill whatever dared to approach them. The thought caused Vanimire's lips to lift in a soft smile. After all he went through, he still paled compared to the renowned Kingsguard. Though he hoped the older man was watching him favourably from whatever afterlife welcomed him.

Vanimire sucked in sharply as the two-legged beast came into view. It was taller than most of the monsters he encountered, and the claws on its elongated arms scraped through the bloodied street that it slowly meandered along. Vanimire could partially make out its head above the roof of the nearby buildings and, to his horror, it appeared to lack both eyes.

Instead, the beast sported an uncountable number of twisted spikes protruding outwards in every direction. The twisted shapes were dripping with fresh blood, and despite feeling the warmth of the blade course through him, Vanimire couldn't help but tremble slightly in terror.

The monster stopped right where the alleyway ended, blocking Vanimire's forward path. The hulking monstrosity leaned its head back, opening its unnaturally wide jaw, before another scream ripped through the night air. Its flesh tore at the edges of its gaping mouth, causing its own dark blood to pour between the rows of serrated teeth that lined its jaw.

Such terrible ferocity shook the buildings. Loose bricks ripped from their holdings, falling and crashing in the alleyway. Vanimire pressed a hand to his ear, desperate to still some of the overwhelming noise that made his very bones rattle in his chest. His other hand lifted the blade overhead, naively hoping any debris would connect with the weapon rather than caving in his head.

Vanimire cast his gaze upwards just in time to see the upper wall of the nearby building rocking from side-to-side. Knowing what was only a few moments away, Vanimire lifted himself upright, lowering his blade to the side before sprinting through the rest of the alley.

The force of the blast tore the upper section of the nearby building from its position, sending it crashing into the alleyway and shooting dust and rocks in all directions. The carnage didn't faze the crimson monster, and despite Vanimire's hesitation to sprint toward the beast, he had no other choice. Staying in the alley would cause the falling debris to crush him, or glass shards to rip through his clothing.

Vanimire reached the end of the alley and leapt to the side, throwing himself to face the blood covered street as the dust and debris ripped through the main street. Vanimire scrambled away, turning his gaze to see the beast was still standing in the middle of the narrow street.

Though the blast lodged countless bits of glass, rock, and debris into the side of its leg, the beast seemed hardly bothered. It raised its head, directing its eyeless gaze toward the crimson moon hanging overhead.

Vanimire slowly lifted himself to his feet, holding the blade between two hands as he pointed its tip towards the monster. Despite being forced from the relative protection of the alley, he managed to have not drawn attention to himself, no doubt thanks to the massive blast that erupted from the falling building.

Despite this, Vanimire formed no plan in his head which seemed smart to him. The beast stood taller than six men combined. Its twisted spikes jut out from multiple parts of its body, creating a monstrosity more terrible than any Vanimire laid eyes upon.

Although terrifying, the two-legged Bloodsmiles were easy to dispatch. By now, Vanimire pieced together their general methods of approach. The winged beasts presented another threat altogether, but they couldn't locate their prey so long as they stuck to the shadows. Yet this hulking monstrosity was unlike anything Vanimire encountered.

He wondered if this was the ultimate form of these beastly invaders, or if it too had larger counterparts. It seemed impossible to him there could exist any monster larger than the one standing before him, and the whole evening was accented by near impossible circumstances.

Vanimire turned his gaze toward the street opposite of where he emerged, desperately looking for a new alleyway to dart into. Standing in one of the main passageways for too long would certainly attract the attention of the winged beasts. To his terror, the fighting in this section of the city was fiercer than at the palace, for much of the buildings lay in burnt ruins. There was another alleyway that twisted towards his destination, but its entrance lay right in front of the hulking monster's foot. It seemed a fool's choice to choose that alleyway. Vanimire had little choice.

Vanimire sighed, peering back towards the alleyway that appeared to be the only solution. The Gods themselves seemed content with making every step of the journey impossibly difficult, and Vanimire could only think they were laughing as they gazed down upon him.

Moving as slowly as possible, Vanimire inched his way closer to the hulking monster. His breath hitched as he drew closer to the shadow of the beast. Vanimire did not know what grasped its attention, which was still lifted upward towards the crimson moon. It lacked the eyes to appreciate the beauty of its terrifying visage, and Vanimire saw no sign of ears or anything else that might have drawn its attention. Regardless, he was content so long as it remained focused on something other than him.

Walking through the main street was hardly an easy trek. To avoid slipping on the blood-slicked stones, or tripping over the widespread debris, careful placement of each step was crucial. Vanimire held the blade before him, watching the monster for any sign of detection.

As he drew near to the monster's leg, it still seemed intensely focused on whatever loomed overhead, and Vanimire hesitantly moved his gaze down towards the alley just out of reach.

Vanimire paused, thinking to himself as he looked back at the distracted monster's leg. There were little signs suggesting the monsters acted like anything that walked the mortal world, and yet, despite his rational conscience screaming at him otherwise, he formed a plan in his mind.

The blade of Einor of Old could cut through the monsters as if they were little more than strands of cloth, and Vanimire couldn't see any reason the larger beasts would fare any better.

To kill the beast would almost certainly bring about his demise, but perhaps he could slow the beast for a time. If any survived the chaos of the Low City for this long, then the inability of the hulking beast to chase them down would undoubtedly be a boon. Every part of Vanimire wanted nothing more than to dart down the alley, consigning the hulking monster to memory as he focused on the ultimate mission at hand.

Vanimire sighed, holding the handle of the blade tighter as he took a careful step away from its leg. Raising the weapon overhead, Vanimire let out a terrible scream as he brought the weapon downwards. The glowing blade hit the flesh of the monster's ankle and immediately cut through it. To his surprise, Vanimire nearly severed it completely in a single strike, though he could not finish what he started.

The looming heavens held the hulking monster's attention until its terrible agony caused it to scream, shaking the earth and buildings. Vanimire clenched his teeth, darting through the entrance to the alleyway as the monster writhed. In its twisting, the beast brought a spiked arm through the surrounding buildings, immediately shattering through them with a terrible blast as Vanimire sprinted through the alley at full speed.

Immediately, the buildings shook and trembled as pieces came loose and crashed into the alley behind him. Darkness covered the alley, though Vanimire wouldn't hesitate to appreciate it for even a moment. Quickly crashing buildings threatened to crush him, and he concentrated on avoiding them.

A crimson light shone at the end of the alley, and Vanimire tried to summon all his strength as he sprinted towards it. He heard not a thing beyond the crashing of the surrounding buildings and hoped that having been severed at the ankle, the hulking monstrosity could not give chase.

The darkness of the alley was quickly giving way as the buildings on either side continued to collide against one another. Despite his intense focus on escaping the wretched alley alive, Vanimire saw the rapidly approaching crimson light. He didn't consider the beast might respond to his provocation by bringing the buildings down upon him, but should he live, it was a lesson he would not soon forget.

Once more, the hulking monstrosity let out a terrible roar, and Vanimire sensed the very earth tremble in fear beneath him again. The sound was quickly drowned out as the buildings crashed into the alley behind him, and Vanimire struggled to stay on his feet as the blast whipped past him.

It seemed he was running on the very winds themselves, for he sprinted through the alley faster than he ever ran before. When at last he emerged from between the crashing buildings, the momentum of the blast sent him hurtling through the air. He hit the ground hard, and a sickening whirl immediately engulfed the world around him as he rolled across the hard, cobbled stone.

Unable to maintain his grip as he collided against the ground, Vanimire sensed the warmth of the weapon subside. He heard it clink and scrape against the stone of the road as he continued to roll. As every bone and muscle in his body screamed in agony, he came to a stop, laying on his back with his eyes wearily cast up towards the night sky. His mind reeled with a mix of both pain and confusion, and though he knew he should scramble to his feet, he found his body would not move.

To Vanimire, it felt like the first moment of peace after a night filled with countless terrors. No stars lined the sky, consumed in a blanket of near total darkness, yet as his mind came to its senses, Vanimire noticed the crimson light which reflected off the winged beasts appeared to almost eerily recreate the night's beauty.

They've destroyed our world, and made it their own, he thought to himself as he lifted a hand upward towards it. Gone was the light of the heavens, and in its stead these monsters created their own terrible, twisted world.

Did the crimson beasts appreciate such beauty? Did they seek to walk beneath the light of the crimson moon with those they were fond of?

No one could answer because soon there would be no one left. Yet despite losing so much already, Vanimire found the most heart wrenching loss was of all that made the world so unnoticeably beautiful.

Unable to bear the sight of the twisted sky any longer, Vanimire rolled his head to the side, hoping the Watchtower was nearby. To his unfathomable delight, he saw the aged tower stretching high over the courtyard that the blast launched him through. There was still a vast distance separating him from his goal, but for the first time in what had felt like a lifetime, Vanimire had hope.

Warmth surged through him as his fingers wrapped once more around the grip of the sword, much to his surprise. He knew the blast had ripped the blade from his hand, but now he undeniably held it. Did he retrieve it in his stupor?

It mattered not, for he braced himself against it and wearily lifted his battered and sore body upright before casting his gaze across the courtyard separating him from the Watchtower.

Buildings that still raged with intense fires lined the courtyard on one side. Even with all the distance, Vanimire sensed the terrible heat raging from the dancing orange flames. Standing opposite the destroyed buildings, on the far end of the courtyard, was the beginning of the city docks.

As he expected, no boats remained, though the winged beasts littered the harbour with debris and destruction. It would seem fate prevented anyone from leaving the city alive, by land or by sea.

Vanimire turned his gaze back to the Watchtower standing opposite him, looming enticingly over the courtyard. The crimson beasts were there once, for bodies twisted in terrible agony littered the courtyard, but none of them remained. All that separated Vanimire was a few minutes of sprinting, and then, at last, he would come to the ancient and aged doors that would mark his success.

It all came down to this, all the struggles, all the loss, all the moments of self-doubt, and all the moments of minor victories. Despite everything stacked against him, and under the watchful eyes of the Gods who seemed fit to torment him, he succeeded. When he passed through those doors, he would undoubtedly draw the eyes of the city upon him, but in his sacrifice, he hoped he would save the lives of countless others. That sprint was all that remained.

Vanimire lifted the blade of Einor of Old, holding it with both hands as he breathed in the warmth and power it provided him. If he lived a normal life, he might have spent it learning more about the weapon, but the searing pain in his left arm reminded him otherwise. He needed to alert the Empire before the next tremor occurred, for it would undoubtedly be his last.

With a scream, Vanimire sprinted into the courtyard, feeling the terrible crimson light of the corrupted moon bear down upon him as he moved. All around him his city, and people, were burned and destroyed. He lost everything to these monsters, and to the Redcloaks who served that wretched six-eyed abomination.

Through this last act of courage and strength, he would earn his revenge. For the friends he knew, and the father he loved, Vanimire sprinted towards the Watchtower. For his people, he would sacrifice himself happily, not so that the historians might label him a wonderful ruler, but because he couldn't bear to see the wretched monsters continue their victory.

Through this, High King Vanimire, the sixteenth of the line of Eineriel, would give his all.

CHAPTER XIV

THE WATCHTOWER

"Seldom few are afforded the opportunity of looking upon their tomb, and yet, as I gazed upon the tower, it was clear to me where I'd find eternal rest."

VANIMIRE MOVED AS IF ACTING ON IMPULSE, HIS BODY ALIGHT WITH NEW life and energy. Through the longest night of his life, he lost so many aspects of his former self. With the betrayal of the Redcloaks, he lost the innocence of his youth. When Daromir threw him from the Gardens, he severed the last familial connection he had. When Ser Ralick died, he lost the only friend that he knew survived. Now, as he came to a stop before the Watchtower, he lost all fear of failure.

Vanimire cast his gaze upwards, panting as he breathed in the impressive sight of the Watchtower. It felt as if it took a multitude of lifetimes to reach it, but against all odds, he did it. The ancient doors looming ahead were all that remained to be opened.

Despite the world ending all around him, Vanimire's lips curled into a soft smile. He proved so many wrong in his journey. He proved his uncle wrong by surviving the fall and proved Syraxis wrong by killing him. Yet, most important of all, he proved himself wrong by accomplishing that which he thought was impossible.

With a deep breath, Vanimire approached the door. Just as his fingers brushed the ancient entryway, he stopped, leaping backwards as he watched crimson blood pour from between the cracks of the stone foundation. Vanimire held the blade close, continuing to put distance between him and the destination of his journey that was so tantalizingly close.

The blood continued to pour from between the stones, moving unnaturally as it formed a pool before the door of the Watchtower. When at last the pouring ceased, Vanimire watched as the pool rippled. To his horror, a figure emerged from it, lifting upwards as it formed the unmistakable shape of an armoured figure towering over the trembling Vanimire.

When the figure reached its full height, the colour of its form finally appeared. The hues of life emerging from the figure obscured the deep crimson of blood, revealing the Redcloak that Vanimire immediately recognized. Ealric stood between Vanimire and the doorway. Just as it was with both Syraxis and Daromir, his red cloak was in tatters, revealing the obsidian arm glowing beneath it.

Ealric gazed at Vanimire with a measure of disappointment, sighing as he took a step beyond the pool of blood which vanished after leaving it.

"So, they were right," Ealric muttered, his voice low and laced with the same disappointment etched into the lines of his expression.

"W...What do you mean?" Vanimire said, trying to appear calm as he furrowed his brow.

"Just before he died, Syraxis spoke of the weapon that was given new life. I suppose he meant you?" Ealric paused, scoffing as he held his hand to the side.

Much to Vanimire's surprise, a weapon seemed to appear from the lines of red lining his stone-like arm. Glowing droplets fell from the cracks, merging with each other to form a long, terrifying blade.

"Syraxis was a fool, and took those beneath him for granted far, far too often. I do not intend on making the same mistakes, princeling. Or should I call you High King? That *is* your title now, isn't it?"

Vanimire struggled to contain himself against the obvious slight. Unlike Syraxis and Daromir, he spent relatively little time in the company of Ealric. Even before the transgressions of the evening, the man was hard to get along with. Where Syraxis was irritating in his overconfidence, Ealric was dismissive and rude. A testament that admittance to the Redcloaks was based on prowess with the blade, rather than the tongue.

"H…How do you know what he said?" Vanimire spat as the man took a step forward.

He was quick to maintain the distance, the tip of his sword levelled toward the former Redcloak as he maintained a safe distance.

"We are all flames in the same endless night, little High King. When one of us dies, the rest quickly notice the absence of warmth." Ealric ceased his approach and instead lifted his obsidian arm towards the anxious Vanimire.

Unlike during the slaughter in the banquet hall, the lines that traced beneath the cracks in the stone-like exterior did not glow brighter. Vanimire leapt to the side, acting on instinct born from the dreadful memory of the slaughter in the banquet hall. He expected the spikes to rip through the air towards him, and confusion gripped him when they didn't come.

Vanimire watched silently as the cracks in his arm widened. He saw the arms twist and contort before, but there was something different about it this time. The small drops of darkened blood that continued to seep through the cracks poured freely as they widened. They pooled beneath the armoured boots of the Redcloak, staining the shattered stone as some droplets leapt upwards and hung in the air.

Much to his surprise, Vanimire watched in horror as the blood streamed up from the pool, twisting and merging as it took shape. As if from the air itself, Ealric produced a long blade, similar to the one Vanimire wielded.

However, its form continued to drip blood onto the ground beneath it, as if the form born of blood was melting beneath the summer sun. Ealric tightened his grip around its handle, lifting it up to face the confused Vanimire.

"I had no love for Syraxis in either of the lives we lived, but in killing him you have inflicted a wound unto us all, and for that, I will exact revenge."

Ealric moved faster than Vanimire could follow. In an instant, just as he finished speaking, his physical form twisted into blood before dropping to the ground. Vanimire instinctively pulled his blade closer to his chest, uncertain of where the attack would come from.

The pool of blood that emerged from the walls of the Watchtower stretched out until it pooled between all the nearby stones of the courtyard beneath them.

Before Vanimire caught his breath, the form of Ealric appeared right in front of him, lurching up from the darkened pool of blood. Ealric brought his sword down upon his surprised foe, but halted with the blade still held high. Vanimire watched as the man's arm trembled, as if he were fighting to control his very muscles.

Ealric's eyes widened and strained, as if he struggled under an impossible weight. The man showed all the clear signs of a struggle, and yet Vanimire had no sense of what might have been the cause. Ealric caught him wholly off-guard, and where a dedicated foe might have ended their battle before it begun, the Redcloak faltered. There was something strange about the moment, but Vanimire wouldn't refuse a gifted opportunity.

Acting on the man's momentary struggle, Vanimire took a half-step backwards as he brought the blade of the sword arcing down. As the blade sliced towards the foe it seemed to crave, the light radiating off the ancient metal intensified. Just as the blade's edge neared the man's shoulder, Ealric's material form shimmered and dissolved, dropping into a pool of blood with a splash.

Vanimire stumbled forward as the momentum of his swing connected with the stone courtyard beneath him. When he regained his footing, he shifted into a more defensive stance once more. It seemed to him an infuriatingly foolish effort to decipher where the next blow would come, for the pool of blood seeped between the cracks of the stone, growing with each passing moment. Vanimire let out a frustrated scream as he swung his blade down against the stone once more.

Though the blood splashed, there was little sign he connected with the hiding Ealric. Where the older man there to witness their bout, Vanimire was certain Ser Ralick would have been disappointed. *'A true knight stands proud, waiting in eager anticipation of any blow that might come!'*

Ealric's hesitation still bothered Vanimire, but before he could dwell upon it, the figure shot up from the bloodied pool, reemerging once more. Seemingly unable to bring the sword against the surprised Vanimire, Ealric instead contented himself with launching a gauntleted fist into his stomach.

Vanimire stumbled backwards. The world immediately became a darkened blur as all the air in his lungs escaped him. It took every ounce of his effort to not let go of the blade and collapse into a fit of wheezing gasps. Doing that would certainly lead to his demise, and he refused to die when he was so painfully close to his objective.

"Give up, little High King. You besting Syraxis speaks only to his incompetence, not your prowess. Even then, our master granted him only a glimpse of his power. A morsel offered to a ragged *mutt.* I, however, was given a taste of it." Ealric approached the dazed Vanimire as he spoke, bringing the gauntleted fist once more down against him.

Vanimire barely kept upright from the first blow and was not nearly as lucky when the second came. Immediately he stumbled backwards, falling to the ground with a crash. He tried to stand defiantly against the Redcloak approaching him, yet even it was in vain, as he was so easily knocked backwards. Though the world seemed barely recognizable through the veil of exhaustion and pain that gripped him, he still felt the warmth of the blade course through him.

How he kept hold of it, he did not know; in some ways, it felt as if the grip were glued to his palm. Yet so long as he felt the faint glimmer of warmth, he knew he stood a chance. The blade represented the strength of Einor of Old, and of the line of Eineriel which followed. It was capable of feats that Vanimire could never have hoped to achieve. So long as it was his to wield, death *may* be bested.

He needed but a single moment, an opportunity like he found when facing Syraxis. Yet when he faced the latter, the opportune moment came only when Ser Ralick sacrificed himself. How could he stand his own against someone who vastly out powered him, and do so without the aid of the experienced competence Ser Ralick provided?

Once more, Ealric raised the sword overhead, clearly intent on bringing it downwards against the man that could barely keep himself upright. Air had yet to find its way back into his lungs, and the world strained as Vanimire tried to force his gaze to focus. He scrambled to his feet only to fall to his knees, unable to find the strength to resist the blow that was certain to follow.

Vanimire could do nothing but watch as the obsidian arm moved down towards him. Ealrics face strained as the arm once more came to a sudden halt. Ealric's eyes once more strained and widened, and his jaw clenched so tightly that Vanimire heard *something* crunch within it.

Vanimire saw his opportunity, and he wouldn't let it slip him by.

Lurching forward, Vanimire brought his blade up from against the bloody pool that stretched out beneath him. He acted as if on instinct, channeling the entirety of his weight into the motion as he sought to capitalize on the moment of hesitation. His body was too weak and battered to act on his own accord.

Instead, he let the warmth of the blade course through him, guiding his hand as if the *weapon* were the one leading the charge. The blade of Einor of Old cut cleanly through the obsidian arm, slicing through it as if it were little more than weightless fabric. Vanimire hoped to sever the arm completely, but in his haste, he slipped upon the blood-slicked stones that crunched beneath his boot.

Though it was not perfect, Vanimire sliced the obsidian arm at the elbow, severing it from the man that now screamed in terrible agony. Ealric stumbled backwards as time slowed. Just as Vanimire was about to revel in his minor victory, he noticed the Redcloak was *smiling*. The hours that passed since their encounter with Syraxis was not enough for Vanimire to learn his lesson, for once more he fell into his opponent's trap.

Ealric twisted away from Vanimire's blade, bringing his armored boot upward to collide with Vanimire's stomach. His vision faltered as pain surged through him, and as he stumbled backwards, he watched as Ealric grabbed the severed arm from the air. Just as it had when he faced Syraxis, the mistake he made dawned on him. He focused too intensely on the power of the obsidian arm, and in doing so, didn't realize that the internal struggle Ealric was suffering *came* from the arm. The moment it was severed, Ealric appeared unleashed. The moments of hesitation came from the side of Ealric that wished to save the High King. The side that Vanimire had unknowingly *severed*.

Before Vanimire recovered from the kick to his stomach, Ealric set upon him once more. Holding the hand that still clutched the crimson sword, he lurched forward, unleashing a fury of swipes at the stumbling Vanimire. To his surprise, he parried most of them away. His head reeled from the pain coursing through him with every movement as his muscles screamed in agony.

He sensed the colours of the world drain, drifting towards the edge of his vision before vanishing completely, like water sucked down a drain. Just as it had when he faced Syraxis, the world immediately blazed in a glory of white. He saw the outlines of Ealric and the Watchtower behind him, their forms without definition, yet Vanimire *felt* where they were.

Time itself paused, leaving the Redcloak, or at least what Vanimire sensed of the Redcloak, suspended in his onslaught. It was only a moment. A blink of something whose existence stupefied Vanimire, and as colour flooded his vision once more, Ealric lurched towards him.

Though he felt more powerful than he did in hours, Vanimire's luck soon ran out. Ealric brought his blade upwards in a different motion, and though Vanimire blocked it, the force of the blow knocked his arms upwards. The moment finally presented itself, and just as Vanimire was keen to capitalize on it, so too was Ealric. He moved faster than Vanimire could follow, dropping his bloodied sword down before thrusting the tip forward.

Pain unlike anything he ever experienced surged through him. The feeling of Ealric's unnatural sword piercing through his stomach immediately caused him to drop his weapon, unable to even form a coherent thought, as the pain was unbearable. The blade sent a chill through him, which was pursued by a hellfire which threatened to consume all his senses completely.

An excruciating sensation rushed over him as he felt his blood pour against the blade that pierced him. Ealric twisted it, sending another unbearable wave of pain rippling through him as he screamed in agony. The noises were a delight to the Redcloak, who watched Vanimire with a curious delight.

"Too slow, High King," he hissed, leaning in so close, Vanimire smelt his terrible breath against his face. "Syraxis was a fluke."

Vanimire opened his lips but could not form any words. His body was alight with agony, and without the warmth of the blade in his hand, he felt his luck ran out.

Perhaps this was his fate all along, to get within a stone's throw of his destination, only to fall at the hands of one who outclassed him in every regard. Blood poured from where the sword still pierced him, and Vanimire sensed an uncomfortable chill grip him. Was it the claws of death he avoided for so long?

The feeling of the sword's removal pulled his mind from its pain-addled musings. Vanimire screamed once more as the shape of the sword disappeared, dropping back into bloody liquid, which was soon lost to the pool beneath them. He wondered how he still stood, though Ealric found his wavering amusing.

"Two High Kings have died this night." Ealric hissed, his gaze still laced with a quiet confusion as he studied the defeated Vanimire. "Though I suppose of the two, you put up the better fight."

Ealric's lips parted in a terrible smile, and Vanimire felt a wave of anger spike in him. The Redcloaks took everything from him, and worse of all, mocked him for his losses at every turn. He hoped to save the rest of his people by activating the Watchtower, yet Ealric robbed him of that. If he could only enact some measure of vengeance upon the wretched Redcloak, then it would provide him with one last dying of comfort.

Vanimire struggled to lift his eyes upward to meet the gaze of the repulsive Redcloak. The colour of the world was hazy, and as his anger continued to rise, anything beyond the form of the Redcloak in front of him drifted away into obscurity.

There was nothing more he wanted, nothing more he could think of, than killing the man who mocked him. Ealric represented all that he lost, and all which was taken from him, and though every breath was agonizing, he panted with increased fervour as he watched the Redcloaks' wicked smile.

Vanimire pressed a hand against his stomach, trying desperately to stop the blood that poured freely with every weary pant that escaped him. Ealric seemed content to watch his conquered foe, his smile growing ever larger with each moment. Though each breath sent a wave of pain coursing through him, Vanimire found himself consumed by a rage unlike anything he ever felt.

The man before him, embodying all that was destroyed, taunted him with a disgusting, nonchalant smile. As he focused his gaze upon the figure driving all his senses into a frenzy, it felt to him as if with each breath he exhaled fire.

Steam seemed to pass through his clenched teeth, and though he had at first thought it to be a product of his exhausted mind, Ealric noticed it as well.

Confusion slowly overtook the Redcloak's expression, his features lifting in silent surprise as he watched the wavering man. Vanimire tried to summon all the strength coursing through him, knowing if he were to die in this moment, he would wish for nothing more than to bring the wretched Redcloak down with him.

Fire surged in his veins, causing all his senses to burn with the intensity of the midday sun. In an instant, all the pain he felt was gone, replaced instead with a blazing inferno he felt through every fibre of his being. His vision roared back into focus as the colour of the world vanished.

Beyond the figure of Ealric, he saw the unmistakable figure of his father emerge from the white veil. The man's face bore no expression beyond the smile tugging at his lips. As tears stung Vanimire's eyes, he saw countless other individuals stretching out beyond his father.

He knew not their names but felt in them a part of himself that spoke to him the truth that his mind was desperate to hear. His actions, his life, and his choices, were looked upon by his ancestors. Wherever they were consigned to, he felt their presence surge through him, giving fire to his veins and spurring his aching muscles into action once more.

The line of Eineriel watched him..

Vanimire let out a wicked scream as he lurched forward, bringing his left hand forward to grip the head of the shocked Ealric. He felt the tremor tear at him once again, and though he was certain it would have been his last, under the watchful gaze of those who came before him, he felt confident in his ability to bridle the oncoming storm.

Time itself slowed as Vanimire held Ealric's head in his grip. His arm glowed with the brilliant light that radiated off the blade of Einor of Old. Its radiance was blinding, yet through it, Vanimire saw genuine fear in Ealric's expression.

Vanimire saw the pain tear through him, the tremor appearing to him like a flash of white that coursed through his body. In that moment, Vanimire felt the hand of his father resting upon his shoulder, and knew he had the strength to overcome the last hurdle separating him.

Vanimire surged forward, pressing the flashing white of the tremor through his arm and into the mind of Ealric. A flash of light instantly engulfed his left arm, causing Vanimire to stumble backward and release the writhing Redcloak. Colour dripped wearily back into the whitewashed world, and Vanimire felt the rage filled power inhibiting him slowly depart.

Confused, Vanimire glanced to his left arm, only to see it was left seared from whatever possessed him. Gone was the cloth of his attire, leaving only a burnt edge wearily clinging to his singed skin. The tremor subsided, and though it seemed to have claimed the ordinary appearance of his left arm, he felt no pain emanate from the burned surface.

As the unspeakable power faded, the warmth from the blade in Vanimire's right hand remained. How it got there he did not know, but he was thankful to feel its comforting presence once more.

Content he was none the worse for wear, Vanimire turned his attention to writhing Ealric. His body twisted and contorted as if gripped by a fit of madness, his scream echoed through the abandoned courtyard. Vanimire watched quietly as the man shook, holding the blade of the sword towards him in case the madness-struck man tried to lurch forward.

Much to Vanimire's surprise, when at last the writhing subsided, Ealric fell to his knees, his body barely able to keep itself upright. All that remained of the obsidian arm slowly burned away, turning from ashes into nothingness as it carried on the eternal evening air. Vanimire took a step closer, pressing the tip of the blade against the defeated man's head.

"We were prisoners," Ealric whispered, his voice broken and weary.

Whatever Vanimire did seemed to have tormented the former Redcloak in a way Vanimire couldn't describe. Ealric's features were softened with pain.

"Prisoners to fate."

"What?" Vanimire muttered, removing the tip of his blade from against the man's head. "Who is it that's speaking? Ealric the Redcloak? Or Ealric the monster?"

Silence fell over the kneeling man, and Vanimire saw his body shook quietly as tears fell.

"There is no difference any longer." Ealric muttered.

"Who is Veristeriax!?" Vanimire screamed, kneeling so he could peer at the defeated Ealric properly. "Who is the six-eyed man!? Please tell me!"

Ealric lifted his head, and Vanimire saw all the pride and terror that inhibited his features vanished alongside the obsidian arm.

"I don't have much time," Ealric whispered. His tears continued to roll down his stained cheeks.

"They will find me soon, and I would not have them use me against you. Please Vanimire. Activate the Watchtower. Find the Order."

Vanimire opened his lips to ask more questions, yet before he could speak, he watched as Ealric's physical form give way to blood before dropping into the pool beneath them.

Vanimire immediately stood up, holding his sword upwards in preparation of another attack, but to his surprise, the pool of blood slowly moved through the cracked stones of the courtyard, until at last they disappeared into the black waters of the harbour.

CHAPTER XV

DESTINY SEALED

"Yet, with fear thrumming in his chest louder than the roaring cannons, he pushed on, intent on facing destiny itself."

Vanimire had not a moment to mourn the passing of the man he once knew before the beasts set themselves upon him once more. From the red skies above, the winged horrors swooped down with renewed vicious hatred as their claws were still wet with the blood of their victims.

Acting purely on adrenaline-fuelled instinct, Vanimire threw himself towards the Watchtower, using all the strength he could muster from his battered body to move the heavy doors.

The massive doors scrapped along the carved floor as dust from the seldom moved cracks fell upon him. Despite giving his every effort, he could not move fast enough. Searing pain shot through him as the winged beasts laced their claws against his exposed back. The wounds cut deep, and Vanimire sensed the warmth of his blood as it soaked his tattered clothes.

When the smallest crack appeared between the doors of the Watchtower, Vanimire threw himself through it, narrowly avoiding the next onslaught, which would certainly spell his demise. He stumbled into the dark hall of the Watchtower, falling to the ground as his momentum carried him desperately towards safety.

He clamoured to his feet, tossing his blade to the side as he once more threw his weight against the doors. To his relief, they ground back into place. As the last vestiges of crimson waned, he wondered if he would ever get to bask beneath the moon's glow again.

The doors to the Watchtower closed with a low boom that echoed through the empty hall. Relief washed over Vanimire as he collapsed to the ground, allowing himself a moment to catch his breath as his eyes adjusted to the low light surrounding him.

Small stones, enchanted centuries ago, held in their sconces, cast the small chamber in a blue light that mesmerized Vanimire. How long was it since he last visited the Watchtower?

He remembered the warm days of his youth when everything seemed both new and exciting. When did that part of him die, leaving only the beaten and broken shell that he now was?

Vanimire braced himself against the doors of the Watchtower, easing himself up with a shaking hand as he realized the extent of his exhaustion. Never did he feel so weak, as if his body were balancing upon the very precipice of life itself. The talons of the winged beasts left their mark, for every slight movement sent a wave of white-hot pain searing through him.

As he stumbled to his feet, one truth became painfully apparent to him: these were to be the last moments of his life. Whether it be the wounds that cut deep into his back, or the next tremor that tore through his already seared and agonizing left arm. He had but a few precious moments to alter the course of history.

The night events altered the course of the entire island Empire. Cast beneath the light of the crimson moon, the fate of the very world itself was called into question. Under the unsettling gaze of the six-eyed figure, the Redcloaks, and the nightmare-born beasts, the Capital City was devastated within hours.

Vanimire couldn't possibly know if any survived the onslaught. After all he encountered, and all the endless struggles he just barely overcame, it seemed unlikely any would have had the same measure of luck.

The Capital City may have been the first to fall, but Vanimire was certain the rest of the empire would follow. Aerturiel would share a similar fate, for the six-eyed Herald seemed intent on consuming all that stood before them.

With one hand bracing himself against the door that was stained with his own blood, Vanimire reached down to wrap his fingers around the hilt of his blade, slowly lifting it upwards as he balanced the tip along the carved stone tiles. Vanimire, using the weapon's strength, inched towards the centre table, having besmirched the blade of Einor of Old in its final moments.

The weapon of legend became little more than a walking stick, helping the battered High King forward. Nameless, departed authors composed the various maps, pages, and other writings that covered the surrounding walls. Vanimire could have spent a lifetime in this room, perusing the various scribblings and learning some of what those who held their vigil before him considered important enough to leave behind. Just as they stole his friends, his family, and his comfort, the crimson moon robbed him of his future as well.

Vanimire crashed into the side of the stone table, resting the blade against it as he braced himself with two unsteady hands. Carved into the very stone-face of the table itself was a depiction of the Empire, with deep sigils and etchings marking the various cities. The table always impressed Vanimire, for he knew there was something unnatural about it.

The carved table the council gathered around seemed little more than a cheap imitation. An attempt at recreating something much older and more powerful. Despite the Watchtower having gone unused for many years, the table's stone face portrayed an accurate image of the Empire, including small towns that were only recently settled in the peaceful years that the Empire had known.

Vanimire ran his fingers along the beautifully intricate depiction of the capital city. Nestled against the mountain, and sprawling out towards the ocean that graced it, the city was all Vanimire ever knew. How strange it was that the city, despite being his entire world, seemed so small in the grand scale of things.

He saw the fields and forests stretching beyond eyesight from even the city's highest peak. Seeing how the rivers twisted and turned from the great mountain ranges, bringing both life and serenity down to the cities springing up alongside them. Held in its stone visage, the Empire seemed so peaceful, as if time itself froze in the gentle warmth of spring.

Yet, Vanimire knew there was a much wider world beyond the shores of the Empire. A world he never got to know.

A terrible scream shook the very building itself, sending dust and pebbles falling down upon the distracted Vanimire. The scream instantly broke his concentration, and tears welled in his eyes as he realized that although the stone table depicted the empire, its tranquil reflection would never again be realized.

Immediately he was pulled from his thoughts, and tears welled as he realized that however the stone table depicted the empire, it could never depict the same tranquil image it bore now. This was to be a snapshot of the empire's last moments. A silent memory of life before the vicious terrors that toppled the capital.

Never again would the gentle days of spring grace the denizens of Aerturiel. Gone were the days of serenity and relaxation, leaving only the endless torment and struggles that were certain to come. Perhaps, Vanimire wondered, death was a blessing. His struggles would soon cease, and he would enter whatever awaited him in just a few moments.

Before that happened, he needed to finish what he started. Though the corners of his vision blurred from the overwhelming pain that wrought him, Vanimire summoned all the strength he had, focusing his attention on the carved table sprawling out beneath his fingers. He knew a system to warn all the other Watchtowers of the Empire was built into the device. Yet, he never thought to ask how it worked. Hells, it was likely his own father wasn't aware either.

Centuries ago, builders constructed the Watchtower to ward off dangers threatening the entire Empire. Yet as the Empire's strength grew, the need for the Watchtowers diminished. They remained only as a relic for the turbulent years of foundation, and now, when the world needed them most, Vanimire realized he had absolutely no idea how to operate them.

Fighting against both the waning minutes of his life, and the fear that threatened to cripple him, he scanned every inch of the table, desperate to figure out how to make sure his entire journey wasn't for naught. His chest rose and fell from panicked gasps, each movement sending a wave of pain tearing through him until at last his fingers moved over a small indent along the base of the table.

Wasting no time, he pressed against the stone, and to his relief, heard a small click.

The carved rune that identified the capital city lifted and moved to the side, revealing a greater indent beneath its surface. Vanimire leaned over as another terrible scream ripped through the foundation of the building. The beasts were clearly gathering in strength, and it would only be a matter of time before they brought the very weight of the Watchtower down upon the last High King.

The low light of the Watchtower was enough to make every quest for insight a struggle. Moving desperately with what little time remained, Vanimire fingered along the newly created opening, trying to feel if there was any sign of a switch or other device. Though clearly undamaged by years of disuse, Vanimire still needed to discover how to operate the table.

Those who crafted it didn't leave behind any explicit instruction. He felt a small slit that sat in the middle of the new opening, and as he moved his fingers along it, a realization sprung forth from the depths of his mind.

The small slit had a distinct shape, and Vanimire realized it wasn't the first time he'd felt it. With a shaking hand, he reached for his neck, digging beneath the sweat-stained fabric of his clothes and lifting out the necklace that he attached his signet ring onto.

Though his hand felt naked without it, in the aftermath of their escape from the palace, the blood and sweat had caused it to slip off, and Vanimire would not lose one of the last reminders he had of his father. The low light of the Watchtower caught on the carved face of the ring, making the curious symbol glow. Lines cut through a small central diamond, forming the shape of a backwards 'E' on its left, and the slope of the mountain where the castle stood on its right.

His father, upon presenting the ring, said it symbolized Eineriel's blood flowing through the mountain's veins, empowering the protectors of the city. To Vanimire, however, it seemed more akin to the twinkling radiance of the north star.

Vanimire took the ring in hand, turning it over and pressing it face down against the slit that appeared beneath the rune of the capital city. To his relief, it fit perfectly, and there was a satisfying click as he pressed the entire slot down onto the table itself. He focused on the glowing carved runes as he pressed the ring into the table causing the world beyond the Watchtower to drift into uneasy obscurity.

Vanimire panted from both excitement and exhaustion as he watched the glowing runes, waiting for something, *anything*, to happen.

Time itself came to a standstill, and yet, despite holding the ring in place, no response came. Vanimire's eyes widened as fear once more clawed against his soul. He pushed the ring into the slit over and over, watching as the runes glowed and withered.

Looking across the stone table, he studied the runes marking the names of the other cities, and yet, no response came. He wasn't sure how it worked, but he hoped *something* would have appeared. If the tables were connected, then he hoped anyone in other Watchtowers would see the glowing runes and realize that *something* was amiss. Despite desperately throwing his plea into the void, no response came.

"Dammit!" Vanimire screamed, bringing a fist down against the table with such ferocity blood splattered across the silent surface. "All these damned struggles. All the people I've lost. Just for... for nothing?!"

He shut his eyes as tears streamed down, bringing his fist down upon the table repeatedly as all the stress, terror, and exhaustion overwhelmed him. His fist, battered and broken, stained the table crimson, but no one heeded his warning.

The fall of the capital would result in the massacre of all its citizens, all to no avail. Any hope that their sacrifice would somehow warn the rest of the Empire was in vain. Time would forget them, and the world would end in the days that followed.

Vanimire collapsed to his knees, his arms sprawled out against the stone table as grief overwhelmed him. His sobs racked his body as he mourned his lost father, the friends surely caught in the chaos, and the people he failed.

If only he were more attentive. If only he considered the weight of his position and not squandered it so selfishly. Perhaps then he might have been the saviour that his people so desperately needed. No, he lived his life as if he were any other noble, enjoying the excesses of life at the expense of his understanding, and in the end, he let an entire generation of his citizens down for it.

As he lay crumpled and devastated against the stone table, a warm light bathed his face just as he thought all hope was lost. Immediately, Vanimire glanced up. The stinging tears blurred his vision, but he painstakingly pulled himself upright, wiping them away as he saw the most magnificent sight he ever seen.

The runes on the table slowly glowed. One-by-one, moving as if a wave spreading outwards from the carved runes of the various cities in the Empire lit up. They held their glow, and Vanimire scrambled to push the pendant back into its slot.

"I'm still here!" He screamed, watching in amazement as all the runes of the cities glowed.

Though unable to learn all that happened in the capital, he conveyed something was wrong. The orange light of the glowing runes alerted the entire Empire that a foe threatened them all once more, and Vanimire was certain they would remain alert.

Warm tears stung his eyes, and for the first time since the beginning of the long and dreadful night, Vanimire sensed hope swell in him. These were not the cold stinging tears of despair; tears for the friends and family he lost. No, these were tears of what might come to pass on the morrow.

The presence of the red moon would no longer signify the passing of days. Having alerted the Empire at large, Vanimire was confident a day would come where the combined might of men would push back against the vile beasts that so deftly destroyed the capital.

The glowing runes on the table darkened one by one, each giving one last burst of light to confirm the message's receipt. When the last rune silenced, and the low light of the Watchtower washed over him once more, Vanimire removed his signet ring, resting it along the side of the table.

"Please don't forget me. Don't forget about our sacrifices." He muttered, the tears stinging his cheeks as another terrible scream shook the Watchtower.

He accomplished that which he set out to do, and now that he managed such an impossible feat, there was only one fate awaiting him. His vision continued to blur, and he sensed the chilly claws of mortality rake against his soul. The wounds on his back were deep, and with no hope of salvation for the devastated city, the Watchtower was to be his tomb.

"I'm scared," Vanimire whispered, cupping a shaking hand over his mouth as he shut his eyes.

Death was always a natural part of life, and never was it more terrifying than when it stood before you. His was a life always intricately tied with death. Death was the ink in which the historical accounts were written, whether they detailed expeditions or the Empire's founding.

Yet, this time, it was not the stories of ancient and remembered heroes, or the records of great triumphs. No, for Vanimire, the last of the line of Eineriel, death was to be the veil that dragged him into obscurity. There would be no account of his demise, no story or legend of his struggles.

In the world that followed, historians would speak only of the significant efforts of the survivors, who, Vanimire hoped, would push back the vile beasts born from the crimson moon.

"I suppose it's time," Vanimire mumbled, his shaking voice failing to inspire some semblance of confidence.

He would ensure he took a few more beasts with him into oblivion, even if history forgot him. He wouldn't cower in the Watchtower, waiting for death to find him. No, he would look towards it with his head held high, and with blade in hand, show the forces of the world the line of Eineriel does not go quietly.

Vanimire reached for the blade, wrapping his fingers around the hilt as he lifted the blade upwards. Even in the low light of the Watchtower, the beauty of the blade did not diminish.

There was an otherworldliness to the design, for in its blade the very light of the stars that were stolen from the skies above them danced. Even holding the blade sent a measure of warmth through him, and, even if only faintly, it instilled in him a measure of resigned certainty.

He *would* die, more than likely soon, but it was a fate destined for all, and one that was unavoidable.

With a silent nod, Vanimire inhaled a deep breath, trying to stabilize his swirling vision as he glanced towards the doors of the Watchtower. The first step was always the hardest, and even having resigned himself to his fate, Vanimire struggled to make his feet move towards his destiny.

His breathing grew ragged as he sucked in a sharp breath, letting out a sharp scream as if to force his body into its reluctant action.

Vanimire forced his body forwards, sensing every fibre of his being scream out in agony as he took the first step towards the fate that awaited him. Yet just as he moved towards the doors of the Watchtower, an unexpected noise caused him to leap in surprise.

In his effort to inspire himself onwards, he didn't notice the low mechanical clicking that echoed from within the large ornate table holding the depiction of the Empire. He was so concentrated that the low clicks and groans went unnoticed until, with a loud scraping groan, the centrepieces of the table retracted inwards.

Vanimire stumbled back to the table, his eyes poring over the moving pieces in desperate hope there was more to its design than he first imagined. Despite having resigned himself to his fate, he hoped some ancient escape route might open itself to him, allowing him to flee the city and nurse his wounds before leading the charge to retake it.

It was a selfishly vain wish, for the rational side of his mind knew he already suffered far too much damage to make travel possible. Even if he didn't take the back wounds into account, he knew the next time his left arm suffered its tremors, it would certainly spell the end of him, regardless.

Vanimire couldn't help but watch in amazement as a large swath was cut through the centre of the Empire. The table comprised countless small squares, each pushing upwards to connect with the others, thus creating the map of the Empire.

The clicks and groans grew louder as Vanimire watched a line through the centre of the Empire lower into the table, and when at last the machinations of the table ceased their movement, Vanimire peered in stunned shock to see beneath the surface of the Empire's depiction lay a massive indent appearing to match the shape of the Blade of Einor of Old.

Vanimire leaned forward, running his fingers over the carved runes that were inscribed around where the blade of the sword would have rested.

By the might of my bloodline, my blade shall bear witness to the golden dawn. See the strength that runs through my progeny. Let the Golden Akura be born anew.

Vanimire's heart sunk as the words echoed in his mind. Despite the indent clearly matching the shape of Einor's blade, the inscription left Vanimire with more questions than he had answers. Time was crucial, and although he wanted to spend weeks studying the inscription's meaning, he knew he lacked that luxury.

Let the Golden Akura be born anew.

In all the tomes and annals he read over the years, never had such a word stuck out to him. Was it possible the table predated the Watchtower, and that whatever this Golden Akura was, it referenced some ancient and forgotten civilization?

Vanimire's breathing quickened as his mind raced for answers. Another terrible scream through the skies overhead reminded him of how precious little time he had left. He wasn't sure what the inscription meant, nor why a resting spot for the Blade of Einor of Old was hidden beneath the table, but there was a part of his soul tugging him towards it. As if the very warmth of the blade itself was urging him towards the indent.

"Dammit!" Vanimire screamed, smashing his fist on the table once more.

In an instant, his hopes for a secret escape vanished, leaving him only riddles and little time to solve them. There was something about the inscription that seemed of vital import, as if figuring out what it meant might offer some measure of salvation.

What if the Golden Akura was an ancient army? Or a device that could destroy the crimson moon itself?

Vanimire shook his head, letting out a hiss of frustration as he lifted the Blade of Einor of Old with both hands, leaning over the table and gently resting it into the indent.

Placing the sword into the indent was a gamble, for Vanimire knew that without it there was no hope in him defeating the beasts that awaited him just beyond the nearby doors. Yet, what did it matter?

Whether death was to find him in three minutes or thirty, it drew ever nearer. If placing the blade into the indent revealed whatever this *Golden Akura* was, then what did he have to lose?

With the blade placed in the indent, Vanimire leaned upright, resting his hands along the edge of the table as he watched with vicious curiosity. The world around him drifted into obscurity, broken only by the sharp screams of the beasts looming beyond the walls of the Watchtower.

Vanimire couldn't help but think that this last discovery was intricately tied with his fate, or what remained of it. The moments passed by in silent uncertainty as nothing appeared to happen. If it were some ancient device, then it could very likely have been non-functional after the long years of maltreatment. What a cruel twist of fate it would be. The key to salvation destroyed because no one knew of its existence.

Just as Vanimire lost hope, a low hum echoed through the Watchtower. Vanimire's breath hitched as the inscribed runes glowed a brilliant gold, which soon bled into the indent itself, encasing the blade in a blanket of such resplendence that it was almost overwhelming. Vanimire raised a hand to his eyes, desperate to block the light that glowed with all the intensity of the midday sun.

The tower itself shook, not from the screams or claws of the terrors that loomed beyond them, but from the very foundation itself. Such light and warmth, unlike anything he ever knew, enveloped him. The still air of the Watchtower crackled and hummed with excitement, as if the winds themselves were singing some unheard song of eager anticipation.

Brilliant yellows and oranges, stronger than the rising sun, quickly consumed the Watchtower. The low hanging lights glowed so brightly the enchanted stones burst. The tower continued to shake violently until at last a massive boom ripped through it.

The explosion of light sent Vanimire flying backwards from the table. He hit the ground hard, rolling along it as light engulfed the entire hall of the Watchtower.

Dazed from the sudden burst, and blinded by the overwhelming light surrounding him, Vanimire could hardly make out what was going on. The sea of light and serenity cast him adrift, and it felt warmer than the gentlest summer day, making time seem askew. Then, just as quickly as it appeared, the light vanished, sucking in towards the Blade of Einor of Old on gusts of wind that ripped all the maps and pages from the walls of the Watchtower.

Vanimire sat alone in the darkness, his chest heaving from ragged, exasperated breaths as he tried to make sense of all that had just happened. The blade of Einor of Old glowed softly, providing a warm sensation that emanated from the centre of the mysterious table.

Summoning all the strength he could muster, Vanimire braced himself against the nearby wall, lifting himself to his feet as he strained to overcome the pain that wrought him once more. Wearily, he stumbled towards the central table, amazed at the newfound resplendence of the blade.

Small wispy tendrils of light seemed to dance from the silver blade, moving lazily and nonchalantly through the air that was still warm from the sudden burst that sent Vanimire stumbling. The air fell heavy over the blade, humming with the power that now imbued it.

Something was different, Vanimire could tell that much, but as for what exactly changed, he could hardly garner a guess.

With his mouth agape in surprise, Vanimire reached out towards the handle of the blade, drawn to it by some innate desire. It felt to him an extension of his very self, and even the bit of distance separating them seemed insufferable. Vanimire needed the blade, and, as strange as it was, he felt as if the blade was calling out to him.

Something linked the two, whether it be the foes they conquered that night, or the blood coursing through Vanimire's veins. So determined was he to feel the warmth the blade instilled in him that all the pain flooding his battered body drifted away. All he needed was a single touch, and he knew all would be right in the world.

He brushed his fingers along the handle, a quiet gasp escaping him as the warmth coursed through him once more. Having experienced it, he wasn't sure how he ever lived without it. His breathing quickened as the soft tendrils of light danced above his hand, moving in more quick and excited fashion. It was unlike anything he ever encountered, but had that not summarized the plight of the entire evening?

The world itself seemed washed against the unimaginable, and for once, Vanimire was simply happy that, in this instance, it was something good.

The warmth surging through him gave him a measure of relief, whether it was vain or otherwise. Vanimire *wanted* to believe that this was the turning point, that all the struggles and hardships which led him this far would lead to something better, undo the fatal wounds that still pained him, and see him through the obstacles that still stood in his way.

With the Blade of Einor of Old in hand, it felt as if such a feat were possible. For the first time that evening, Vanimire felt something he thought the crimson moon stole from him: hope.

Suddenly, the wispy tendrils paused, their movements growing erratic as they multiplied before Vanimire's very eyes.

"W...What?" Vanimire muttered, suddenly feeling a sense of dread wash over him as he recoiled his hand from the blade.

Realization washed over him in an instant, and the dread that ensued was far worse than any wound he had suffered.

"N…No!" He screamed, feeling the tremors in his left arm begin once more. "N…No please! I…I was so close!"

Pain seared through him as the golden light again overwhelmed his vision. Immediately, Vanimire dropped to his knees, clutching the searing arm as he screamed in bloodcurdling agony. The intense burning sensation ignited all his senses, ensuring he felt every bit of pain.

He writhed along the stone floor, his fingers pressing so tightly against his arm that he thought he might very well break it. The intense light consumed him. Its brilliance overwhelmed him, even with his eyes shut. He could not escape it.

Each second felt like an eternity as he writhed and screamed along the floor of the Watchtower. His body felt as if it was lit aflame, and the fingers clenching tightly against his left arm were certain that the pain had seared through the layers of flesh, burning, and cracking it as if he had cast his arm into a pit of coals.

Blood pooled beneath him as he twisted, screaming into the void for some measure of relief. He was so close to salvation, so close to finding a way through the wicked despair the crimson moon wrought. What a terrible trick from the Gods it was, allowing him to brush his fingers against greatness only to rob it out from beneath him.

Vanimire's vision quickly faltered as he felt his body speed towards the precipice of mortality. Every fibre of his being seared through him, sending so much pain through his battered body that as his vision darkened.

So intense was his agony that no words could form through the screams that echoed in the hall. He wished only for death to grab hold of him.

There, writhing pitifully against the stone floor of the Watchtower, the last High King of the line of Eineriel lay in the darkness of the forgotten building. As darkness quickly enveloped him, his breathing slowed. Feeling his soul's last vestiges surrender, he thought only of how close he came to saving his people and, however, here he would be known only as a failure.

As a tear crept down his cheek, he saw their faces in the

darkness. His father. His friends. The mother he'd spent most his life missing. They all waited for him beyond the veil, waited to be reunited once more in the warm, blissful eternity.

Gods, he missed them.

CHAPTER XVI

A CERULEAN DANCE

"Darkness consumed me, and Vanimire, last High-King of the Rhyserion Empire, and proud child of Aerturiel, died."

EVEN THE SICKENING LIGHT OF THE CRIMSON MOON COULD NOT ROB HER of her birthright. She flew through the twisting narrow streets of the devastated city, carried on the winds of her own momentum.

A glowing streak of sapphire followed in her wake, fighting back against the oppressive darkness that fell over the ruins of the capital. Through flame and smoke she soared, whistling on the winds as she raced with the familiar, all-enveloping sense of powerful warmth. Her flight drowned out the cries of man, the monsters, and the terrified sense of devastation.

Her focus was unwavering, and as the shadows of yet another horde of winged beasts appeared overhead, she twisted through the air, moving as if it were little more than water itself as she held her left hand towards them.

Blue light exploded from the cracks in her arm, arcing through the air like arrows as they soared towards their targets. The beams broke and multiplied, tearing through the army of winged beasts with an explosion that shook the buildings racing alongside her.

A lifetime of training culminated in this moment, and yet, now that hell itself ripped across their world, she couldn't help but feel disappointed. The stories of old painted their foes to be much, much more imposing than they turned out to be. Where were the World enders?

The beasts with jaws so large they could consume entire cities with ease. Compared to them, these mindless hordes were little more than vermin, so easily crushed beneath the weight of her boots. Yet despite her disappointment, she was careful to remind herself that such attitudes came only from the luxury of her inheritance.

For even these mindless hordes were far, far too devastating for the average citizen. A terrible crimson stained the streets beneath her, a constant reminder of her fortunate inheritance of a power that rivalled the Gods themselves.

Her glowing azure eyes flicked to the shadow looming before her, the figure growing rapidly closer as she soared through the narrowing streets.

"Kanah, aid me!" She thrust her sword forward, spinning through the air as it glowed a brilliant sapphire.

The massive, hulking beast barely had time to respond to the glowing light before she tore through its chest. The blade cut through skin and bone with ease, and as she passed through its disgusting form, the light of the blade exploded, sending azure arrows ripping outwards.

She landed on the stone walkway, flourishing the blade to her side as the hulking monstrosity erupted behind her. The sapphire arrows slowly vanished, burning the remains of the monster that stood taller than the houses surrounding it.

How many innocent civilians did it feast on before she cut it down?

She grit her teeth. If only she were more cognizant, more aware. If she acted even a minute or two sooner, she might have saved tens or dozens more from their fate.

'You weren't able to save the ones in the chapel.'

No, there was a time and place for such consideration, but only after her mission concluded. To falter for even a moment would certainly bring about her demise, and though she loathed the notion that Kellear was quick to remind her of, her death would cost the world much more than those whose broken bodies lined the surrounding streets.

With her sapphire gaze cast up toward the crimson skies, she clutched her fingers tighter around the grip of the blade. The monstrosities tearing through the city would scarcely give her a moment to catch her breath, and just as she expected, another swarm was quick to descend upon her.

They acted not on individual instinct, but as some mindless collective. She was certain her presence alone caused the hordes to become alerted to her position, for they were desperate to overwhelm her.

To the beasts' misfortune, she woefully outmatched them. For hers was an order that always lived within the folds of the world, content to maintain their silent vigil until the day came where they could remain idle no longer.

The crimson moon unleashed more than just the terrible beasts upon the world. It caused them to awaken as well. A blessing, though it mattered little to those who'd succumbed to their fate already.

"Kanah," she whispered, feeling the blade hum in response to her call.

It was a sensation like no other, as if two souls intertwined beyond recognition of separation. Even if Kanah often looked upon her antics with dissatisfaction. She was as much the blade as the blade was her, and it was a power unlike any of their foes ever encountered.

With both hands wrapped around the handle of the elongated blade, she stood in the open square, waiting for the horde of winged monsters to descend upon her. They had some semblance of learning, for they tried to attack her in significantly greater numbers.

She could not understand to what extent they acted beyond the direction of those that controlled them, but until that moment of understanding presented itself, she was more than content to drown the streets in their wretched blood.

The storm of winged beasts descended upon her like hellfire. The beating of their countless wings was so loud it shook the very earth beneath her feet. Their approach was simple in its design but devastating in its effect. The beasts soared downwards, moving with such vicious speed one could blink and lose sight of them.

The woman closed her eyes, letting her senses dance amidst the sapphire waves swaying gently in her mind. Beyond the confines of her essence, the world was aflame with chaos and despair. Deep inside the walls of her own subconscious, there was an unshakable peace.

Confidence was as strong as the weapon she bore between her hands, and it was a flame whose embers never extinguished. If the beasts hoped to overwhelm her with terror, they did not know what awaited them. After all, she felt and overcame the terror that was inspired by their masters. Compared to them, these beasts were little more than vermin.

The cracks on her left arm shone a brilliant sapphire as the horde unleashed itself. The winged beasts raced towards her, screaming with such ferocity the stones beneath her feet trembled. Colour drained from her vision, pulled towards the edges as that brilliant, all-encompassing white consumed it.

Gone were the lines that defined the beast from the building, but it mattered little. She could feel where they were, could see them as black, wretched splotches against a white canvas. Time slowed, and though the beasts lurched towards her, they moved at a crawl, as if one were clamouring through mud.

She lingered, but methodically, arcing the blade around her as her corporeal form vanished and moved with all the ease of water flowing downhill. Each small motion was deliberate, and time seemed lost in the space between life itself. Though it required more finesse than handling some common thugs in an alleyway, these beasts were little more than a warmup for her by now.

Just as quickly as the light enveloped her, the colours of the world dripped back into focus. Small droplets of glowing sapphire hung in the air, marking the path she took in that space between consciousness. Time itself caught up, snapping like a band, and with a flick of her blade to the side, the droplets exploded.

Bursts of sapphire ripped through the open square, consuming the winged beasts in a torrent that destroyed them before they realized what happened. In the blink of an eye, she moved nearly twenty paces away from the spot they flung themselves towards. In her wake, she left a small example of all that her order was capable of.

She hardly appreciated how easily they dismantled such a massive force before another attacked her. This time they attacked her from both ground and air, intent on overwhelming every avenue of approach. Despite herself, she smiled, amused by their unsuccessful attempts to defeat her.

With the blade held to her side, she lurched forward, sprinting along the cracked stone of the open courtyard as her sapphire gaze brightened. She sensed the familiar warmth of power course through her as she moved with inhuman speed.

She swiped her arm through the air, unleashing a barrage of sapphire shards that ripped through the skies. The winged monstrosities didn't expect such a rapid assault, for the shards ripped through their wings before exploding in the surrounding air.

The beasts hardly had enough time to let out their wretched agonized screams before the blast consumed them. Unstoppable, she pressed her rapid advance against the enemies, trying to stop her.

Deprived of aerial support, the advancing monsters presented a minor distraction. After all, she was Eliira, inheritor of the Azure Akura. With the edge of her blade held towards them, she moved at an inhuman speed, leaving only thin glowing sapphire lines in her wake that crackled and buzzed with palpable excitement.

For the first time in many years, she felt free as the breeze rolling above her. Although the world itself teetered on the precipice of disaster, she couldn't help but smile quietly. This is what she spent a lifetime preparing for, and now that the moment presented itself, she was going to relish in every single moment of it.

No longer would she have to spend her days meandering through the twisting labyrinthian catacombs of the Capital City.

As she expected, the ground assault quickly opened itself as the monsters moved towards her at different speeds. The smallest of their kind could move as fast as a horse spurred to action. Yet such speed denied them the overwhelming power that the larger of their kind possessed. Dispatching these smaller foes required little effort on her part.

As she moved, the world itself seemed to slow once more, and she swung her blade through the air with unnatural ease. She soared past the smaller monstrosities, leaving in her wake their stumbling and devastated bodies. Her blade moved faster than the eyes of her foes could track it.

The blade hummed between her fingers, exulting in the blood it shed. Eliira giggled softly, glancing down to the blade, which appeared insatiable for the foes that dared to stand in their path.

"Having fun?" She muttered, raising a playful brow as she flicked the blood off the long blade.

Kanah hummed in turn, its wordless response evoking another quiet giggle from the woman who wielded it.

"Still no sign of it," she continued, glancing around the square surrounding her. The glow of her eyes softened as the cracks along her left arm dimmed.

"You felt it, though. Not long after, all this carnage began. So, it *must* be somewhere, right?" Her face scrunched in frustration, a response that earned a soft hum from the blade. "Where in the hells could it have been brought to?"

She had always been a woman of action, content to let the softer and more astute minds ponder the tomes and records that their order maintained. The time spent practicing with Kellear, honing her abilities, was far more memorable than the long hours spent studying with Faelwin. The sapphire light coursing through her left arm was created for a purpose, and it would be a waste to spend her days locked in the archives.

"We'll give the district one last sweep, Kanah," she said with a sigh, flourishing the blade through the heavy air as she felt the warmth of power surge through her once more.

"Faelwin won't like it, but I suppose, if need be, we can call on the others to help us scour the island. Hells, maybe it won't be necessary. It's been ages since the Order was united, anyway. What's one missing blade and Akura? We're already missing members as is."

Her boots clicked along the carved stone path as she set off into her stride once more. Devastation and destruction raged around her, and despite her instinct to save as many as she could, she knew such a pursuit would be in vain.

Hours passed since the light of the crimson moon appeared in the sky. Though she was late to make her ascent to the castle, she bore witness to the destruction that was wrought.

She was too late to save the High King and moments too late to rescue his heir. The line of Eineriel perished, and though no historical tomes would mention it, she was there to witness it all.

Even if she found the missing blade, tonight was a failure the likes of which she would never forget. No other in her order would taunt her for her mistakes, for each of them knew how deep an invisible wound the night carved in her.

What good was a shield if it couldn't deflect even a singular blow?

She must have grown languid during the days of her silent vigil. Her mind grew too easily intrigued by unsubstantiated rumours.

Beset only by the smaller monstrosities, she moved through the twisting alleys of the lower city with ease, her mind focused on her failures as she cut down countless enemies daring to stand in her path. Her boots barely touched the stone path beneath her as she soared upon the wind itself. Her body glided like the storm's breeze carried droplets of rain.

The walls and pathways racing around her bore the extent of the capital's devastation. It would have been a miracle if even a fraction of the population escaped, for the armies of the crimson moon descended and wrought its devastation instantly.

The attempt to save the capital's citizens failed, but she hoped to salvage Aerturiel from utter destruction. Though the banners of the Empire may burn, there was still time to save the world, and that was a pursuit she would never waver in. An avenue whereby she might manage to eek out a measure of redemption. *An apology to those whose blood pooled around her boots.*

She came to a halt in the centre of a small opening, and the wispy tendrils of light she left in her wake caught up with her. Despite her time spent in the shadows of the capital, she still struggled to wrap her head around its layout.

She wholly believed the story which claimed the city's builders intended to confuse anyone lost in its twisting and turning alleyways. Despite such unfamiliarity threatening to consume her, there was something strange about the air.

She squinted, letting the colour of the world pull towards the edges. Once more, an overwhelming veil of white light consumed her surroundings. Even in the unseen world, she could not make sense of the strange sensation.

It was as if the air itself danced in rapid excitement, moving frantically and vigorously around her. She let the colour drip back into her vision, not willing to exert herself with an unnecessary blink through the world unseen.

For the first time since the crimson moon appeared, she felt exposed, as if the world expected something that her mind could not fathom. She turned around rapidly, casting her glowing gaze across the square surrounding her as she raised her blade. Though she certainly looked a fool, it was all she could do to prepare for whatever was poised to break upon her at any moment.

A loud blast ripped through the skies above her, silencing the otherwise deafening devastation that gripped the city. Immediately, her gaze shot towards where the sound bellowed from. To her surprise, she saw a beam of light rip through the crimson skies, piercing the clouds and smoke that had formed a canopy of despair overhead.

"W…What the…" she muttered, lowering her hand as she gazed in awe at the tower of light emanating from elsewhere in the Low City.

The ground beneath her shook as a wave of warmth raced outwards from the source of the light. Eliira watched as the beam vanished, only to flicker a few more times before its glow returned in full radiance.

A chorus of screams which threatened to burst her eardrums quickly broke the silence that fell over the city. Though she wasn't sure what caused the tower of light to appear, the forces of the crimson moon were not pleased with it.

Once more, the air of the city changed, yet this time she could taste the searing hatred that warmed the surrounding space. It would be but a matter of time before the forces of the crimson moon would descend upon the tower of light, clearly finding in its existence a slight that deserved nothing but complete and total devastation.

It seemed to her the last sign needed to make her departure. The armies of monstrosities would likely regroup before they assaulted the last bastion of defence. Her responsibility weighed heavily on her, and though she yearned to join the final stalwart guardians, she knew she could not perish with them.

Not yet.

Just as she prepared to turn her back on the glowing tower of light, its overwhelming resplendence diminished once more. She couldn't help but feel a tinge of sorrow pass over her at what she suspected was the demise of whoever activated the tower.

The strands of fate appeared ever to surprise and confuse her, for just as she was about to depart from the ruined city, another blast ripped past her, sending her stumbling to the ground.

This one felt different. She sensed the air tremble with excitement, but no light shone against the oppressive crimson light. Her heart raced as she blinked, letting the colours of the world fade and be consumed by that veil of overwhelming white. The blast didn't come from the tower. It traveled through the world unseen. It had called out to *her*.

"H...Here?!" she screamed, clutching her blade tighter as she gazed toward the distant, faint glowing golden light in disbelief.

"Now!?" Her jaw clenched. "Curse the Gods!" she hissed, blinking her vision back into the familiar crimson world.

"All this time searching, and it reveals itself NOW?!"

She sighed, glancing down to the blade that hummed with so much excitement it nearly pulled itself free from her grip.

"You felt that too, didn't you Kanah?" The blade hummed. "That was *far* more than we felt earlier. That could only mean..." She shook her head, lowering the blade to her side as she cast her gaze once more towards where the tower of light had shone.

"Well. Let's see what awaits us then, hm?"

The corner of her lips lifted in a gentle smile as the cracks in her left arm glowed a brilliant sapphire.

Her vision swirled as her corporeal form glowed in unison, and, as if drops cast amidst the rolling breeze, she vanished. Her physical form reduced to little more than raindrops as she vanished from sight.

CHAPTER XVII

THE FORGOTTEN WATCHTOWER

"There was no applause, no mourning, and no terror. The beasts of the crimson moon silenced the screams of the world."

THE SHADOW OF THE WATCHTOWER STRETCHED ACROSS THE OPEN courtyard that sprawled out beneath it. Even here, the same devastation that plagued the city stained the quiet waterfront. Bodies of slain monsters lay strewn about, indicating a fight took place rather recently. The air burned with an unusual energy, and as her body slowly materialized from the winds that carried her, she couldn't help but sense a steady measure of excitement swell.

This is what she was searching for, if her and Kanah's suspicions were correct. Beyond the looming impressive doors of the Watchtower lay the single thing that might allow her to clutch a measure of success from the jaws of the otherwise overwhelming catastrophe of the evening.

There was but one problem. Resting between her and the Watchtower stood a tall, armoured figure. Blood stained his appearance from head to toe, but even through the thick, disgusting veil she made out his left arm, deformed and twisted, as black as the pre-crimson night sky. She realized this foe would not let her pass, and the tattered remains of a red cloak told her of the experience he wielded.

"Who are you?!" she hissed, clutching the blade tighter as she held its tip towards him.

"You and I aren't so dissimilar," he muttered, peering at her with a gaze that seemed to blaze with hatred.

He rolled his shoulders, flexing his left arm, which appeared more fitting on the monsters rather than on a man.

"You must be mistaken." She shot back chidingly.

Despite her own left arm being consumed by the stone-like exterior of the Akura, there was a beauty in its deliberate appearance. Like his, hers consumed the entirety of her arm, but there was a grace and fluidness to the sapphire that glowed beneath the cracks of her arm.

"We both bear the weight of power long since forgotten." As if on command, the crimson that rolled beneath the cracks of his arm shone brighter. "We both know what it means to toe the line between humanity and…greatness."

She scoffed at his words, finding in his pompous self-righteousness an overwhelming sense of disgust.

"You're little more than a cheap imitation," she hissed, narrowing her glowing sapphire gaze upon him. "The Gods themselves have preordained me. I was born to bear witness and shepherd the very Song itself. You simply imitate a power you do not understand."

Her smile only widened as she saw her words found their mark. The man's teeth clenched tightly as a low growl escaped him.

"*You* will be forgotten!" He spat, clenching his fist as the crimson glowed brighter. "The Gods are dead! And their wretched Akurien's are not far behind them!"

She paused, a curious brow lifting above her glowing sapphiric gaze.

"Where did you hear that word?"

Now it was the man's turn to smile.

"Hit a nerve, have I? Worried that the shadows your wretched order clings to aren't as dense as you once thought? Yes, my master knows all about your kind."

She tried to appear as nonchalant as she could manage. What he said *was* worrisome, but it would be a matter for the entirety of her order to contemplate when she returned. She already exchanged blows with another of his order.

Rhamun may have gotten away, but the former Redcloak had revealed much of how they fought. Perhaps in time Eliira would have to thank her. Before she executed the irritating woman, at the very least.

"What's your name?" Eliira asked, focusing her mind back on the matters at hand.

Though he possessed a cheap imitation of her arm, he was without a blade akin to Kanah, if even such a thing could exist.

"Does it matter?" He growled, tensing his left arm as he sensed the time for discussion rapidly reaching its conclusion.

"I only wish to know whose family I was robbing a son or father from," she replied.

Her smile widening as he once more growled in response to her chiding response.

The man paused for a moment as she raised her blade to prepare for the attack that was expected. Much to her surprise, the glowing crimson light seeping through the cracks of his abominable arm dimmed.

"In life I was Daromir, proud Redcloak and brother to the High King himself." He spoke with such clarity and softness it seemed to her as if a different person now stood before her.

The shadows that caught and danced in the hardened lines of his expressions seemed to wane. Though he maintained his stoic and cautious posture, there was a dejected sorrow lingering over him in those brief moments.

"What happened Daromir?" She asked, lowering her blade slightly as her glowing eyes strained to get a better look at him. "Who gave you that horrifying arm?"

Daromir stood silently for a few moments, letting the low breeze roll across his features. The scent of death and devastation filled the air, almost overwhelming the senses, revealing the extent of the city's despair. He finally muttered, glancing towards the woman with an exhausted gaze.

"The Six-Eyed Herald controls our fate."

"The Six-Eyed Herald?" She muttered, her brow furrowing as she tried to make sense of the cryptic words he spoke.

"I came here in search of that which should have died by my hand. I...I suppose I hoped the whispers through our order were true, and that his blade would free me from my torment. I hoped that…" His words stopped abruptly as his body seized and tensed, and he clutched his head, screaming sharply.

When his right hand lowered, the woman sensed whoever it was she was speaking with no longer stood before her. She lifted the tip of her blade once more towards him, watching as the crimson light shone brighter from his battered form.

"I will convey your message, Daromir of the Redcloaks. Even if you cannot hear my words, I, Eliira, known to those of my order as the Azure Akura, will seal your fate."

The time for talking concluded, and Daromir was clearly intent on concluding their duel as quickly as it began.

Large spikes erupted from the crimson light, roaring with vicious excitement as the obsidian layer of his arm cracked. The spikes shot towards her as Daromir charged, a strategy that resembled, to an almost pathetic degree, her own.

Eliira scoffed as she flourished her blade, deflecting the first spikes racing towards her as she lurched forward. Deliberately placing each footstep, she charged towards the approaching Daromir, weaving through the barrage of spikes as if she were the wind itself.

Her arm glowed with increasing brilliance. A ray of azure set against an overwhelming sea of crimson as she surged towards the former Redcloak.

She lurched to the side, ducking under another barrage of spikes as she swiped her left hand through the air, launching her own barrage of droplets that soared towards the approaching man.

Daromir, for his part, lacked the graceful fluidity his counterpart so masterfully exhibited. For Eliira, their duel was a dance pitting two celestial forces against one another. A confrontation that echoed the tense state of the world itself. Rhamun showed her much of what the corrupted Redcloaks could do. She *would not* let another slip away from her.

Daromir moved like a tumultuous wave battering the shoreline. He raced towards the approaching barrage of raindrops, moving with an irritating nonchalance as the small beads connected and detonated against his exterior.

Were Eliira any less experienced, she might have thought their confrontation over before it even began. Daromir emerged through the debris cloud from her explosion, seemingly unaffected as he held his glowing crimson arm across his chest. Even as he moved, spikes continued to twist and pierce through the rough exterior, falling from the broken cracks and hurtling towards her as the distance between them rapidly closed.

Eliira surged towards Daromir, blinking quickly to get a glimpse of the unseen world as she ducked under another barrage of spikes.

If there were any secret to his existence, it was not to be found in the world cast beneath the overwhelming veil of resplendent light. Even there, in the world whose brilliance shone so brightly it completely drowned out the colour, his crimson arm appeared twisted and vile. It was a cruel and wicked mockery of the gift she inherited. The very sight of it sent waves of irritation through her.

The familiar colours of the world bled back into focus as she reached Daromir. Kanah seemed to scream with excitement as she arced it towards the enraged Redcloak, moving the blade as if it were an extension of her arm.

Daromir appeared cautious of the blade, for even as the two came face-to-face, he opted to duck under the swing rather than meet it with his arm. He moved with a speed which equaled her own, and just as he ducked under her blade, he curled his obsidian fist and lurched forward.

Eliira saw the vile smile clinging to his lips. It dripped with a cockiness that only served to further irritate her. Kellear wore a similar one in the early days of their training, but there was a fondness and affection that was wholly lost on the Redcloak.

Daromir believed he outsmarted the Azure Akura, but if he was hoping for a quick confrontation, he would be sorely disappointed.

With a flash of sapphiric light, Eliira's corporeal form glowed. The Redcloak's curled fist punched clean through where her chest was only a moment before, but where skin, flesh, and bone had once stood, it punched through the watery visage she left behind.

She materialized behind him, her blade already moving quickly as she spun on her heel. Her movement resembled the rolling of an ocean wave. Daromir, surprised at how quickly she appeared behind him, and felt the sting of Kanah rip across the back of his legs.

Screaming as he stumbled forward, Daromir turned to face the foe who had appeared from the water that pooled between the cracks of the stone courtyard. The carved stone beneath them sizzled as his dark blood splattered across it. He struggled to lift his arm upwards to defend himself against the onslaught that followed.

Eliira was far too hesitant when facing Rhamun. Though the Redcloak escaped, she provided enough insight for Eliira to act with recklessness that the other members of her order would have chastised her for.

Except Torveck. He would have enjoyed it.

She moved with grace, bringing Kanah down in a flurry of blows against the stumbling Daromir. Every time the blade sunk against the flesh of the Redcloak, Eliira vanished, dropping into a pool of water only to materialize a moment later at a different angle.

Daromir screamed as the stones beneath him burned with his darkened blood, yet despite the searing agony, he tried to ensure Kanah did not connect against his twisted arm.

Eliira felt the surge of excitement course through her as she eviscerated her foe. Dancing between the veil of the world of colour and the unseen world required a lifetime of practice, and even then, it was both exhausting and dangerous. She pushed herself to her limits through the evening, drawing upon a well of energy and strength that had long lay dormant.

When the first wretched night concluded, she would certainly spend many weeks in recovery, but it could wait. She could not maintain the dance for long, but the Gods themselves would struggle to stand against her onslaught.

The resolve of the Redcloak surprised her, for even as her onslaught was nearing its conclusion, he stayed on his feet. His existence was an insult to all she represented, but he was clearly not a foe to be taken lightly. Dark blood poured from the countless wounds Kanah inflicted. As Kanah drank greedily, the glowing crimson light on his arm intensified.

Realization came too late for Eliira, who danced upon the precipice of the worlds. As a Redcloak, Daromir was one of the greatest swordsmen in the entire Empire. Now, the vile power granted by his abomination of an arm elevated him far beyond mortal comprehension. He lured her into the confrontation, allowing her to get close and unleash her fury, for he knew she thought herself superior to him.

Though she danced between worlds, he danced between life and death itself. He gambled with that which no mortal could conceivably offer: his own body. The agonizing pain that Kanah inflicted was not a deterrent, but an inspiration.

The crimson light flashed with such intensity that Eliira was nearly blinded, and a barrage of spikes ripped across her faster than she could drop her corporeal form. Though she stepped between worlds once more, appearing a dozen paces away from the Redcloak, the spikes inflicted their damage.

With the tip of Kanah pressed to the ground, she braced herself on the sword. Her chest rose and fell from ragged, pained breaths as the wounds seared with an almost overwhelming agony. These were not the cuts of a blade or a mortal weapon. These were much, much worse.

"How does it feel?!" Daromir roared, his human hand pressing against his side to stop the dark blood pouring freely from his wounds. "Yours is not the only gift that can inflict agony incomprehensible to mortal minds."

The colours of the world swirled before her eyes as she fought her body's instinct to flee to the unseen world. Her survival instinct poised to overwhelm her, lest she be careful. The searing wounds intensified as the spikes dug deeper into her exposed skin.

She knew something vile and wicked coated anything born from his twisted arm. How the wounds continued to sear was a cause for concern, and though she knew she could nurse her wounds with time, there was no way she would manage a prolonged fight any longer.

"You are still nothing more than a cheap imitation. An attempted copy crafted in the dark workshops of hell!" Eliira spat, straining to lift herself back up to her full height as she stood before him. "You might stand against the Azure Akura, but you'd be little more than a rodent when faced with the others."

Eliira inhaled sharply, feeling the cool air swell between her clenched teeth. She needed the fight to reach its conclusion so she could investigate whatever awaited her beyond the doors of the Watchtower. With her senses set ablaze by the spikes, she could not concentrate fully, limiting her ability to walk between worlds.

In her order, only those gifted with the legendary powers of being a *Dominant* could move between the worlds with ease. Though she had a surprising aptitude for it, she was still a full-armed Akura wielder.

As she stood there, silence fell over the world, consumed in chaos surrounding her. Daromir continued to gloat, his arms stretched out to either side, but his words fell on deaf ears, for something caught Eliira's attention.

The chaotic frenzy of their deadly dance consumed her, and she gave little thought to what she noticed in the unseen world. There, awash amidst the sea of overwhelming light, Daromir appeared as little more than an outline of himself at first. Though formless, he appeared as a dark stain against the otherwise resplendent unseen world.

Yet as they clashed and the unseen world became part of her dance, there was an ominous feeling that came over her in those few moments spent in the unseen world. There, beset against the maelstrom of light, it felt as if a shadow loomed over her.

"No. Not over me," she muttered.

The sounds of the world consuming her once more as her focus returned to the Redcloak who still screamed before her.

"I've got it!" She whispered, the corner of her lips twisting into a strained and weary smile.

Daromir interpreted the smile as a vain act of confidence, for he immediately screamed in frustration, holding his arm towards her as the crimson light shone brilliantly once more.

"Die!" He screamed, and another barrage of spikes twisted forth from the cracks on his arm.

Eliira pushed through the waves of pain threatening to overwhelm her, moving with intense speed as she held her own arm up. With a swipe through the air, she sent forth another wave of droplets hurtling towards the roaring Redcloak.

Whistling on the winds that carried them, the shining specs of blue light danced and hummed with excitement, ever eager to carry out the unspoken orders they were given. Though he was content with holding his position stalwartly, she raced towards him, moving behind the droplets that connected with the spikes.

An explosion ripped through the square as dust and debris raced up towards the crimson moon, watching over their duel in ominous silence. Eliira vanished into the dust, leaping upwards and soared on the winds that were her birthright.

Daromir glanced up, brandishing his arm towards the woman glowing a resplendent azure. She saw the spikes form, piercing through the stone-like exterior as he prepared for another onslaught of spikes. Yet just as quickly as she appeared through the dust and debris, she vanished.

Eliira carried on the winds of her momentum, soaring through the unseen world towards the black stain that represented the confused Redcloak. The passage of time in the unseen world was not bound to the constant laws governing the world of colour. She saw the spikes slowly twist and form from the cracks in his arm, clearly building towards a wave that would hurl itself towards her.

There, set against the canvas of light shining with an almost ethereal intensity, the Redcloak appeared a tainted, and wretched spot of darkness. Warmth enveloped her, and though her senses became so overwhelmed with the unmitigated brightness of the world unseen, there was a sense of nostalgia that came with it.

Long were the hours of her training, and through it all, the world unseen became akin to a second home for her, even if she could only bask in it for a few moments at a time.

Consumed by the overwhelming light, one felt their senses burn as they strained to maintain themselves against the waves of resplendence battering against them.

Mastering movement through the unseen world meant learning how to push down those feelings, locking them away as to not distract from the purpose of your journey. With how far Eliira had come, and how much she lost, she would not let this moment escape her.

Not again.

Kanah moved effortlessly to swing before her. The blade found purchase with its target, cutting through it with such ease that Eliira worried she had been wrong in assuming its existence.

Despite the feeling of doubt that grasped her for but a moment, she sensed something change in the Redcloak as she soared overhead. Kanah did not cut through the dark stain that represented the Redcloak, but through the shadow looming around.

With a blink of her eyes, Eliira emerged back into the seen world, rolling along the stones behind the Redcloak as her momentum carried her roughly down onto the battered ground.

The world around her swirled as colour drifted back into her gaze, combining to overwhelm the senses almost to the point of nauseating. She put every ounce of her effort into that one blow, and she knew if she was incorrect in her assumption, then it was at the risk of her very demise.

Daromir stood motionless, his head cast towards the crimson moon foreboding overhead. Eliira watched with ragged, weary breaths as his obsidian arm lowered to his side, and the crimson light that shone from it slowly vanished. Cutting the shadow leveraged some effect on the wounded Redcloak, though she prayed it would be enough to bring their fight to its conclusion.

Her hope vanished as his right hand reached for the 'Mercy-blade' which clung to the back of his waist. Redcloaks were given the narrow, ornate blade, which they only used against defeated foes clinging to life. Its purpose, as its name, was to shepherd worthy opponents to the lands beyond life.

Eliira watched the crimson light dance against its blade. Her heart sank as she realized her efforts weren't enough.

Daromir turned to face her, clutching the blade tightly in his hand. He hobbled over towards her, his obsidian arm hanging limply at his side as he painted the stone beneath him with his darkened blood. Small pools formed where the two dealt blows to one another, a stain upon the square which would be a testament to their almost celestial clash.

Eliira could not herself up off her knees as Daromir approached. Though Kanah screamed at her to rise against their foe, her body, beaten and broken, would not heed her call.

Knowing how close she came to breaking through the Watchtower hurt her more than any wound she ever experienced. As Daromir towered over her, she saw in the blade only the reflection of her monumental failures.

"You have saved me from my fate," Daromir grumbled.

The fingers of his obsidian arm curled and stretched, as if trying to pull from beneath its cracked and abominable form one last vestige of strength. Eliira flinched as he rested the obsidian hand against her head. Her heart raced at the thought that these might be the last moments of her life.

She grit her teeth as her wounds seared through her once more. Her screams echoed through the open square as the shards that pierced her set senses ablaze. To her surprise, he removed his obsidian hand from her head after the pain subsided, pulling the shards out with it.

Eliira glanced up with weary, ragged eyes as Daromir dragged his arm back from against her. He took a step backwards, peering down at her with a faint measure of respect as he nodded slowly.

"As I have saved you from yours," he added.

Before Eliira mustered the words, Daromir lifted the mercy-blade upwards, bringing its sharp blade roughly against where his twisted arm met his torso. The scream escaping him was unlike anything Eliira ever heard. It shook the very ground beneath her as he cut through the arm with an agonizingly slow motion.

The blade moved through obsidian flesh as if some unseen hand fought against every small jerk. When at last it was severed, the obsidian arm fell to the ground between them, the familiar dark blood pooling beneath it as Daromir let his mercy-blade fall to the stone. He clenched the wound with his other hand, glancing at Eliira with a bloodstained smile as he barely kept himself upright.

"I...If the rumours were true." Daromir whispered.

His words strained as if each one required the entirety of his remaining strength.

"Tell Vani that I...I'm sorry, and that by your blade, I was killed."

Eliira watched as the fallen obsidian arm turned to embers, as if set ablaze by some unseen flame. Daromir staggered, barely able to keep himself upright after losing so much blood. Even now it poured freely from the self-inflicted wound, and though his fate seemed grim, Eliira sensed a measure of calm acceptance wash over the former Redcloak.

"I will," Eliira said.

A million questions wracked her mind, but she possessed neither the strength nor the time to ask them. For just as she delivered her promise, Daromir gave her one last nod. His physical form shifted and dropped into a pool of blood, leaving Eliira alone in the open square.

The blood splashed upon broken and battered stones, pooling between the cracks like the rainwater which fell from the overhanging canopies of the Low City.

She watched as the blood pooled beneath the cracked stone, moving towards the Sea of Storms that stretched out as far as the eye could see.

A sense of peace emanated as the remnants of Daromir made its retreat. She knew that no matter what the outcome was that awaited him, he stole for himself the right to decide his own fate, and that was something she admired.

With one final strained effort, she lifted herself up to her feet, feeling the strength slowly return now that she had the corrupted shards removed from her body.

With one hand still tightly clasping the handle of Kanah, she reached down to pick up the discarded mercy-blade, the last memory of the man that came so close to defeating her. Then, with eyes glowing a re-surging azure, she turned her gaze towards the Watchtower, and her corporeal form dropped into a pool of water. She snaked through the cracked stone, drawing closer to the doors.

With eyes gazing towards whatever future destiny held, she pressed through the cracks of the Watchtower door.

CHAPTER XVIII

DAWN OF GOLD

"But in that silence, the Golden Dominant was born."

WATER, EPHEMERAL, COOL, AND BEAUTIFUL, UNLIKE ANY FOUND IN ALL the brooks and rivers of the world, seeped through the cracks of the battered Watchtower door.

In his efforts to reach that which was relayed to him only through rumours, Daromir unknowingly provided an easy pathway for the Azure Akura to finish what she started. She moved effortlessly into the low light of the Watchtower, pooling at the base of the door before the glowing water lifted upwards and her corporeal form emerged.

She did not yet fully recover from the confrontation with Daromir, whose fate seemed intricately tied to the crimson moon blazing beyond the cool stalwart walls of the ancient Watchtower.

Writings and scribblings from countless authors that were now lost to the sands of time surrounded her. She felt an overwhelming sense of awe as her glowing gaze scanned across all that was gathered. It took a long time for her eyes, still seared with the overwhelming light of the unseen world, to grow used to the now low light embracing her.

She deciphered only fragments of the collected information. Many of the ancient pages were penned before the island Empire ousted both dwarves and elves. She was amazed to see whispers and rumblings of a mysterious order that supposedly acted as guardians from the shadows.

'Hells, they were onto us back then?'

This was, as she was so often reminded, the true purpose of their existence. Those they watched over were free to ponder and assume, but it was imperative that they never come to rely on the help of those with whom such gifts of power were granted.

If the kingdoms of the world were to grow accustomed to their existence, they would languish under the weight of their own laxness. Ineptitude flourished in the gardens of those unwilling and uncaring to ensure their own survival. Faelwin was quick to instill *that* tenet early in the days of Eliira's studies.

As her glowing gaze slowly became accustomed to the low light of the Watchtower, Eliira marvelled at all the inscriptions surrounding her.

How long did such a trove of contemplation and mystery sit below her very nose?

She clicked her tongue as she cursed her own oversight. Wandered through the expansive hall, she immediately saw the faint glowing runes on an ancient, unexpected table.

"By the Gods!" she gasped, immediately bolting towards the table. "A table of the ancients, here?!"

She rested Kanah against the edge of the table, her fingers tracing over the cool carven stone that depicted the Empire. Of all the places she expected to see such an ancient and important relic, she could hardly believe that one rested in the old and forgotten Watchtower. The table hummed with excitement, and the fingertips on her left hand left traces of light emanating from the otherwise silent stone.

Splendour and amazement overwhelmed her senses, blinding her to anything beyond the unexpected treasure. Kanah seemed to equal her revelry, for the blade hummed and buzzed with such fervour that Eliira could barely keep hold of it.

"Kanah?" she muttered, gazing at the blade with a curious brow. "Sure, the order knew that a table must have existed in the empire, but to find it here? Well, it's all rather…"

Her words trailed off as the blade continued to buzz. As if heeding the weapon's unspoken call, she turned her gaze away from the inscriptions and saw the cool silver blade silently laying in the centre of the table. Eliira's heart skipped a beat as she gasped, her fingers pressed to her lips as she looked upon the golden blade with shock. Though its light dimmed, the resplendence of the blade was unmistakable.

"Telerach." she whispered.

The ancient name of the missing blade felt heavy upon her lips as she marvelled at the sight of the faintly glowing blade.

"Was that light the Watchtower activating? But that still doesn't line up with…" Her eyes traced the length of the blade.

Telerach, named after the man who first wielded it, resembled Kanah only in the otherworldliness that emanated from the length of its blade.

Where the blade of Kanah was thin, Telerach boasted a warrior's strength, more suitable for even the fiercest of battlefields. Both weapons shared in the elegance and prestige of their design. Though the sleek, flowing design of the handle shone gold, where Kanah's more muted and elegance, held the deep azure of the ocean.

She saw depictions of Telerach, for her order arranged the halls of their citadel with countless murals and recreations of the blade's previous owner. However, no one in her order had seen it in person. The blade of Telerach had long been lost to the annals of history. A relic that countless lifetimes were spent chasing after. Yet here it stood, as graceful and resplendent as the day it left their order.

Eliira yearned to reach out to the blade, drawn by the aura of its elegance, but a thought quickly consumed her, causing her to recoil her hand. *Who activated the Watchtower?*

Blades like Kanah and Telerach were otherworldly in many respects, but, as far as she was aware, they could not sprout wings and command themselves. *'Well, Kellear's might.'*

Those who awoke to their power controlled them, and as she stood at the edge of the table, she realized someone awakened Telerach. Kanah sensed it earlier in the evening. The blade felt its companion awaken. Which meant that…

From the shadows of the far wall, a man groaned, causing Eliira to practically leap upright as she spun to face the agonizing noise.

"Who's there?!" she called, feeling the handle of Kanah move between her fingers.

She lifted the blade upwards, taking a few cautious steps back from the table as her glowing gaze trailed along the shadows of the Watchtower.

Hesitant, she crept her way around, searching for whatever, or whoever, made the noise. If one of the Redcloaks snuck in before her, then it was possible whoever awakened Telerach already met their fate.

She blinked into the unseen world, carefully examining the hall of the Watchtower. As lines and definition were consumed by the unwavering white light, she saw no darkness or shadow that suggested the company of a crimson monster. There was, however, a faint glimmer that immediately caught her attention.

A faint golden hue glowed against the overwhelming whiteness of the unseen world, like the last vestiges of sunlight dancing across the tumultuous waters of the ocean. Eliira blinked away the light, letting the colour seep back into her gaze. Her breath hitched as she lowered Kanah.

There was a warmth emanating from the glimmering gold that was not unfamiliar to her, though it strained with each passing moment, as if it were a candle on the verge of extinguishing.

Eliira raced around the table, falling to her knees as she approached the groaning man. His chest rose and fell from deep, ragged breaths, and his eyes strained as if grasping to stay alive. A flickering golden glow, which struggled to maintain its resplendence, consumed his unfocused gaze. One moment his eyes held the waning gaze of the Crown Prince. The next, a glow, similar to Eliira's, enveloped it.

"V-Vanimire!?" she cried, studying the face that she'd only ever seen at a distance.

Though she was trained for this very circumstance, seeing it firsthand was terrifying. Her mind raced with a million questions, but she had precious little time to change the course of history forever. Her glowing azure gaze traced along his battered form, seeing in the tattered silken clothes the story of a confrontation against insurmountable odds.

Grave wounds covered him, for the ancient stones of the Watchtower floor were awash in the slick, warm crimson that pooled beneath him. Yet it was the state of his left arm which caused her most concern and curiosity.

"B...By the Gods." she gasped, running her fingers gently along the skin that was burned and cracked.

She saw the formation of the familiar stone-like exterior that beset her own arm. Where hers stretched up to her shoulder, his stopped at the elbow.

"A Dominant Akura, here?!" Her hand trembled as she ran along the broken and uneven exterior that formed. "The Golden Akura reborn as a Dominant!?"

Her breathing quickened as excitement and terror flooded her senses. It wasn't uncommon for one to struggle when awakening to their powers. For the Akura to be born, one was subjected to the unfiltered majesty of the Song itself. Countless died in transition, and those who survived were taught how to aid the process of others. To unleash the Akura on one's own was a remarkable feat, almost as rare as a Dominant being born.

Seldom few were born with the innate instinct to channel the Song through them and solidify it against the binding laws of the world that were intent on eradicating those which did not belong in the material plane. The mystery of how the Redcloaks managed their vile imitations and how their beasts escaped instant hellfire remained unsolved for her. Though she bet the appearance of the crimson moon was at least partly responsible.

If the Akura's were themselves a rarity, then a dominant was to them what the commoner was to the Gods.

"Kanah!" Eliira screamed, holding her hand to the side as the blade heeded her call.

She felt the familiar warmth course through her as she wrapped her fingers around its handle.

"You're lucky, Princeling." she called out to him, hoping the words could be heard through his torment.

Her voice wavered as she tried to contain the emotions surging through her like a maelstrom.

"If any other were to have found you, the Watchtower would have become your tomb. But, as long as I'm here, there's still a chance."

She breathed in sharply, moving her fingers to push aside the disheveled strands of his hair from across his face. The pain in his expression made her wince. She remembered the agonizing pain of her own awakening, as if it were fresh in her mind. Though she didn't quickly forget such agony, the reward for enduring the pain made every second of torment worthwhile.

"Hang in there," she whispered, biting her lip as she raised herself up to her full height.

Eliira never assisted in another's awakening, but the process was drilled into her by Faelwin. Though the process was largely beyond her control, she couldn't help but feel a measure of fear that she would fumble and consign to the halls of eternity the single weapon that might help tip the scales against the crimson moon.

If the armies of humanity were to stand any chance against the oppressive foes that beset them, it would only be possible with the aid of a Dominant, for even the Akura would eventually falter.

"Kanah." She called, pulling herself from the thoughts racing through her mind like a torrent. "I know it's foolish to say, but... please, lend me your aid."

Relief washed over her as the blade silently answered. Eliira couldn't help but smile as she felt some of her fear vanish. There was a bond the two shared that was indescribable, but having grown so accustomed to the blade, she wasn't sure she would ever survive a day without it.

"I'm sorry, Princeling." she muttered, glancing down to the boy who still twisted and seized in agony. "But things must get worse before they can get better."

Vanimire gasped, his eyes still flickering with the faint golden glow.

"P...Please!" He groaned, finding a moment of clarity in the whirlwind of torment that consumed him.

Eliira nodded, and, allowing no more time to be wasted, lined the tip of Kanah above the chest of the agonizing Vanimire before plunging the blade downwards. The tip of the blade shone brilliantly as it shed its physical form.

The silver edge of the blade became transparent and watery as it pressed down against the chest of the agonizing Vanimire. Like water seeping through cracks in the earth, it plunged, not physically piercing through the man's chest, though it didn't save him from the agony which soon followed.

Vanimire seized and writhed in renewed agony. His screams echoed through the hall of the Watchtower, revealing the torment that enveloped him throughout his entire body. Eliira winced as she watched the boy thrash against the stone floor.

His fingers curled and pressed so tightly against the stone that his nails cracked and broke as he sought an escape from the pain. She could remember her own transformation well, could remember the weeks spent in recovery.

Golden light blazed in Vanimire's eyes, though it vanished as the boy danced upon the precipice between worlds. Eliira could remember the all-consuming agony that threatened to overwhelm with each passing moment. Like flesh thrown in the depths of the hottest fires, it never dulled nor faltered.

To fully awaken to the godlike power of the Akura, one needed to shed much of what constricted them. A part of your humanity died, but it was a sacrifice to claw at the power of the Gods themselves. Blood pooled beneath the boy as Eliira maintained his grip on the blade. Kanah would assist in the awakening, but its success hinged entirely on Vanimire's strength alone.

WAS HE DYING? WAS THIS HOW HIS STORY WOULD REACH ITS conclusion?

He had the faintest memory of seeing someone else in the Watchtower. Though his mind strained to conjure any coherent thought amidst the sea of agony gripping him, an otherworldly beauty enveloped her outline, which he could barely make out.

Did she really exist, or was she simply a messenger from the Gods above, sent to retrieve another tormented soul?

None of it seemed to matter now, for just as quickly as the thought surfaced, it burned away beneath the waves of torment. Time itself lost all meaning as he writhed on the floor of the Watchtower. He knew not whether this last episode of anguish lasted a few seconds, or an eternity.

He sensed his body breaking down, sensing every fibre of his being rejected, and fought against the blazing inferno. Only to be battered down and replaced with the embers of something that was in equal parts new and familiar.

He longed for death. Craving an escape from whatever was pulling on him. He felt a prisoner in his own body, forced to wallow in a sea of blinding light and blazing agony. With every flicker, he smelt the searing, burning skin on his left arm, sending fresh waves of pain through him. He smashed the arm on the stone floor of the Watchtower, desperate to end his agony.

His mind raced to make sense of his demise, trying to figure out what exactly he was going through. If this was death, then the process was far more agonizing and prolonged than he had ever expected. Desperate to be freed from his torment, the rational side of his mind knew that there was something more going on here.

Something pierced through him.

He knew that much with certainty. For though he writhed and twisted, some strength kept him pinned down through his chest. It wasn't cool and searing like any blade or weapon, but it felt as if it pierced through his very soul itself.

Whatever it was, it left something in him, he sensed traces of an eerie coolness dance alongside the waves of agony that wrecked him. They moved as if guiding the pain and torment, leading it forward to consume that which evaded the claws of its anguish.

ELIIRA CONTINUED TO WATCH IN SILENT DISCOMFORT AS THE BOY twisted and writhed along the stone floor. Though Kanah pierced through him for a matter of moments, she knew far too well how one's perception of time twisted when subject to a level of agony that was beyond the sense's capabilities.

To awaken to the Akura was to feel the power of the Heavens course through one's own body. Opening oneself to the splendour of the Song and feeling as it rewrote and reconfigured all that made the recipient whole to allow them to wield such extraordinary strength and power.

Heavenly light flooded one's body, imprisoning the soul until the transformation was complete. Only then did the pain subside, and one could wield that which was divinely instilled in them. Through pain and torment that would break the will of any regular mortal, the Akura was born.

The seconds passed in an uneasy strain as Eliira kept Kanah plunged through the writing boy. She did not relish in seeing the pain she partook in inflicting. Though it would, hopefully, save his life, she never revelled in seeing another in the worst moments of their life. Her glowing sapphire gaze continued to study the boy, examining how his left arm seared and burned as he awoke to the power he wielded.

An almost blinding light consumed his left arm, burning away its humanity until it resembled the resplendence of the unseen world. From there it quickly solidified, becoming stone-like in appearance as the binding laws of the world tried to eradicate that which should not belong.

Golden light shone brilliantly through the cracks of his stone-like arm, pulsing like a beating heart before growing dim. She withdrew Kanah, stumbling backwards and falling to the ground as she panted heavily.

"I…It's done," she said, feeling her head swirl as exhaustion threatened to consume her.

The boy's screams silenced, his eyes shut, and she knew it would be a matter of weeks before at last he awoke. He would desperately need the aid of a healer. Though the power that now surged through him would tend to the wounds he received, it would need to be coaxed out whilst he slept. Faelwin had to be the one to oversee his recovery.

Kanah, too, partook in the relief. Eliira sensed the excitement dancing through the blade as the droplets of water returned and it took physical shape once more.

The Golden Akura, long thought lost, awakened the Crown Prince to its power. Further, unlike any her order encountered in centuries, he possessed a Dominant.

She might have failed in saving the capital from its fate, but in awakening the Golden Akura, she might have altered the course of history forever. Despite the achievement, she was too selfless to consider herself anything more than she was, the wielder of the Azure Akura.

If the prince was to save the world from its fate, he would achieve salvation through his own actions. She would be content to guide and assist him.

"K…Kanah," Eliira whispered, feeling the earth shake beneath her. "We need to get out of the capital. Think you can convince Telerach to activate the table?"

She flicked her glowing gaze to the blade, waiting for the

wordless response she grew accustomed to. The blade hummed, and Eliira let out a quiet, weary chuckle.

"I knew I could count on you."

Eliira strained to lift herself up to her feet, bracing herself against the blade as she staggered towards the table in the centre of the room. Kanah hummed with excitement as Eliira leaned over the table, examining the carved sigils that glowed softly.

Of all the places that might have housed a point of convergence, she never expected it to be in the heart of the empire's capital.

The order was aware of few convergences, and even fewer were operational. In the years before they opted to observe from the shadows, the convergences acted as a method to respond to threats that arose throughout Aerturiel. Yet as power coalesced in the hands of the kings and emperors, they saw the convergences not as a tool for safety, but as one for betrayal.

Why was the capital's convergence which the scholars of the order believed destroyed remained in secret working condition?

It mattered little to her now. A terrible screech ripped through the air, shaking the very foundation of the Watchtower. Before the dust settled, the Watchtower shook once more from repeated blasts.

Clearly word spread through the forces of the crimson moon to where the mysterious azure warrior disappeared to, and all their efforts were now devoted to bringing the Watchtower down upon her.

Eliira placed Kanah down on the table, letting the blade hum with excitement as it silently communicated with the other blade. Telerach was a blade of legend and renown, two facts which it seemed very aware of.

As she pressed the carved sigils in a specific order, Eliira sensed frustration bubble up within the blade. Telerach, it seemed, was reluctant to offer its help to those who were unworthy to bask in its presence. The blade seemed to possess a bitterness, perhaps having been far removed from its rightful place of prestige.

The blades each possessed a personality that differed wildly, never ceasing to amuse the exhausted Eliira. Where Kanah was almost motherly in how it cared for its wielder, Telerach was stoic and proud.

The blade supposedly experienced the heights of prowess and might. Though it slumbered for many-a-years, it didn't forget. If the boy wielded it this evening and survived its awakening, he would have quite the difficult time proving himself worthy of the blade and an even more difficult time winning its affection.

As the weapons silently bickered amongst themselves, Eliira moved with a renewed sense of urgency. The crimson monsters continued their assault against the Watchtower, slamming against the ancient stonework with reckless abandon. Fuelled by fury, the mindless hordes willingly sacrificed themselves to complete their orders.

Twenty-six was the sequence of sigils that needed to be pressed to activate the ancient pathways of convergence. If Eliira pressed even a single sigil out of place, the entire sequence would end, and she would have to begin from the beginning.

Thankfully, even though she rarely used the ancient convergences, the sequence was drilled into her during the months of training. As she pressed the sigils in sequence, she couldn't help but feel a pang of nostalgia wash over her.

Faelwin stressed the power of the ancient convergences when Eliira first awakened to her ability. They could bend the very fabric of the world itself, allowing for one to travel halfway across Aerturiel in the blink of an eye.

The order were the watchers and inheritors of the convergences, and all the other relics which were entrusted to them when the order first formed. Eliira didn't think herself worthy to experience the might of the convergences. However, in a night full of unexpected twists and turns, this one seemed hardly monumental.

The lights of the Watchtower glowed brighter as she neared the end of the sequence. It seemed the two blades came to some measure of understanding, for though Kanah maintained her silent frustration, Telerach recognized the necessity of his help. Eliira knew Kanah would vent the frustration to her later, but for now, they raced against the hordes that descended upon the Watchtower.

As another massive blast rocked the Watchtower and sent Eliira to the ground, the last sigil was set in place as the walls buckled around her. Her vision swirled as she eased herself up to her feet, reaching for Kanah as the air of the Watchtower electrified around them.

With all the reverence it deserved, she eased Telerach out of the carved slot, gently carrying the heavy blade over to its newly awakened wielder. Despite Telerach's bravado and haughtiness, she sensed the blade release a measure of relief as she placed it against its wielder. Even the most ancient blades could not resist forming a sense of concern and care for those who wielded them.

The foundation of the Watchtower hummed with excitement as the lights of the hall intensified. Using the ancient convergences stealthily was impossible, and activating it would announce its use to all observers.

Eliira dropped to her knees, running a hand gently over the disheveled hair of the now slumbering Vanimire. Pain and exhaustion clung to the lines of his soft expression. Though the masters of her order would nurse him back to health, she knew he would forever remember their escape. He was the High King, after all. He would not spend his entire reign in exile.

Even now, as the crimson hordes continued to batter the Watchtower, Eliira sensed it was only a matter of time before they returned to save that which was stolen from them that evening.

The Watchtower continued to rock as the ancient convergence neared activation. The hordes beyond its walls realized something was going on, for the intensity of their assault redoubled. When at last the lights of the hall reached their zenith, Telerach and Kanah glowed with staggering resplendence. They were to act as grounding rods, ensuring that neither Akura was lost amidst the ethereal sea during their retreat.

Kanah hummed silently, and Eliira understood the ancient convergence was now ready to be used. It came not a moment too soon, for as she tightened her grip on the handle of the blade, one last blast rocked the side of the Watchtower. The force of the collapsing Watchtower propelled dust, debris, and rock from their ancient resting places.

"To the Citadel! Now!" Eliira commanded.

Just as the walls of the Watchtower came down upon them, both Akura glowed brilliantly and disappeared from sight.

End of Book One

EPILOGUE

NEVER WAS THERE A MORE BEAUTIFUL SIGHT THAN THAT OF THE WORLD teetering on the precipice of destruction. Seen from the upper terraces of the capital's castle, the city seemed little more than streaks of black, orange, and crimson, splattered upon the canvas of destruction they wrought.

How beautiful it seemed.

The countless flames dotting the city danced as if to praise the crimson light that consumed them. Terror was to be the chorus of the world's demise, yet to the ears of the six-eyed figure, it was as if the Gods themselves were singing their harmonies.

To say the night was a success would have been a grave understatement. They openly declared war not just on the Rhyserion empire, but upon the very Song itself. In one night, they managed to not only drown the world with the blood of sinners, but they summoned that which would oversee the creation of a new era.

Were he any less pious, then the six-eyed figure might have thought the evening went too smoothly. Yet he saw their resounding success as a testament to the strength that faith in their Lord could provide. Her design ensured the summoning's success, and it was her plans that would see the dawn of a new era of peace and tranquility for the world.

The birth of a new Song.

With hands clasped behind his back, the six-eyed figure cocked his head to the side as the sound of boots echoed along the stones of the garden.

"Speak!" He growled when the approaching figures came to a stop.

He knew immediately these were not the children he adored. As silence fell over the palace of the capital, they were sent forth into the city itself, each entrusted with specific orders. He need not glance at the figures who approached to know they were the simple acolytes that served those who served him.

Even with their hooded heads held low, they appeared to him as vile and disgusting creatures. For the time, the Redcloaks required the acolytes, as their wide dispersion prevented operation without liaisons. Yet each of his children knew the moment the acolytes were no longer needed, the volunteers would serve as further sacrifices to sate their master's endless lust for blood.

"I...I am in service to Ealric, master speaker." The first one muttered.

The six-eyed figure had long grown used to the fear that carried on the voices of the unworthy acolytes when they spoke in his presence, yet he couldn't help but sense that the acolyte was more terrified than usual. He turned to face the robed figures, letting the weight of his burning gaze fall upon them. He revelled in seeing how they winced when faced with his unwavering gaze, a constant reminder of how unworthy they were to live in the world he deigned to create.

"I said speak," he repeated, clenching his hands behind his back.

It was difficult to see the acolytes as anything more than cattle. Few of them ever seemed to possess any qualities that made them stand out from those that the crimson horde now devoured.

They were useful for sending messages between his children and devastating when his tempers burned hot. Beyond that, he could think of no further purpose for them. They were unfit to bear any gifts from his father and were certainly unfit to step foot in his new world.

"I...I bring bad news, lord speaker." The acolyte continued, finally finding the courage to continue the simplest of tasks.

"Speak quickly then!" The six-eyed figure spat; their timidness tried his patience at the best of times, but he couldn't bring himself to bear it when there was something amiss.

"Y…Your child, Ealric," the acolyte began, barely able to string together his words as fear completely took hold of him.

Beneath the oppressive gaze of the six-eyed figure, he couldn't help but shake.

"He was defeated."

"What?!" the six-eyed figure roared. Taking a step towards the hooded acolytes, who immediately fell to their knees in terror. "How!? By who!?"

The acolytes pressed their heads against the stone of the gardens, begging for mercy and understanding as the temper of the six-eyed figure blazed. Despite a wavering, cracking voice, the messenger summoned the courage to complete his report of bad news.

"The Azure Akura."

"Damn it!" the six-eyed figure screamed, and in the blink of an eye, the acolyte who delivered the report burst into flames.

His screams of terror and agony drowned out the Herald's roars of frustration. The other acolyte could only keep his head press low and deferentially as his companion writhed and twisted along the ground next to him.

Every scream of mercy and forgiveness fell on deaf ears until at last his writhing stopped, and he lay a burnt and devastated mess upon the quiet stones of the garden.

"You!" the six-eyed figured screamed, turning his gaze back upon the remaining acolyte. "To whom do you serve?"

The acolyte continued to keep his head pressed lowly against the stone, not daring to earn any further ire lest he join his companion in twisted and terrible agony.

"Daromir, master speaker."

"Daromir, Daromir! A name born from the Song of old! He was reborn as Diametrix, vermin. Don't get it wrong! What of Daromir?! Pray tell the bastard Akura hasn't taken my beloved Diametrix from me, have they?!"

The remaining acolyte seemed to have learned from the mistakes of its companion, for he swallowed back his terror to the best of his ability before speaking.

"He faced the Azure Akura outside the Watchtower, master

speaker. Though he was defeated, we brought the Watchtower down upon the Azure Akura. We believe she is…"

"Did you see her die?!" the six-eyed figure screamed, taking another step towards the bowing acolyte.

"We did not, lord spe…" His words were cut short.

Spikes sprouted from the ground beneath him, surging upwards and impaling the acolyte as the Herald screamed in frustration.

Lifted off the ground by the spikes that devastated him, the acolyte's lips continued to move, though no words broke through the blood that poured from him. He silently went still, unable to scream or writhe on account of the spikes that had pierced through his lungs.

"Damn it all!" The six-eyed figure screamed, turning his back on the dead acolytes as he hurried back to the ledge of the gardens.

He brought a curled fist down against the cool stone. The pain coursing through his arm was hardly felt compared to the pain of losing two more of his children. Replacing the former Redcloaks proved difficult, unlike replacing the acolytes that served them. They were scouted, followed, converted, and trained specifically to carry out the orders of their slumbering master.

Losing even a single of his children was more devastating than losing a million of the crimson hordes.

"Yathriel!" the six-eyed figure screamed, his gaze still burning with renewed hatred as he looked down upon the city in ruins.

Yathriel was, to him, what the acolytes were to his children. Unlike them, however, she was irreplaceable.

"Yes, my lord." The stoic and calm voice called out.

Her words always soothed him, even when he was in the depths of his frustration.

"Gather my remaining children. Send word through their wretched acolytes, if you must. I want every one of them to search for the Azure Akura. I care little for the useless Princeling. We must kill the Akura. All of them!"

"Of course, my lord," Yathriel responded.

The six-eyed figure sensed a faint warmth emanate from her as she closed her eyes and began her ritual. Though he knew not why she was instilled with the gifts she had, he would not question the decisions of his master.

"What else would you ask of me, my lord?" She hummed when at last her ritual was completed.

The six-eyed figure continued to bask in the beauty of the devastated capital. It might have consumed his children, but he would not let their deaths be in vain. He would drown the fields of the empire in the blood of sinners, set fire to the wretched abominable villages that housed them, and when the last of their kin begged for his mercy and forgiveness, it would be for the deaths of Ealric and Daromir that he denied them.

"The empire will fall." The six-eyed figured growled, breathing in sharply as he took one last glance at the devastated capital. "Too great a loss were the souls that partook in the festivities here. We'll leave our children to man the armies and see to the death of the remaining lords."

He pushed himself off the ledge of the gardens, turning to face the slender and ghastly woman that awaited his command.

"I send you to continue our master's commands in the Kingdom of Kandila, across the Sea of Storms. The Northern Realms will fall, but Kandila must be the first to go. I will see to the Numerien Republics in the South. For too long, their greed has blinded them to the world beyond their borders. They are unfit for the world we are creating. Unfit to hear its *melody*."

Yathriel inclined her head in silent acceptance.

"Very well, my lord." She turned to leave but was stopped by the gentle hand of the six-eyed figure who turned her to face him once more.

"Don't be a fool, Yathriel. Carry out your orders then return to my side; do I make myself clear?"

She paused, the corner of her lips twisting into a gentle smile.

"Of course, master Sarkreth. I will meet with our brother Kolvith and we shall return to you when the fields of the Kingdom run red with the blood of sinners."

Sarkreth, six-eyed herald, lord speaker for their slumbering master, nodded, giving her shoulder one last squeeze before he released her from his service. Yathriel wasted little time in departing, for she knew the journey to Kandila would be long and arduous, even with the forces of the empire consumed and devastated.

Left alone beneath the glowing light of the crimson moon,

Sarkreth turned to take one final glance of the city that was consumed by flames.

"Do you hear the song of your children, oh slumbering beloved? Do their cries sound to you like the trumpets and horns of jubilation, calling you from the depths to return to the world that so desperately desires your guiding hand?"

Silence fell over him as he spoke. His words carried on the breeze that rolled over the destroyed capital. He found in that silence the exact answer he long awaited. Warmth washed over him, caressing and embracing him with such splendour that tears welled in his six eyes.

"Thank you, my love." He muttered, then, with a renewed sense of hatred and guidance, he turned his back on the city that he had destroyed.

DAROMIR WATCHED AS THE DYING EMBERS FINALLY SUCCUMBED TO THE oppressive breeze that danced through the cracks of the cavern walls, leaving him lost in the shadows of the spacious underground sanctuary. He reclaimed his mind, but in doing so, had lost far, far more than it was worth.

If only he stole that single moment of strength when it mattered most. He witnessed the death of his brother, threw his nephew from the highest ring of the castle, and yet, it was in saving the Azure Akura that he finally stole his mind back from that which claimed it.

He deserved torment and anguish for his inability to rectify any of the evils which occurred under his watch, and yet, despite an overwhelming desire to feel the cold steel of his mercy-blade pierce his flesh, he cauterized his wounded arm in the embers that grew silent.

How long was he the product of such twisted dualities?

To crave the punishment of death, he deserved yet saving himself from its talons.

When he pulled the poison from the body of the Azure Akura and severed that which had marked him as an abomination, it was his every intent to escape to this curiously placed subterranean cavern and await the fate he deserved. His only solace was that the Azure Akura very well might have saved Vanimire, if the boy lived.

Yet, much to his surprise, he was not the only Redcloak who sought such an outcome.

To the wonderment of the aged Redcloak, Ealric escaped from his clutches and retreated to the cavern as well. There the two discussed in depth all that had occurred, trying to make sense of the tumultuous maelstrom that was the recent weeks.

Ealric told Daromir how he encountered the wounded, but miraculously strong Vanimire, and how he fell to the crown prince. Yet Daromir could find no joy in the story, for Ealric painstakingly told him of the wounds he had inflicted on the young boy before departing.

Were Vanimire not looked favourably upon by the Gods, then his demise was almost certain.

Daromir pushed the thoughts from his mind as he heard the thick liquid pour through the cracks, dropping onto the stone of the cavern floor before Ealric's shape appeared from the pool.

"I've returned, Lord Commander." Ealric muttered softly.

"And?" Daromir asked, turning his unseeing gaze through the darkness towards where the shadows danced against the armoured Ealric. "What did you uncover?"

Silence fell over the pair, broken only by the metallic sounds of the younger Ealric lowering himself down onto the cavern floor.

"The speaker and his emissary departed the city three days ago." Ealric began. "The acolytes informed me that our former kin were to lead the infernal armies against the other lordships in the Empire, whilst the speaker departed for the Republics. His emissary was sent to the Kingdom of Kandila, although to what ends, they did not know."

Daromir let the words sink in, trying to figure out the intention behind such actions. That his fellow Redcloaks were to lead their armies against the remaining bastions of the Empire made sense, for it always was the speaker's intention that the empire itself should fall first, but why then depart to the republics? Was there something secret that awaited him there? Something so precious and important that he dared not tell his most trusted servants?

When Daromir borne the name Diametrix, he was privy to the speaker's most confidential and important plans, and yet, now that he freed himself from the crimson arm, so little of it remained in his memory.

"Damn it," Daromir hissed, slamming his remaining fist against his armoured leg. "It all dances on the edges of my memory, lingering just beyond the veil of understanding."

Ealric shared in his frustration, letting out a deep sigh as he leaned against the cool stone of the cavern wall.

"And what of the acolyte?" Daromir asked. Even though he knew the answer, he needed to hear the confirmation.

"Dead." Ealric muttered simply. "He told me what he knew, and then I pressed the mercy-blade through his head."

Daromir nodded, despite the complete darkness absorbing such primitive notions.

"Good." He added, letting out a sigh of frustration. "Any word on the Akura?"

Ealric clicked his tongue. "None. The acolyte claims the Watchtower fell upon them, consuming the Akura and anyone else that was inside the Watchtower. Though he claimed a bright light emanated from it just as the walls collapsed, they believe it was nothing more than the enchanted light stones erupting."

Daromir chuckled, running his hand through the hair that was still slick with sweat.

"Do they believe that?" He asked, lifting a brow.

"So, it would seem." Ealric added, disbelief and humour lacing his words. "Only a couple of our brothers were left to maintain the City and have departed for the other bastions of the Empire yesterday."

"Finally, some good news." Daromir said with a sigh, leaning his head back against the cavern wall. "I refuse to believe the Azure Akura I faced would die in such a pitiful way. The fate of my nephew weighs heavy on my mind and soul, brother, but I know the strands of fate have something in store for him. The Vanimire you faced was not the one that I remember, even if my last memories of him are hazy."

Ealric nodded, running his armoured gauntlet over the wound that the crown prince had inflicted.

"Poor boy probably thinks he's killed me." He said wistfully, sucking back a quiet chuckle. "Instead, he saved me."

Daromir nodded, caring not for the darkness that still hung over them.

"Aye. For now, it's best we leave him to what the fates have ordained, I think, though it will pain us both. If Vanimire lives, he certainly is in the company of the Azure Akura, for which there can be no safer place in this wretched world we created."

"On that, we agree," Ealric said with a huff, leaning forward as he slowly set to work, rekindling the slumbering fire.

It would take a long time before he grew used to life with just one hand, for even the simple act of starting a fire was both cumbersome and time-consuming. When at last the first flames appeared, and light cascaded against the two battered, armoured men, he leaned back against the cavern wall, letting the warmth dance across his weary face as he looked to Daromir.

"What should we do then?"

Daromir held his chin in hand, thinking to himself as the flame's light danced against him. How long was it since he felt such genuine warmth?

For too long, he lived as the pawn of another. Though he loved his brother, the Redcloaks were little more than a blade in the High King's arsenal, carrying out duties that, while he was happy to do, were rarely of his own design.

Then, on that wretched day, his strings were passed to another, more foul master. Though the plans of the speaker were lost in the haze of his memories, the atrocities he committed were not. No, when he severed his arm, he severed with it the strings that had bound his fate to other masters.

"We head to Kandila, in the Northern Realms." Daromir finally muttered, flicking his gaze to the surprised Ealric. "Searching for the speaker in the Republics would be a fool's errand. He is but one wretched man amongst a sea of multitudes, but if we can find his emissary, she will undoubtedly lead us back to him."

Daromir saw the cogs in Ealric's mind turned, and the sense of the plan finally settled in.

"Find the emissary and learn all that the speaker has planned." He muttered to himself, speaking more as if to convince himself of the plan rather than repeating it back to Daromir.

"Aye." Daromir hummed, his mind still moving like a tumultuous river as he pondered all their approaches. "If she heads to the Northern Realms, then it's the High Court that she will eventually look to dismantle. If she is to head there without the infernal armies, then she will certainly look to settle herself somewhere in Kandilas itself. The capital will be a flood of terror and confusion, and that will be all she needs to corrupt others to her side. Once Kandilas falls, so too will the kingdom. The Northern Realms will consume themselves in its wake, and they will be one step closer to bringing about that wretched melody."

Ealric listened intently, running his fingers along the handle of the mercy-blade that rested against the cavern wall beside him.

"We leave Vanimire hoping his fate is now entwined with the Akura's, and support him from the shadows."

Daromir nodded, his lips slowly lifting into a weary smile, the first genuine emotion he had felt beyond despair in a long, long time.

"Exactly. If our paths are to cross again, then we can hope to redeem our wretched existence by aiding him with information."

"It won't be easy." Ealric started licking his lips as his gaze became unfocused. "The prestige of the Redcloaks is certainly diminished, and people will fear us if they see us approaching. It will take only a matter of days before the Redcloaks will be known as the commanders of the infernal armies."

"We'll leave the marks of our sin here." Daromir countered. "Wearing only simple attire and bearing what weapons are necessary. If we move under the cover of darkness, whatever darkness that wretched moon provides at least, then we should hopefully cross into the Northern Realms with little issue. We need only to move faster than the infernal armies can conquer."

Ealric nodded silently, still mulling over the intricacies of the proposed plan.

"We can cross the border near Estling." He muttered. "The river is deep there, but we should be able to book passage on a fishing vessel. Sneak into Kandila and make straight for the capital."

Daromir gave a quiet nod. In the years of the Redcloaks, Ealric had always been slow to adopt plans. He was, for better or worse, a meticulous over-thinker. Though these traits had afforded him a fast position among Daromir's most trusted companions, Ealric's presence ensured that no plan would ever be quickly agreed upon.

His mind worked mysteriously, for he could envision a proposed plan and evaluate the varying degrees of danger that be encountered along every step of the way.

Daromir knew better than to interrupt the former Redcloak

when he was deep in concentration, for it only meant that the process would have to start again from the beginning.

As Ealric contemplated, Daromir cast his gaze towards the crackling fire that lay between them. Though his mind was freed from the claws that had sunk deeply into it, he could still feel the faint traces of that unsettling voice which invaded him.

Forced to bear witness to the vile actions that his body performed, all the while unable to do anything to stop them. It was a torment and agony unlike any he ever experienced, and it was one that he hoped he would never endure again.

It was impossible to stomach the guilt that he felt, especially since his mind still freshly bore the images of the brother he lost, and the nephew he had condemned. His screams and pleas in those moments fell on deaf ears, and he was forced to witness as all who he loved and fought for were stolen from him.

The crimson moon was to be the mark of his sins made manifest, and only when it was torn from the very skies itself would he allow himself the reprieve from death. No, until the moment came where he could right some wrongs he unleashed, he could not, would not falter.

"Daromir." Ealric called, pulling him from the river of thoughts that threatened to drown him.

"W…What?" Daromir asked, focusing his gaze on the Redcloak that lifted himself upright at some point.

"Are we ready?" Ealric offered his remaining hand to the seated Daromir.

He wasn't sure how long he was lost amidst his thoughts, but clearly it had been enough time for Ealric to calculate the extent of the proposal.

"Sure." Daromir muttered, happily taking the proffered hand and lifting himself upright.

His senses swirled as the extent of his exhaustion and pain manifested once more, and he clenched his teeth tightly as to not cry out. The spot where he severed his arm was freshly cauterized and agonized him with every minor movement. It would take weeks for him to recover, but it seemed a small price to pay for what he had done to Vanimire.

"What's the best plan, then?" Daromir asked, stamping out the fire with an armoured boot to distract himself from the agony.

"We head to the Halls of Healing in the City." Ealric began. "We've stayed death's hand for the moment, but we're going to need supplies if we are to survive our trek to Kandilas. Estling still offers the best chance of navigating into the Kingdom, but I think it best we make our way there through the dense forests of Talmire. At least then we are out of sight and, with some favour of the Gods, out of the way of the infernal armies."

Daromir nodded, holding his chin in hand as he considered the proposal. In all the years of working together, Ealric never proposed a terrible plan, though he was prone to occasionally proposing dangerous ones.

Despite the world itself ending around them, his proposed plan seemed as safe as one could manage. The heart of Talmire was dense; the tall trees would offer protection from the winged monstrosities, and the thickets and roots below would ensure the armies wouldn't dare traverse through them in great number.

With any luck, the occasional forester communes would offer them a mat to sleep on, until at last they could buy their vessel in the small town of Estling.

"Very well." Daromir said with a huff, rolling his neck as he tried to coax his muscles into preparing for the long adventure that loomed ahead of them. "Let us not waste time."

The pair exchanged a nod in the cavern's darkness before their corporeal forms dropped into pools of thick crimson. The liquid snaked along the walls of the cavern, pouring through the cracks and meandering through the twists and turns of the earth until at last they seeped through the stone paving of an alleyway. There they dragged themselves up from the pools, their shapes taking form once more as they quickly took stock of their surroundings.

Wielding only the mercy-blade that had ushered him from one torment to another, Daromir cast his weary gaze up to the crimson moon looming overhead. It was impossible to gauge the time of day, for the moon hung at its zenith, imposing, and daunting all that looked upon it.

If there was solace to be found in the wretched abomination, it was that wherever he might be, Vanimire would look upon the same moon.

"Stay strong, nephew." Daromir whispered, the crimson light of the moon dancing in his weary gaze. "Our roads will cross in time, but until then, find strength and solace with the Akura. You always were the best of us, Vani. From the moment you were born, we knew one thing: *this boy will change the world."*

Ealric squeezed Daromir's shoulder, pulling the older man's gaze back from the heavens towards the hell that surrounded them.

"Let's go," he muttered, giving Daromir one last nod before the pair turned and took off through the crimson nightmare they created.

AUTHOR'S NOTE

If you're reading this, then you have finished reading 'Dawn of Crimson'.

That, or you have skipped to the back of the book, curious to see how many pages it is, or if it ends on some monumental cliffhanger. If that is the case, then to you, I can only ask:

Wasn't it strange how Vanimire's fate at the end of the book was…

Okay, I think that scared them off.

Vanimire's journey, and the world of Aerturiel itself has been the product of years, and years of discovery, redefining, and excitement. Born from an idea nearly ten years past, Vanimire's journey is one that has been constantly adjusted, tweaked, and altered.

Aerturiel itself is a world with history, faces, and names in such an abundance that it becomes difficult to often decide where best to begin, and who all to include. The most exciting adventures often begin with such uncertainty, and ever is the pen sketching out the path that lays just ahead of one's feet.

All this to say, thank you.

Where Vanimire's path leads, no one can know for certain. Other than myself, of course. It would be quite the conundrum if that wasn't the case, given my penchant for over-planning.

The story of Dawn of Crimson began over five years ago and sat collecting dust for some time before Vanimire reached through the void and called to me once more. It has been a learning process, and with each page turned, I have striven to improve.

All that excited me about Aerturiel, and Vanimire's adventures, increases with great magnitude in the books that are to follow. The lands beyond the Rhyserion Empire are vast, and rife with things to see, and explore.

From the bottom of my heart, thank you. If even one mind is

enchanted by the world of Aerturiel, then I will have considered it a success. Though, if you grow attached to a character and they're killed off, that isn't my fault.

Or is it?

Sincerely, the one staring into Aerturiel and shaking it like the crazy snow-globe that it is,

Kyle Scarlett

P.S. I would never kill off a beloved character. That would be cruel.

P.S.S. To write is to craft a lie that holds up just enough to become believable. Only time will tell the extent to which I am to be believed. Until then, grow attached. Surely nothing bad can happen.

ABOUT THE AUTHOR

© Kyle Scarlett

Kyle Scarlett began his literary journey over a decade ago, inspired by the enchanting stories found in books and games. His passion for fantasy deepened with every new tale, leading him to create his own worlds filled with magic, adventure, and bold characters. Alongside his love for storytelling, Kyle pursued a master's degree in history, merging his academic interests with his creative pursuits. The result is a writing style rich in historical detail and imaginative depth, where vibrant characters meet the echoes of the past.

Outside of writing, Kyle is an avid speedrunner and a seasoned Dungeon Master, guiding friends through thrilling tabletop campaigns with a flair for the unexpected. His love for immersive storytelling shines through in every session, captivating players and readers alike. When he's not crafting new adventures, you'll likely find him with a cup of coffee in hand, dreaming up his next tale—one sip and one story at a time.